**Praise for Diane K. Shah's
first Paris Chandler Mystery,
AS CRIME GOES BY**

"A sensational first novel about Hollywood in the Forties
. . . the best part of this book . . . is its impeccable,
character-revealing dialog. It's a first-class read."
—*Playboy*

"Some fun is had with an earlier Hollywood era in *As
Crime Goes By* . . . the period is convincingly rendered
with a flair that goes beyond research."
—*The Wall Street Journal*

"The story is constructed well, and it passes the ultimate
test of a mystery: Shah kept me guessing right up to the
last pages . . . a classy, highly readable blend of '40s
mystery and modern character development."
—Los Angeles *Daily News*

DYING
CHEEK
TO
CHEEK

◆

DIANE K. SHAH

BANTAM BOOKS
NEW YORK • TORONTO • LONDON • SYDNEY • AUCKLAND

*My heartfelt thanks to KTLA's estimable news
reporter, Stan Chambers, for taking me back to that
first year when the fledgling TV station operated out of
an old Paramount garage.*

*This edition contains the complete text
of the original hardcover edition.*
NOT ONE WORD HAS BEEN OMITTED

DYING CHEEK TO CHEEK

*A Bantam Crime Line Book / published in association with
Doubleday*

PUBLISHING HISTORY
*Doubleday edition published May 1992
Bantam edition / March 1993*

ISBN 0-553-29628-0

Published simultaneously in the United States and Canada

PRINTED IN THE UNITED STATES OF AMERICA

RAD   0 9 8 7 6 5 4 3 2 1

DYING
CHEEK
TO
CHEEK

1

♦

It was a Santa Ana kind of day, typical for this time of year, when the ground is parched and the brushfires stand waiting in the wings. Always the hot winds arrive without warning, blowing in over the San Gabriel Mountains sometime during the night. The temperature steadily rises and you find yourself licking sandpaper lips and touching skin that feels like old brittle paper. As the dry, dusty days drag on, you walk around with your teeth on edge. I was crabby enough already.

The sky was sapphire blue.

I had overslept. And then I had wrestled with my closet, unable to find anything to wear. Actually, I didn't know what to wear. Neither did Emily Post, whose book I had riffled for unimpeachable correctness. The funeral had been held in New York a week ago and this was a memorial service for people on the West Coast. In the end, the navy Dior suit with the dropped hemline and the nipped waist wound up the winner.

"Do you want to be right on time?" inquired Andrew from the front seat of the Bentley.

I stared at the back of his peaked cap. "I don't mind."

I gazed uninterestedly at the houses on Highland, and then I glanced down at the newspaper on the seat beside me. The story still claimed the front page of the *Los Angeles Examiner*, where I worked. I pulled off my white gloves and lifted the paper. But I just stared at it, too.

We turned onto Third Street and skimmed the edge of the Wilshire Country Club before turning left on Muirfield Road, one of the prettiest streets in Hancock Park. Half a block up the car stopped at the curb. Andrew did not switch off the engine but turned and looked out the passenger window at the broad, manicured lawn and the two-story stone and wood house set well back from the street. A shiny green Buick, a sagging black De Soto and an important-looking gray Lincoln had staked out the circular drive. The mahogany front door stood open, ready to admit what promised to be an impressive cast of mourners. A dozen men in dark wrinkled suits, with boxy cameras dangling from their necks, stood ready, too. I could hear Andrew's breathing, along with mine.

"You won't want your picture taken," he said.

I licked my lips but did not reply.

"Shall I escort you in, Miss Chandler?"

I put down the paper and picked up my gloves. "No." I hesitated. "I don't know how long I'll be."

I dug out the compact from my purse and studied the mirror. I looked pale. I pinched my cheeks and put the compact away, just as a long black Cadillac dove into the curb in front of us. The back door flew open and out stepped Mayor Bowron. Two other men hurried to flank him, then all set off at a clip up the drive.

"I'll go in now," I said.

Andrew came round to open my door. "Are you sure you don't want . . . ?"

"Yes."

I walked quickly up the cement driveway, past a bed of forlorn freesia and droopy roses. The mayor had stopped to pose for the photographers, as I knew he would, giving me the chance to sneak by. I climbed the steps and walked into the house.

The black-and-white marble floor in the round foyer had been polished to a high luster and the crystal chandelier that hung from the soaring ceiling glittered with a reflected sunlight that slanted through the living room windows and came pouring under an archway to the right. The walls in the foyer were still the faded yellow of some long-ago occupant.

In the living room, six or seven people struck self-conscious and somber poses while a string quartet filled the air with sad Broadway melodies. A white-haired man and a Mexican woman, both in black uniform, stood at either end of the room holding trays of glasses filled with what was probably sherry. Behind me, I could hear the mayor's party entering, just as a woman in a black taffeta dress stepped through the archway to the left. For a moment, she looked startled.

"Mrs. St. Clair? I'm Fletcher Bowron," the mayor said.

The woman nodded distractedly and extended her hand.

"The mayor would like to pay his respects, Mrs. St. Clair," one of the lackeys jumped in.

"Oh," said the woman, smiling slightly. "Mayor . . . Bowron? Sorry, I am a stranger to Los Angeles."

The mayor, still gripping her hand, slid his meaty left hand on top of hers. "We all share your pain, Mrs. St. Clair. And I want to assure you, everything possible is being done by our fine police force to get to the bottom of this uh . . ."

"Murder," Mrs. St. Clair supplied.

The mayor dropped her hand. "If there is anything we can do . . ."

"Please come in, if you like, Mayor Bowron. Excuse me."

Mrs. St. Clair turned rudely away and then she spotted me. I took a deep breath as I started toward her. "Mrs. St. Clair, I'm Paris Chandler. With the *Los Angeles Examiner.* I was told it would be all right for me to come."

She studied me with indifferent black eyes. A wing of raven hair dipped over one of them. She was shorter than I, and rounder. The scoop-necked taffeta dress and narrow rhinestone belt accented her voluptuous figure. She wore high-heeled black suede shoes. Emily Post hadn't helped her either. Or maybe black taffeta and rhinestones were all the rage for mourning in New York.

I said, "I am also on a show once a week for the TV station and I knew your husband. I'm so terribly sorry. It's a shock to us all. I mean, if it's possible, he had already become a fixture here." I paused. "He was a nice man."

Mrs. St. Clair continued to gaze at me. "If you'd care to join the others now. I must see to the kitchen." And she walked away.

The mayor cleared his throat. "Miss Chandler, I'm Fletcher Bowron," striding over, giving me the smile. "Obviously, she's in shock."

Bowron had thinning white hair and black eyebrows that shot out from behind his rimless glasses. His dark suit didn't hide the substantial girth beneath it. Down at City Hall, the reporters called him "Old Chubby Cheeks." I grinned. "I didn't expect the mayor to be *here,*" I said meanly.

"Well, my dear. It's a terrible thing for our city. Our first TV newscaster gunned down in his own home. People will think it's not safe to live here. As you know, statistically . . ."

"Right," I said.

"But I must tell you, Miss Chandler, I've seen your show, in fact, I try never to miss it. You and that Nick fellow. My wife and I should have you two over sometime." He beamed at me.

I stepped closer. "Sir, the investigation has turned up so few leads. If there is something you could tell me that I could slip in tonight. You know, by the by?"

"Tonight?" His heavy eyebrows rose unevenly, like two slithering black worms. They flattened. "Ah yes, you're on tonight. Well I haven't spoken to Chief Gladstone today, but . . . by the by, they're looking for the gardener."

"The gardener?"

"A Japanese man. Still bitter about the internment camps. Lost his house and now he's resentful . . ."

"A Japanese gardener," I said, "who wore red lipstick?"

"Er, apparently there's no connection."

"The police still don't know who she is?" I watched his face with interest. That had been the big clue in the days following the murder. Two cigarette butts with red lipstick marks had been found in an ashtray on James St. Clair's bedside table. Mrs. James St. Clair had been on the *Twentieth Century Limited,* en route from New York.

"You'd better speak to Chief Gladstone," the mayor said. "A pleasure to meet you, my dear."

Soon the living room and the foyer were overflowing with politicians, people from KTLA, a handful of stars, including Betty Hutton and Linda Darnell, a flutter of movie starlets, spotlight moochers and whatever few real friends James St. Clair may have had. The Reverend Thomas Macom, God's minister to society, sobbed out a eulogy for a man he had never met.

Mrs. St. Clair stood in the archway between the living room and the foyer, expressionless, perhaps the only dry-eyed mourner in the house. But maybe there comes a point when the tears simply run out. Eleven days ago she had stepped off the train at Union Station and was met by two L.A. cops who welcomed her with the news that her husband was dead. She spent two days at the Hollywood Hotel waiting for the autopsy and the coroner's report, then climbed back on the train with the casket for the long miserable journey home. A funeral there, then another trip here to tidy up the business end of James St. Clair's life.

Or maybe she was simply feeling inconvenienced.

"She's a cold, selfish woman," Jim St. Clair had once confided to me. "A nice Italian girl. You know, religious. Before our first anniversary she had taken a lover."

It was no secret at the television station that they had

quarreled bitterly over his move to L.A. He was thirty-six, and already at the top of his profession, broadcasting nightly out of New York for NBC Radio and lending his stentorian voice to the *News of the Week* reels in the movie theaters. Then last January, KTLA went on the air as L.A.'s first commercial TV station. When it decided to hire a newscaster, James St. Clair was the man it went after. He delivered his first newscast in July, beginning, "Good evening. This is James St. Clair, reporting to you live from KTLA studios in Los Angeles, July 8, 1947."

Two and a half months later he was dead.

"If I were a betting man, I'd bet my bucks on Brooklyn," said a tall man with wire-rim glasses, whom I recognized as city councilman Mike Flanders. "Chrissake, Harry. With the whole country listening, you don't think Jackie Robinson is going to hog the show?"

"Forget it," said Police Chief Gladstone, loosening his tie. "My money's on the Yankees. Figuratively speaking of course."

"Well they ain't gonna win today," Flanders said, lifting his glass. "Branca's pitching."

"The Yankees have Shea." Gladstone frowned. "You know anything about this Shea, Mike?"

"Chief Gladstone?" I said.

"Spec Shea," recited Flanders. "Fourteen and five. Gets a little wild is what I hear."

Gladstone gave me an appraising look. "Whaddya think of this Shea against Branca?"

"I haven't the foggiest idea."

"But you like the Yankees?" The police chief looked at me as if this were an important consideration for him.

"Better than the Confederates. Could I ask you a question? I'm Paris Chandler with the *Examiner.*"

He brightened. "The girl on TV?"

I smiled.

"Scuse me, fellas." Harry Gladstone put his arm around me and whisked me through a French door out onto a brick patio. Underneath the brown wool suit, I could feel the muscle. He was a square-shaped man with a matching jaw, a tan face and measuring eyes. His mouth meant business. Mayor Bowron had installed him as police chief in an attempt to clean up the not-so-clean LAPD. From what I had heard, he was doing the job he was supposed to.

"So," he said, "Miss Paris Chandler. I see your show all the time. You look real cute doing those Rancho Soup commercials. You ever worry you might spill some, raising that spoon to your mouth?"

I just looked at him.

"Anyway, I was wondering," said Gladstone, resting his highball glass on the patio table. "You know I have my own radio show?"

"Uh huh. Monday nights. Eight-fifteen."

"Yeah, well, what I was wondering . . ." He cleared his throat. "How can I get on TV?"

The chief straightened the knot in his tie and raised his chin as if demonstrating his telegenic appeal. It didn't send me.

"Why that's a wonderful idea," I said carefully. "You being on TV."

"Yeah?"

"Oh yes. Why don't you let me help you? I can talk to my boss tonight. Would you like that, Chief Gladstone? I don't mean to be too forward."

"Actually, I would be most grateful, Miss Chandler. Perhaps we should talk more. Are you free for dinner soon?"

"Not tonight. I have the show tonight. Which reminds me. I would love to mention something about the investigation into Jim's death. People are beginning to think the police have lost interest." I moved a step closer. "You haven't lost interest, have you, Chief Gladstone?"

"I had no idea your eyes were green. Light green. Unusual."

"The lipstick marks, for instance. Surely you have *some* idea where they came from."

"I'm afraid not. But what I can tell you, Miss Chandler, and you mustn't let on where you got this, we're looking for the gardener."

"You found fingerprints in the house?"

"Lots of 'em. But none are on file. We have to collar the Jap then print him, see if there's a match."

"But Jim was killed in his bed."

"Jim was killed not in his bed." Gladstone gave me a hard grin. "You put me on TV, I'll tell you exactly where the body was found."

"Tell me now. You'll sleep better."

"Meaning what, Miss Chandler?"

"Meaning you'll enjoy the World Series more. I don't really follow baseball. But I do know about DiMaggio. Your money looks safe to me."

"What you overheard was hearsay."

"The papers said in his bed."

"The papers don't know nothing."

"Where?"

"You tell me."

"In the kitchen?"

"You're getting colder."

"In the rotunda?"

"You're smarter than you look."

"But nothing was stolen. Wouldn't the gardener steal?"

"Come with me to Reno. I'll get a divorce tonight." He leered.

"What is the gardener's name?"

"We only know they call him the Jap."

I edged my way around Bob Hope and Dorothy Lamour, who were talking with Klaus Landsburg, the general manager of KTLA. Hope had hosted KTLA's first commercial telecast last January, with Tupman Motors paying four thousand dollars to sponsor the hour-long show. It had not been the highlight of Tupman's career, or of Hope's. *Variety* panned the show, saying, "Tupman Motors must go down in local video history as a pioneer of strong faith if not a martyr." The picture was blurry, the entertainment lightweight. Not even Cecil B. DeMille's appearance could save the night.

But less than a month later, there had been an explosion at an electrical plating plant on Pico Boulevard. KTLA was on the scene within twenty minutes, camera on a flatbed truck. Standing amid the rubble of leveled houses while ambulances raced in and out to retrieve the dead and injured, Dick Lane interviewed eyewitnesses, scooping the newspapers and radio. More sponsors signed up.

I kept going, edging between people in the marble rotunda, wedging through more in the packed dining room, on into the kitchen.

Mrs. St. Clair was sitting at a beat-up wooden table smoking a cigarette. A glass on the table in front of her contained ice cubes and not much else. Behind her, at a counter, the Mexican woman was loading finger sandwiches onto a tray. The widow's eyes came up to meet mine. I felt my throat tighten.

I said, "May I speak with you for a moment?"

She nodded listlessly in the direction of a chair across the table. I sat down, noticing her pale skin and the rhinestone collar she wore around her neck. Pearls would have been more appropriate. But then, insisting the memorial be held here, in the house where her husband had been shot, was even less appropriate.

"The police don't seem to be making much headway," I offered.

"They don't care. The only one who cared was the sergeant who tried to molest me."

"Molest you?"

"He stuck his hand down my blouse. Of course, he still had his sunglasses on, so maybe it doesn't count." She gave me a skeptical look. "What's your interest, anyway?"

I selected an answer that contained part of the truth. "As I told you, I worked with your husband at the station. I don't mean to sound insensitive, but his murder was major news. Usually the police jump on cases like this one. I don't think they're jumping."

"So?" She picked up her glass and drained the last drops.

"I was just wondering if you gave them any information they're not acting on."

"Me? I was only out here once. You!" She waved her glass at the white-haired man in the black uniform. "A refill, please. Scotch. I came out in August to look at this awful house. I told Jim fine. And then I went home."

"You had no interest?"

"I knew I would be a prisoner here. I don't drive. And Jim isn't the kind of husband who comes home to care for his little wife." She burped. "I mean he wasn't."

"Do you mind if I have one of your cigarettes?"

She nudged her pack of Lucky Strikes across the table. I reached for a book of matches and lit one. The matches were from Chasen's. I wondered when she had found the time to go there.

"They told you about the gardener?" I said.

"I asked the neighbors next door. They never saw a gardener."

"Would you know if anything was taken?"

"All he had here were his clothes. And whatever furniture was still in the house when he rented it. What was there to steal?"

"Money maybe."

"The police asked me that. Unless he changed his ways, Jim never got to the bank, so he rarely had much cash on him. In New York, I had to advance him cab fare all the time." She made it sound like a major grievance in her marriage.

"I can't imagine he had any enemies," I said.

"You're obviously too naive."

"Oh?"

"The neighbors saw a blonde leaving the house the night he was murdered. The only enemy he had who wasn't blonde was me." She laughed.

I shifted uncomfortably.

The butler put down a drink in front of her, but Mrs.

St. Clair jumped up. "I'd better see to all those bereaved people out there." She gave me a charming smile. "So nice to make your acquaintance. I'm sure."

"Likewise." I returned her smile. But my heart wasn't in it.

2

♦

Appearing on TV is not really what I do. But try explaining that to someone. Especially in L.A., where anyone who isn't famous feels enhanced by knowing a person who is. Lots of people I encounter these days seem thrilled to know me.

What I really do for a living is quite the opposite of enhancing people's lives with my fame. I am a faceless, nameless legman for Etta Rice, the feared and revered gossip columnist for William Randolph Hearst's *Examiner*. Etta is from the old school of barge-in journalism. All over town, bellhops, nurses and waiters are only too eager to clue her in. And Etta, audacious and unrelenting, thinks nothing of busting into a room at the Beverly Hills Hotel and giving a piece of her mind to an actor or actress quaking under the sheets with an illicit lover. Just as brazenly, she will ring up Sam Goldwyn or Louis B. Mayer and wangle a contract for a promising young talent. She can make careers or destroy them, and has. Etta is syndicated nationwide and can be heard on the radio coast-to-coast two nights a week. The real power in this town is not Mayor Bowron, or Police Chief Gladstone or the maître d' at Mocambo. It is dumpy, well-dressed, over-bejeweled Etta Rice.

For $57.50 a week, I help her dish the dirt.

I hadn't scooped up much, though, at James St. Clair's memorial.

A pile of phone messages had collected on my desk by the time Andrew dropped me off at the *Examiner*. I removed my gloves and began sorting through them. The first that caught my eye was from the producer Roy Del Ruth. Joe DiMaggio, according to Del Ruth, was expected in Hollywood after the World Series to test for the role of himself in *The Life of Babe Ruth*.

Test for the role of . . . himself? What if . . . he botched it? I began to giggle. Another slip of paper heralded the impending arrival from Honolulu of Joan Crawford. "Gone two days, homesick" read the rest of her press agent's message. I sighed and began to place calls. By four o'clock I had learned that Tyrone Power would leave Johannesburg next Friday to pay a personal visit to Emperor Haile Selassie in Ethiopia and that Esther Williams still wasn't out of the woods with her ear infection. Rita Hayworth and Orson Welles were proceeding with their divorce and had reached a financial settlement. Rita was off to New York.

I dialed Etta Rice. Etta worked out of her house in Holmby Hills and was last known to have visited the office on V-J Day. Not that I blamed her. The *Examiner*, built in 1915, had an impressive Moorish exterior to match Hearst's castle at San Simeon, but an interior better suited to the neighborhood—Skid Row. The word was that *Examiner* reporters operated like characters out of *The Front Page*, which was fine for our circulation. Unfortunately, the sagging and rickety wooden desks, cracked linoleum floors and peeling paint were of the same vintage as the 1931 movie, which was not fine. The floor moppers came twice a year.

Nick Goodwin, the handsome scoundrel who served as Etta's other legman, worked out of her house as well. When I was hired nearly eighteen months ago, I was inserted into The Society Department, due less to a lack of space at Etta's, I suspected, than to her neurotic insecurity. Etta was counting on me to serve as her spy at the paper.

By now she would be pacing back and forth across her priceless Oriental rugs, barking out Items to one of her two secretaries. She broke off to come on the line. After I told her what nuggets I had dredged up, she cried, "Sensational!" and hung up.

I lit a cigarette. The Society Department had reached its usual pre-deadline cacophony; typewriters clacking, phones ringing, voices hitting a panicky pitch. I rolled two pieces of copy paper with a carbon between them into my typewriter and began to hunt and peck my way through the Items I had culled. At five o'clock, a messenger would leave Etta's house with her column and deliver it here to the copy desk, where someone would add punctuation. Etta was too arrogant to bother with periods and paragraphs. My Items would be inserted, according to Etta's illegible notations.

This system actually worked.

"My dear, tell me about the memorial service, tell me *everything*."

I looked up from Rita Hayworth's financial settlement into the flushed face of Constance McPhee Estevez, the tall, glamorous society editor who was married to some vague Chilean royalty and who cowered at the mention of Etta Rice.

I punched out a "–30–" at the end of my copy and rolled the last page out. "It was like a theme party," I answered, "only everyone forgot the theme."

Constance patted her long blond hair. Usually she wore it in a stylish bun, but today it was combed back behind her ears. From her lobes dangled silver poles with large glittery globes attached. She frowned. "You mean nobody toasted the departed?"

"Nobody even mentioned the departed. Except Reverend Macom." I lit a new cigarette. "It's possible I went to the wrong address."

"Really?" Constance began chewing on her polished fingernails.

"I did talk to Mrs. St. Clair. She acted like she was at the wrong memorial."

"Ooo, what does she look like?"

One of Constance's problems is that she doesn't listen. I said, "She looks like a bitch."

"Paris! How delicious."

"She said the only enemy her husband had who wasn't blond was herself. Her hair is black."

"*I love it.*"

"I thought you would."

"We must do a story on her, don't you think? We'll take a picture of her smirking. Does she smirk?"

"I think she meows."

"Hmm." Constance turned and surveyed the department, debating who should get this plum assignment. Her eyes fell on Abigail Longhorn, the gawky fashion editor known as "The Hat," then on chubby, gray-haired Theresa McKenzie, who wrote up parties as if they were scenes out of D. H. Lawrence. The mopey advice-to-the-lovelorn columnist, Prudence Penny, had already left for the day. Dolph Mann, the mysterious restaurant critic, penned weekly columns but could have been Roy Rogers for all anyone knew of him. Constance's eyes came back to me.

"Nick?" she said.

"Exactly," I said.

"You'll tell him?"

I handed her the phone. "You can reach him at Etta's now."

Constance handed the receiver back to me. "Get him on the line, dear. I'll be right back."

I got Nick on the line.

"I was about to call you," said Nick. "Are you ready for tonight?"

"How come you weren't at Jim's memorial?"

"Did I miss anything?"

"Just the police chief betting on the Yankees."

"You're kidding," Nick said. "He didn't take Brook-lyn?"

"Should he?"

"They lost 5–3. But they'll pull it out."

"You mean you bet on them, too?"

"Yeah. In six."

"Six what?"

Nick sighed. "So we'll meet at the studio?"

"Fine. But first Constance wants to talk with you."

"And then we'll have dinner?"

I hesitated. "All right."

I turned the phone over to Constance, who was stand-ing deskside, chewing on her lip. Then I picked up my purse and walked down the hall to the rest room. I fooled with my lipstick, brushed my hair and went down the marble staircase to the ornate, frescoed lobby of the *Examiner*, which was the only presentable part of the building. Andrew, looking immaculate in his black chauf-feur's uniform, was leaning against the circulation counter, conferring with a short, unshaven man wearing a flannel shirt and soiled cotton pants, who was scrib-bling in a reporter's notebook. A wheezing dalmation sagged at his feet.

It was Benny the one-eyed Bookmaker. "Service while you wait."

3
◆

KTLA operates out of an old garage across the alley from the main Paramount Studio gate. KTLA is actually owned by Paramount, but it is considered a poor relation indeed. Every afternoon, a guy named Gus wheels over a dolly of props from the studio and, based on the props sent, the writers for *The Garry and Larry Show* create their fifteen-minute comedy. Other than that, Paramount treats us like some kind of bizarre and possibly dangerous experiment, as if we might be inventing The Bomb.

When I walked in under the huge raised garage door shortly before six, the test pattern was still on the large ten-inch TV that sat on a table just inside Studio One. Behind the TV, three rows of folding chairs were lined up for the "studio audience," or anybody curious enough to walk in off the street. Programming ran from quarter past six until ten, starting with a fifteen-minute newscast and usually ending with wrestling.

Studio One, the main television studio, and two smaller ones, illogically known as B and C, were located in the front of the garage. Already the hot, glaring lights were turned on and the crew was getting ready to go. Bernard Wexler, who had taken over Jim's newscasts, was sitting behind his desk with a bib on, head tilted back as May Rivers dabbed makeup on his face. Behind the desk was a fake fireplace, built for no reason anyone could think of. To the right of Bernard's shoulder, propped on a stand, was a large map of Europe. Other props—a wooden globe, a calendar and an ashtray— were arranged on the desk where he delivered the news. To the left, three microphones on poles stood in a row. During commercial breaks, the camera would swing around to one of the announcers hawking Ovaltine, Tupman Motors or Lucky Strikes, our three big sponsors.

"Watch the wires, cutie."

I smiled at Ed Drake, an engineer with a knack for troubleshooting and the smile of an angel, waved to the others, but kept walking toward the back of the garage.

After eight months of commercial operations, KTLA still resembled a gypsy camp, liable to pack up and move out at any time. The few small offices that existed were partitioned by long white sheets hung from the rafters. I passed two before entering the enshrouded newsroom. Four desks with two telephones were bunched together in the middle of the area. Along the perimeter stood two metal file cabinets and the clattering AP and UPI wire service machines. Jim used to sit at his desk writing his newscasts from the wires. When he needed more fill, he would choose segments from Hearst's Metrotone news-reels, which arrived at least three days after an event. With the TV camera focused on the newsreel, Jim would read copy that made it sound like the event had occurred only hours before. TV was a tricky business.

As I walked through the sheets, one of the phones was ringing. Truman Stone, the sly, laconic news director, was on the other one. I lifted the receiver. "KTLA."

"Yeah, hi. Who's this?" came a man's voice.

"Paris Chandler."

"Hi, Paris. This is Bill Greenwood. Over in Culver City?"

"Uh huh."

"Honey, my picture's going up and down. I been fiddling with it for the last hour. What do you suppose is wrong?"

Three hundred TV sets in L.A. County and I figured I'd talked to half the owners in the two months that Nick and I had been on the air.

"I'll have one of the engineers phone you," I promised. I wrote down his number and hung up.

I sank into Jim's cushioned swivel chair and stared at Mr. Greenwood's number, feeling suddenly immobilized. After a while, I began to scribble on a piece of paper, trying to look busy. Eventually, Truman finished his phone call and went up front to watch the newscast. I knew I would have the office to myself for fifteen minutes. I slid open the top drawer of Jim's desk. The police had been through the desk, but I wanted a go at it one more time.

I knew the contents of the top drawer by heart. Sharpened pencils, an eraser, a scissors, a roll of three-cent stamps, a World Series ticket stub autographed by Stan Musial and several typewritten pages of phone numbers of city officials whom Jim frequently called. Those pages were gone.

Curious, I began working the three side drawers. Jim had met someone for dinner the night he was killed, I knew that. But he hadn't told me who it was. I assumed it was someone connected with the freeway construction project, a pet story he had been chronicling on the air. Now, remembering his widow's sniping remark about blondes, I began to wonder. Could it have been a woman?

I suddenly realized my fingers were ice cold as they continued to rummage through the drawers. If Jim had been found in the foyer, had he heard a noise and come down? Or had someone rung the doorbell, sometime after ten-thirty, someone Jim was expecting? Or someone, he may have assumed, who had just left, only to return?

I slammed the bottom drawer shut and went over to the file cabinets. The bulging folder marked "L.A. Freeways" was still there. I pulled it out and stuffed it into the shopping bag I had brought, and tried to remember the last time I had seen those missing phone numbers. Then I walked further back along the hall to the makeup chair, glancing at my watch. Wondering where Nick was.

"All right, kiddies, five minutes."

"So I'll open with Greer Garson making her first public appearance since her divorce by going to hear Sophie Tucker at the Florentine Gardens," Nick said triumphantly. "I'll use the line about her telling Sophie she'd been crying so hard, she came to see her just so she could stop." Nick adjusted his tie for the umpteenth time. "And then you can bring up the Bogart and Bacall thing."

The director was now conferring with the cameraman, who was stationed only five feet away. Nick and I were sitting on a couch with a coffee table in front of us. I was having a hard time concentrating.

"I'm sorry," I said to Nick.

"You know. How Bogie's call from his boat to Betty in Beverly Hills on the shortwave was intercepted by Ida Lupino." Nick crossed his legs and pinched the crease in his pant leg. He looked up with a sudden grin. "How risqué do you suppose we can get?"

"Risqué?"

"I won't mention names obviously, but at the John Huston party, a lady walked into the bedroom to get her coat and found two people were already in it."

"Two people were in her coat?"

"I mean they were on the bed under the coat. A director and an actress. You'd know their names. Everyone would."

I laughed. "You do that, Nicky, and next week it won't be *Nick and Paris on the Town*. It will be *Paris on the Town.*"

"You think so?" Nick tugged at his French cuffs, making sure the gold lion's head cuff links showed. I couldn't help but smile. As often as I wanted to kill him, I was still, after a year and a half, a sucker for him. It was Nick who had somehow gotten us this fifteen-minute show on television.

"Three minutes, kids."

He was a real operator. From Princeton, Nick had studied one year at Fordham Law, then, after writing propaganda for the war effort, had followed a girl to the West Coast. How he landed a job with Etta Rice I did not know—it was a year before I arrived—but once installed as legman, he played the role for all it was worth: Mr. Man About Town. He could jive with the best of them. His face, on anyone else, would have been called nice looking. But Nick's boyish charm made him cuter than he was. Our relationship had begun, and remained, as a kind of hide-and-seek flirtation, though at the moment, we seemed to have stalled out. Possibly because he had recently taken up with another in a long line of golden blond bathing beauties. When that wore off, he would undoubtedly come seeking me. Given my frame of mind these days, I wasn't in much of a hurry.

"And then we'll talk about the premiere of *Forever Amber*," Nick was saying.

"Which was boring." I licked my lips. "The police chief betting on the Yankees is not."

"You're gonna?"

"Ten seconds. Paris, put that cigarette out."

The lights were a blinding glare and I felt that sudden, pulsating magic that always flooded through me at airtime. I stubbed out the cigarette, cleared my throat and sat up straight.

"You bet," I said. And turned on my 100-kilowatt smile.

I talked Nick out of going to O'Blath's, the noisy hangout around the corner from the station. I wasn't in the mood for a crowd. Instead we found a back booth at The Grotto on Melrose, a more refined watering hole at the edge of the Paramount lot. I was on my second Perfect Manhattan and picking at a lamb chop, still not able to concentrate.

"How did you know about St. Clair's body being found in the foyer?" said Nick, referring to my little scoop on the air.

"Gladstone."

"Well well. You and the chief certainly got on." Nick's eyes flicked past me to see who had just walked in.

"He wants to be on TV," I said.

Nick put down his fork. "You strung Gladstone along? Paris, you're shameless. What else went on?"

"They're trying to peddle the idea that the gardener did it." I picked up my drink. "But I don't buy it."

Nick flashed one of those grins that lasted just a second too long.

"What's the matter?"

"I suppose," said Nick, "you've been reading Miss Marple. Tell me." He leaned across the table. "Was it the butler?"

I put the glass down. "I don't think anything was taken, Nicky. And the people next door said they never saw a gardener. I could do without your wisecracks for once."

"Have another Manhattan."

"I'm sorry," I said. "It's been a long day. The memorial was . . . tough."

"Which brings up the subject of Mrs. St. Clair."

"You're going to do it?" I was surprised.

"Of course. A byline is a byline," Nick sang.

He was referring to our ghostlike jobs. Legmen were known at the studios, the restaurants and among the Beverly Hills social climbers—but not to the public. A hundred people could contribute to Etta's column, but it would still appear under her name. Nick was hungry.

I smiled. "Good luck." And reached for my purse.

"You're leaving?" Nick look aggrieved.

"I'm tired." I stood up.

"And a little sad." His tone softened. "What's the matter, Paris?"

For the second his baby blue eyes held mine, I could see genuine concern in them. Then his eyes shifted.

A vampish brunette carrying a cigarette holder had pulled up to the booth. "Say, aren't you Nick Goodwin?"

Nick grinned.

"Yeah, I saw you on television once. At my friend Deedee's house. She has one. A television, I mean." She took a deep breath. "I'm Carmel."

"I'm gone," I said.

Nick stood and reached for my elbow. "You sure you're okay? You look pale."

Carmel had already slid into the booth and was checking her face in a small mirror. She ran her tongue over her lips.

"It's the Santa Anas," I told him. "They drain the color right out of me."

Andrew dropped me off at the front door before pulling the Bentley into the garage. He lived above it. I had acquired him more through genetics than free will. My mother, a B-movie actress of the thirties, and stuck with a Victorian frame of mind, had hammered into me the inviolable notion that proper ladies didn't drive. Why I had bought into that argument, when I had rejected most of her others, was unclear. Why I had hired Andrew was inexplicable altogether.

Although he was a chauffeur to me, in his eyes, he was a promising actor always on the verge of the Big Break. At twenty-seven, he needed one. Although attractive, with sandy hair, perfect features and a dimpled smile, Andrew had been saddled with a high, nasal voice. Whether he could actually act was unknown. But he definitely had the instability for the profession. Whenever he felt depressed, he changed his name. I had hired him as Martin. For nine months we then endured Bret. Two weeks ago, he sent me a formal notice—through the U.S. Mail—announcing he was now Andrew.

I plucked the mail from the wall rack over the telephone table in the entrance hall and walked into the library. I headed straight for the red leather wing chair with the matching ottoman and sank into it. For a while I

stared at the curlicues in the Oriental rug, then I stared
at the floor-to-ceiling bookshelves. I considered putting
a record on but somehow I couldn't get myself to move.
Perhaps *I* needed a name change.

I sank deeper into the chair. The room, my favorite in
the house, had been designed and mainly occupied by
my late husband, Russell, before he went to war. He was
a Chandler, and expected one day to run his family's
business, the *Los Angeles Times*. But three years ago last
week they had rung my doorbell and delivered the news:
Shortly after the liberation of Paris, my husband went
bicycling in search of a bistro he had remembered from
his youth. He was hit, head on, by a deliriously drunken
cabdriver. This left me with a lovely house on North
Maple Drive in Beverly Hills, which, since Russell didn't
have a will, the Chandlers were trying to reclaim, a black
1939 Bentley with a Park Ward saloon, and a thirty- or
forty-year stretch I didn't begin to know how to fill.

I had fired all of the servants except for Mrs. Keyes
and the then-Martin and rumbled disconsolately around
the house for eighteen months until, by chance, I was
seated at a dinner party next to the editor of the *Examiner*. He knew my parents. My mother, still shamefully
gorgeous at forty-nine, had remade herself into a social
lion, while my father maintained his own prominence as
a screenwriter under contract to Warner Bros. With my
connections, the editor said, why didn't I go to work for
Etta Rice?

Which is how I came to know Nick. And through
Nick's maneuverings, how I landed at KTLA. And met
James St. Clair.

We had actually met in July, soon after his arrival from
New York. KTLA, so proud of its status as the city's first
commercial TV station, had taken out full-page ads in
Variety and *The Hollywood Reporter* to trumpet Jim's de-
but. The trumpeting was heard less by the Hollywood
community, which had decided to ignore TV, than by the
city's leading hostesses, who were instinctually poised to
ensnare anything faintly resembling a new celebrity.

It was at Agnes Greenhall's intimate sit-down dinner

for forty, which I was sent to monitor for Etta, that Jim had come up to me saying, "Hi. I know we've met before."

And I had said, "I hope you deliver the news better than you just delivered that line."

He didn't smile. He just stood there studying my face, biting his lip. "Indiana," he declared at last. "You taught at the two-room schoolhouse, the older kids, fourth through sixth grade I think. I was the man next door."

Now it was my turn to study him. Tall, athletic build—even at his publicized age of thirty-six—dark wavy hair, brown eyes, full lips, nothing that particularly sent me. But he had one of those wonderfully deep radio voices that made you want to hear more.

"Yes, why of course," I replied. "The man who was always complaining that the kids made too much noise. You—were recovering, right? From a war injury, and everyone thought you were the grumpiest man they had ever met." I smiled.

"You deliver your lines just fine. Are you an actress? Or does that notebook you're holding mean what I think it does?"

"I'm an actress pretending I'm a reporter." I paused. "Do you think I'm convincing?"

At which point, Agnes Greenhall, deciding I had tied up more than enough of her prize's precious attention, barged in and hauled him off, like a tugboat guiding a cruise ship through the shoals.

"I thought I heard you come in. Tea?"

Mrs. Keyes, a continual sight if there ever was one, stood in the doorway, hands on hips, eyeing me accusingly. My housekeeper ran my home as if I were the help, expecting me to announce my comings and goings to *her*. She was obviously irritated that I had failed to do this when I came in.

Tonight she had outdone herself. Next to a fetish for polishing, her second favorite thing in life was to change her hairdo. First came the dyed red hair, followed by the frizzy permanent, which had mercifully almost grown out. Sometime after I had left the house that morning, Mrs. Keyes had apparently dumped a bucket of peroxide over her head.

"How, er, *blond,*" I enthused.

"You like it?" She was wearing, as if the hair didn't offer enough shock value, a slithery black caftan that fell over her narrow body like a collapsed tent. Furry white slippers peaked out from underneath like scared rabbits.

"It's, uh, fine, Mrs. Keyes. I'm just not quite used to it yet."

She grinned. "I figured we could jazz up the house with two blondes now. When men come to call, I can get them in the mood."

"Ah," I said. "Well."

She began twirling a bleached curl with her finger, like a bad imitation of a flapper. "Did you say you wanted tea?"

"That will be fine." I glanced at my watch. "I still have some reading to do."

My eyes traveled to the shopping bag on the floor at my feet. But when Mrs. Keyes brought the tea, I went upstairs to bed. Thinking, as I got undressed, that tomorrow was October.

And they had both died in September.

4

♦

The *Times* and the *Examiner* were on the breakfast table when I came downstairs the next morning. I went over to the stove and poured a cup of coffee from Mrs. Keyes's sparkling pot, pilfered two Fig Newtons from the cabinet and sat down. The front page of the *Times* was dominated by two large photos, five columns across, one on top of the other. The first showed downtown L.A. on a rare clear day, the second on a typical smoggy day, the outlines of buildings barely visible through a dark soup. Below was a story about Dr. Louis C. McCabe, the county's newly appointed "smog control" chief.

"He arrived yesterday aboard the Union Pacific's *City of Los Angeles,*" the story said, "to find visibility poor."

The *Examiner* had a different kind of front page. Next to a story about yesterday's first game of the World Series, was the headline: GARDENER ARRESTED IN NEWSCASTER'S DEATH.

According to the story, the arrest was made early last evening by a Sergeant William Baxter, who had found the man cleaning up a toolshed in Hollywood just off the

27

Cahuenga Pass. He was identified only as a twenty-six-year-old former resident of the Manzanar internment camp. Additional information was to be provided at a press conference at police headquarters at ten o'clock. It was now eight. I went back to the *Times,* found a similar story on page two, then flipped to Hedda Hopper's column to make sure she hadn't scooped Etta. She hadn't.

I took a fresh cup of coffee upstairs, climbed back into bed and began sifting through the papers in the freeway file.

Jim had started in on freeways his first week on the air.

It had happened as the result of a "technical problem." To allow Jim to deliver the news while looking directly at the camera, some clever fellow had hit upon the idea of putting Jim's newscast on a roll of paper. The copy Jim had written was transferred onto the roll, using a special typewriter with large letters. A pole was inserted through the roll and the whole thing was rigged up under the camera lens. A man sitting on the floor under the camera pulled the paper down as Jim read.

But on this evening, with two-and-a-half minutes to go, the pole slipped off its hinges and clattered to the floor, dumping the paper in a tangled mess. Without missing a beat, Jim finished the last lines of the story he had been reading. He then began to improvise. Having just arrived from New York, he was rather dumbfounded, he said, to watch Los Angeles shovel both dirt and people aside to lay down superhighways. The system could only lead to more noise, smog, traffic deaths and congestion. For all the millions of dollars being spent, why not fix up the popular streetcar system, known as the Red Cars, and the buses, which, though dilapidating, were efficient. And if the city wanted to play with its erector sets, a subway system seemed a much more practical answer. Without one, L.A. was doomed to remain a dusty, second-class town located in the middle of a bean field.

Jim had delivered this impromptu editorial with a smile and a sense of humor. The newspapers, which were dispatching reporters to the studio on a daily basis to cover "picture news," brought Jim's comments to far more people than would have seen him on TV.

Angry politicians attacked Mr. Know It All, and Jim, enjoying the furor he had created, wouldn't let the issue die. In subsequent editorials, he began referring to the Hollywood Freeway as the Hollywood 500, calling the home relocation plan "freeway interruptus," and urging the Chamber of Commerce to name Los Angeles "the country's first All-American Parking Lot."

Mr. Landsburg, KTLA's general manager, was in a quandry. While Jim's spirited remarks were bringing welcome attention to his infant station, the sponsors of the news program were being pressured by oil companies, Firestone Tires and determined local officials to pull out. Some politicians had gone so far as to petition the FCC to clamp down on KTLA for violating the Mayflower Doctrine, which prohibited broadcasters from advocating a point of view. It was a mess.

Jim managed to quell the storm somewhat by injecting even more humor into his editorials and by taking the side of "the little guy," who watched the state tow his house down the street and into a new neighborhood, out of the path of the "oncoming, house-eating, fume-belching freeway." Soon he was delivering his editorials three nights a week, always beginning with the middle-class hero, Charlie Paycheck, trudging home from the factory only to discover he had just missed his house by five minutes. The sponsors stayed.

Jim wrote out his editorials and kept them in a special folder, along with detailed notes of his telephone interviews with public officials. I had seen the folder on his desk many times. But what I had swiped from the file cabinet the night before was not that folder.

This one was filled with letters, mostly handwritten, from people commending Jim for his campaign, castigating him for attacking modern advancement or offering belabored personal stories of freeway dislocation.

I tossed the folder aside and got up.

Shortly after six, on the night he died, the phone had

rung in the newsroom. I was standing there, talking to
him. He turned and answered it, said, "Which freeway?"
Then he had laughed. I hadn't listened further, except at
one point, I thought I heard him say, "Barbie." Later, as
he went hurrying off to Studio One, he called out, "Got
to meet someone for dinner, Paris. I'll tell you about it
later." Only—he never did.

I put on a pair of black gabardine slacks and a red
military-style jacket. Then I went out to find Andrew.

He was nowhere to be found.

Police headquarters was located in City Hall, at the corner of Temple and Spring. The mayor entered his offices
from Spring, the chief of police from Temple. Depending
upon the political winds, they could cross paths or not.

I entered through Temple Street, waltzed across the
marble floor and scampered down a flight of stairs. By
the time I hit bottom, the city coffers had run out. The
basement was drab gray concrete, highlighted by naked
light bulbs screwed into the ceiling wherever there was a
gap in the tangle of wires. My high-heeled footsteps
click-clicked ominously on the hard floor. Halfway along
the hall, I stopped at a door with a pebble-glass window,
turned the greasy knob and walked in.

Six pairs of distracted eyes swung reflexively in my direction, returned automatically to their keyboards, then
did a double-take back to me. Two typewriters fell silent.
An audible intake of collective breath sounded in the
stale room.

"Low, inside, ball three," said a radio on the far table.
Another typewriter stopped clattering. Competing with
the radio came the tinny sounds from the squawk box,
coded calls being sent out to squad cars. Six men, spaced
around long tables bordering the square room, were
hunched over their afternoon stories. Cardboard cups of
coffee rose above balled-up pieces of copy paper. Pictures of women in seductive poses were taped to the
peeling walls, along with a torn, faded column by Damon
Runyon.

The man closest to the door sized me up. "Ladies' room's upstairs," he grunted.

I walked past him to the back of the room and slid into a folding chair next to Don Wilsson of the City News Bureau. "Can I talk to you?"

Don was a rangy Minnesota Swede I had met on saloon runs with Walter Ainsley, a former crime reporter at the *Examiner* who had been my first office friend. Don held up his hand then went back to banging a furious tune on his keyboard. After a while, he stood up and walked out of the room. I followed.

He tilted against the wall and stuck a fresh cigarette between his teeth. "Whole damn town's shut down cause of a ballgame. Call any office. No one's there." He struck a match.

"They're at the bars," I said.

"Yeah." He inhaled deeply, dropping the match on the floor. It flared briefly and went out.

"Were you at the press conference, Don?"

"Why? You filling in so your guy can listen to the game?"

"No. I'm just asking." Thanks to my chauffeur's little hookey play, I had relayed between two buses to get downtown and had arrived too late to hear what I had come for.

"They arrested the Jap gardener. Tommy Nakamura, or something."

"Did they say how long he had worked for Jim?"

Don snapped a fat blue suspender. "You looking for a reference, or what?"

"Supposedly there was no gardener. What did they have on him?"

"A couple of oxford cloth shirts they say belonged to St. Clair and fifty bucks."

"Did they find the gun?"

"Yep, that, too. Standard .38 automatic. The guy ain't talking."

"They're saying what—the gardener rang the doorbell, Jim answered and . . ."

"They're saying St. Clair hears a noise, maybe like the

garage door opening. Goes out to investigate. Sees this gardener, who pulls a gun."

"And then goes into the house to shoot him?"

"Hell, Paris, there's no score."

I grinned. "So where's Gladstone listening to the game?"

"The Downtown Athletic Club. But I wouldn't try busting in there." Don twisted his heel into the burning cigarette butt. "He's listening with J. Edgar Hoover."

I walked the eight blocks to the office, the hot, dusty air catching in my throat and coating the insides of my mouth. The cars parked along Broadway looked as if they had been identically painted in shades of brown dust. A woman in a housedress leaned out of a second-story window, languidly moving a torn rag across droopy begonias in a flower box. In an hour the leaves would be grimy again. For once, the office looked hygenic.

It was noon and Society was deserted. I glanced at the phone messages on my desk before taking a pass through the newsroom. It, too, had lost most of its personnel to the lunch hour, which probably meant plenty of action across the street in the bar of the Cabrillo Hotel. A copy boy hurried in carrying a stack of afternoon papers, just off the press. I picked one off the pile and wandered back to Society.

The arrest of the gardener was splashed across the front page. Although the *Examiner*'s policy was to give bylines only rarely, I recognized the handiwork of George Healy, our brash young crime reporter, who was a snake. He had presented only what Gladstone had said at the press conference, but George had written it as if it were a scoop. Bully for him.

I scanned the rest of the front page. The weatherman made the startling prediction that October would be cooler than September. The director of the Florida Safety Council theorized that many automobile wrecks were caused by husbands after eating burnt breakfasts cooked by their wives and a woman was granted a de-

fault divorce on the grounds that her husband criticized
her clothes in public. "And I had to support him, too,"
grumbled the woman. "Is he retired?" asked the judge.
"No," said the woman. "Just tired."

The phone rang.

"Paris? Truman Stone." There was a pause. "Got a
minute?"

"Sure," I said. And pulled a burnt orange crayon out
of my chipped coffee mug. I began drawing a piece of
toast.

"A woman's been calling for you. A Lucille Wills."

"Uh huh."

"She wants to talk to you about Jim."

I put down the crayon.

"May have something to do with the broadcast last
night. You mentioned that his body was found in the
foyer. She phoned right after you left. And she called
again this morning. Twice."

"She didn't say—anything else?"

"I told her I was the news director, could I help?
Nope, she wanted to talk to the pretty lady on TV."

"You don't suppose she meant Sparkles?" Sparkles
was the chimp who appeared in the six forty-five time
slot on Thursday nights.

"If she did, call me. You want her number? It's Morningside 4768. Let me know if it's anything impor—*Oh-
no!*"

"What?" I said.

"Lindell just doubled." And the line went dead.

Lucille Wills said she would be happy to meet me downtown so I told her to turn up at Gallagher's, the coffee
shop across the street from the *Examiner*. I told her to
turn up at four o'clock sharp.

She was one of those people with a mismatched voice.
On the phone it had sounded low, serious and deep,
conjuring up the image of a middle-aged librarian or—a
spinster. Lucille Wills may have been both but gray hair
and glasses weren't part of the package. She came

wrapped in a beige cashmere dress, her hair in short loose ringlets about her heart-shaped face. It was a face that had seen thirty and didn't mind it.

She was watching the door from a seat toward the far end of the counter. Two men in shiny business suits and snap-brim fedoras sat near the front arguing whether Jackie Robinson could take the heat.

I slid onto the worn leather stool next to her and said, "I'm Paris Chandler."

Hazel eyes flicked anxiously over my shoulder. Then she turned them on me. "You're prettier in person." She raised her coffee cup and took a sip.

"Thank you." I signaled Ruth to bring me a cup, too. "So," I said, "how can I help you?"

There was something in her manner that made me not want to help her with anything, a kind of superiority that came through in her perfect posture and the slight tilt of her chin.

"Lewis, stop it," Lucille Wills said.

I turned around on the stool and noticed a small boy crawling up the leg of one of the men in the shiny suits. The man tried to shake Lewis off. I looked back at Lucille.

"Lewis, darling, come *here.*" She extended a slender hand toward the boy, but he just grinned and trotted to the front of the coffee shop. "Lewis!" He crawled under an empty booth. Lucille Wills jumped off her stool and marched over to him. She grabbed his hand and dragged him back over to me. "He's at that horrible age of three. There, there, precious. You sit with Mommy now. I think I'll kill him."

She climbed back on the stool and arranged Lewis in her lap. "I'm sorry, Miss Chandler." She extricated her right arm from Lewis and raised her coffee cup. "I don't want to be a suspect." Lewis grabbed at the cup. "Darling, you're making Mommy angry." She slapped his hand away.

"A suspect?" I repeated.

Lucille opened a large handbag and pulled out a worn

gray bunny with one ear. "Darling, take this over to the booth and play. That's a good boy."

Lewis scampered away and Lucille sighed. "I couldn't find a sitter on such short notice so I had to bring him with me."

"What do you mean, a suspect?"

"I'm afraid the police will think I did it." Lucille flashed a can-you-believe-it smile and leaned closer. "That's why I called you. I need to get my letters back."

"You wrote letters to James St. Clair?"

"I thought you could look for them at the TV station. Lewis! Get off the floor. You know, in his desk. From TV, you seemed like the kind of person who would understand." She gave me a quick, appraising look to see if her judgment held up in real life.

"What kind of letters?" I said uneasily.

"Personal. Very personal letters." Lucille Wills blushed.

"You knew him?"

"Quite well. We met at a freeway meeting."

"When was that?" I heard myself saying.

"Early August, I think. In Los Feliz. There was a rumor the freeway was coming through and people from the neighborhood were upset. They asked James to come."

"You live in Los Feliz?"

"As a matter of fact, I do."

Lucille Wills cast a concerned eye toward Lewis, who was sticking his tongue out at Ruth.

"I see." I drank some of my coffee.

Lucille lowered her voice. "It was just one of those crazy things. Frankly, I don't know what got into me."

"Uh huh."

"You can understand my position, Miss Chandler. I have a husband and a son. I don't want the police finding my letters." Lucille hopped off the stool and went to remove a salt shaker from Lewis's mouth.

When she came back, she opened her handbag and dug out a quarter. "Coffee's on me."

"Mrs. Wills," I said, "when was the last time you saw Jim?"

"We were supposed to have dinner the night he was murdered, but I had to cancel. My husband was actually going to be home." She shuddered. "Can you imagine? I might have been there when the murderer came and—" She narrowed her eyes. "The lipstick marks. Do you know who it was?"

"How would I?"

"Lewis! We're going now, honey. Put that candy bar *back.*" She gave me a faded smile. "I guess I wasn't the only girl he was seeing."

I told her I guessed she was right.

5
♦

I crossed 11th Street and stopped at the corner of the *Examiner* building. Through the large plate glass windows I could see the presses, monstrous metal machinery, silent now and still, like slumbering dragons. Within an hour these behemoths would be going full throttle, *clacka-clacka*ting with a deafening roar, churning out tomorrow's early edition, which would hit the streets at six tonight. In the back, men in smeary aprons were setting the type with thick, sure fingers. Someone had posted a hand-lettered sign in the window: Yankees 10, Bums 3.

I pulled away from the windows and moved along the sidewalk. A squad car was parked at the curb by the *Examiner*'s main entrance. As I drew nearer, a uniformed cop jumped out of the passenger seat and peered at me. "Chandler?"

I kept walking.

"You Paris Chandler?" He was young and dark-haired and bold in his crisp blue uniform.

"Perhaps," I called out. "Perhaps not."

I tugged open the front door.

The cop was on me in a flash. "Chief Gladstone wants to see you, Chandler. Hop in."

I looked over at the squad car. The driver cop had come round and opened the rear door. I said, "Oh really? What about?"

The blue suit at my elbow flashed his teeth. "Maybe he wants to crown you Rose Bowl queen."

"I'm booked." I pulled the door open wider.

The cop grabbed my arm. I just looked at him. Then he decided to switch to the charm channel. "Look, miss. The chief wants to see you. It must be important. Chief don't send chauffeur service just for anyone." He worked on getting his smile straight.

"No," I agreed. "Just for criminals."

"Come on, lady."

I pried his fingers off my arm. "All right. But I have about a half-hour's work to do. Can you wait for me here? I promise I won't climb out the second-story window."

The second-story window did, in fact, see a lot of commercial traffic. If you walked through Society and ventured into the back storage room, you could usually find someone hovering at the window, lowering a bucket on a rope into the alley below. It was where Mark the Mark, Benny's bookie competitor, operated. *Examiner* staffers would place their markers in the bucket, naming their picks, and send it plummeting down to the slippery-fingered Mark. Collections and payoffs were made the same way. But I wasn't about to lower myself down in a bucket to avoid Gladstone.

I had an agenda of my own.

"So," said Harry Gladstone, straightening a stack of files on his desk. It was a nice desk. Big slab of mahogany with a brass plaque that said "Chief of Police Harry M. Gladstone." I wondered how much that brass had cost the taxpayers and whether it was there to remind Gladstone who he was, or to inform visitors, who undoubtedly knew anyway. Behind him, growing out of the floor like exotic trees, were three flags: America's, California's and the LAPD's. Gladstone looked up suddenly. "I am not a gambling man."

I crossed my legs in the leather club chair across from him and said nothing.

"I could arrest you for dispensing hearsay."

"It's called slander, and you'd have to sue me." I flicked a strand of hair out of my eyes. "Besides, it makes you seem more human."

He leaned forward and switched on his intercom. "Miss Percy? What do you drink, Paris?"

"Am I on duty or off?"

"Miss Percy, bring a Scotch. Will you join me?"

"Great," I said. I hated Scotch, but I didn't want to risk arrest for that, too. "And water, please."

I opened my purse and found my cigarettes. "Look, I apologize, Chief. I was trying to liven things up. Mentioning you is a lot more interesting than another boring Betty and Bogie bulletin." I lit my cigarette and carefully blew the smoke away from him.

Gladstone grunted. "I forgive you." He said it solemnly, like a priest forgiving a sinner. His face brightened. "Now. Tell me what your boss said."

Miss Percy entered carrying a wobbly tray with two poured drinks, a pitcher of water, an ice bucket and a bottle of Chivas. She sort of lurched toward the desk, holding the tray in front of her, as if it were propelling her forward. She somehow managed to get everything where it belonged, then she tottered out.

"She's been working for the chief of police for forty years," Gladstone said resignedly. "A little dotty, but . . ." His voice trailed off. "Cheers," he said brightly, raising his glass.

"To your health," I recited.

"Now," he said eagerly. "Tell me."

This, of course, was the point of the exercise—his TV future. Which I had suspected all along. I cleared my throat. "I was only able to catch Mr. Stone for a minute last night. But his eyes kind of lit up. I think you're onto something, sir. Really I do. And we're going to talk more tomorrow." I took a swallow of Scotch, hoping to wash the fib out of my mouth.

"Really? No kidding! He looked interested, eh? Gee, that's great." Gladstone leaned back in his swivel chair and folded his hands across his stomach like a man who'd just gorged himself on a five-course meal. It must have been a secret vein of vanity that transformed him into such a sap. He was not a sap when it came to throwing out lieutenants and sergeants who had been caught with their hands in the wrong cookie jars.

"Actually," I added, "I lied a bit. I told Mr. Stone it was my idea. I hope you don't mind."

"Don't be silly, girl. He'll think you're brilliant."

"Thanks." I risked another sip of Scotch. "Oh, that reminds me, sir. I'm supposed to ask you something."

Gladstone beamed over his stomach at me. "Anything, hon."

"We seem to be missing some stuff at the station. Mr. Stone thinks maybe the police took these things from Jim's desk."

"Really," said Gladstone. He glanced at his watch.

"Is it possible to check the list of items you took, sir?"

Abruptly Gladstone stood up. "The World Series. It used up the whole day. I had no idea how late it was."

I sipped my Scotch.

"I'm supposed to be at the Fireman's Benefit Ball—" He looked at his watch again. "Now." He leaned over and pressed the intercom. "Miss Percy? Bring in my tux immediately, thank you." He looked at me. "Sorry about this, Paris. Call me tomorrow, will you? We'll, uh, carry on." He winked.

I stubbed out my cigarette in his ashtray, put my glass on the desk and stood. By then, Gladstone had my elbow firmly in his grasp. At the door, he said, "Love ya!" The door closed behind me.

I stood in the outer office wondering how I'd let that happen. A *tut-tutt*ing sound brought my attention to Miss

Percy. Either there was no tuxedo, or Gladstone's request hadn't registered.

She was sitting at her desk, staring blankly at the wall.

"You had an audition," I repeated, "at ten o'clock this morning. That you forgot to tell me about? Forgive me, but I find it hard to believe you had an *audition* at ten o'clock in Los Angeles when everybody knows it was one o'clock in New York. What I'm trying to say is . . ."

Andrew turned his head and smiled sheepishly. "I didn't think you would understand, Miss Chandler. I'm sorry. I just knew that some important people would be there and—"

"Where," I said, "is *there*?"

"The Guild. And I was right. Howard Hawks showed up and Billy Wilder. Plus like Clark Gable and Jimmy Stewart."

"It's not as if we don't have a radio in the car," I said peevishly.

"It's staticky," said Andrew defensively.

Chief Gladstone's chauffeur service apparently extended to comings but not goings. My escorts were nowhere in sight when I stepped out of City Hall. But the familiar black shape of the Bentley was hovering across the street. The same unfathomable logic that impelled Andrew to disappear on whim, also, somehow, caused him to reappear in places where he had no possible way of knowing I'd be. Police headquarters, for example.

"You could get it fixed," I pressed.

"I stood next to Clark Gable for a whole inning," Andrew said.

The YWCA in Hollywood has the kind of outside that doesn't make you want to go inside. Unless, possibly, you have an assignation with a mobster.

The three-story white frame building stands between two vacant lots and sags under a shingle roof. It is on a side street off Hollywood Boulevard that is so question-

able it doesn't have street lamps. I climbed out of the
Bentley and told Andrew to stick around.

I walked across the warped wooden floorboards, up a
flight of dark, creaky stairs and into a locker room. At
least it had lights. Bright lights, illuminating sunny yellow
walls fitted with scratched metal lockers. A wooden
bench, running down the middle of the room, supported
a chubby, middle-aged woman rolling up her stockings.

I did not stop at my locker, but kept walking through
the damp, smelly room to a far door. I tugged it open
and entered the gym.

Theodora Jones was lying on a mat doing leg lifts. She
wore navy shorts and a white T-shirt, but all you tended
to notice was the wavy red hair fanned out under her, all
the way down to her waist. The cast had finally come off
her left arm and, as I approached, I could see the discol-
oration from the elbow to the wrist. It was the arm of a
wizened old lady. As I drew nearer I could hear her
grunting.

I barked, "Full extension. Straighten those legs, Tee.
You're cheating. More!"

"Go to hell," said Tee, not looking up.

Over against the mirrored wall, two women with unusual muscle configurations were making faces as they
lifted barbells. "I'd rather just go," I said.

Tee flicked me a glance. "You haven't changed yet.
Hurry."

"I'm not going to today. I don't care about my muscles. How many more?"

"Fifty-six, fifty-seven," Tee huffed.

She would go to one hundred. The place gave me the
creeps. But when Tee broke her arm climbing out a second-story window, the goods on the couple inside recorded in her camera, I started showing up to boost her
morale. She had talked me into joining this wretched
gym and went with me to buy shorts and gym shoes. I
used them once. I wasn't into muscles and was suspicious
of women who were. Except for Tee, who was a striking
five feet ten and needed them. She was a private eye. I
forgave her the muscles.

"Sixty-five, sixty-*six.*"

I sat down on a stool. "I need something," I said.

Grunt, Tee said.

"From Police Chief Gladstone."

Tee gave me a quick glance. She returned her attention to her legs.

"Specifically, a folder," I continued. "I think the police took it when they went through the newsroom. I asked if I could see a list of what was taken and Gladstone practically pushed me out the door." I paused. "You have friends."

"Gladstone isn't one of them."

I watched Tee carry on with her leg lifts. I had met her through Nick. There wasn't anybody, it seemed, Nick Goodwin didn't know, though how exactly they had met was somewhat unclear. "Why aren't you working on your arm?" I prodded. "You're not doing what you're supposed to. And besides, you can get that list from somebody else."

Tee groaned.

Two small girls came tumbling into the gym followed by a mother. The girls, giggling, raced over to the trampoline in the far corner and began jumping up and down. I watched them until I began to grow dizzy.

"You don't want the list." Tee sat up and began jiggling her legs. "You want the folder. What's in it?"

"Interview notes and commentaries about the freeways."

"Do me a favor, hold my ankles."

I scooted down and grasped Tee's ankles. She began doing full sit-ups. "So?"

"I'm not sure, Tee. But most of Jim's research was in that folder."

"Uh huh."

"I'm just curious."

Tee sat up. "Am I missing something here? I know you feel bad, Paris, but—" She fixed me with those large rootbeer-colored eyes. "You're not going to start looking into freeways, are you? It's a bit downtown for you, I should think. Now hold tighter."

I dug my fingers hard into her ankles. "I asked you for a favor, Tee, not an inquisition."

"Fifteen," Tee said.

"How much longer will you be?" I was feeling tired again, and irritable. "You could come over for dinner." I paused. "Mrs. Keyes is a blonde now."

"Oh Lord." Tee grimaced. "I wouldn't want to miss that. But I'm having dinner with Nick, sorry."

Behind me the girls had begun to shriek. My eyes traveled to the side of the gym where the muscle twins were now standing at the ballet barre doing knee bends. Their eyes were glued to their images in the mirror. I wondered why Tee and Nick couldn't include me.

"This place gives me the creeps," I said sullenly.

Tee sat up and began blotting her face with a towel. "I told you. You're not a downtown sort of girl," she said.

6

♦

KTLA wasn't far from the Y, so I had Andrew route me there before heading home. The lights were off in Studio One as I entered. It was either boxing night or wrestling night, I couldn't remember which, and the station would be televising live from one of the two arenas. I walked toward the back of the garage. When I got to the news office, however, I saw that Truman Stone was talking to two men in business suits, so I continued along the narrow hallway to the Coke machine.

It was located against the back wall, right beside the fire escape hatch. The escape hatch, a four-foot-wide horizontal chute, had been chiseled into the wall to satisfy safety regulations because there wasn't room for an emergency door. The chute, which opened two feet above the floor, could be unlatched in case of a fire. Supposedly, the metal door would open wide and a person could hop in and roll out of the burning building, into the alley behind. So they said. Each month, KTLA scheduled a fire drill, but to anybody's knowledge, there had never actually been one.

I found a nickel in my purse, dropped it into the machine and pulled a Coke out of its slot.

"You wouldn't have another nickel, would you, sis?"

I turned. One of the suits from the news office was standing there jiggling a handful of coins. He had slicked-back dark hair, a sharp nose and not a wrinkle on him anywhere. "Mr. Barnathan wants a Coke." He glanced up from his coins. "I'll give you a quarter for a nickel."

"Who's Mr. Barnathan?"

The man blinked. "You're not serious. Matthew Barnathan? Where've you been, girl?"

"Not where Mr. Barnathan has. Excuse me. You're blocking my way."

He held up a quarter the way a master holds up a bone to his dog. "For a nickel? That's a four hundred percent profit right there. Can't do better than that, girl."

I put down my Coke on a cardboard packing box and opened my purse. I took the quarter out of his hand and gave him a coin in return. I picked up my Coke.

"Say, this is a dime!"

"That's okay. Three hundred percent is plenty for me."

"But I need a nickel!"

"The machine gives change, mister." I winked. "For a quarter."

I left the heel standing there and detoured round to the one rest room men and women had to share. By the time I got back to the news office the suits were gone. Truman, his white shirtsleeves rolled up to the elbow, tie askew, was standing over his desk rummaging through various piles of papers. A glass of Alka-Seltzer fizzed noisily within grabbing distance.

"Hi," I said. "Got a minute?"

"Yep."

He picked some papers off one stack and transferred them onto another.

"You are busy."

"Naw, sit down. I'm going over the budget. Don't," said Truman, opening a folder, "ask for a raise."

I sat down in Jim's chair. "Twenty-five dollars a show, I'm not complaining. But is there enough for Harry Gladstone, too?"

Truman looked up. "The police chief?"

"He wants to be on television. He's been hounding me."

"Doesn't everyone?" Truman sighed and sat down. "Couple a swells just left. They want to be on TV, too."

"Who are they?"

"Matthew Barnathan and one of his slick salesmen. They thought we might expand the *Shopping at Home* show to half an hour. The last fifteen minutes, they sell real estate."

"In that case, I'd better run out and buy a TV," I said with sarcasm.

"They cost four hundred at J. N. Ceazan's, but we can probably get you a discount."

"Real estate?" I repeated.

"Barnathan's a big developer in the Valley. Tract housing. He wants to show pictures of houses and talk about how many johns they have." Truman opened a desk drawer and pulled out a paste pot. He began snipping a wire service story, which he then pasted onto a sheet of copy paper. I supposed he was doing this to alert Bernard Wexler to items he might use the next night. "It's not a bad idea actually."

"Make it an hour show," I urged. "You can have Gladstone auctioning off confiscated loot."

From somewhere down the hall I could hear the whine of an electric sweeper. Truman looked up suddenly. "So what else?"

"I was in the neighborhood."

"Uh huh."

"And I want to ask you something. Did the police give you a list of what they took from this office?"

Truman began pasting again. "I think so. Why?"

"Jim's freeway folder isn't here. I thought . . ."

"You thought?" Truman put down his paste brush and gave me a stern look.

I smiled. "I always think it's funny how children grow up to be adults with serious jobs and they end up using scissors and paste."

"You thought what?"

"I met Lucille Wills. The woman who was calling me."

"I knew it," declared Truman with satisfaction. "Just another nut with a freeway story. You know we've been getting pressure, don't you? I'm glad we're dropping the whole thing."

"Lucille Wills may be a nut but her interest was not in freeways," I emphasized.

Truman raised an eyebrow cautiously. "She knows something?"

I lit a cigarette. "Lucille Wills told me—no, she alleged to me—that she was having an affair with Jim. She said she was hoping I could get some letters back that she had written to him." I inhaled. "She's married."

"Nonsense. There was no affair. She's just another publicity hound." His eyes drifted back to the paste pot.

"You know her?" I was dubious.

"Of course not." He glanced at a new piece of wire copy. "The President's citizens' food committee says we have to eat less bread, meat, poultry, eggs and grain so we can ship more food to the starving people of Europe. And my butcher's *still* out of steak half the time." He looked up and sighed. "Just run along home and forget it, Paris."

"How do you know he wasn't having an affair with her?"

"Jim wasn't having an affair with anybody," Truman said with certainty. "He told me."

I stubbed out the cigarette. "His wife thinks he was having more than one."

Truman put down the story but he kept the scissors raised in his right hand. "And what do you think?"

"Jim didn't tell me. Why should he tell anybody?"

Truman grunted. "Men tell each other things. We were close. We played handball." He hesitated. "We talked about tempting women." He gave me a bland look. "Your name came up."

I grinned. "Truman, I had no idea."

"Not me, sweet pea. He. He said it was too bad he was married." Truman finally put the scissors down. "Anyway, if Lucille What's Her Name wrote mash notes to Jim, let her worry about them." He stood up. "I'm going home."

I watched him walk over to the coat rack and remove his jacket and hat. I said, "Not even a little interested?"

Truman put his hat on, but folded the jacket over his arm. "Don't be silly," he said dismissively, moving toward the sheets. "You look like you could be my daughter."

The sheets flapped as he disappeared through them. Truman was fifteen years older than me. He had a torch singer for a wife. He didn't have a daughter.

For the next ten minutes, I stood over the AP and UPI wire machines, reading what they had to say. Which was mainly excruciating detail about the Yankees' fifth inning. Eventually, I wandered back to Truman's desk and started going through it. Truman's idea of drawers was that they be used for anything he couldn't quite decide to throw out. I sighed and dug in with both hands. It took all of my willpower not to toss out the Hostess Twinkie wrappers. I sorted through news stories, bills, letters, job applications and scrawled reminders in pencil. Then I dumped the whole mess back in and went on to the second drawer.

The annoying whine of the sweeper grew louder. The second drawer contained two Rancho Soup cans, unopened, five packets of Saltine crackers, a crusted spoon and more papers. Among the papers were the pages of telephone numbers that had disappeared from Jim's desk. After sifting through several letters from viewers, I found the list of Jim's belongings the police claimed to have taken. I skimmed it.

Out of the corner of my eye, something seemed to move. I turned. But it was only one of the sheets flapping. The electric sweeper had hit a piercing whine. The items on the list were enumerated by letter. Under "M" it said: *"Papers. See Appendix B."* The single sheet of onionskin paper had a staple in the upper left-hand corner. But whatever had been attached, was gone. A sudden stillness came over the office. The sweeper had been turned off.

I plunged back into the drawer but could not find the appendices. The bottom drawer contained a bottle of aspirin, a pair of rubber boots, two paste pots, a box of paper clips and two packs of Juicy Fruit. I stood up.

There were footsteps coming down the hall. I stuck my head through the sheets but the hall was deserted. The electric sweeper stood unattended halfway between me and Studio One. I went over to the file cabinet and began poking through the folders. Maybe the freeway folder had been haphazardly shoved inside another.

I paused. More footsteps. This time they seemed to stop right outside the sheets. "Hello?" I called out.

I jumped as the bell on the AP machine rang three times, signaling an important story. The machine began to chatter furiously. Instinctively, I went over to see what the fuss was about.

The first sentence told me.

LT. ART BOLSKY OF THE LOS ANGELES POLICE DEPARTMENT SAID THE HUNT FOR THE MYSTERIOUS BLONDE IN CONNECTION WITH THE SHOOTING DEATH OF KTLA NEWSCASTER JAMES ST. CLAIR HAS BEEN INTENSIFIED.

There was only one other sentence.

LT. BOLSKY, WHO IS HEADING UP THE MURDER INVESTIGATION, RE-FUSED TO SAY WHETHER TOMMY NAKAMURA, A GARDENER TAKEN INTO CUSTODY LAST NIGHT, PROVIDED ANY INFORMATION ABOUT THE WOMAN SEEN LEAVING ST. CLAIR'S HOUSE ON THE NIGHT OF HIS MURDER.

Uneasily, I returned to the file cabinets and continued sifting through the folders.

Nothing turned up. After twenty minutes I left. The electric sweeper was still in the hallway.

The house on Muirfield was lit up like a Halloween pumpkin. Light blazed through every front window.

"Do you want the front door?" Andrew asked carefully.

"Yes, of course. Pull right into the driveway."

We rolled past the lanterns spaced along the drive and stopped at the brightly lit front door. Andrew started to get out.

"That's okay," I said, opening my door and sliding out. "I won't be long."

I smoothed my gabardine slacks, straightened my jacket and climbed the front stairs. I felt a hollowness in my chest as I rang the bell.

The chimes echoed loudly inside the big, empty rotunda. If the freeway folder was not gathering dust in the loot department downtown, this was the only other place I figured it could be. Hesitantly, I rang the bell again. Still nothing. I turned and looked at Andrew, slumped in the driver's seat.

"Hallo, yoo-hoo! She isn't there."

The face of a woman floated ethereally on the other side of the hedges bordering the St. Clair property. The lanterns spaced along the driveway helped me make out limp, dishwater blond hair and a plaid collar. The face turned sideways, toward her house. "Billy, if you're going to come out, put on a jacket." Then the head swung back to me. "If you're looking for Donna St. Clair, she left a few minutes ago."

Intrigued by this monitoring system, I walked down the three broad steps and turned toward the hedges. "Oh dear, what bad timing. You—wouldn't know when she'll be back?"

The woman disappeared. Arriving at the hedges now, I could see she was bending down to zip up the jacket of a young boy. He had the same dirty blond hair, with bangs falling into his eyes. He looked at me solemnly.

"I have no idea," the woman replied. "I just happened to see her leave with a gentleman about fifteen minutes ago." She straightened. "I suppose she went out for dinner." The woman gave me an expectant look, as if she were hoping I'd give her some juice.

I gave her my name. "I was just stopping by to see how she was doing. I'll come back another time." I turned.

"You look familiar to me," the woman said.

I hesitated. I was tempted to just keep going, get in the car, drive away. But I stopped and turned back. "I worked with Mr. St. Clair at KTLA."

The woman's face lit up. "Yes, of course. I *knew* I had seen you before. Billy, this is the lady we've seen on TV."

Billy continued to watch me gravely, but said nothing.

"I'm Claire Boronski. Sometimes Jim would let us come over and watch his TV. We don't have one. My husband says the radio is good enough. Oh. This is Billy."

"How do you do?" I said formally. Then I addressed the woman. "Why you must be the neighbor who told the police you didn't think Tommy Nakamura worked for Mr. St. Clair."

"He didn't. So I did. I don't know why Jim didn't hire a gardener. Maybe it's on account of him coming from New York. New York doesn't have gardens, I'm told."

"Er—"

"But Tommy would have been a good choice. He takes care of a number of people on this street."

"How odd," I said, "that they arrested him then."

"You want my opinion? They're covering up for the real person who did it. The woman."

"You think it was a woman?"

"I absolutely do. Billy saw one coming out through the front door not ten, fifteen minutes before the gun went off."

We both looked at the boy. I said, "Gee, you must have been up kind of late, Billy. Are you—ten?"

"Nine," declared Billy. "I get to stay up late."

"You do not get to stay up late," his mother admonished. "Billy's bedroom is right up there." I followed her pointed finger to a window on the second floor. "That's how he saw her coming out."

"But if she had left—did you see anybody else, Billy?" It was a dumb question and obviously the police had asked it right off.

"Lots of times they come in through the back door," said Billy knowingly.

Mrs. Boronski laughed nervously. "Mr. St. Clair always had people coming and going. Once, the mayor came with a city councilman. Messengers came, people from the TV station, in and out all day long."

"The ladies came at night," Billy cut in. "Through the back door."

"Hon, you go on in," chided Mrs. Boronski. But Billy didn't move. He kept his eyes on me.

"It was nice meeting you, Billy," I said.

"Yeah," he said. And reluctantly trooped off.

"He's only nine," Mrs. Boronski reiterated. "I think he makes things up."

"Sure. I understand."

"Cause from his window, you can't see the back door. But I hear him talking to his little boyfriends about girls. I think they put ideas into his head."

"The night of the murder—you didn't see anyone?"

She raised her chin indignantly. "I don't spy."

"No, of course not," I said quickly.

I hesitated as a new thought drifted through my mind. Jim's garage was on the other side of the house, behind the kitchen. If Jim had indeed heard a noise and gone out to investigate, he could have used the kitchen door. In which case, if the murderer had corraled him back into the house, he would, naturally, go through the open door. But if Jim had used the front door, going out into the driveway and around back, and was shepherded at gunpoint into the house through the front door, why hadn't these nosy neighbors seen *anything*? Maybe not before the gunshot. But surely the noise would have caught their attention and sent them running to their windows.

"Mrs. Boronski—you didn't hear a gun go off?"

"Oh yes, we did. We certainly did. My husband and I came running out. We'd been in the parlor listening to *Doorway to Life,* but you couldn't mistake that sound."

She paused and tilted her head slightly as if listening for the noise to repeat in the night. She began nodding, as if to confirm she had just heard it. "Why we were the ones who found poor Jim lying in a pool of his own blood."

"How did you get inside the house?"

"The front door was standing wide open. As soon as we ran up the steps we could see Jim lying there. Ralph, he told me to call the police."

I wondered how much Billy knew that he wasn't telling. If he had seen me leaving only twenty minutes before, wouldn't he have heard the gun, even assuming he had fallen asleep?

Inadvertently, I glanced up at the second story. I caught a fleeting image of a pale face at the window. Just before it vanished behind the thin, white curtains.

7

$\blacklozenge$

I unlocked the front door, dutifully announced my arrival to Mrs. Keyes—"Hallo! I'm home!"—and sulked up to my bedroom, wondering why all this had happened to *me*.

He had been available and I had been alone too long. I had avoided men I shouldn't have, because none of them was Russell. This one was glamorous and charming and—very safely married. We began having dinner after work, joining the crowd at O'Blath's or squeezing round a table of friends down the street at Lucy's. Often we stayed on, just the two of us, sipping brandy and sharing intimacies until the restaurant closed and sent us off. So when it happened, late on one of those nights, him saying, "Paris, do you mind stopping by the house? I want to show you some fabric the decorator dropped off," I went, knowing full well the invitation came with the inevitable, unspoken punchline.

I stayed until nearly dawn, entwined in his arms, listening to his stories about covering Patton in Europe for NBC Radio and dwindling down to revelations about the

55

sad state of his marriage. From then on, I would either
meet him at his house or ride over with him after dinner.
If I showed up on my own, Andrew would park in the
alley behind his house. I would go through the gate and
in through the kitchen door. When I drove with Jim, we
would pull into the garage and walk the few feet to the
kitchen door. I never stayed the night. Often, quite late,
the phone would ring and Jim wouldn't answer it. Which
should have tipped me off. But what went through my
mind was the image of Donna St. Clair alone in New
York, needing to hear the sound of her husband's voice.
I never suspected there was anybody else.

I missed him terribly. What my feelings were at the
time, I couldn't say. I never had a chance to sort things
out. I just knew that Jim was warm and fun and passion-
ate and that he escaped the Russell comparison because
he wasn't a threat to replace him. But the murder—the
murder stoked all kinds of feelings. I managed to duck
them, as I had when Russell died, by focusing on something else; in this case, keeping my affair with Jim out of
the papers. Gossip columnists—or their legmen—were
not supposed to be the subject of gossip. My parents
would be humiliated to boot. No one, except Andrew,
knew. And if the police had my fingerprints, which they
undoubtedly did, they had no way of matching them to
me . . . But what if they did? Could they possibly suspect me? No, I was not going to indulge my fears even
more. I was Jim's colleague; why shouldn't I come by?

Sometime soon, I reassured myself, the police would
nab the murderer and I would go on with my life.

But the police had nabbed not the murderer, but a
convenient, short-term scapegoat. Whatever improvements Gladstone was making downtown, they did not
carry over into murder investigations. The sensational
Black Dahlia murder last January had commanded the
biggest investigation ever, and still her killer had not
been found. They had to be growing desperate, as evi-
denced by their little vaudeville show, starring Tommy
Nakamura.

I got off my bed and went over to the window seat.

Anybody could have shot James St. Clair. A vindictive woman, as his wife insisted, or even, somehow, his wife. Or a nut. For some reason, I had the feeling it might have been the person he dined with that night. He had scribbled notes as he spoke on the phone. His folder lay open under the sheet of paper he was scribbling on.

Something caught my eye. A figure in black.

A figure in black weaving down the middle of North Maple Drive. No, not weaving, gliding; gliding along on roller skates. The street was dark but I could see him quite clearly as he moved in and out of puddles of light thrown by the street lamps. He was wearing black pants and a black turtleneck sweater and some kind of leather helmet that came down over his eyes and nose—like Zorro. A long black scarf, wrapped around his neck, trailed gossamer ribbons in his wake. Slim and lithe, and using his arms for balance, he moved in wide graceful loops. There was a joy, a giddiness about the movements; a bird soaring. And then he stopped.

Slowly, lazily, he made figure eights, gradually tightening the loops until he began a dizzying twirling routine, dropping into a crouch, rising, dropping again, round and round like a top. He finished with a flourish, arms thrown over his head. As a finale, he bowed.

I sat there for a long time staring through the open window into the hot, wind-blown night.

All I could see was that nosy little brat with his telescopic eyes.

The Downtown Athletic Club, at Sixth and Olive, was not exactly high on my list of destinations in life. I was neither athletic, nor male, two characteristics shared by its entire membership. The truth is, I wasn't even sure what the DAC was.

"It's where a lot of snooty old men play handball and swim and steam a lot," Andrew informed me as we blew down Sunset the next morning. "And I'm not coming in," he added darkly. "I think this whole thing is stupid."

"I can't disagree with you," I offered.

"Then why can't you just agree with me? You never agree with me, Miss Chandler. It hurts my feelings sometimes."

"It does? Sorry. I guess I've just become a querulous old biddy."

"You're twenty-nine," replied Andrew scornfully.

"Which is old."

"It is not. It is not old."

"Okay." I grinned. "There, I agree with you."

Why these men would want to come down here at 8 A.M. for coffee and sweet rolls and game two of the World Series was beyond me. Game two happened yesterday, as everyone in the free world seemed to know. But someone in New York had loaded kinescopes of it onto a transport plane yesterday and the kinescopes were being shown in six area locations today. It would be the first time anyone here had seen a World Series game on TV.

Which should have been enough of a thrill for one day.

But oh no.

After watching a game they had undoubtedly *heard* the day before, the DAC membership was then invited to stick around to listen to game three on the radio. It seemed unlikely a whole lot of work was going to get done.

Andrew stopped the Bentley in front of a brick building with a dark green canopy stretching out to the street. A perfumed guy in a uniform whisked open my door and helped me out. But that was about as helpful as he intended to be.

"Yes, ma'am?" His beady eyes managed to avoid my face.

"Paris Chandler, from the *Examiner.*" I adjusted my green wool cape. "I'm expected."

"Yeah, for what?"

"Only the baseball game." I smiled. "I won't be having a steam bath today."

He bent slightly and peered through the window at Andrew. Andrew was combing his hair in the rearview mirror. The guy straightened and planted his feet. "No dames allowed."

Of course no dames were allowed. That's what I had told Etta Rice when she woke me at 6:45 A.M. with my marching orders. I had suggested Nick as the better candidate to do this Item. But Nick, Etta explained, without explaining, was otherwise occupied. Besides, she informed me, she had already phoned ahead. The men would be delighted "to receive me."

I said, "Your membership is delighted to receive me. Run along in and ask. I'll wait."

The guy's beady eyes shifted as a car door slammed. An oily smile cracked his face. "Good day, *sir.*"

"Johnson. Good morning. I . . . Paris Chandler?"

"Mmm. I adore your timing, Chief Gladstone. Would you mind escorting me in?" I smiled. "I'm expected."

Gladstone took my arm. "I heard."

"You did?"

"We voted. I just hope you don't turn green at the language. Some of the boys get a little worked up. Johnson, open the door for god's sake."

Gladstone led me down a dreary wood-paneled hall cluttered with framed pictures of guys with goofy grins clapping each other on the back. There was a trophy case and finally two curtained doors that led into—The Room.

Round tables were scattered about, most of them filled with manicured men in suits, a litter of coffee cups and crumbs already soiling the starched white cloths. The air was heavy with cigar smoke but not with conversation. All eyes were glued to the TV.

"Strike one."

It was balanced high on a podium, a big ten-inch screen fitted with a bubble-shaped magnifying glass. The picture, distorted on the sides, was amazingly true if you stood in line with the middle of the set. A gray figure in a baggy uniform was swatting flies at the plate. I stifled a yawn.

Gladstone squeezed us in at one of the close-up tables, shook everyone's hand and announced, "Miss Paris Chandler, our lovely and honored guest."

A white-jacketed waiter drew up on the double. "Screwdriver? Bloody Mary?"

"Driver," said Gladstone.

"Um . . . me, too."

I looked around the room. I recognized Superior Court Judge Thomas Ambrose and a prominent physician from Beverly Hills. But I needed a famous face. Someone good for a quote or two; a piece of news, a joke, *something* for the column. "Who are these people?" I whispered.

Gladstone leaned close. "Next table you have Donald Wells, owns parking lots. He's with the heir to Helm's bakery. Next table over are some stiffs from the State Highway Commission."

"From Sacramento?"

"They're down checking out the freeway sites. Supposedly. Next table you got a bunch a goddam lawyers, one in the red jacket cheats at golf."

My eye roved across the room to Van Johnson, who was sitting with the agent Charlie Feldman, David Selznick and Peter Lawford. Charlie Morrison, who owned Mocambo, was at another table.

I leaned toward Gladstone. "Tell me about Tommy Nakamura," I whispered.

"Christ," said Gladstone. "Did you see that curve?"

"Oh yes. Oh my." I had no idea what a curve was. I leaned closer. "Harry?"

"Hm?" He tore his eyes from the TV.

I smiled. "The gardener."

"He's being questioned. Don't you read your own paper?" He gave me one of those granite-eyed cop looks.

"I can't read what's not in the papers. Can I, Chief?"

"Lieutenant Bolsky is running the investigation. Read him."

I didn't have access to Bolsky. And the chief of police did. He would know every detail Bolsky was digging up. I sighed and tried to watch baseball.

By the fourth inning, men were drifting back to the

buffet table, playing musical chairs. I took this opportunity to slip in next to Van Johnson.

"Have you finished *State of the Union*?" I asked.

"No, next week. Another screwdriver? And I can honestly say I don't look forward to the end. You have no idea what it's like working with Frank Capra and Spencer Tracy *and* Katharine Hepburn." The actor rolled his eyes. "You realize they've all won Oscars."

"That's right."

"So maybe I'll win by association." He laughed.

"Tell me your favorite story of the week," I prompted.

"You want gossip, Paris?"

"Tracy and Hepburn?" I said hopefully.

Johnson smiled. "No, no. Now don't say where you got this, but the other night I was at Otto's party and . . ."

"Otto Preminger?"

"Yes. And you should have seen Gene Tierney and Orson making eyes at each other."

"Not Orson Welles," I gasped. "Come on."

"Listen, it's true. I mean, he came with Greer, but she's still moping about her divorce. I think she was his beard."

I grinned. "Thanks, Van."

After he moved away, I found myself sitting with two men I didn't know. I introduced myself. "Hank Armstrong," said the larger man, touching the knot of his brown bow tie. "And this is Norm Wills. But we're old fogies. You should go talk to the livelier set."

I scanned the room but didn't see one. I pasted on a new smile. "So tell me, fellas, are you betting with the Chief—the Yanks to win the Series?"

"We're taking the Yanks," said Wills, a trim man with a center part and horn-rimmed glasses, "but not quite so grandly as our esteemed police chief."

"I suppose it's just friendly bets among—friends. Among each other, here," I said.

Armstrong grinned. "I'll tell you a little secret. Johnson, the doorman? He's our bookie."

"No—really?"

"Speak for yourself," said Wills quickly. "Johnson may

take care of the high-rollers. But us government men tend to play the sawbuck tune." He paused. "Armstrong is a banker."

"Gee, that's swell," I said. "I bet I can't guess which bank."

"Los Angeles Savings," Armstrong supplied. "I run it."

"Then I know exactly who to call when I need a loan."

"You need a house, call Wills."

"Real estate?" I inquired.

Armstrong guffawed. "Freeways."

"I hadn't exactly considered buying a freeway. Are there any for sale, Mr. Wills?"

"She's cute," said Armstrong.

"Look, Shotton's taking Lombardi out."

"He'd better," sighed Armstrong.

"Possibly I could buy an off-ramp," I broke in. "A small one."

Wills said, "Why not?" and reached into his pocket. He found a business card and handed it to me. "You get serious, young lady, give me a call. Excuse me."

I glanced at his card. *Norman Wills, attorney, Division of Contracts and Rights-of-Way (Los Angeles)*. I looked up. He was across the room going through the door marked "Men."

"Why, I believe I know his wife. Lucille?" I turned to Armstrong.

But the banker had already walked away.

8

♦

Like the Dodgers, I was gone by the eighth inning.

As it turned out, my dishy Welles-Tierney Item was buried halfway down the column, thanks in part to word from Buckingham Palace that Princess Elizabeth would vow "to love, cherish and obey" Lieutenant Philip Mountbatten at their wedding next month, and would not, as hotly rumored, delete the "obey"—and to news that Gregory Peck would not, after all, star in *The Robe*, a minor scoop Etta had dredged up later that afternoon.

As for the intriguing Mr. Wills, I learned nothing more. He returned to the game and sat down with the Highway Commission before somehow disappearing during the Dodgers' dreadful seventh. Gladstone was deep in conversation with the Hollywood table and I was getting a headache from trying to watch a picture that developed snow and showed me nothing at all I cared to see.

The afternoon picked up.

I phoned the L.A. office of the State Highway Commission. I told the woman on the other end I was a reporter with the *Examiner* and could someone explain to me how the division of contracts and rights-of-way worked? She had me hold. I picked up a scarlet crayon. A man came on the line. "Larry Robinson speaking. How may I help you?"

I repeated my question.

"It's easy," he said. "The division comes into play when we have to move people out of the path of a freeway."

He made it sound like a noble cause.

"We send a right-of-way agent into the neighborhood. He negotiates with the owner of a house. Now two things can happen. If it's judged to be structurally sound, we'll hold an auction to sell the house, leaving it up to the purchaser to move it. If it isn't, we will pay the owner for the property and have the house demolished. Each removal requires a contract and we have a team of lawyers that draws them up."

"Mm hm," I said.

"It's an enormous undertaking, miss. Over the next ten years we'll move ten thousand buildings and twenty-five thousand people. That's like moving Beverly Hills. But everything's going smooth as molasses. Most of the relocated people are happy as bedbugs in their new locations."

"Who sets the prices for the homes?" I asked.

"Our right-of-way agents appraise the land and the structures. Let's say yours is worth one thousand dollars. We pay you the money. Again, two things can happen. At auction, you can try to buy it back and probably you'll get it for less than we paid you for it. So there's a little profit there. But it becomes your responsibility to move it within an area of eight miles. If there are tenants in the building, you must provide for them for six months at a cost of fifty dollars per person, and see to their relocation. You may not want to bother, or financially, if you have a lot of tenants, you may not find it worthwhile. In that case, you won't bid on your house, and hopefully someone else will. The buyer then takes on the relocation responsibilities. Or, if the house is deemed not in good shape, we'll demolish it."

As with most bureaucrats, I didn't understand a thing he was saying. I said, "Right."

"Now, if your house can't be moved, we foot the bill to relocate you into a similar house."

"And if the owner thinks your price is too low?"

"We negotiate. We have a bit of room to maneuver. But we rarely have a problem. We come in at good value. Believe me, we're not trying to stiff anyone."

I thanked Mr. Robinson and hung up. Wondering how many people had already been stiffed.

I thrashed through the papers on my desk until I found the scrap with Lucille Wills's number on it. I dialed. She answered on the third ring. Pinching my nostrils, I droned, "Long distance calling for Mr. Norman Wills. Is he in, please?"

"Who's calling, operator?"

"Mr. Johnson in Sacramento. Is the party there?"

Sounding annoyed, she recited a number and hung up. It was the same number that appeared on Wills's business card.

Well well. I now had a matched pair. An interesting one at that. The wife of a man who relocated people from the path of oncoming freeways had been playing nookie with a man who publicly condemned freeway removal.

I liked it. I just didn't have any idea what to do with it. Freeways, like natural disasters, were things that happened to other people. Since they weren't bulldozing through Beverly Hills, at least not along North Maple Drive, I hadn't followed their progress. Now I feared I would have to.

I stood up, checked the seams of my stockings and walked down the hall to the morgue.

The morgue was a dark, dreary set of rooms, dominated by rows of wooden file cabinets and more rows of bookshelves. Which were a waste of furniture. Dozens of magazines, dog-eared file folders, snipped articles and yellowing newspapers were strewn everywhere, giving the place a kind of after-the-earthquake effect. Or, to put it more sinisterly, if the Commies dropped the Big One here, nobody would know the difference. The morgue was the paper's library and contained—or was supposed to—a copy of every *Examiner* ever printed, ditto the *Los Angeles Times,* reference materials, editions of *Time, Life, Look, Newsweek, Saturday Evening Post* and other magazines, though most were missing. It also contained Penelope Potts, librarian, better known in the newsroom as "the old flower pot."

Penelope was five feet tall, five feet wide, and manned her desk in the corner like the keeper of the flame. She wore horrid print dresses, smudgy eyeglasses and two ancient flowered hats; one for winter and one for summer. Her face resembled a bulldog. On the minus side, she had body odor.

But nobody in the newsroom, not even the city editor, knew more about Los Angeles than Penelope. And no piece of information was too esoteric to find permanent lodging in her brain. Which is why everyone politely suffered her eccentricities and brought her roses and chocolates on Valentine's Day.

I approached her desk as a commoner would a king's, on tiptoe, and dripping obsequiousness. She was wearing a purple and orange print thing highlighted with shocking yellow triangles, unsightly even by her standards. A droopy black felt hat with a sprig of plastic cherries embedded in a profusion of silk daisies bobbed up and down behind the *Iowa Grain and Oats Quarterly.* "Hi, Pen," I breathed. "New dress?"

"What's Etta want now?" not even looking up.

"Er, nothing."

She looked up.

"I need some information on freeway removal and right-of-way agents. I need a fast course on what's been happening."

Penelope put down her magazine, placed one hand on either side of her brim and shifted the hat to the right. She sniffed. "Try the last pile. Over there."

I followed her gaze to the wall, where three high

stacks of *Examiner*s were listing precariously. I looked back at her. "You haven't clipped them yet?"

"I'm behind. You people keep me too busy." She said it accusingly, as if she were Cinderella and the rest of the staff her evil stepsisters.

"Er, how far back do they go?" The stacks were waist high.

Penelope worked her considerable jaw, thinking. "June. Possibly May."

I sat down on the corner of her desk and inhaled her aroma. "But you've read the stories, Pen. Tell me. Who are the bad guys?"

Behind her smudged lenses, Penelope blinked. "I won't do your work for you, any of you. But if you can read, start with September. First sections only. And don't keep pestering me."

She readjusted her hat and picked up the grain quarterly. Reluctantly, I went over and sorted out a stack of Septembers. Then I sat down at the table farthest from the unpleasant odor of Penelope Potts.

Two hours later, streaked with newsprint, red-eyed and cross, I had filled three pages on my scratch pad with notes. Most of the stories concerned planning meetings, progress meetings and attempts by citizens to find out if a freeway would be heading into their neighborhood. As I read, I wrote down the names of the officials involved. It wasn't until the last week of September that anything but a rosy story appeared. Then, on the bottom of page three, five paragraphs reported the arrest of a man for posing as a right-of-way agent in an attempt to entice a homeowner to sell cheap.

"The deal was fair and square," protested Fred R. Akins, the accused man. "It wasn't like I was gonna steal."

A spokesman for the Highway Commission urged homeowners to ask anyone saying he was a right-of-way agent to show proper identification.

I yawned. I had to be on the wrong track. Or, I thought wryly, in the wrong lane. I lugged the papers back to their piles and turned to say good-bye to Penelope.

She was digging something out of her teeth with a toothpick while deeply engrossed in *Sci-Fi News and Galaxy Report.*

I crept out of the morgue and went looking for an aspirin.

"So what are you doing?" I said into the telephone. It was six o'clock and I was getting ready to leave the office when I thought to check in with Nick.

"Judy Garland's toothache," Nick said. "They rushed a dentist over to MGM. Judy, she goes to the barbershop, where she sits in one of those chairs, thinking it's like a dentist's chair. The dentist wants to pull the tooth immediately. Judy has a fit and stomps off to her bungalow." Nick paused. "She won't come out."

"Aren't you the lucky stiff. First you get Mrs. St. Clair. Now Judy Garland. I'm green."

"What a dame that woman is."

"Mrs. St. Clair? Tell me."

"I can't. Etta's having a nervous breakdown. Her arches have fallen."

"Later?"

"Can't. Jennifer has the croup. I'm going over to make her soup."

"I'm sure I didn't hear you correctly," I said. "They should really do something about the phones here."

"You think I can't make soup? Or Jennifer doesn't have the croup?"

"No, no. Of course she has the croup. Though I must say, my favorite was the vapors." Jennifer Lowe was an actress, naturally.

"Meow, meow," said Nick.

"Look, I once had my tonsils out," I confided hopefully. "Does that interest you?"

"Possibly. But you'll have to show me exactly where they were. Will you?"

"Canned soup," I said. "Or homemade?"
Nick hung up.

Canned soup is what I ended up with for dinner. Vegetable soup with an overcooked chicken breast. I ate in the kitchen while listening to Eddie Cantor. Then I parked in the red leather chair in the study with the file of letters. Mrs. Keyes lit the logs and I dropped some Glenn Miller on the phonograph. My grumpiness did not melt. I poured a glass of brandy and filched two chocolates from a box I kept in the record cabinet. Then I put my feet up on the ottoman and began to read.

The twelfth letter I read twice. It was from a Mrs. Edna Herbert in Silver Lake and recounted how she had sold her house to a Miss Martens. A week later she learned the freeway was coming through. When she asked Miss Martens about this, Miss Martens acted surprised that Mrs. Herbert didn't know. A few weeks later, Mrs. Herbert discovered that a woman fitting Miss Martens's description had also tried to buy the house of a neighbor, who had refused to sell.

Thinking it might be worthwhile to find out more, I went into the hall, dialed the number on the letter and made an appointment to see Mrs. Herbert the next day.

I had just hung up when the doorbell rang.

I glanced at my watch—nine-oh-five—and opened the door.

"Hi," said Nick sheepishly.

He was wearing pleated pants and a white V-neck sweater over a blue plaid shirt, loafers, no socks, and he was holding a brown paper bag. He handed it to me.

"Clam chowder," he announced.

"She's eaten," Mrs. Keyes reported, from somewhere behind me.

"Come in, Nick."

"Miss Paris, it's *very* late."

Mrs. Keyes had once tried to lecture me on the proper way to receive gentlemen callers, though I sincerely doubted she had ever had one. I got her through a news-

paper ad, just before Russell went to war, because I felt
sorry for her. Her husband, she had explained, had run
off with a lizard-tongued lounge singer, or something to
that effect, and she needed a place to call home. She
swore she could cook. Although my mother had
schooled me in the art of knowing how to do nothing for
myself—except hire others who could—I still had not
developed a knack for picking help.

Nick shifted from one loafer to the other. I was trying
not to giggle. "Don't worry," I said. "We'll be quiet. Go
to bed, Mrs. Keyes."

In the study, I poured Nick a brandy, replaced the
Miller with a Hoagy Carmichael, and sat down beside
him on the couch.

"I probably shouldn't have dropped in like this."

"It's okay. Mrs. Keyes was under the wrong impression. She thought you were a gentleman caller."

Nick grinned. "That would be a stretch, being a gentleman. Were you expecting one?"

"I'm afraid not. So you'll have to do." I sipped my
brandy. "Just as I have to do for you. What happened?
Did the croup regroup? Or didn't she like your soup?"

Nick reached for the silver lighter on the coffee table
as I shook a Chesterfield out of the pack. He leaned over
and lit it. "It doesn't seem fair," he said.

"What doesn't?"

"Three guys hanging around Jennifer when we should
be over here, making a play for you."

"Three? Oh dear. You didn't pull straws, I hope?"

"No. I just decided to leave. And come here."

"The trouble with dumb women is they can't recognize
quality merchandise," I said, trying to cheer Nick up.

"You're not dumb. What's your excuse?"

"I really don't care to discuss this." I lifted my brandy
glass. "I'm not in the mood."

"Somehow you never are."

"You might try a different approach. Booking me as
the first act instead of the impromptu finale."

"Well why don't you write it down for me. Step by
step, including sample dialogue."

"What's that supposed to mean?"

"It means, I think you have everything all worked out in your head. I miss a cue, I get the hook."

"Oh, really?" I got up and walked over to change the record. But when I reached the cabinet, I couldn't remember why I had come over. I turned back angrily.

"Let me tell you something, Nick Goodwin. If we didn't work for Etta, we'd have nothing to do with each other. Nothing. You're not my type."

Nick had been putting his brandy glass on the table. He looked up with surprise. "I'm not? What is your type? No, let me guess. Kind of mysterious and shadowy. That's it. I'm too lifelike for you."

I said, "Huh?"

"Ghosts. I think you go out with ghosts. I mean, I've never seen you with anyone. When was the last time you had a date?"

"Recently," I said. "A few weeks ago."

"A few weeks ago!"

"Yes. I was seeing someone for a while. But now I'm not. Are we through?"

"Who?" said Nick. "Who was it?"

"It's none of your business." I remembered now why I was standing at the record cabinet. I squatted down and pulled out a Louis Armstrong. A loud, noisy Armstrong, and put it on. I didn't return to the couch. Instead, I plunked myself down in the red chair. "I'm tired."

"Why aren't I your type?" Nick asked uncertainly.

I sighed. He was exactly my type, that was the problem. But something always prevented me from letting him know. "I like men of substance, that's all. Men who are grown up and who know how to treat women nicely."

"Ah," said Nick. "I should have brought chicken broth."

"Anything," I said, "but chowder. You don't know how it feels, being brought the very same soup that was rejected only a few hours ago. It makes me feel . . . cheap."

Nick swallowed the last of his brandy and stood up. "I don't know if you're joking, but I suspect you're not. So

I'll leave now and set about righting this dreadful wrong."

He walked to the door of the study, paused, then hesitantly turned back. "Tomorrow? Dinner at eight. Champagne. Dancing cheek to cheek. It will be a starry night. A faint scent of jasmine in the air. A stolen kiss in the moonlight. And"—he gave me his most adorable smile—"a poem by Shelley or Keats. How's that?"

I just stared at him. This one was a major piece of work. He raised an eyebrow questioningly.

"I think I'd prefer Dylan Thomas," I said.

9
◆

The Santa Ana winds blew through the night, clearing out the smog that had suffocated the city the day before. It was leaf-burning season and small bonfires dotted the lawns of Beverly Hills, adding to the dirty air created by the endless procession of cars that continued to roll into the city. Hundreds of thousands of servicemen and defense workers had decided to stay on after the war and Los Angeles was struggling to make room for them. Given the serious housing shortage, Jim had argued, to demolish existing apartment buildings for freeway construction was just one more ill-conceived, lame-brained scheme typical of myopic politicians.

I lifted the receiver.

For twenty minutes I had been debating—should I call, or simply show up? The peeping kid next door had me spooked. Even though he should now be at school, I didn't trust him. I dialed the number.

She answered on the first ring. "Yes, hello?"

"Mrs. St. Clair, it's Paris Chandler." There was a silence. "From KTLA."

"KTLA? Who . . . I'm sorry. What was your name?"

I realized then I must have awakened her. "Paris Chandler. We met at your husband's . . . um, memorial. I'm sorry if I woke you up."

"Everyone wakes me up. The hours here don't suit me. Thank god I'm leaving at the end of the week."

"Perhaps I ought to call back."

"Don't bother." She yawned. "I'll never get back to sleep."

"I'm looking for a file folder, Mrs. St. Clair. Jim kept freeway information in it. We can't find it at the station and I was wondering if he might have brought it home."

Mrs. St. Clair did not reply. But I heard a quick intake of breath, as if she were inhaling a cigarette.

"It contained information we'd like to have back. I thought you might have seen it somewhere."

"I think I did. Somewhere."

"Would it be all right if I stopped by later?"

"Somebody already stopped by. Anyway, what's it to you?"

"Well I . . ."

"Look, I know who you are. You do that gossip show with Nick Goodwin. What do you care about a news file?"

She was quicker than I thought. Most grieving widows wouldn't have cared who came by to pick up a useless file. I wondered what else she knew about me.

"I don't care for myself," I answered. "But I help out in the newsroom as well."

"Aren't you the little Girl Scout," Mrs. St. Clair said.

I ignored the remark. "Would eleven o'clock be convenient?"

"No it wouldn't, as a matter of fact. I have no idea where it is. It may be gone for all I know. It will take me forever to straighten everything up. And frankly, that folder is the last thing I care about."

"I'm sorry. I thought you said you had seen it."

"Maybe I did, maybe I didn't."

I should have just gone over there, I thought. I was

getting nowhere fast. "Mrs. St. Clair," I tried again, "the folder we want is clearly labeled 'freeways.' It's . . ."

"I don't care what it's labeled," Mrs. St. Clair snapped. "Someone broke into the house last night and tore the place apart. *I* have to straighten it up. So if you'll excuse me."

"How awful. Perhaps—"

"The answer is no. I don't need any help, no. But I'm sure an old lady somewhere could use an arm crossing the street." Mrs. St. Clair slammed the phone down.

I put the phone back on the table and sat on the stairs mulling over what she had told me. With all of the publicity surrounding Jim's murder, the memorial service and the presence of Mrs. St. Clair in town, any cat burglar could have targeted the house. But if the freeway folder was the desired loot, then my instincts were correct. The file contained something terribly damaging to somebody. But who, besides me, could have known that?

I glanced at my watch. It was nine-thirty. My appointment with Mrs. Herbert was at ten.

The Crestmont Arms was wedged diagonally onto a lot near the corner of Sunset and Griffith Park Boulevard, as if it were an eyesore the neighborhood was trying to hide from view. The four-story stone apartment house may have been elegant at one time, but that time was long before mine. Yellow water stains streaked the front of the building. The wrought-iron grillwork that enclosed the balconies on the higher floors had sprouted ugly rust spots. Brown patches of grass marred the lawn and the black painted front door creaked when I pulled it open.

Pungent cooking smells, heavily laced with garlic, permeated the small lobby. An elderly man sat on a sagging, flowered sofa, his hat in his lap, patiently waiting for life to go on. The tile floor needed a good scrubbing.

"Have you come to see Mrs. Ardst?" The old man looked at me expectantly.

"No," I said.

"Cause she died two days ago."

"I'm sorry. Could you tell me, is there an elevator?"

"Keeled over just about where you're standing now." The man nodded sadly. "Her husband had been giving her trouble."

I didn't see an elevator, though surely the building had one. I smiled at the man and started up the stairs.

"He ain't here either," the melancholy voice echoed. "You're wasting your time if you're looking for Harry Ardst."

I was looking for 4D, which I found at the front of the building. I knocked on the door. After a moment, I heard the chain guard clink. Slowly, the door swung open.

I was looking at a gray-haired woman of medium height who had grown quite plump with age. Tight curls framed a wrinkled face anchored by bright blue eyes. She was wearing a navy dress with a narrow matching belt that fit snuggly above her protruding stomach. A white handkerchief had been folded into the breast pocket of her dress and a strand of pearls, good pearls, encircled her neck.

"Mrs. Herbert?"

"You must be the Chandler girl. You look different from TV."

I smiled uncomfortably. "Thank you for letting me come by."

"Hardly anybody does anymore. Who'd want to come visit an old lady stuck up here like an owl in a tree?"

She turned and I followed the path of her thick black shoes saying, "You must be used to living on the ground. I . . . oh what a lovely view. You can see the reservoir in the distance."

"I get nose bleeds if I stand too close to the window. Martha Cox thinks I have some kind of phobia, but I forget which one."

She had stopped in front of a faded chintz sofa, which was parked, like a barrier, a foot from the double windows that framed the distant shimmering blue reservoir. It was a small apartment. A dining alcove jutted out from the far side of the square living room and beyond it, I could see the kitchen. Off to my right, a doorway, not far from the sofa, must have led to the bedroom. Mrs. Herbert seemed to follow my eyes. "It isn't much. But the people in the building are nice. Make yourself comfortable while I get the coffee. Do you take cream?"

"A little, yes."

The couch, a coffee table and two worn armchairs took up most of the living room. I walked over to the bookshelves on the wall opposite the windows. There was a collection of Sherwood Anderson, *Moby Dick*, some Dickens and a book about Walter Winchell. Two shelves were given over to the *Reader's Digest*. A framed eight-by-ten photograph of a younger Mrs. Herbert with a man, presumably Mr. Herbert, was flanked by two smaller photos, each showing a bridal couple. On the console below the shelves was a maroon-leather photo album, a Bakelite radio and a menagerie of colored glass animals.

Against the neighboring wall stood a card table with a jigsaw puzzle in progress.

"Please sit down, Miss Chandler."

Mrs. Herbert was carrying a metal tray with difficulty. I took it from her and put it on the coffee table. Two cups of coffee, a bowl of sugar and a plate with a carmelized cake on it.

"Oh," said Mrs. Herbert. "I forgot the plates."

"Let me get them. This is really very nice of you."

The kitchen was barely large enough to turn around in, but like the front rooms, immaculate. The cabinets were the old-fashioned kind with glass windows, and the plates were stacked in the one to left of the sink. The top plate was sparkling clean. But the plate under it was coated with dust. Other stacks of dishes were the same; clean on top, dusty underneath. The glasses were dusty as well, except for the one in front. Mrs. Herbert obviously ate alone, washing up after herself and using the same service over and over again.

I wiped off the second plate and found her sitting on the couch, turning pages in the photo album. "Sit next to me, dear. I want to show you the house I'm talking about."

She tapped a square fingernail on top of a snapshot showing a two-story white frame house on a scrap of lawn. The picture was taken from the street and included a telephone pole that looked as if it had bisected the front door.

"My husband and I bought that house in 1928, just before the Crash," she said fondly. "We put down fifty dollars and had to get a loan for twelve hundred. We always joked about our bad timing. If we had known the Crash was coming we could have waited and probably gotten the house for next to nothing." She turned suddenly and gave me a stern look. "Twelve hundred was a lot then."

"I can imagine."

"Fourteen twenty-two Bellevue," she said gazing at the picture. "We had two small children at the time."

I made the appropriate noises, sipped my coffee and listened. Her husband, Sam, had died two years ago of a heart attack. Her children were married, and with a bit of arthritis beginning to limit her movements, she had decided to sell the house on Bellevue Avenue and find an apartment. She was fifty-four. There was no reason for haste; but sometime in the next few years, she would move.

"Then one day Miss Martens knocked at my door." Mrs. Herbert closed the album and put it on the coffee table.

"When was that, exactly?"

"Back in April. First or second week. She said she was looking for a home in the neighborhood and liked my house from the outside. She hoped I wouldn't think her rude, but she'd just decided to knock on the door and ask if I might be planning to sell."

"How odd."

"I thought so, too. But she seemed like a lovely person. Young, well dressed. Like you." Mrs. Herbert squinted at me, as if to double-check. Satisfied, she nodded. "She told me she was about to be married and that her fiancé's mother lived several blocks over on Edge-cliffe. He wanted to be near her. And what with the housing shortage, she thought maybe by taking this approach she could surprise her fiancé and find a house."

"I see."

"So I told her to let me think it over. I wanted to call Marilyn Kent to see about vacancies. She lives right here in this building. She found out Mr. Long, who was in this apartment, was going to live with his daughter and I could rent it come June."

"How did you negotiate the sale of your house?" I asked.

"Miss Martens brought a real estate man with her the next time she came. He said he thought fifteen hundred was a fair price. The place needed painting and sprucing up, he said. I told them I wouldn't sell for less than thirty-five hundred."

I grinned. "Where did you get that figure?"

"I didn't know any fancy real estate people like Miss Martens did. I just decided I wanted double whatever they said. And that's what they finally paid me. Double."

"Then you got three thousand?"

"I did indeed. Don't you like my coffee cake?"

"It's delicious. But I had a big breakfast. Do you by any chance remember the man's name or his company?"

"I have it in the kitchen. He did the paperwork. He said it would be simpler if we both used him. That way we could split the commission. It came to one-and-a-half percent each."

"So you feel like you got a fair deal?"

"I have no complaints. But when I found out that this same Miss Martens was trying to buy other houses, also where the freeway was coming through, I began to wonder what was going on. I mean, it seemed odd that she never even brought her fiancé around. Can you imagine? So I did some investigating."

Again I smiled.

"I know what you're thinking. That I'm a nosy old lady. And the truth is, I have more time on my hands than I'd like. But what I think happened is that Miss

Martens bought houses cheap and sold them to the state for a profit. Of course I can't prove it. So I wrote letters to the newspapers but nobody wrote back. Then I decided to try Mr. St. Clair. Marilyn Kent's children bought her a TV and I watch it evenings with her. Anyway, Mr. St. Clair was the only one who seemed interested."

"You heard from him?"

"He called me one day and thanked me for the letter. He said he was pretty busy but he'd get back to me. He never did though. It's a shame. Cause I believe something's going on here and it doesn't seem right to me."

I put my empty cup back on the table. "I must go, Mrs. Herbert. But I want you to do something for me. Make a list of your neighbors who either sold to Miss Martens or who were approached by her. And give me the name of the real estate man."

"You'll do something then?"

I stood up. "I don't know what I can do, to be honest. But I'm collecting information. Seeing where all this is leading. Only I'm late for work now. Do you have that man's name?"

She walked into the kitchen and came back with a business card. It said "Richard Walken, Realtor." There was an address on Glendale Boulevard, and a phone number.

"He wasn't with a company?"

"Not that I know of. When I called him once, a woman answered. I guess she was the secretary."

I thanked her and took another look at the bright blue reservoir outside her window. It was a shame Mrs. Herbert didn't care for the view.

10

◆

When I arrived at the *Examiner,* I took off my hat, hung up my white wool suit jacket, fluffed my hair and headed for the morgue. Just for fun, I wanted to check the card catalogue to see if we had run anything on Richard Walken or Miss Martens. Penelope Potts was at her usual station, snipping stories with giant scissors while listening to *Perry Mason* on the battered radio that commanded a corner of her desk.

"Hi, Pen."

"Shhh!"

According to my watch, it was eleven twenty-three. Perry had seven minutes to unmask the culprit. Which gave me seven minutes to kill before I attempted a conversation with our temperamental librarian.

The dog-eared card catalogue turned up no entries for either Walken or Martens, so I shut the drawers and timed my arrival at Penelope's desk just as a commercial, delivered by a dulcet-toned man, came on for Revlon lipsticks.

Snippets of newspaper flew through the air as she chop-chopped an *Examiner* to pieces. "Pen?"

"Hold it." Chop, chop.

Her dress today looked like last night's meatball and spaghetti dinner. The man was still intoning about creamy-smooth Apple Cheek Red. The scissors landed with a thud on the desk and papers began flying. "It's here somewhere. I cut it out for you. Ah!"

Triumphantly, Penelope handed me a clipped news story. The headline read, BLIND WOMAN FINDS FRIEND IN AGENT. I scanned the story quickly. An elderly woman, blind, was going to be removed from her apartment, which stood in the path of the Hollywood Freeway. Because she knew her quarters so well, she was able to live alone. But how could she manage somewhere else? According to the story, a right-of-way agent consulted the woman and her family and, after scouring the area for a month, found a similar apartment with low rent to which she could be relocated. *"This illustrates,"* a highway official noted, *"the care and preparation that goes into our efforts to keep the program moving with as little inconvenience to people as possible."*

I looked up. "How touching." And dropped the paper in the wastebasket.

"You told me you wanted relocation stories," Penelope said belligerently.

"I do. But you can't tell me it's all sugar and spice. These are government people we're talking about, Pen."

"Right."

"So?"

Penelope blinked at me through her smudged glasses. "You want dirt, dig it up yourself, dearie. You won't find it in Mr. Chandler's paper or in Mr. Hearst's. They're both big boosters of the freeways, in case you couldn't guess. And anyone connected with building them is a holy saint."

"Even if something crooked is going on?"

"Paris, you're not very smart today. Mr. Hearst gets irritated when he drives down from San Simeon and has to fight the traffic. The word is out to boost the freeways.

Same thing with smog. It hurts his throat. And as for Mr. Chandler, if he thinks something is good for local business, he supports it. You of all people have to know that. Now let me work."

"Okay. Just one more thing, Pen. Who covers freeways for us?" As usual, the stories I had read didn't carry bylines.

Penelope leaned across her desk and began fiddling with the radio dial. "No one is assigned. Just whoever is available to attend a meeting that day. Which should tell you something."

Her hand hesitated as the voice of Red Barber broke through the static saying he would be talking to the manager of the Yankees, "when we come right back." Penelope switched off the radio with a scowl.

Perhaps there was hope for her after all.

A block and half along Broadway, near Olympic, was Romeo's, where for twenty-five cents, they would give you all the spaghetti you could eat. Penelope's dress had put the idea in my head. With the *Examiner* for company, I walked into the restaurant and was led to a table in the back. A kid wearing a white paper cap and tomato-stained apron put down a basket of bread and a glass of water. "Yes, ma'am?"

"Blue plate special, please."

"Coming up."

I flattened out the *Examiner* on the table. I hadn't read it at breakfast because I had skipped breakfast. Now, as my eye slid down to the bottom of the front page, I found myself staring dumbly at the headline: POLICE LET ST. CLAIR SUSPECT GO.

Late last night, the story said, Tommy Nakamura, a gardener arrested in the shooting death of KTLA newscaster James St. Clair, was released following intensive questioning by Los Angeles police officials.

Glumly, I read the rest. Tommy's story, which the police believed, was that he had found the two shirts and the gun stuffed into a trash bin behind a house two blocks away. He found them the day after the murder when he was dumping grass and leaves in the bin. The shirts apparently had laundry tags on them and Tommy, thinking he could use a couple of nice, fresh shirts, had kept them for himself. He also took the gun, he told police, hoping to sell it. The fifty bucks he had on him, the cops confirmed, had been paid to Tommy Nakamura the day of his arrest by several of his customers. At the time of the murder, Tommy claimed he was home cooking his dinner. Although police could not confirm his alibi, they said they did not have enough evidence to seek an indictment.

"Police officials reiterated they were still looking for the mysterious blonde," read the last line of the story.

The kid put down a steaming plate of spaghetti and a bowl of grated Parmesan cheese.

I began to read an accompanying story reviewing the details of Jim's murder. Two bullets, .38-caliber, one in the chest, which felled him, the other in the head, as he lay gasping on the floor. The approximate time of death, between ten-thirty and eleven, the neighbors weren't sure, and the telltale evidence that a woman had been present: the two cigarette butts upstairs and an ashtray in the den, filled with ashes but not, oddly enough, any butts.

I put down the paper and looked up as three reporters and city editor Fred Dickinson sat down in a nearby booth. One of the reporters noticed me and nodded curtly. I was not a favorite in the newsroom. The way I had been hired—by the executive editor—on whim—and inserted into Society, didn't sit too well with the hard-core staffers. Some had come back from the war to find their old jobs taken and only lesser beats available. Some had been turned away altogether. And though it was doubtful any of these men would have wanted my job, the fact that I had been given it—an ex-deb who could not type and who didn't know a pyramid lead from a police blotter—was not overlooked.

I stared at the uneaten plate of spaghetti. I put down a

quarter and a ten-cent tip and walked out. I let Romeo's make a profit on me.

When I got back to the office I found a phone message from Mrs. Herbert, which was the good news. A copy of the afternoon edition, fresh off the press, was the bad news. There had been more developments. The *Examiner,* not one to practice subtlety, ran a screamer across the top of the front page, announcing them: COPS SEEK BLONDE IN GETAWAY CAR.

Anxiously, I read the following:

> On the night television newscaster James St. Clair was murdered, a dark Rolls-Royce was seen driving up Muirfield Road. According to Lt. Art Bolsky of the LAPD, Arthur Chase was walking his dog when the car drove by. The right rear window of the Rolls was lowered part way and Chase claims he caught a glimpse of a blonde in the backseat lighting a cigarette. At the time, the car was three houses north of St. Clair's, moving at moderate speed.
>
> Chase, an insurance man, said he had arrived home only minutes before, and had immediately let out the dog. He was only out for a few minutes. He went back inside and began quarreling with his wife. He did not hear the gunshots, which, he said, could have occurred before he got home or during his wife's histrionics.
>
> Police confirmed that the blonde seen leaving St. Clair's house by the next-door neighbor at about the same time was, quite possibly, the same woman as the blonde in the Rolls.

My stomach was in knots.

At least, I thought gratefully, Arthur Chase could not distinguish a Bentley from a Rolls. On the other hand, I reflected gloomily, the police undoubtedly could.

I dropped the paper on my desk and walked back to the Home Cooking Department to fix a cup of tea. The Home Cooking Department consisted of a small kitchen that was supposed to be used by our food writer to test recipes. No cooking had ever been witnessed as far as anybody knew. Occasionally someone would stash a

sandwich in the refrigerator, then forget it for months. I
had never spotted a soul in the kitchen other than me.

I put the kettle on the stove, found a chipped cup in
the cabinet and dropped a Lipton's tea bag into it. While
I waited for the water to boil, I tried to calm down.

The front door loomed in my mind. I never used the
front door of the house on Muirfield. But that night, Jim,
in driving up the circular drive en route to the garage,
had noticed a package outside the front door. He had
stopped to pick it up and then heard the phone ring. He
went into the house to answer it, leaving the car in the
driveway.

I had arrived some time after and come in through the
kitchen. Later, as I was dressing, he had sleepily asked if
I would mind locking his car doors on my way out. He
had left his briefcase on the front seat.

So I had gone out the front, brought his briefcase into
the foyer, locked the door on my way out and walked
around back to the alley, where Andrew—who was then
Bret—was asleep at the wheel of the Bentley.

From his vantage point, the boy could not have seen
me go out the front door. He might have seen me open
Jim's car door, though that is not what he told the police.
He said he saw a blond woman walking out of the driveway. Rather than cross the dark front lawn and creep
along the far side of the house to the alley, I had taken
the sidewalk. I had passed one house, Jim's other neighbor, turned the corner and walked up the block to the
lighted alley. I didn't think the boy's window would allow
him to see the alley. But even if he had watched me get
into the car, he must have then fallen asleep—otherwise
he would have told the police what else he had seen—
leaving nobody who could testify that I did not, in fact,
return to the house and shoot James St. Clair.

Except Andrew. My paid employee.

The whistling of the teakettle interrupted my bleak
thoughts. I watched the tea steep, threw in a petrified
lump of sugar from the chipped pink bowl in the cabinet
and decided I was going to have to break my silence.

The one person in the world I could trust, and who

could actually be helpful in a pragmatic way, was Theodora Jones.

Tee would know just what to do, if anyone did. I walked out of the kitchen, feeling better already.

"This is what I dug up," Mrs. Herbert was saying over the phone. "Esther Lubinow was one she called on, right down the block from me. Esther's number is Morningside 7234. Next door to her is old Mr. Grimes. The word is he agreed to sell then found out about the freeway. Instead of running scared, he decided to wait it out. He got a good price from the state, they say. Anyway, he's in St. Theresa's Nursing Home on Pico. I got two more to track down."

"Thank you, Mrs. Herbert. By the way, do you recall Miss Martens's first name?"

"I sure do. Ursula. Ursula Martens. Whoever heard of a name like that?"

I spent the rest of the afternoon on the phone. Tee said I could stop by her office at five-thirty. Nick called to confirm our "evening of experimental bliss," as he put it, and wondered if the flowers should be sent to the office or my house. And sometime between calling Darryl Zanuck to confirm that *Forever Amber* really did cost $6 million, the most expensive picture Zanuck had ever made, and tracking down the juice about the Maharaja of Cooch-Behar's cocktail party, Lucille Wills got through the line.

"I've been on pins and needles wondering if you'd found my letters," is how she began.

"Gee," I said, "I hadn't."

"Have you, ah, looked?"

"Yes, I did. I went through his desk. But they aren't there. It's possible, Mrs. Wills, the police have them."

There was a sharp intake of breath. Then, "But they can't, they just can't. I must have them, I really must."

"If the police have them," I pointed out, "I wouldn't be able to help you. But I wouldn't worry. I suppose the worst they could do is question you."

"Oh god," Mrs. Wills said.

"From what the papers say, they're looking for a blond woman."

"I don't care if they're looking for a blue-haired midget," Mrs. Wills said sharply. "If the police question me, everyone will know. It would get out somehow. And then . . ."

"Mm, your husband." I hesitated. "Are the letters *that* incriminating?"

"I'm afraid so."

"I see."

"But it's not just that. Norm . . . I could somehow patch things up with him. He loves me. He . . . needs me."

"Uh huh," I said. "Well."

"He's . . ." Mrs. Wills halted as if debating how much to reveal. "A public figure," she finally breathed.

"Ah."

"That is, he's a lawyer with the Division of Highways. This kind of thing could ruin his future."

It could ruin all of our futures, I thought, though I wasn't sure how it applied to Mr. Wills. "Well look," I said. "Maybe I've alarmed you for no reason. We don't know the police have your letters. Maybe they're somewhere else. Or—"

"What?" said Mrs. Wills expectantly.

"Maybe Jim threw them away. Yes, that's probably what he did." I paused. "Don't you think?"

"No I don't. Jim would have saved them. But I really must go. Please, Miss Chandler, continue your search. I'll be happy to pay you generously if you find them and return them to me. Very, *very* generously."

I told her I would continue to look—and hung up.

Wishing I had told her what she could do with her generosity.

Tee Jones rents an office on Hollywood Boulevard, in an Art Deco building one block west of the Pantages Theatre. Andrew dropped me at the curb and the uniformed elevator man took me up to the fifth floor. I walked down the hall and knocked on the door that had *Barney Feldman Investigations* stenciled in black on the glass. I went in.

The anteroom was empty. The door to Tee's office was closed and I could hear her muffled voice, so I sat down on the Victorian olive green velvet couch that Tee claims she bought off the MGM lot. It looked like something out of a bordello, which was more likely. Tee was a woman with a past. The past stretched back to New Orleans, where she grew up in a brothel—her mother's— and where she ignored child labor laws and went to work at fourteen. By sixteen, she was the star attraction. One cold December night in 1939, she was attacked on the street by two drunken Marines, one of whom wound up knifed to death. Tee never explained how, but the next day she hopped the *Southern Crescent* for Los Angeles and, in one of those success stories you don't find in *The Christian Science Monitor,* was soon "the managing directoress" of a certain establishment run by the famed del Gennio family. In a mansion high above Sunset, she played madam to city officials, entertainment figures and mobsters, banking a lifetime savings of goodwill by listening attentively and keeping her mouth shut.

After the war, she quit the business and moved in with the vice cop she had been paying off weekly. The cop, Barney Feldman, took early retirement and opened a detective agency. Tee found idle life a bore and began to tag along. She learned the ropes quickly, but her life with Feldman soon soured. In the end, Tee bought him out and now she answered to no one.

The door flew open. "Paris? Sorry, I was on the phone. Come in."

I followed Tee into her office. She had refinished the secondhand furniture herself, producing a polished walnut desk, two upholstered club chairs and a flowing green velvet drape, tied back with a sash over the large square window. Potted plants and an assortment of fresh flowers gave the office the fragrant odor of a florist shop.

"It's after five," said Tee. "Shall we?"

"I'd better not. I have this, uh, date tonight. I think it's going to require sober concentration."

"Who?" said Tee, opening the top drawer of her file cabinet. "Who, who, who?"

"I think the story is best saved for the sordid atmosphere of the gym."

Tee raised an eyebrow, took out a bottle of whiskey and poured herself a shot in one of the glasses she kept handy. She sat down behind her desk. "Boy, what a day. This palooka comes in. He's wearing dark glasses and a false mustache. Sweating like a pig. Says he wants a woman followed. Says he thinks she's spending her afternoons in the bed of another Joe. So I say, what makes him think so? And he says—listen to this, Paris. He says, 'Well, her tan's faded. She always has this swell tan.' And I say, that's it? I mean, it's October. And he says, yeah, well, it was gone in September, too."

I laughed. "Sounds like the first chapter of your book, *How* Not *to Cheat on Your Spouse.*" I opened my purse and fished out a cigarette. "So did you take the case?"

"Wait, there's more," Tee said. "So I ask him, what's with the fake lip fuzz? And he smiles happily and says, 'It worked! You didn't recognize me.' Turns out the guy is on radio." Tee grinned. "He's worried someone's going to recognize his *face.*"

"Are you going to do it?"

"Sure. His money's not fake." Tee pushed an ashtray across the desk. "How was your day?"

"Not good. I . . . need a favor."

"Shoot."

"Remember I told you about the freeway file I was trying to find?"

Tee lifted her glass, nodding.

"I spoke to Mrs. St. Clair this morning. I called to ask if she had seen the file at the house."

"Really," said Tee.

"She said she might have. But last night someone broke in and turned the house upside down. She said the last thing she cared about was finding the file."

Tee put down her glass.

"So I wondered if I could hire you to look for it."

Tee said nothing.

"Will you do it?"

"What is it with you and this file? Did you leave your grocery list in it or something?"

"That file may contain important information. There are things I haven't told you. I—"

"Don't tell me." Tee stood and walked behind her desk to open the window. "If I were you, I'd forget this folder."

"I can't forget it, Tee. I really need you to get it for me. It's . . . critical."

"I can't help you."

"I could be in trouble. Why can't you do this for me?"

Tee turned back from the window. There was a sadness in her reddish-brown eyes that I hadn't ever seen before.

"Paris," she said softly, "I want to help, but I can't. Even if I found the folder I couldn't turn it over to you. Do you understand what I'm saying?"

I shook my head.

"The other night I had dinner with Nick, remember?"

"Yes," I said woodenly.

"He brought along Mrs. St. Clair. She isn't happy with the LAPD."

I felt my stomach grow queasy.

"I can't reveal the names of my clients. But I can tell you, I've been hired to find James St. Clair's murderer."

I licked my lips. "By Mrs. St. Clair?"

"Mrs. St. Clair thinks the police know who the mysterious blonde is and are covering it up. Mrs. St. Clair suspects that a woman killed him. She thinks the woman figured she could lure Jim away but that he made it clear he wasn't going to leave his wife."

"So she shot him?"

"That's what Donna St. Clair seems to think."

"Donna St. Clair. Who may or may not be your client," I said.

"Exactly," Tee said.

. . .

The card that arrived with the two dozen long-stemmed white roses said: *"At 7:30 I will be there. To begin the beguine with one so fair. Nick."* I decided he must be trying out a new scene for the long-suffering screenplay he claimed always to be writing and submerged myself in the bathtub, wishing I had never agreed to this lunacy.

"I think your strapless navy taffeta sheath with the cape jacket would be safe," said Mrs. Keyes cheerfully. "Considering you don't know where you're going."

She was perched on the toilet seat, fluttering her fingers, trying to get the orange nail polish to dry. In a few minutes her sister would come to take her off to the movies, as she did every Friday night, not returning her until Sunday afternoon. Her sister lived in Garden Grove with one of those large, messy families I didn't care to hear about.

"I was thinking more along the lines of flannel pajamas and a bathrobe and telling him I'm ill," I said.

"And pearls," said Mrs. Keyes doggedly. "I have to check and see how your navy silk shoes look."

"I could get dressed," I continued. "And then when he arrives, I could feel faint." I blew some bubbles off my chin and glanced over at Mrs. Keyes. "What do you think?"

"I think he'll see through that in a minute." She stood up. "Tell him you've got the croup."

I shot her a look.

"I'll lay out your dress now and then I'm going. Don't dawdle. You'll have to answer the door yourself."

"Have a nice time," I called after her. And sank back into my gloom.

The stupid briefcase. The ill-timed telephone call. The dopey kid lurking behind his bedroom curtains. And Tee. How could Tee abandon me for—*her*?

Maybe somewhere in the world there really was a slow boat to China. And I could board it.

Or maybe, who cared at this point, I would just get

blotto with Nick and go into a swoon when he whispered his silly poems at me.

I pulled the plug on the bathwater and thought why the hell not.

Red lips glistening, wrists dabbed with Chanel No. 5, and taffeta swishing, I glided down the stairs when the doorbell chimed at seven twenty-six.

But it wasn't Nick Goodwin standing on my welcome mat.

"Miss Chandler?"

I stared at the two uniformed cops.

"Chief Gladstone would like a word with you."

I looked between their squared shoulders at the empty patrol car docked in my drive. "Where," I said suspiciously, "is he?"

"You'll have to come with us."

"Now? That's impossible. Tell him I'll see him on Monday."

"I'm sorry, ma'am," said the one on the right. "He wants to see you right *now.*"

"But—"

"It won't take long," said the one on the left. "Probably."

"Couldn't I phone him? He can tell me what he wants over the telephone."

"He wants to question you," said the one on the right. "About the murder of James St. Clair."

In the kitchen I used the intercom to tell Andrew to come down to the house immediately and explain to Nick when he arrived that I would be back as soon as I could. "Make him wait," I said. Then I got into the back of the police car and went sirening into the night.

We did not, as it turned out, go to police headquarters. We went to an address on San Marino, two blocks south

of the Ambassador Hotel. "Friday night poker game,"
came the explanation from the driver cop. "He'll see you
in his study."

I said, "How charming."

My anger at being abducted swamped whatever ner-
vousness I might have felt. If Gladstone had positive
proof that I was the notorious blonde, I would own up.
But if this was a dumb fishing expedition, he would get
nothing out of me. *Nada.*

"We'll go around back," mumbled the driver, as he
parked the car on the street. "Chief said to."

It looked like a nice house. A two-story pseudo-Victo-
rian with lots of lawn and trees. We followed a flagstone
path around to the back, passed through a gate, skirted
the lighted pool and entered a small guesthouse which,
apparently, Gladstone used as an office. It was comforting to know the Los Angeles police chief lived in a manner befitting his civic position.

I sat down on a worn beige couch and waited while
one of the cops went into the main house to summon
Gladstone. The office had apparently been furnished
with secondhand goods. Weathered beige carpeting, a
cheap desk and a big Philco radio. A gallery of photos of
the chief hung on the wood-paneled walls. I didn't
bother to get up to see whom Gladstone was posing with,
but from their even teeth, I supposed they were movie
stars. I lit a cigarette.

"Good evening, Paris. How lovely you look."

Gladstone filled the doorway. He was wearing a yellow
V-neck golf sweater over a white shirt and brown trousers. Brown leather boots poked out from under his
droopy pant legs. I tapped my cigarette into the ashtray.
"Yeah, hi," I said.

"Boys, wait in the car. Paris, a drink?" Gladstone
came into the room and closed the door.

"No, thank you."

He sat down on the couch beside me. "This isn't an
official interrogation. If it turns out we need one, we'll go
downtown, have a stenographer present and a lawyer, if
you want one."

"Do I want one?"

Harry Gladstone smiled. "I wouldn't think so."

"Good," I said. "The other thing, which you ought to mention, is that I don't have to answer your questions unless I'm under arrest. Am I under arrest, Chief Gladstone?"

"Don't be ridiculous. This is just a friendly chat."

"You won't mind if I take off my cape. It's a bit warm in here."

"Go right ahead."

"I'm having a little trouble untying the knot. Would you help me, please?"

Gladstone leaned toward me and awkwardly began pulling the knotted cords. He grunted. After a moment I placed my fingers on his and removed them. I pulled one of the cords and the knot came untied. I let the cape slip off my shoulders onto the couch. Then I leaned forward, extinguished my cigarette and straightened. I smiled. "You first."

"Uh—"

"You start the friendly chat." I crossed my legs and looked at him expectantly.

Gladstone cleared his throat. "On the night of September sixteenth, were you at the house of James St. Clair?"

"No."

"A woman fitting your description was seen leaving the house at around ten-thirty."

"Really? And how would you describe me?"

"Medium height, shapely, blond hair, green eyes."

I touched the mole above my left breast. "Any identifying marks?"

"Not that one would notice."

"Look closer," I said. "There's a small scar on my forehead. Just a pale pink line."

"I never noticed that before."

"And this," I said, sliding my skirt up my leg. "A birthmark. Can you see it? Right above my knee. I just hate it when I have to wear a bathing suit."

"It's very faint. No one would see it."

"Probably not at ten-thirty when it's dark. But anyway, someone told you that a woman of medium height who was—shapely did you say?—had blond hair and green eyes was seen leaving Mr. St. Clair's house at ten-thirty. Is that right?"

"Not exactly. She was described as a young woman with blond hair, your length roughly. And we believe she smoked the cigarettes found in the ashtray in the bedroom. St. Clair didn't smoke."

"At least not when he was wearing lipstick," I said.

"Stop screwing around. Was that you, Paris?"

"Me and a depressing number of other medium-height blondes who smoke. We all smoke. You can't have dragged me down here just for this."

"You were known to be quite friendly with the victim."

"Yes."

"Were you having an affair with him?"

"If I were, do you think I'd shoot him? I'm not sure I would even know how to pull the trigger, let alone aim right." I put my elbow on my knee and my chin on my hand. "Perhaps," I said coyly, "you simply fancy me and want an excuse to sit with me, close like this on the couch."

Gladstone didn't even blink. "You were having an affair with him."

"I'm not going to respond to that."

Gladstone stood up and walked over to his desk. He opened a drawer and pulled out something black. When he held it up, I saw it was a negligee. "Then maybe you'll respond to this."

I sat up straight but said nothing.

"This may not be yours," Gladstone said. "But it's the same style as the one James St. Clair bought for you. He bought it at Saks, charged it and had it sent to your address. Men don't send women nightgowns if they're not sleeping with them."

He tossed the nightgown into the drawer and came back to sit beside me. I made myself sit perfectly still. Gladstone and I stared at each other. "It's possible," I said finally, "that such a nightgown might be found in my closet. It's also possible that there is an entirely different explanation. Is our friendly chat almost over?"

"No. Did he ever mention to you a woman named Barbie?"

"Barbie who?"

"I don't know. But we found a slip of paper in his car. Said Barbie, seven o'clock."

"Did it say she smoked cigarettes? Barbies have been known to hit the peroxide bottle."

"She may know something. She may have been with him at the house."

I grinned. "Deputize me. I'll find out."

"You can't take fingerprints off a nightgown. Did you wear it at his house?"

"Perhaps I'll have another cigarette. Anything else?"

He watched me light a Chesterfield. It took all my control to keep my fingers steady. As I dropped the match into the ashtray, he said, "Paris, if you tell me the truth now, we can cross you off our list and get on with our investigation. You have nothing to fear, honestly. Look at me."

I turned and gazed into his dark appraising eyes. I couldn't read their message. He reached across and touched my cheek. "Tell me what happened, cookie." His fingers slid down my neck and began massaging my bare shoulder. "I'll help you. You know that."

Right. He had said "cross you off our list." If I gave in and told him what happened, he wasn't going to cross me off his list. I couldn't think straight and I needed to. He had the nightgown connection, but what else? He had neglected to mention the Rolls-Royce. Was there anything more he had or could get to put me in Jim's house that night?

"Chief Gladstone, because of our friendship I have been very patient. But now I must tell you. I think you are playing games with me. I think you are harassing me. If I am on your suspect list, then you better tell me I'm a suspect. In that case, maybe I ought to retain an attorney. But I must say I'm really disappointed in you. The police! Surely the police can't be this incompetent."

Gladstone's massaging hand suddenly became a steel vice. The sharp pain made me suck in my breath and I began choking on the smoke I involuntarily inhaled. Gladstone let go and clapped me on the back. Then he put his arm around me, not speaking at all. The yellow golf sweater smelled of stale smoke.

"I'd like to go now."

"Paris, you will probably be brought in for questioning sometime next week. When you are summoned, bring your attorney. I was hoping we could avoid this. But now I think you look forward to the publicity."

He stood up and walked out of the guesthouse without a backward glance.

For a while, I sat there numbly, staring at nothing. I listened to the ticking of the big triangular clock on his desk. An open window let in the insane chirping of the crickets. The room felt suddenly damp. Carefully, I put out my cigarette, slipped into my cape and blew my nose. Then I walked to the door and stepped out.

A soft wind ruffled my hair. I could smell the night-blooming jasmine and the bougainvillea. The kidney-shaped swimming pool twinkled like a giant's precious gem. Across the pool I could see into the house. Gladstone was sitting at the dining room table with three men. One was shuffling cards.

I listened to the crickets and watched the cards being dealt. I wondered if Gladstone's luck that evening was better than mine.

I had gambled. And I had just crapped out.

11

◆

Nick, naturally, wasn't there.

Why I expected him to be, two hours later when I went clumping into my house, I didn't know. But I was so depressed after talking to Gladstone that I hardly even cared.

Though he could have at least left me a note.

I turned off the downstairs lights and stood in front of the mirrored doors to my bedroom closet staring at my sad-eyed self. Behind the doors, in one of the built-in drawers, was the black negligee. I wondered if I should burn it. I wondered how many other drawers contained black negligees dispatched across the city by James St. Clair. "Wear this when you're at home and think of me," the gift card had said.

There were also the pearl earrings. But those he had given me in person and they presumably could not be traced.

I took off the cape and hung it up. I started to unzip my dress, then stopped. I walked over to the phone beside my bed, sat down on the gray satin spread and dialed Nick. He was probably grumping around his apartment waiting to hear from me.

The phone rang nine times before I gave up.

After a moment, I lifted the receiver and dialled the operator. I needed to reach a Walter Ainsley in Sacramento, I told her. Could she please get me his number? Also, I added, I would like the number for the *Los Angeles Examiner* Sacramento bureau. She said she would call me back.

After I hung up, I lay back on the bed and tried to picture Walter. He looked like the prototype of a U.S. Marine recruitment poster, tall, thick-chested, Popeye arms with tattoos. The last time I saw him, his dark hair was clipped in a crewcut. But the most distinctive part of Walter were his dark, piercing eyes.

He was—or had been—the *Examiner*'s top crime reporter and was considered by most to be the best in the city. He not only beat his competitors, he often beat the police. Three times, the Walter legend went, he had hauled in a villain himself. His sources inside the LAPD were matched only by his connections with the Mob. Walter had all the bases covered.

But something had snapped during the war. He had been in the Pacific, and despite returning home with a Navy Cross, a Silver Star and a Purple Heart with a gold star, he never got back on track. He became a boozer. In time, he was relieved of his beat and shifted onto the copy desk, where he kept a bottle in the bottom drawer and used his gifted pencil to make other reporters' stories read like poetry. Except when he went on a bender. Last January, after creatively rearranging a bar, he was given the word by the editors: Dry out or get out. Walter theoretically dried out. Then, by some convoluted thinking that editors are so capable of, Walter was assigned to cover the state capital, where, it was determined, he would be "safer."

Had Sacramento no bars?

I hadn't the foggiest notion. All I knew was that Walter was the only person at the *Examiner* who believed I might have a sliver of a brain in my head—the only one who took me seriously during my occasional forays into "real" journalism.

I needed to talk to him, I suddenly realized, badly.

I debated ringing the newsroom. It was nearly ten o'clock and the editors would be racing to meet the eleven P.M. deadline. Still, maybe Walter had a story for tomorrow's paper and would be calling in. I dialed Richmond 1212 and asked for the copy desk.

"Yeah, Rogers."

"Mick, it's Paris Chandler. I'm trying to reach Walter. Do you have a number for him? Or could you give him a message if he calls in?"

"He called twenty minutes ago, but hang on." The phone headset clattered to the desk and I could hear margin bells ding over the clacking of typewriters and voices shouting: "Where's the goddam dictionary?" "Copy boy!" "Hank, you got the paste?" "What's the headline count on City Hall?" "Copy!" "Say, Lewin's on the phone." "Where's the—?" *"Cop-py!"*

"Paris? Try Avon 4-3476."

Regretfully I clicked off the sounds of a newspaper and got a new operator. She told me the lines to Sacramento were tied up and she'd ring me whenever she got through.

Which could be tomorrow.

I realized then I hadn't eaten and my head felt light. But once downstairs in the kitchen, my stomach churned at the sight of food. I fixed a cup of hot cocoa and drank it with a piece of toast.

Then I went upstairs and did what I had wanted to do all along. I put on a pair of flannel pajamas, climbed into bed and felt ill.

A loud ringing jolted me awake.

I fumbled for the lamp, blinked at the clock and carefully lifted the receiver. "Hello?"

The dial tone buzzed loudly in my ear. Another ring. I realized groggily it was the doorbell.

I stumbled down the stairs, switched on the light in the foyer and cautiously opened the door.

Nick was standing on the welcome mat. His black dinner jacket was hanging open. He was tieless and his white shirt collar was unbuttoned. Wordlessly, he handed me a paper bag.

"More soup?"

He smiled stiffly. It was too bulky for soup. I pulled out a bottle from the bag. "Mm," I said. "Moët et Chandon. Nice." But he was already down the front stairs.

"Nick?" He kept going. "I told Andrew to make you wait, though I was gone longer than I thought and I don't blame you a bit for leaving."

He had reached the right-side door of his green MG, the driver's side of the little foreign import.

"I was all dressed up, waiting for you. I had on, well, not what I have on now. It was a nice dress. Won't you at least talk to me for a minute?"

Nick leaned against the car, folding his arms across his chest, and just looked at me. I felt suddenly self-conscious. I hadn't bothered to wash my face when I went to bed. My hair would be a mess. The pajamas, probably ten years old, were really fit for viewing only by Mrs. Keyes. I thought of how my mother would have locked herself in the bathroom and methodically slit her wrists before she'd ever let anybody see her looking like this. But then, my mother would never look like this.

"Are you drunk?" I called to Nick.

"Unfortunately not." He looked at me grimly. "I went to a movie. I ate a large popcorn, a Baby Ruth, a thing of M&Ms and a package of peanut butter cups. And a Coke. Then the movie started. I bought more peanut butter cups and another Coke."

"Poor Nick. You must be starving. Come inside."

He didn't budge.

"I'll wash my face, if that will help. And brush my hair, okay?"

He stared at me.

"I hate this. Please say *something*."

The arms unfolded.

"Only if you promise you won't change out of that adorable little outfit," Nick said.

When I came out of the powder room, Nick was in the study, pouring a brandy. A fire was crackling behind the glass doors on the hearth. "If you want champagne, I'll open it," he said.

"I don't think I'm dressed for it. Brandy will be fine." Nick poured a discreet amount of Courvoisier into a snifter and handed it to me. I smiled. "I feel a kind of time warp. Like it's still last night, only twenty-four hours later."

Nick clinked my glass. "So much for your recipe for the perfect date. I followed it, to a T. And I'm still standing here feeling like a dope."

"You are?"

"Is it all right to sit down? I feel I have to ask before I do anything."

"Oh, you *are* angry. Yes, let's sit down. I feel funny, too. I mean I really did get all dressed up. And now, when I finally see you, I look like this. Maybe I'd better get a robe."

"What I'm really hoping for," said Nick, "are the fuzzy pink slippers."

"I don't have any."

"Then that's one Christmas present taken care of." He swallowed some brandy.

"Don't be angry, Nicky. I couldn't help it. Where were we going to eat?"

"La Rue."

"Really? I sort of had you pegged for Dolores's Drive-In."

"Well I tried to get in there," Nick said, "but the clip-on trays were all reserved."

We sat there awkwardly. "Some music?" I said eventually.

"If you want."

"Okay." But I didn't get up. "So," I said, "you never

told me about Mrs. St. Clair. When is the story running by the way?"

"Sunday. And why do we have to talk about Mrs. St. Clair?"

"All right." I sipped my brandy, though it didn't taste particularly good, and watched the flames in the fireplace.

"Where did you go tonight?"

"Andrew didn't tell you?"

"Called away on urgent business is what I believe he said."

This surprised me. I figured Andrew would have given a dramatic rendering of my being stuffed into the police car and whisked away. I said, "It doesn't matter, Nicky. I wouldn't have left if I didn't have to."

"How comforting."

"Maybe we could just move on. I blew the champagne and dinner portions of the evening. But we still have the poems."

"No, we don't."

"I guess I don't look very inspirational, huh?"

"Unfortunately, Dylan had a previous engagement. He was already checked out of the library."

"Oh well. You never could count on Dylan anyway."

I got up and went to sit on the floor near the fireplace. I hugged my knees to my chest and tried not to think about Gladstone. But he was there, in that room, worrying me to death. I desperately needed someone to talk to, but I couldn't bring myself to talk to Nick.

After a while he came over and sat beside me. "Paris, do you want me to go?"

I looked at him. A strand of light brown hair had fallen across his forehead. I could see the old confusion in his eyes. We were stuck in the same place we always were, like two characters trapped in the frame of a movie while the projectionist went out to lunch.

"No. Please stay. I'm sorry, I can't think what to talk about. But I like having you here."

He got up, and a few moments later he had Sinatra singing "I Only Have Eyes for You." He brought the brandy decanter back with him and refilled both glasses. "Can I ask you a dumb question?"

"All right."

"Do I make you uncomfortable?"

I looked at him in surprise. He was watching me with those baby blue eyes, searching for an answer in mine. It was a question I had never considered and it seemed to lie there, like a card, face down on the table. Would it be picked up and change the course of the game or—would the game move along without it? I sensed the projectionist returning; hand poised on the switch.

I turned back to the fire. "A little."

"Is it because you think if you care for me I'll die?"

I shifted uneasily. That I had never been able to talk about Russell had always bothered Nick. I wasn't afraid that the men I might love would die. Rather, I was afraid I wouldn't be able to love anyone again.

"No," I said. "I'm not afraid if I love someone he will die."

"Do you know why you're afraid of me?"

"I don't, Nicky. I never thought about it, truly."

"Well I'm a little afraid of you, I admit." He paused. "What do you think we should do about it?"

I stole a glance at him, then, feeling shy, had to turn away. "Let's see." I listened to Sinatra and thought again of the projectionist in some hidden room upstairs, gazing down at us, his finger still on the switch. I said, "We could lie on the floor like children and turn out the lights and tell ghost stories and get really scared."

"We could," said Nick. "But the lights are already out. It's the fireplace that's on."

Sinatra drifted away. A shower of sparks flew up and fell to the hearth. I slipped my hand into Nick's.

"Then why don't we go upstairs," I said softly. "Where it is dark."

12

◆

The discovery of Nick Goodwin in my bed in broad daylight sent me reeling into the bathroom in a dither. I sat down on the edge of the tub, shut my eyes and panicked. *What* had I done?

After a while, the icy porcelain made me stand up. I switched on the light. A cotton robe was hanging on the back of the door. I slipped it on, pausing to look in the mirror. My lips were swollen and my chin felt raw. My eyes looked abnormally bright. I smiled at myself. Then I sank back down onto the edge of the tub and watched my toes turn blue on the cold pink marble floor.

Bang. Bang. Bang. "Paris, how long are you going to stay in there?"

"Um. Nick? There's another bathroom off the guest room, okay?"

"I don't want a bathroom. I want you to come out."

"Oh." I stood up and opened the door a crack.

Nick was standing on the other side, shirt and slacks on, jacket draped over his arm. "Good morning," he said.

"Hi."

He smiled. "Open the door and come out and say good-bye to me."

I opened the door wide. "You're leaving?"

"It's my weekend to work. You're off, I'm on. Remember?"

"Sure." We alternated weekends. Since Etta's column ran seven days a week, one of us always had to be at the office. Nick would take two days off during the week and next weekend I would work. "Can I make coffee?"

"I seriously doubt it," Nick said.

"Funny."

"I'd better go." He tilted his head sideways and looked at me appraisingly. "Maybe you could manage a little smile?"

"It will cost you," I said, stepping into the bedroom.

The kiss seemed to go on for some time, getting my blood going, all the way down to my wiggling toes. "That," he said, "is a deposit for the next time."

He turned and walked toward the bedroom door.

"Nick?"

I could see the tension in his shoulders, in the instant before he turned back around.

"What are we supposed to do now?"

He held up his dinner jacket, shook it and wrestled the car keys out of a pocket. "Nothing, I think."

"Nothing?"

"We'll have dinner Tuesday, after the show. By then you'll have figured out what we're 'supposed to do now.' "

"Don't you want a say in this?"

"Sure. But for the moment, I think I'll stay in the wings. Watching you." He sketched a good-bye, and then he was gone.

I sat on my window seat and followed his MG out of the driveway with my eyes, replaying his final words.

Whatever they meant.

13

♦

"Take an airplane," I said to Walter Ainsley. "Are you joking?"

"Serious. I used to joke, but now I'm sober. Now, I'm always serious."

"You mean delirious. I am not getting on an airplane."

"It won't bite you, Paris. I'll pick you up in 'Frisco. We'll have a nice lunch. You'll fly home. I'll drive back to Sacramento." He paused and I could hear voices in the background. He must have had the radio on. "Cause if you take the train, you'll never get to work on time Monday."

"Walter, I took the plane once. To New York. It took twenty-four hours and I was almost always sick."

"Fine," said Walter. "Call the Port of Los Angeles. There must be a boat leaving sometime this week. Or have Jimmy Cagney drive you."

"Andrew. Bret is now Andrew. I don't know how to take an airplane. What do I do?"

"Jesus," said Walter. "I actually missed you one day. What a waste that was. I'll call you back."

"No—wait. I'll . . . find out. I'll call you when I get to the airport and tell you when the flight gets in . . . is supposed to get in. Do they ever get there on time?"

"Yeah," said Walter. "When the wings don't fall off."

Taking an airplane wasn't that complicated.

Andrew drove me to the Los Angeles Airport on Sepulveda and left the Bentley outside the terminal. I made him come in with me and stand there while I filled out the flight insurance forms. "I'm leaving the car to you, so you can stop peeking over my shoulder, okay?" I said crabbily.

"I wish I were going," said Andrew dreamily. "There's an open audition for a pilot on Wednesday at Twentieth Century-Fox. I'm pretty sure now that I'll go to it."

I gave the forms to the woman behind the counter, took my sunglasses off and put them in my purse. I was wearing my navy wool Norman Norell suit, a roll-brim navy hat and carrying my mink stole. "Don't forget my travel case," I called to Andrew as I marched off.

I found a telephone booth and rang Walter, using four quarters and waking him up. "I'm leaving now," I announced. "Nine-thirty. Western Airlines. It gets in at noon. They say. Will you be there?"

There was a loud staticky noise, which I realized was Walter clearing his throat. "Yeah, I'll be there. Look for me at the gate. Tall, handsome fellow, often mistaken for Clark Gable, in case you've forgotten."

"I must have the wrong number," I said and hung up.

Andrew tried to coax me upstairs to Mike Lyman's Flight Deck for breakfast. Failing that, he went over to the newsstand and bought me two magazines and a package of Doublemint, which I assumed he would bill me for at the end of the month. At the gate, a woman in a beige suit with a Bullock's badge on her lapel stood behind a table selling box lunches for sixty cents. "You'd better get one," urged Andrew, whipping out a dollar. "You'll need nourishment."

"No, I won't."

"And don't forget your Dramamine, Miss Chandler. Bye-bye."

Supplied and duly instructed, I walked out the door onto the tarmac and climbed the stairs to the plane. I chose a seat midway down the aisle, next to a gray-haired man with a bulbous nose who was reading the sports section of the L.A. *Times*. He introduced himself as Ed Cameron, helped me put my travel case on the rack above and politely asked if I might like the window seat. To which I replied, "Heavens no."

I opened the cardboard box and found two sandwiches in wax paper, an apple, and a package of Salerno butter cookies. "Maybe you would like this," I said to Mr. Cameron.

"Thanks, I have one."

When the stewardess came round with the Chiclets, I asked for a glass of water. I swallowed two Dramamine, strapped myself in, grabbed onto the armrests with fingers of steel and hoped the end would come . . . painlessly.

"Why don't you roll down the window? You look a little green."

"Ball two, low and inside. Branca not liking the call one bit."

I rolled down the window of Walter's decrepit green Packard and looked across Mason Street at the entrance of the Fairmont Hotel. A woman in a pink wool suit came out tugging on a leash attached to a recalcitrant matching pink poodle. At the top of the stairs, the poodle went into fourth gear, forcing the woman to grab the handrail and come bumping down at a precarious pace. "How come they always have poodles?" I said. "They're horrible little dogs."

"With two men on, here comes Joltin' Joe."

It was a bright, clear San Francisco Sunday and there

was a freshness to the air not often found in L.A. any-more. The headache I had when I lurched off the plane seemed to be abating. I removed my pearl hat pin, took off my hat and shook out my hair.

"One swing, folks, he could tie it up," the radio said excitedly.

"Could you turn that down, please?"

Walter was gripping the steering wheel, staring out the windshield. He was dressed as he always had been, black slacks, white shirt and an Ernest Hemingway safari jacket. The pointed end of a paisley tie flopped out of one of the pockets. Even with the tie knotted properly around his neck, I wasn't sure the restaurant would let him in.

Walter said, "Driving two and a half hours on a nice Sunday to get here is one thing. Not listening to the World Series goes into a whole other debit book."

"Which, I imagine, is already overflowing."

"There it goes! Long fly ball! Deep into the left field corner. Little Al Gionfriddo is racing back—he'll need jet propulsion to get this one—back, back—seventy-four thousand people are on their feet—he is . . . reaching over the fence. Oh my! Does he have it? He does! Holy Chicago! DiMaggio is robbed! *Ooh, doctor!*"

Walter was pounding the steering wheel with both fists, grinning like a lunatic. "Way to go, *Al-fray-do*!" he boomed.

"Is it over now?" I said, brightening.

Walter stared at me as if I were a cockroach crawling across his plate. "Look, why don't you go for a nice walk, huh? Get your color back. Three more innings, we'll go inside, have lunch." Walter grinned. "Yeah?"

I put on my hat and opened the door. "Just as long as it doesn't go into extra innings," I said.

It didn't. But it did go three hours and twenty minutes. That Gionfriddo person was some kind of substitute and stealing DiMaggio's home run was like "bringing down a B-17 with a slingshot," is what Walter said. He insisted

on replaying the great moment for me as we sat in the
Venetian Room of the Fairmont, listening to two violins
and one piano and waiting to be served. Well into "The
Blue Danube," a waiter in a black suit and bow tie
floated up to us. He smoothed the white damask tablecloth before inquiring what our drink choices might be.

"Two Bloody Marys," sang Walter. "Only take my
vodka and put it in her drink. So you're bringing one
Bloody Mary with two vodkas and another Bloody Mary
with none."

"What?" said the waiter.

"I think the gentleman was asking for one Bloody
Mary and one Virgin Mary," I cut in. "Thank you."

Walter grunted.

"You look good, Walter. I expected you to be all shriv-
eled up and gray, with nose hairs and maybe a wen on
your face. Instead you look—"

"Healthy," said Walter aggrievedly.

"You're not playing tennis or anything, are you?"

"Handball." He peeked under the napkin covering the
bread basket and pulled out a roll. "I was thinking of
growing a mustache."

"I wouldn't."

"Well of course you wouldn't." Walter tilted his head.
"Would you? Ex-deb launches new career as lady in the
circus. Life can't be that bad."

"I think I'll have a roll."

The waiter brought the drinks. We clinked glasses and
lit cigarettes. "So," said Walter. "I'm all ears." He wiggled them.

Through two Bloody Marys, a center cut of roast beef,
vegetables and a salad, I told him my story. When I got
to the night of the murder, Walter put down his knife
and fork and sat perfectly still, staring at me with his
piercing eyes.

"So you can see the mess I'm in," I said. "There's a
noose around my neck and Gladstone is tugging on it."

I lit a Chesterfield, leaned back and waited for Walter
to tell me what to do and how everything would be all
right. Instead he unfastened his eyes from me and sig-

naled the gliding waiter. "Please remove these plates and bring us two coffees. Also a selection of cigars. Paris, I hope you won't mind. But this is more than a cigarette situation."

I felt a knot in my stomach. "Meaning?"

"Meaning—" His eyes seemed to drift to another table where a man in a baggy suit was reading *The Chronicle* and forking into a piece of pie. Walter's eyes swiveled back to me. He chewed on his lip and waited until the waiter had poured coffee from a silver urn into two flowered china cups.

"All right, let me go over a few things. First, where did you leave St. Clair that night and what was he doing?"

I tapped my cigarette into the ashtray. "He was in bed. He had turned on his lamp and seemed to be getting ready to read. Why?"

"What do you mean, seemed to be?" Walter said.

"The phone rang and Jim picked it up. It was on his bedside table. He waved good-bye and I left."

"I thought you said he didn't answer the phone when you were there." Walter began stirring sugar into his coffee. He looked up. "Do you know who it was?"

"I don't."

"So you go downstairs, open the front door, get the briefcase out of the car, bring it in, right? Is he still on the phone?"

I put down my coffee cup and tried to think. The bedroom was at the end of a long hall. Jim's voice would have been barely audible downstairs in the rotunda.

"I don't know. But—yes, I think he was. I remember now. I heard a noise in the kitchen, a creak or some other small sound. I thought he had come down and I called his name. But there was no answer. And if the light had been on in the kitchen, it would have shone through a little into the dining room, which you can see from the rotunda. I didn't call loudly, but he might have heard me if he hadn't been on the phone. Does it matter?"

Walter's eyes drifted over to the man eating the apple pie, then swung up to take in two women in print dresses and flowered hats who were strolling by. The ensemble was playing "Someone to Watch Over Me." "You'd think our waiter swam to Havana," Walter said angrily. "All right. So you leave the house, locking the front door as you go. You don't walk across the lawn, along the house to the alley, because it's dark. Instead you go out to the sidewalk, walk all the way around the house on the corner, and back into the alley. Let me think. If you had cut across the lawn, would you have passed by the kitchen?"

"Yes."

Suddenly Walter brightened. "Well, look who's here."

The waiter arrived, setting down four cigar boxes on the table. Walter leaned over and eagerly opened each box like a large child making a big decision about a candy bar. At last he chose Monte Cristo number three, fishing out two. "We could be a while," he said meekly.

"I don't understand what you're getting at, Walter."

"Pipe down." Walter allowed the waiter to snip the end of one of the cigars and light it. He leaned back in the upholstered chair and puffed happily.

"What about the kitchen?" I persisted.

"You entered the house through the kitchen, right? So what I'm wondering is how come you didn't leave that way. Instead of walking around the corner."

"I don't know," I said irritably.

Walter was watching me with that intense stare that I knew so well, but it could have been the stare of a look-a-like stranger. I hadn't seen him since April, when he stopped by the *Examiner* after spending six weeks drying out at some sanitarium in the desert near Indio. He had come by to collect his belongings before heading up to Sacramento. We had exchanged several letters. But the time and the distance had put a bigger space between us than I realized and I was feeling slightly off-balance.

"I guess I wasn't thinking." The violinists had left the piano and were strolling through the dining room, stopping at tables to ask for requests. "I put the briefcase in the entrance way and was concerned about locking the front door. Which I did. So I couldn't go back in, could I?"

"Not through the front door," Walter said.

"Are you saying I went back in through the kitchen and shot him?"

"Could you have?"

"Shot Jim?"

"Gone back into the house through the kitchen. Lower your voice. When you went in originally, did you lock the door?"

"No. I always locked it when I was leaving."

Walter grunted. "You see my point."

"No, I do not see your point."

"Then listen. The police could say you reentered the house through the kitchen. Nobody would have seen you. Or, you could have rung the front door bell. He comes down, lets you in. You shoot him and you run out the kitchen door to the alley, and into the car. Again, no witnesses. Your driver is asleep. He doesn't know anything until you open the rear door and rap on the glass."

"Are you saying, Walter Ainsley, that you think I shot Jim? Because if you are—"

"I am not." Walter picked up his cup and slurped his coffee. "I am merely making a point. You could have done it. Or," said Walter signaling the waiter, "so could someone else."

"Someone else going in through the kitchen?"

"And St. Clair hearing a noise, like you did, coming down the stairs, seeing the guy, getting it in the chest."

I took a deep breath. The violinists arrived at our table. I shook my head. "Play 'When My Baby Left Me,' " Walter said, handing one of them a dollar. He turned to me. "He could have been in the kitchen while you were there, kiddo. Or he could have been outside, waiting, seeing you leave. Then ringing the bell."

"Or *she*," I put in.

"And your only alibi is the dozing chauffeur."

"Yes, but if a gun had gone off, Andrew would have heard it. It would have awakened him. Maybe he wouldn't even have known what woke him up, but he would have been up. And when I got to the car, he was definitely asleep. I had to tap him on the shoulder."

"This is Bret, the actor, we're speaking of? The major talent who died in the first scene of *The Sunrise Kid,* to speak of his most celebrated credit."

I stared at Walter. "Are you saying Andrew heard a shot and *pretended* to be asleep?"

"To protect you, as any loyal servant would."

"Oh for god's sake, Walter."

"I'm only trying to think like the police. Old habits die hard." Walter looked at his water glass sadly.

The waiter arrived and silently took Walter's order for more coffee and a club soda. It was three-thirty and the Venetian Room was emptying out. The man across the way was still reading his newspaper, but seemed to have lost interest in the pie. The women in the print dresses were drinking tea and whispering confidences that caused them to burst into giggles. Nearby, a family of four was squabbling noisily, sounding like a cage full of finches.

"What concerns me more, if we can slip back into reality here, are the cigarette butts."

"Forget the butts. But do switch brands."

"I'm speaking of my fingerprints. If they bring me in this week, they'll fingerprint me and see the prints are the same."

"Paris, look at the way you're holding your cigarette. Between your index and middle fingers. It's doubtful you made a full print on the butt. Besides, there's no way to prove those cigarettes were smoked the night St. Clair died. They could have been smoked the night before, maid forgot to empty the ashtray."

"The maid only comes once a week."

"Perfect. Jeez, the guy's getting another dessert. You want a dessert?"

The waiter, before bringing us our drinks, stopped to give the man with the newspaper a slice of lemon meringue pie. It made my mouth water. "I guess he didn't like the apple," I said, watching the waiter pick up the half-eaten piece of pie. "I'd better not eat anything more. Uh, plane ride back."

"Of course," Walter said.

The waiter poured our coffees and floated away. As did the violinists. I leaned forward. "So what do I do? Can I go to Gladstone unofficially and tell him my story and trust him to keep it out of the papers? I mean, if he drags me in . . ."

"Keep your voice down," Walter whispered harshly. "And no, you can't trust him. He'll go for the big headlines. Run along to the ladies' room now while I pay the check. We'll talk in the car."

"I don't need to go to the ladies' room."

"Yeah, you look swell." Walter grinned. "That green thing in your teeth is a nice touch."

I grabbed my purse and fur and stalked out of the dining room, across the Oriental rugs in the lobby and into the ladies' room. A Negro woman in a white uniform sat on a stool staring dreamily into space. I leaned across the marble vanity and bared my teeth at the mirror. There was no "green thing" that I could see. I powdered my nose and applied fresh lipstick. Then I dropped a dime in the dish beside the attendant and returned to the lobby.

Walter was coming out of the dining room. He stopped and motioned me over.

"So, kid, this is it. I'm running a bit late. But you still have time. There's an arcade on the other side of the lobby. Nice shops. Stuff you might like to look at, ten or fifteen minutes. And at the end of the arcade, you take the elevator to the terrace level and go out onto California Street, catch a cab there. Okay?"

Walter raised his eyebrows, questioningly. He still had the cigar in his mouth. He put it in his breast pocket and squeezed my shoulders. "Okay?"

I nodded uncertainly.

"Tell the boys in the city room I say hello." Walter hugged me. "And next time, give me a little warning. I'll take you out to a club."

I smiled. "Take care of yourself, all right?" I kissed Walter on the cheek and walked toward the arcade. Without looking back.

14
♦

Fifteen minutes later, I stepped out onto California Street and slid into the front seat of Walter's car. He made a quick, and illegal, U-turn and parked on the other side of the street. A moment later, the double-dessert man from the dining room pushed through the revolving door onto the sidewalk. He looked both ways before noticing Walter, who waved cheerily at him. Walter then stepped on the gas and the Packard sputtered off with a violent lurch.

"What is going on? Who is that man?"

"You can ask him yourself." Walter checked the rear-view mirror. "On the plane."

"The plane?"

"He got off it with you. He followed you here. When you went to the rest room, he walked out and parked in the lobby." Walter gave me a sidelong glance. "Probably he was headed for Omaha. Caught sight of you at the airport in L.A. Fell in love."

"That's it," I said.

"All right, Paris, listen. You trust me or you wouldn't

118

be here. So trust what I'm going to say. If I were still on the beat, I could probably do something for you. But when you're off the beat, the cops don't know you anymore. I can make calls, find out some things. But I can't get you off the hook."

I stared at the Bay off to the left, sparkling under the late afternoon sun. A couple of sails bobbed tipsily on the horizon. "I've always wanted to be scandalous," I said miserably.

"You always were. So listen. Let Gladstone haul you in. But don't tell him squat. He's got nothing on you, believe me. You probably got more on him. If the Yanks win the Series, you can name his bookie."

"Oh swell."

"Meantime, follow your leads like a good girl. That Mrs. Whazzhername sounds interesting. So does her old man, the contracts guy. Keep digging. You'll turn up something."

"For this I had to take an airplane?"

"And smoke Luckys. Or those little brown cigars. It's a cute look."

"Gladstone's seen me smoke Chesterfields."

"And keep in touch." Walter pulled on the hand brake. "Okay?"

I hadn't realized we had turned into the airport. Suddenly I didn't want to leave Walter's car. Sometimes he could be a lunatic, but I believed he wouldn't let anything bad happen to me. I looked at him and saw the worry in his eyes.

"Can't you come back?" My anxious words hung heavily in the air between us. Walter rolled down his window, as if to let them out. But he was only looking for a porter. He turned back to me.

"If I can—I'll try."

There was another silence as we both watched the cab door in front of us spring open. The man in the baggy suit jumped out. Without a backward glance, he hurried into the terminal.

I looked at Walter. His face, for just a brief moment, seemed sad. I realized then that by asking him for something he could not do for me, I was reminding him of how he had failed. Come back from the war damaged, and maybe not repaired still.

"I'm sorry," I said. "I've been so wrapped up in my own problems that I haven't really asked you how it's been. Are you all right?"

"I'm fine. Now run along and let me know what happens with Gladstone." He squeezed my hand.

"Do you have friends up there, a girl?"

"No girl. They tell you to lick one problem at a time."

"So what do you do at night, if I may ask?"

"Movies. I've seen *Bulldog Drummond Strikes Back* five times. Last night I caught *Dark Passage*. Bogart. I listen to the radio, read."

"Do you sleep well?"

Walter shook his head.

"Is it the war? Do you still think about it?" Once, in a rare moment of semi-inebriated confession, he told me about the nightmares.

"*Think* about it? I can still *smell* it. Now run along. And stop worrying. You're not the kind of girl trouble takes a shine to."

I said, "Sure."

Walter shouted at a passing porter. "And that guy in the suit. Go sit next to him. Otherwise, you'll be a wreck the whole flight, guy back there spying on you. Just plunk yourself right down next to him. He gives you any trouble, you know what to do."

"I do?"

Walter grinned.

The porter opened my door. I handed him my travel case.

"Barf," Walter said.

"Gin," the man said.

"No—already?"

He smiled, showing his crooked little teeth. "Lucky hand." He snapped his cards, fanned them and tossed them onto the tray.

"That's your third lucky hand in a row. You wouldn't be peeking at my cards?"

"No, ma'am. If you don't want to play, that's fine with me."

"I don't have much money, I'm afraid." I sipped my Coke and looked at him. "I keep thinking I've seen you somewhere. Have we met?"

"No. You saw me having lunch at the Fairmont. I was at a table across from you."

"So you just came up for the day, I suppose."

"Business. But the guy didn't show. How do you like that? As if I have nothing better to do in the world."

"What *do* you do in the world, Mr.—?"

"Brown. Al Brown. I'm in sporting goods. Play another hand?"

"Twenty-five cents a game? Okay. Maybe one more."

"You look well heeled enough, Miss—?"

"I'm sorry. Cassandra Blake."

"Would that be—Mrs. Blake?"

"No."

"The man you were having lunch with. A beau?"

I smiled. "He's my uncle. My aunt died recently and I thought he might like some company."

"Mm." Brown dealt the cards. He was a stocky man with a square jaw, thinning hair and a nose that took a couple of wrong turns before getting where it was going. He also had dark beady eyes, which, automatically, made you not trust him. He looked like a politician.

He glanced up. "So how does an unmarried girl afford plane tickets and fur stoles, if you don't mind my being nosy."

I put down my cards and leaned toward Mr. Brown. "You remember Edward Doheny? The oilman? Well I'm part of that family. I just don't care to talk about it, given the scandal and all." Mr. Brown stared at me. "The Teapot Dome Scandal, surely you've heard. Anyway, my mother is a Doheny. I'll take that card if you don't mind."

By now I was convinced that Mr. Brown was not a cop. For one thing, he had dirty fingernails and cops were always meticulous about their hands, for some reason that escaped me. Secondly, he hadn't slipped in any cop words like "accomplice" or "family members," which, according to Walter, cops did without thinking.

Actually, I was beginning to doubt Mr. Brown was following me at all. He didn't seem rattled when I sat down on the aisle seat beside him. He just sort of grunted and went back to his magazine, *Collier's*. When the plane began taxiing, he put the magazine down and gripped the armrests as pathetically tightly as I did. Once we were up in the air, I began to laugh—a nervous reaction —and soon he laughed, too. After a drink, he told me how he had gone to a six o'clock mass that morning. "First time I've locked into a pew in fifteen years."

"Well," I said, discarding a queen, "gin."

"Jeez I couldn't get anything going. Here, two kings, a ten, an eight and a deuce. You got forty points, miss."

Mr. Brown excused himself and went to the rest room. Casually, I reached down and opened the briefcase he had put on the floor. In it, I found a checkbook. The name on the checks said Albert Aubrey. There was also a small leather address book. I slipped that into my purse along with a business card. Then I closed the briefcase and sat back in my seat, debating.

I had lost a dollar twenty-five already.

And we still had a nerve-wracking ninety minutes to go.

15

♦

"So. What do you think it means?" said Constance McPhee Estevez, rattling the *Examiner* in front of my nose.

It was not quite nine. I had come into the office early, hoping to sneak into the morgue and check some things out. But for a reason known only to her, the society editor had swept in long before her usual arrival time. I moved aside my cup of lethal coffee, brewed by a sociopathic copy boy with an intent to kill, and flattened the newspaper across my desk.

DUKE OF WINDSOR, ALONE, IN ENGLAND, the headline read. Following a Dover, England, dateline, the story said:

The Duke of Windsor arrived today for a visit of about 10 days in England "on private business." The Duchess, the former Wallis Warfield Simpson, for whom he renounced the throne, did not accompany him from Paris.

I looked at Constance. "I don't know," I said.
She was wearing a powder blue wool suit and a black

123

straw hat with a brim that could have provided shade for
the entire Society Department. She bit her bottom lip,
making a small indentation in the wild strawberry lipstick.

"Probably nothing," I added.

"They could be separating. Do you think? I mean,
we'd have to get somebody on it right away. Mr. Hearst
knows those people."

"Everyone knows those people," I said. "And everyone will have the story before we do. Stop worrying,
Constance. I should think the bigger news is that Gary
Cooper is not going to Paramount. He's already signed
secretly with Warner's."

"No!" exclaimed Constance. "Seriously?"

"Yes, I'm pretty sure." I smiled. "I could check it out,
okay?"

"Lord, yes, check it out. Good heavens. Paramount
must be dying."

I handed the paper back to Constance. She started to
walk away, then came back. "About the Duke and Duchess. I mean, if they do divorce, could he become king
again?"

"I'm sure not. Princess Elizabeth is next in line. You
know how the British feel about protocol." I hadn't the
foggiest idea how the British felt about protocol, or
whether Edward could become king again. I reached for
my cup. "Go have some coffee, Constance. It will perk
you right up."

With a relieved sigh, I watched her walk away. I knew
about Cooper because my father, who is under contract
to Warner's, gave me the report after I got home from
the airport Sunday night. He had called especially to tell
me, he had said. He had been at Jack Warner's for
brunch and the studio chief was ecstatic. So was I. Now I
could let Constance think I was working on the Item all
day.

When, in fact, I had no intention of doing so.

·   ·   ·

"Good morning, Wells Fargo Bank."

"Hello, this is Miss Canton with the Federal National Mortgage Association."

"Uh huh," the woman said.

"I'm running a check on an applicant, a Mr. Albert Aubrey. Is there someone who might help me?"

"I'm afraid, Miss Canton, we don't give information over the phone."

"Of course. But I only need to verify that Mr. Aubrey is a customer of your bank, that he keeps a balance of over five hundred dollars, and—"

"All right, one moment please."

The business card I had glommed from Mr. Aubrey-Brown's briefcase had been for a Morris Smith, painter, whom I did not think was Mr. Aubrey-Brown. Before I began poring over Aubrey-Brown's address book, I decided to see if he was going to be worth the trouble.

"Miss Canton? This is Lester Pherson, assistant branch manager. You were asking about Mr. Aubrey?"

"Yes. He gave your bank as a credit reference."

"He's had an account with us for several months. No bad checks so far. Other than that, I can't tell you anything."

"Could you tell me if he maintains a solid balance— say, five hundred dollars?"

"No, I couldn't say that."

"Is his balance substantially less?"

"His balance fluctuates quite a bit. Sometimes it's in the thousands, sometimes, well, it has dipped below one hundred dollars. But as I said, we've had no problems with Mr. Aubrey."

"And you have him working at—um. Oh dear, where did I put that paper?"

"Consolidated Developers."

"Ah. Yes, that's it. Well good enough, Mr. Pherson. Thank you so much."

I hung up. So he had lied to me, not only about his name, but about his occupation. Which didn't mean a thing. For I was no more related to the Dohenys than I was to the Duke of Windsor.

The thought made me glance over at Constance. She was sitting behind her desk, a look of fierce concentration straining her facial muscles, as she briskly filed her fingernails. I grabbed my purse and beat a path out of there.

Across the street from the *Examiner,* on the edge of the parking lot, stood Henry's hamburger joint, a wooden shack built by Henry himself. It was just big enough for a Formica counter, eight stools and the greasy grill that produced a steady stream of burgers, fries and—if you could stomach them—tacos. I stood outside the spattered windows, peering in, and talking into the pay phone.

St. Theresa's Nursing Home told me that Mr. Grimes was not feeling well today and probably could not speak with a visitor. But Esther Lubinow said she would be happy to see me anytime.

I hung up.

Tony, the lanky parking lot attendant, was backpeddling along a line of cars, a battered mitt raised over his head. "DiMaggio take a big swing. Oh-oh, it look like trouble. But wait! Gionfriddo's going back. Still going back . . . *ooof*!"

Tony went splat against a shiny black Hudson and the ball, tossed up and swung at by his cousin Hector, dive-bombed onto the car's roof.

I glanced nervously at the Bentley, stowed at the back of the lot. "Where's Andrew?" I called out.

"What a catch, huh? You listen to the game? Robbed DiMag blind."

"I heard," I said. "Where is he?"

Tony began walking toward me. "You think the Bums gonna win it?"

Just then I caught sight of Andrew strolling out of the alley alongside the *Examiner.* I watched him cross Broadway.

"I think Brooklyn's gonna do it," Tony said with certainty.

"Hi," said Andrew. He was practicing what I guessed was his Robert Taylor smile today.

"Who did you bet on?" I asked. He had obviously been visiting Mark the Mark.

"Brooklyn. I got inside information."

"Such as what?"

"DiMaggio's got a bum arm. But nobody's supposed to know."

I looked up. Dark, threatening clouds were moving fast. The forecast was for rain. Just as it had been yesterday. And the day before. I wondered if the weatherman got inside information, too.

"Your secret's safe with me," I said.

Bellevue Avenue was a long, rambling street that ran east to west, south of Sunset. Esther Lubinow's house was located not far from Echo Park. It was a single-story, postage-stamp-sized frame structure with a deep front veranda. I left Andrew at the curb and walked up to the front door. I rang the bell.

Miss Lubinow must have been standing on the other side because the door swung open immediately. "Miss Chandler?" she said. "Please come in."

She was younger than I had imagined. A skinny, frail-looking girl, she had long brown braids that framed a plain, square face; her eyes were a weary gray. She wore no makeup. Her white round-collared blouse was wrinkled and her print cotton skirt was unfashionably long. She had a nice dimple when she smiled.

"You're going to walk in on a mess," Esther said cheerfully. "I've been so busy taking care of Mama, I haven't had time to straighten up."

She led me into a cluttered living room. The smell of stale air laced with medicine portended imminent doom. A standing radio dominated the room but to reach it required a nimble step across and around shoes, magazines and many balls of brightly colored yarn. Yarn also was strewn across the frayed rose-colored couch.

"Why don't you sit on the sofa?" Esther said. "Just move the yarn. I'm making a quilt for Mama and—"

"Esther!" came an angry voice. "Who are you talking to?"

Esther turned and walked through a doorway. "It's okay, Mama. My friend, Miss Chandler, has stopped by for a cup of coffee."

"I don't know Miss Chandler," snapped the querrulous voice.

"I'll bring her in soon." Esther closed the door and came back and sat down in a rocking chair. A worried look crossed her face. "I think we're out of coffee."

"That's okay. Is your mother ill?"

"It's hard to say. My dad never came back from the war. He was on the Bataan Death March. We got word that he survived from another Marine. Then he disappeared. Missing in action. Mama kept waiting for him to come home. Then she just took to her bed." The girl bent over and picked up a knitting needle. "I know we have tea."

"Nothing, please. I just wanted to ask you about Miss Martens. I understand she tried to buy your house. I'm looking into some of these freeway transactions." I paused. "As I told you, I work for the *Examiner.*"

I had chosen my words carefully. I didn't actually say I was looking into this *for* the *Examiner.* It was one of those little white lies that journalism had taught me to tell.

"Well it was queer," Miss Lubinow said. "She just rang the doorbell one morning and asked if I would be interested in selling my house. She had inherited a little money and liked the neighborhood."

"Did you know she had approached Mrs. Herbert?"

"Not then. But I told Miss Martens I wasn't interested." Esther lowered her voice. "For myself, I'd be gone in a minute. But with Mama, it would be impossible. She keeps thinking Daddy will come home."

"But don't you have to move anyway? I thought all of these houses were going to go."

"Yes. But I didn't know that at the time. Two weeks

later, we got a letter from the government, explaining that the Hollywood parkway was coming through and that a right-of-way agent would stop by to appraise the house. We have to be out of here in a month." She gave the living room the once-over, as if measuring how it might fit into a moving truck. I didn't envy her the task.

"Did Miss Martens say what she would pay you?"

"She got kind of pushy, telling me I should at least consider her offer. I said I didn't care what she offered. Then she insulted me. She said I was acting awfully high and mighty, given the house was such a wreck. She said two thousand dollars was a very good price."

"Esther!"

Reluctantly, the girl turned and looked at the closed door.

"Did she ever follow up?" I asked.

"Coming, Mama! Yes, she was back here two days later. She said twenty-two hundred fifty was her final offer if I agreed on the spot. She said she liked another house down the street just as well and she wasn't going to waste any more time on me."

"Did the right-of-way agent make a similar offer?"

"Esther! Open the door. I'm suffocating."

Miss Lubinow jumped up. "That's what's so queer. Twenty-two hundred fifty. Mr. Walken offered the exact same amount."

Walken Realty was located in an odd, two-story gingerbread building on Glendale Boulevard. It looked like it had been dropped from an airplane that mistook L.A. for the Alps. Given the smog, I supposed it was possible.

I sat in the back of the Bentley staring at the fake old English sign and tried to make sense of what I had just learned.

A Miss Ursula Martens had purchased Edna Herbert's house going through a broker named Richard Walken. She had then tried to purchase the Lubinow house. Turning down her offer of twenty-two hundred fifty, Esther two weeks later accepted an identical offer from the state, issued by one Richard Walken, right-of-way agent for the California State Highway Commission. What I didn't know was whether the state employed local realtors to evaluate properties, or whether Mr. Walken had engineered a scam.

"Mr. Flaherty must be some guy," said Andrew from the front seat. He held up the *Examiner* and rattled it at me. "You know him, don't you, Miss Chandler?"

Vincent X. Flaherty was our renowned sports columnist. From the dateline being waved in my face, I gathered Mr. Flaherty was at the World Series. "I don't know him at all," I replied.

"Well listen to this." Andrew cleared his throat. " 'People on the West Coast never see a World Series, unless they travel East for the show. Series games in the East have often collided with cold weather and rain and sleet and snow. In Los Angeles, the series could be guaranteed better climate at this time of the year. I'd like to see baseball do something about it.' "

Andrew paused. "What do you think of that, Miss Chandler?"

I reached for the door handle. "I think Los Angeles is going to the dogs."

One was barking as I entered Walken Realty.

It was a German shepherd, which ushered me into the office. There were no humans in sight. L.A. was slipping faster than I realized.

The office had seen better times, I presumed. Off to the left stood two chairs and a table in a kind of "sit down, we'll be right with you" configuration. Beyond it, the foot of a staircase jutted out from behind a solid wall. Two cluttered metal desks elbowed each other for the rest of the office space. The only decorating touch that caught my eye was a blown-up map of Silver Lake that commanded one side wall. It was crawling with thick marks made by different colored crayons. I moved closer, trying to decipher what the Xs and circles meant. The dog continued to bark.

"Hello?" I called. No one answered.

I stood in front of the map. It was a plait map. Properties were ringed in one of three colors: red, blue or black. I was trying to locate the Lubinow and Herbert houses when, suddenly, heavy footsteps sounded on the stairs. I moved toward the landing. A voice said, "Have it done by the time I get back."

Just then a man appeared. Tall, thin, black hair with too much pomade. A long neck with too much aftershave. He froze.

"Who are you?"

"Mr. Walken?"

"Yes." He said it curtly, as if the fact annoyed him.

"I didn't mean to startle you. I called out before and I was beginning to think no one was here."

The dog began barking again. "What do you want?" Walken said angrily.

"I'm looking for a house."

"You've got the wrong place." He glanced at the dog but did nothing to make it shut up.

"There's a sign outside that says Walken Realty. I should think you'd be thrilled that someone actually came in."

He looked haughtily down at me over a beaklike nose. "We're closed."

"Really? Business must be swimming. Miss Martens could have saved me a trip by telling me you're so . . . overwhelmed. Well, perhaps another time."

The stupid dog began licking my leg. I backed away. "Just a minute," Walken said sharply. "Miss Martens sent you *here*?" He made it sound as if I had waltzed into a strip joint. "I find it hard to believe that Miss Martens sent you here."

"Personally, I didn't care much for her. Perhaps I'll run along."

I started to reach for the door, but the dog parked itself at my feet and began to growl. I looked back at Walken. He was staring at me coldly. I felt the chill shoot straight up my spine.

He took a step closer. "Who are you?"

"Please remove your dog."

"Where did you meet Miss Martens?"

"In the neighborhood. Are you going to remove your dog?"

Walken took two more steps. I felt fumigated by his after-shave. "Whoever you are, I'd advise you not to come back. This office is not open to the public. Sit, Jessie!"

The dog sat. It had drool hanging out of its panting mouth. I opened the door. The scene needed a parting shot, but I couldn't decide if it should go to Walken or the dog.

In the end, I held my tongue. And just walked out.

Andrew was parked half a block down the street. "Ready?" he said eagerly as I got in and slammed the door.

"No. Let's wait a bit."

Someone had been upstairs. I was betting it was Miss Martens. I hoped to catch a glimpse of her. Walken had said he was going out. If he left, I would go back and try to shake Miss Martens loose.

I turned around in the backseat, gazing through the rear window. A few minutes later, Walken came striding out, carrying a briefcase. A blue Chevy was parked behind the Bentley and I hoped it wasn't his. Just before he reached it, he turned right into an alley. A car door slammed, an engine rumbled and a black Ford came sailing out. Walken made a right-hand turn and drove past, but he didn't seem to notice us as he went by.

I turned back to the realty office. I would wait five minutes before trying to scare out Miss Martens. But suddenly, the door flew open. A man stepped out. He bent over quickly to shoo the dog back inside. When he straightened, he glanced first to the right—my direction —then to left, before hurrying across the street.

He yanked at the door of a faded maroon Packard, then began patting the jacket of his double-breasted suit. He found the keys in his pants pocket, unlocked the door, climbed in and started the engine. Without so much as a cautionary look, he muscled into the traffic flowing south on Glendale Boulevard.

I glanced again at the door to Walken Realty. It remained firmly shut. From behind it, the dog barked furiously, as if he objected to my looking. I turned and faced forward.

"We'll follow the maroon car," I said.

The driver was the cardsharp Albert Aubrey-Brown.

16

♦

We trailed the Packard down Glendale and east on Sunset until Aubrey-Brown turned into the parking lot at Taylor's. A big specially printed sign on an easel at the driveway entrance proclaimed: WORLD SERIES SPECIAL—THREE-COURSE LUNCH—65 CENTS. BEER 15 CENTS. EVERYONE WELCOME.

I glared at the sign. "The World Series is ruining everything. Isn't it ever going to end?"

"This afternoon probably," Andrew said dryly. "It's the seventh game."

I sat there debating. If I sort of bumped into Mr. Brown, I doubted I would accomplish anything. I considered sending in Andrew, thinking he could strike up some kind of baseball conversation at the bar and find out more about this man. But if Aubrey-Brown had indeed followed me to San Francisco, he might have noticed Andrew at the airport. In fact, if he had reason to follow me to San Francisco, he probably knew I rode in a Bentley driven by Andrew. Which meant he might have heard me talking to Walken or seen my car when he came out onto the street—and pretended he hadn't.

"We'll go back to the office now," I said.

On the way, it finally began to rain.

The *Examiner* looked like the Lost City of the Incas.

Once a thriving culture, it had been suddenly abandoned. All that remained of its civilization was a radio, which the last native out forgot to shut off.

"*. . . for the Yankees is the rookie right-hander Spec Shea, who's returning to the mound after only one day's rest. More than seventy thousand fans . . .*"

The disembodied voice dogged me along the cracked linoleum floor to Society like a spirit calling from The Other Side. I sat down at my desk with the feeling that at any moment tourists from a future century would arrive and I would be cited as the tribe's last remaining soul. *And to your right is old Miss Chandler, gossip columnist to the dead.*

I reached for my phone. It was just after twelve. The odds were slim that anyone would be at work. But maybe the government was. Stranger things had happened. I dialed the local office of the State Highway Commission and said I wanted information about right-of-way agents. After being passed to several wrong or absent parties, someone named Dahl Hegrem caught me on the run.

"I can only talk for a minute," he snapped.

"I'm Paris Chandler with the *Examiner,* Mr. Hegrem. My question concerns right-of-way agents. Do you use local real estate brokers or do you bring in your own people?"

"Our people are very capable," Mr. Hegrem answered.

"Of course. But my question is, who are they?"

Mr. Hegrem seemed to hesitate. "Is this concerning a civil or a criminal matter?"

"Pardon me?"

"We have one hundred and fifty-seven agents in the

Los Angeles area alone. We should have twice that number. They are terribly overworked."

"So you use local realtors to help out?"

"Actually," Mr. Hegrem said, "we don't. I've tried to effect a change in policy, but—ha ha—you know how bureaucracies are."

"In other words, there's a policy against using local brokers?"

"No, not at all. Did I say that? I didn't say that, Miss Chandler. You're misrepresenting my words."

I sighed. Of all the people in America who weren't getting ready to listen to the World Series, I had to get this one. I cleared my throat. "Then tell me, sir, why *don't* you use local brokers?"

"We do not use local brokers," said Mr. Hegrem, raising his voice, "because they are not, sad to say, patriotic Americans. If they were patriotic, they might pass up the profit motive for once and do their community a valuable service, if you know what I mean."

"Mr. Hegrem," I said wearily, "I haven't a clue what you mean."

"What I'm saying is that there's nothing monetary in it for them. They are not allowed to take a commission for a property sold to the state."

"Ah."

"I have been trying to get that order rescinded but to no avail." There was a pause, as if he expected me to applaud his noble effort. I didn't. "You can quote me on that," he prompted.

"Thank you," I replied formally. "Now let me get this straight. The right-of-way agents are employees of the state, paid regular government wages?"

"That's it. You have the story in a nutshell," Mr. Hegrem declared.

After I hung up, my brain was too tangled to sort through the conversation, so I wandered into the newsroom in search of a telephone book. Telephone books did not thrive well at the *Examiner* and generally vanished without a trace. Society had one, from 1945. But it had been missing for three weeks.

"*. . . they say DiMaggio fields by ear. That the sound of the wood against leather tells him everything he needs to know. His judgment of batters . . .*"

Along the length of the newsroom, under the wall of windows overlooking Broadway, I scrounged through the low bookshelves, accompanied by the tinny blare of the national anthem. A phone began to ring. That meant someone was downstairs manning the switchboard; another soul had surfaced.

I grabbed the phone for companionship. "Hello?"

"Who is this? Is this the *Examiner?*" came a cranky old voice.

"Yes, this is the *Examiner.* I'm Paris Chandler."

That news produced a lengthy silence. Then, "Never heard of you."

"No one has. I work in Society."

"Society! Did I call Society?"

"No. You called the newsroom and I just happened to answer."

The man had to think this over. The only people still in their offices, I concluded, were dodos. I was about to simply hang up when the man said, "Well anyway, this is Mr. Hearst."

I stared at the telephone. "Mr.—Hearst?"

"William Randolph Hearst and I want some cookies."

"Uh—"

"Everyone there knows where I get my cookies. I'd like three dozen sent up here immediately."

"Sent up—to San Simeon, sir?"

"Sent up to heaven, if you keep on dawdling." The line went dead.

I took a quick look around the newsroom to see if someone had sneaked in and was playing a joke. I took a waltz through Sports as well. I had heard stories about Mr. Hearst and his long-distance demands, but I had no idea where he got his cookies or how to deliver them to San Simeon.

"*The lineup for the visiting Brooklyn Dodgers, leading off . . .*"

I picked up the phone, dialed the switchboard opera-

tor and asked for the Colonel's office. The Colonel was
Mr. Hearst's "man" at the *Examiner,* known, officially, as
The Assistant to The Chief. Mainly he bombarded peo-
ple with annoying notes, like a general's aide-de-camp,
demanding, "The Chief wants . . . !" A woman with a
British accent answered and announced, "Colonel J. J.
Willicomb's office."

I explained my problem. She exacerbated it. "Betty
Brown's Sweet Shoppe, Seventh and Hill. Three dozen
chocolate chip." She hung up.

For one brief moment, I considered ignoring the request. For an even briefer moment, I considered delivering the cookies myself. But that would mean, among
other annoyances, having to listen to the stupid game
while Andrew drove. In the end, I decided to dispatch
Andrew alone. I looked out the windows and saw, to my
amazement, that he was actually standing in the parking
lot across the street.

*"And now . . . for the New York Yankees . . . leading
off and playing . . ."*

"Oh shut up," I growled.

The radio ignored me.

I returned to my desk and tried to think. It didn't take
me long to realize I had forgotten to ask Mr. Hegrem the
key question.

I dialed back and was told he was gone for the day.
"Then please transfer me to personnel," I said.

A woman with a head cold answered, "Persoddel."

"Hi. I'm trying to find out if a Richard Walken is employed as one of your right-of-way agents," I began.

"Surely, if you can hag on. I'b here by byself."

"Thank you. I'll wait."

While I waited I selected a violet crayon and began
drawing an ugly dog. I made its hair stand on end. The
longer I waited the more the dog began to look like a
porcupine.

"Hello? Sorry it took so log. But we have dough Richard Walken workig here, biss."

I thanked the woman and hung up.

I had no idea what Walken was up to and even less idea if he connected at all with James St. Clair.

". . . So. At the end of one half inning of play, ladies and gentlemen, it's the Dodgers nothing, the Yankees . . . coming to bat."

It was one-thirty. Time was running out for a lot of us.

Before the day ran out on me, the following transpired.

The local association of realtors confirmed that Richard Walken was a member—or had been a member; it was sorry, but records and dues-keeping chores had been overwhelmed by the weight of the booming real estate market since the end of the war.

All contracts involving real estate transactions between an individual and the state were to be recorded and kept on file at the Hall of Justice. But due to . . . etc., etc., records had fallen behind. The file clerk at the Hall of Justice said December sales from 1946 were still in a pile over at the State Highway Commission offices. Anything from 1947 . . . she couldn't even begin to guess.

Nailing down the Gary Cooper "scoop" proved stickier than I thought. Jack Warner refused to come to the phone. I didn't have Cooper's home number. This left me falling between the cracks. The publicity office at Warner's told me Cooper was not under contract there, try Paramount. The press agent at Paramount, Manny Schwartz, hadn't a clue what was transpiring, and said, "I'm not sure Coop's officially re-signed, Paris. You know how long these things take."

Right. Finally, I had a secretary source at Warner's tell me the studio architect had begun decorating the star's new bungalow on the lot. Under the bright, anxious eyes of Constance McPhee Estevez—and to the reluctant praise of Etta Rice, who couldn't hide her chagrin that Gary hadn't called her personally—I polished off my Item.

.   .   .

And . . . oh yes. The Yankees beat the Dodgers, 5–2, to win the World Series.

The world went back to spinning on its axis. I went home.

17

◆

Sadie Brown, the lobby receptionist, through some magic incantation, actually spirited a cab to drive me home. Andrew, presumably, was somewhere between Hearst's *Examiner* castle and the San Simeon one.

I used the ride to reel in some scattered thoughts. By the time we peeled off from the jammed traffic snaking west on Olympic, turning at San Vicente and heading north to Santa Monica Boulevard, I concluded that I didn't know what I had latched onto, if anything. Even if Richard Walken were pulling a scam, it may have had nothing to do with James St. Clair. Lucille Wills may have been sexing it up with Jim, but it could have been coincidence that her husband worked on contracts for freeway removal. The guy on the airplane wasn't necessarily following me, despite what Walter said. Furthermore, I was hardly equipped to go tearing around Los Angeles hunting down murderers, I told myself. I was just . . . yes, here was the truth . . . trying to protect my own reputation and avoid a possible murder rap.

At Santa Monica and Doheny, I decided to let the whole thing drop.

And instead—closing in on North Maple Drive now—turn my thoughts to . . . Nick.

I handed the driver $3.50, and walked slowly up the driveway. In the early evening twilight, the smell of damp grass and bougainvillea spiced the rain-freshened air and lifted my spirits. Mrs. Keyes had not yet switched on the outside lights and when I turned the knob, I found the door locked. Possibly she was in the back of the house committing another unspeakable hair act. I fished out my key and opened the door.

"Hello!" I called out obediently. "I'm home."

No one cared. I turned on the hall lights and collected the mail from the vertical letter holder hanging on the wall above the phone table. I became aware that no sounds of clanking pans were coming from the kitchen, nor any mysterious cooking odors.

"Mrs. Keyes?"

Perhaps she had quit. I began walking down the hall toward the kitchen. No, I couldn't be that lucky. Her room was off the kitchen; maybe she had fallen asleep.

"Mrs. Keyes?" I repeated.

I walked into the kitchen, reaching automatically to flick on the lights. "Mrs. . . . ." I skidded to a stop.

She was sitting at the breakfast table staring at me with terrified blue eyes. An orange rag had been wrapped around her mouth and her hands were tied to the back of the chair. A faint yellow ironing stain on the front of her gray housedress somehow contributed to her look of utter helplessness.

There was a footstep. I whirled around and nearly bumped into a pointed gun.

"If it isn't Cassandra Blake."

I stared into the beady little eyes of Albert Aubrey-Brown under the brim of a crisp tan fedora. Then into the muzzle of a large black revolver. Instinctively, I stepped back.

I found my voice. "Put that gun away. I can't imagine what you think you're doing."

"Siddown, Miss Chandler. Or should I say Blake? You think I'm a fool? I don't like being taken for a fool, okay?"

"As if I'm going to tell a complete stranger on an airplane my real name. I'm not a fool either, Mr. Brown. These days, who knows who you're talking to?"

He took a step forward and slapped my face. I staggered from the force of the blow, nearly losing my balance. Behind me, Mrs. Keyes began to make little mewing noises. I touched my tender right jaw and said nothing.

"Better. Now siddown and keep your trap shut."

I sat, and ran my tongue along my teeth. They all seemed attached and accounted for. Aubrey-Brown walked over to the counter and switched on the radio. *Tonto, did you see where they went?"* the Lone Ranger said.

Aubrey-Brown turned up the volume.

"No, Kemo sabe. But . . ."

"Mr. Brown, if you intend to rob me," I said, raising my voice over Tonto's, "I will give you what little cash I have on hand."

He sat down at the table and waved his gun at me. "Let's get this straight, sister. You robbed *me*. Now give it back or the crazy lady bites the dust." He turned the gun on Mrs. Keyes, who rolled her eyes and moaned.

"We've got to find them before dark," the Lone Ranger intoned heavily.

"I robbed *you*? Is that what you said? As I recall, you took five dollars and twenty-five cents off me on the airplane. But," I continued airily, "I'm willing to let that go."

"The address book, sister. And I'm late for dinner, so make it snappy."

I said, "The what?"

Brown was on his feet in a flash. He got behind me and yanked my hair until my head was jerked all the way back. He put the barrel of the gun to my nose. My heart stopped.

"I said I'm late for dinner."

"Kemo sabe, there they are!" Horse hooves pounded the dirt.

"I'll do whatever you say," I heard myself telling him. "But I don't have your address book."

Brown pulled back the gun. But only so he could slam it, handle first, into my nose. An unidentified sound came up from my throat. Dark, roiling colors with bright red splashes sprang up before my eyes. I felt waves of nausea and a dampness on my lip.

"Then explain what you were doing at Walken Realty. You got that address outta my book."

I shook my head carefully. When I stopped, I felt cold metal poking into my neck.

"I said *explain.*"

"I'll explain. But . . . could you please sit down? I'm having trouble thinking with a gun in my neck."

"You'll have more trouble thinking with a hole in your neck. What's your game, Chandler?"

I licked my lips. They tasted salty. "My cousin sold her house to Mr. Walken recently," I said, wincing from the pain. "Now she thinks she got a raw deal. I went there to speak to him about it. But he was so mean, I lost my nerve and left."

"Sure," said Brown. "Right." But he stepped back and the cold metal peeled off my neck. Suddenly, there was an explosion of gunfire. I screamed.

Boom. Boom. I dove onto the floor.

"Tonto! It's an ambush!" the Lone Ranger cried.

I opened my eyes and stared dumbly at the radio.

"Get up." Aubrey-Brown stood over me, sighting down his gun.

Shakily, I got to my feet.

"Now you and me, we're going to take a look-see. I find that book, one of you is fish food. March, sister." He grabbed my wrist and hauled me out of the kitchen.

The book was still in my traveling case, sitting on the chair in my bedroom. Surely, he'd make me open the case.

"I don't have your address book. How could I have it? You're going to miss your dinner engagement for no reason and I've got to tell you," I said saucily, "Mrs. Keyes is a terrible cook."

We reached the foyer. Brown's eyes kept going, down the long hall toward the living room, back to the telephone table, then up the stairs. I ran a finger across my upper lip and stared at the blood. He jerked my other arm and pulled me into the study.

I froze. The drawers had been wrenched out of the Queen Anne desk and dumped on the floor. Dozens of books, including some from Russell's priceless first-edition children's collection, lay scattered about the Oriental rug. The Tiffany desk lamp was tipped over on its side.

"My God," I breathed. "What have you done?" I looked at him. "Are you insane?"

This time I saw it coming, the closed fist, flying. I ducked. He came after me, grabbed my shoulder and knocked me onto the couch.

"You gonna tell me where the book is. Huh?"

By now I was afraid to admit my culpability. "I don't have it," I pleaded. "Go away."

What went away was the gun. He stuffed it into a shoulder holster under his worn tweed jacket. Then he removed his jacket. I could hear my heart pounding like the wild beat of a savage drum. He tossed the jacket onto a chair and began rolling up his sleeves.

"Before the war, I fought the undercard at the Olympic." He grinned nastily. "Wanna see?"

I was half-sprawled on my side, my feet on the floor, too scared to move. The first punch went right to the stomach. I heard a loud "whoosh" before I felt the sickening pain and saw—literally—a galaxy of stars. I heard myself sucking in air, just as a fist crashed into my left ear. My head flew back and hit the armrest. I stopped moving, overcome by pain and immobilized by sheer panic. The ringing in my ears was jarring. I opened my eyes and saw him looking uncertainly toward the leaded glass windows behind the desk. The ringing, I realized, was the phone. Aubrey-Brown looked at me angrily. "Answer it."

I tried to move but couldn't. He grabbed my arm and hauled me up, dragging me over to the desk. I swayed. He pushed me down into the chair and handed me the phone.

"Lo."

"Paris? Were you asleep?"

I held the phone awkwardly. I could hear myself breathing hard.

"Look, are you all right?"

"Oh," I said thickly. "Chief Gladstone. I must have dozed off." I glanced up at Brown. He was pointing the gun at my head. "I totally forgot you wanted to see me. Is it too late?"

"Paris, what's the matter with you?" demanded Tee.

"Sure. I can come downtown, but . . ." I was feeling faint. "Uh, I just remembered. I don't have a car right now."

Aubrey-Brown cocked the gun, making a loud clicking sound. I felt like I was going to black out.

A voice urged, "Say the words seven-thirty if you need help."

"Huh?" I said blankly.

The receiver was yanked out of my hand. Aubrey-Brown listened for a moment then slammed it onto the cradle.

He glared at me. "I hate beating up dumb dames, okay? It's like eating tapioca. You finish, you think so what?" His lips parted and I could see the small, uneven teeth. "But you, sister, ain't dumb. And this is only round one."

I saw the fist coming, exaggerated and in slow motion, like a Tom and Jerry cartoon. I waited to see what the cat would pull next.

But I didn't see anything at all.

18

♦

I came to hanging over the arm of the desk chair. I had the feeling I wasn't positioned properly, but I didn't have the strength to do anything about it. I felt numb. Except for my nose, which seemed to be dripping. I opened an eye and noticed red spots on the rug. I heard footsteps. But they seemed far away. I closed the eye and hoped I'd remember to tell Mrs. Keyes about the spots in the morning.

"I can't possibly be on television tomorrow."

Carefully, I touched the bridge of my nose and winced. "How bad is it? Hand me a mirror, I want to look."

"Don't look," said Tee, sitting cross-legged at the foot of my bed. "You'll slit your throat."

"Am I—disfigured?"

"Of course not. But you'll still want to kill yourself. I know you."

"Oh." I touched my nose again. "I don't think it's broken. I can't feel anything mushy. But I'm having trouble breathing."

Tee unfolded her long legs, which had jeans on them, and came over to the side of the bed. "Lie still." She began probing my mid-section.

"Ouch!"

She straightened. "Probably a broken rib. I think we'll go to the hospital after all."

"But what would I tell the hospital?"

"Right." Tee went back to the foot of the bed. "Tell them what you told me. That you were riding in a cab. If they believe that, since no one's sighted a cab in about fifteen years, you can continue with the part about the driver slamming on his brakes. Personally, I'd give serious thought to the walking-into-the-door-how-clumsy-of-me story."

I was sipping iced tea through a straw. I put the glass down on my bedside table. "What did Mrs. Keyes tell you?"

Tee had found my housekeeper first. I had no idea what Mrs. Keyes had babbled to her.

"Well it wasn't a cab and it wasn't a door." Tee paused. "It was bigger than a bread box."

I sighed. My stomach ached, my rib cage hurt, my head throbbed and my nose stung. "Perhaps I'd better have two more aspirin," I said.

"Not until we take you to the hospital."

And the hospital needed a story. My eyes drifted past Tee to the chair. The travel case was not on it. "Why he took it," I said indignantly. "He must have come up here and taken it. It was a Gucci, too."

"What was?"

"My traveling case. He must have come up here afterward, the filthy crud."

"Who," said Tee. "The cabdriver? Or the door?"

I began playing with a corner of my sheet. "All right. It was a man."

Tee's eyes widened. "Really?"

"Yeah. He was a burglar."

"A burglar," said Tee. "Why would he take your traveling case?"

I glared at her. "Maybe he thought it was a bread box."

"Fine. Let's go. I'll help you get dressed." But she didn't move. She was still standing at the foot of my bed.

"Okay. He wasn't a burglar. Exactly."

"Mm."

"Listen, Tee, I can't go into this with you. You're working for Donna St. Clair and this is related to that, I think. Even if it isn't, I got into it because of that. And you told me yourself you didn't want to hear about it."

Tee put a knee on the bed then whipped her other leg around and ended up cross-legged on the gray satin comforter.

I glanced at the clock, ticking loudly on the nightstand. It was nearly eight. "What am I going to do about my face?"

"Paris . . ."

Her hands were folded and held up just below her chin. Her skin was milky white against her dark green flannel shirt. She gazed at me levelly. "Did you shoot him? Was it an accident?"

"Of course I didn't shoot him. Do you honestly think . . . my god, is that what you think?"

"No." Tee grinned. "A girl who would walk into a door couldn't possibly shoot a gun. And if you didn't kill him, I'm not looking for you on behalf of Donna. So tell me what happened."

I reached for the iced tea again. For one brief moment, the cold liquid in my mouth made me feel better. I put the glass back. "I took his address book," I said.

"What are you talking about?"

"We were on the airplane and when he went to the rest room, I opened his briefcase and took the address book." I wiggled my toes and was pleased that they worked. "I guess he came looking for it."

"Was there something special about this man and his address book, or were you just bored stiff?"

I found that by craning my neck I could see my reflection in the mirrored closet doors beyond the foot of the bed. I groaned. "I'll have to call Nick and the station. What will I tell them?"

"Tell them tomorrow. Tonight, you're talking to me."

"Okay. But you talk first. Have you learned anything about Jim's death?"

Tee began playing with a strand of her long red hair, twirling it around her finger. "Like the police, we're looking for the blonde."

"You really think she did it?"

"Like the police, we know a blonde was seen leaving shortly after ten-thirty. Unlike the police, we know when she arrived."

My breath caught in my throat. "When?" I said cautiously.

"A little after eight."

My mind raced. There had been no other car in the drive beside Jim's, and none in the back alley. I couldn't remember if anything was parked on the street. And I hadn't arrived until twenty to nine. Inwardly I sighed with relief. Someone had made a mistake.

"She was seen getting out of the car with Jim, a little after eight."

Tee stopped playing with her hair and began rubbing her left forearm, the one that had been broken. "I've been thinking about that night. I had to go the hospital and have the big cast taken off and the smaller one put on. It was a Tuesday and I was mad cause I wouldn't get to see you on TV. The hospital doesn't have one."

Tee did. She had bought a seven-inch Crosley Spectator during the summer and the day it was delivered she invited Nick and me over to watch it. She had served frozen turkey dinners, a new product that had suddenly become all the rage.

"And then you and Bret picked me up at the hospital and drove me home." Tee fixed me with her big reddish-brown eyes. "Remember?"

"Sure," I said. What was she getting at?

"By the way, where *is* Bret?"

"Andrew. Didn't I tell you? He's reinvented himself. Again."

Tee began nibbling on the side of her thumb.

"He went on an errand. Actually, he went to San Simeon. Mr. Hearst wanted his cookies."

Tee arched an eyebrow.

"I'm sure he'll be back any minute."

Tee resumed playing with her hair. "Anyway, I wanted you to come in and stay for a while. I was blue. My arm hurt and I was going nuts not being able to work. And you seemed so happy. So full of yourself, the way you get after being on TV. I felt like I needed some of that spirit. But you were tired and wanted to go home."

"I'm sorry," I said. "Really."

"Don't be. I went in the house and looked at the clock. It was almost eight-thirty. I checked the schedule KTLA mails out, to see what was on. Wrestling." Tee made a face. "So I climbed into bed with a Sherlock Holmes."

I smiled, which hurt. "Did you figure it out before he did?"

"I fell asleep."

"Boring case."

"But first I went into the kitchen to make some hot chocolate. Only . . ." Tee grinned. "I was out of milk."

"That kind of day, I guess." Tee was not a prattler. I felt myself getting tense.

"So I called you to see if Bret could pick up some groceries for me the next day. But Mrs. Keyes said you weren't home." Tee stretched her arms languidly over her head, looking up, studying her unpolished fingernails. "I guess you must have stopped somewhere for something to eat."

So that was it. She was telling me she knew I wasn't the blonde who arrived at Jim's shortly after eight because she had looked at the clock when I dropped her off. But then, what had happened to me? She had given me an opening. I had never told her about my affair with Jim. But Tee was a clever girl. And she knew me. Was I ebullient that night because of the adrenaline rush from TV, or because I was going to meet Jim?

I realized then she would not question me directly. Instead, she had taken another tack: two friends sharing confidences. If I had anything to offer her concerning that night, she would be grateful. But she wasn't going to force it out of me.

I said, "Gee, I honestly don't remember. We might have stopped at Schwab's, sometimes we do."

Tee smiled and got off the bed and came round to help me up. The moment was over.

I wasn't going to tell her about that night, after all.

I hoped she would understand.

19
◆

I slept until nine the next morning, thanks to a little help from a compound of aspirin and codeine. The hospital bought my story about tripping and falling down a flight of stairs, thanks to a little help from Tee. I had one hairline crack in a rib, which was heavily taped. My nose was not broken, the bone just badly bruised. The other lumps and bruises would mend on their own, I was told. And— heh, heh—watch your step, I was also told.

I struggled out of bed and gimped into the bathroom to check the damage in the mirror. My face, I decided, did not look great in purple. My nose was that of a clown. I gimped back to bed and phoned Constance McPhee Estevez. The flu, I said. Nick was not home. Truman Stone never showed his face at KTLA before noon. But I reached the news director at his home. I said, "the flu." That done, I lay back on my pillows and allowed myself, for the first time, to digest Tee's information. The eight o'clock arrival—now who was *that*?

Was this the dinner companion I had been searching for? Was she the one who had phoned him at work and talked to him about freeways? Could this be the illusive Barbie? Certainly it fit. Jim and I were supposed to have dinner that night. He had phoned me around noon saying he had been invited to a cocktail party, which District Attorney Terry Riley was hosting, and would I meet him after? I assumed that meant dinner. But then came the mysterious phone call. "Change of plans," Jim said. "I have to meet someone. I'll tell you about it later."

The day after the murder, when the police came round, I had told them I thought Jim was going to a cocktail party after his newscast. They checked, and he hadn't shown up. Where he had been between six-forty when he left KTLA, and shortly after eight, was still a mystery.

Lucille Wills claimed *she* was supposed to have dinner with him that night, but had canceled. Is that when he had phoned me?

I twisted under the sheet, trying to find a position that wouldn't hurt. And for the first time, I began pulling down the blocks that I had built up around James St. Clair. How could I have been so wrong about him? So many women, and I hadn't even a clue. Or were the clues right there, out in the open, while I, needing what he was giving me, refused to see them?

The door edged open and Mrs. Keyes blew in. "I thought I heard you moving around, how are you this morning?"

She paused for a moment, her eyes scanning my face. Then she set a tray on the bed. "Orange juice, toast, milk," she announced unnecessarily.

The woman was dressed to kill. She had on a red wool dress that hit mid-knee, a bit short for the season, and a boxy jacket to match. From someplace, I couldn't imagine where, she had gotten hold of a pair of red patent leather flats, which were a bit too orange for the cherry red of the dress. I had never seen my housekeeper looking like this. "Where are you going?"

"I'm not. I was thinking we might have, um . . . company."

"Company? What kind of company?"

"You know. Reporters. The police." She touched her metallic yellow hair self-consciously. "I want to photograph good."

I sat up so fast I nearly knocked the orange juice over. "You didn't call anyone, did you? You better not have, Mrs. Keyes. What happens in this house is not for public consumption."

"Of course not the *public*. I was only thinking of the press."

"Did you call anyone? Tell me the truth, tell me what you've done."

"Nothing. Honest. I just figured they'd naturally come by."

"Well they won't naturally come by. The press does not *naturally* come by."

My housekeeper's face reddened. "You have no idea what I've been through and you don't care," she said indignantly. "What do you care that a fiend held me prisoner in my own home? I'm surprised the police haven't been here already." She sounded slighted.

"That's because I didn't report the robbery. And I'm not going to."

"Robbery! You call that a robbery?"

"He stole my travel case. I'll never get it back."

"You only think of yourself," said Mrs. Keyes furiously. "What about me? You have no idea what his intentions were before you showed up. He was going to . . . I can't even mention it. You're just trying to steal all the glory."

I said, "Huh?"

"What would he want with your old travel case anyway? There was nothing in it worth taking."

"You looked?"

"It was on the chair. I thought maybe there were some things that needed laundering. I didn't even know you'd gone away, you didn't bother to mention it. But all that was in it was magazines and an old address book."

She seemed offended. I had gone away and hadn't told her. But I was already climbing off the bed. "What did you do with it?"

"I put it away, what do you think?"

"And the address book?" I was gimping hard toward the closet.

"I didn't touch nothing," said Mrs. Keyes, offended. "I never do."

I was holding an ice bag on my nose with one hand while trying to read letters from Jim's freeway file with the other. I thought maybe now, knowing more than I did the first time through, I'd find something else of interest. The worn leather address book lay on the blanket beside me. I had gone through it lickety-split. But all it contained were the addresses and phone numbers of building supply companies, plumbers, electricians, glass men, framers, roofers, tilers, etc.

The phone rang.

I fumbled for it. Before I could say anything, I heard, "Miss Chandler?"

"Yes." It was a woman with a clipped accent.

"This is Miss Highsmith in Colonel Willicomb's office. I wanted to let you know Mr. Hearst just phoned."

"Oh. Were the cookies all right?"

"Mr. Hearst's cookies never arrived. That's why he phoned. He's terribly upset."

"But I sent my . . ." I hesitated. "I sent someone to deliver them yesterday, yesterday afternoon. I'm sorry, I—"

"Well they didn't arrive, Miss Chandler. Mr. Hearst is most displeased. I thought you should know." The phone went dead.

Slowly, I replaced the receiver. I wondered if I could get fired over Mr. Hearst's cookies. It seemed unreasonable. But then everything that touched me was beginning to seem unreasonable. I made a mental note to go see my psychic, Mr. Paul.

I pushed the intercom button. When Mrs. Keyes picked up the kitchen phone, I asked her to send Andrew up immediately.

She said Andrew wasn't there.

"And he hasn't been here, as far as I can tell, since yesterday morning."

Two hours later, the Bentley drooped into the driveway. It sighed to a stop in front of the garage door. From behind my bedroom curtains, I watched a disheveled Andrew roll out. I scrambled down the stairs and out the front door.

"Good morning," I sang out. "Uh, excuse me. Good *afternoon.*"

Andrew, who was about to open the garage door, smiled thinly and began trudging toward the house. His black wool suit and white shirt looked as if he had plucked them off the floor of somebody's garage sale. His cap was tilted back on his head. His face was streaky with dirt.

"Let's see," I said. "The car broke down, ah, what? Thirty miles north of L.A.?"

He reached the front stairs and stopped. His jaw dropped. "What happened to you, Miss Chandler? Are you okay?"

"I will be, at some point. If I don't lose my job. Come inside."

Andrew seemed to hesitate. I realized then that he never came in through the front door. "It's all right," I said. "This time."

Stubbornly, my chauffeur shook his head. "I'm quitting, Miss Chandler. And I might as well quit in the driveway, where I've spent most of my life anyway."

Reluctantly, my eyes swung back to the Bentley. "You didn't wreck the car?"

"I would never wreck the car. And I made sure they didn't wreck it either. I watched them like a hawk."

My eyes swiveled back to Andrew. "Who?"

"The stupid cops. They went over every inch of it," said Andrew pointedly, "after they went over every inch of me."

"Where? On the highway?"

"At the police station, Miss Chandler. Where do you think I've been? Out for a drive in the country?"

"I see. Well come sit down and tell me what happened."

Andrew eyed me warily and didn't move.

"Are you hungry?"

He nodded.

"All right. Why don't you go clean up and I'll have Mrs. Keyes fix you something to eat. Okay?"

"Thank you," said Andrew formally. "But I don't think you want her sticking around. You won't want her to hear."

He turned and began walking toward the back of the garage, to the stairs that led up to his room. He walked with an authority I hadn't seen before. I had the feeling I wasn't going to want to hear what he said either.

After sending Mrs. Keyes on an errand run, I scrambled two eggs, fried three strips of bacon and made toast, without burning it too badly. While Andrew ate, I told him about the cardsharp's visit. He glanced up occasionally but said nothing.

"I know what you're thinking," I said, swiping a piece of his toast. "I know exactly."

Andrew finished his milk, blotted his mouth and slumped back in the kitchen chair. "They picked me up just before Ojai and made me come back downtown. They wanted me for questioning."

"I figured they would at some point."

Andrew raised an eyebrow. "Then you should have told me what to do, Miss Chandler. But as usual, you only think of yourself."

"Right," I said. It was becoming a universal complaint.

"When they got me downtown, they put me in this smelly room and tried to grill me. Where was I the night of the murder? Had I driven you to Mr. St. Clair's house? Did I drop you off, did I wait, did I leave and come back. What did I see. Blah, blah, blah."

"And you said—*what*?"

"Nothing."

I sat up straight. "Nothing?"

"Of course not. I knew they'd questioned you, but I didn't know what you'd told them. You never said."

"Then how did you answer their questions?"

"I said I was always driving you places and how was I to know who was inside them? I said I had no memory of what I did that night. It was just another night."

"But how come they let you get away with that?" I said, amazed.

"I knew they couldn't do anything to me unless they charged me with something. And they didn't. And if they did, I would get to have a lawyer."

"You knew that?"

"Of course. It's in all the movies. All they did was detain me. That meant they had to come up with something or let me go. They put me in a cell with two thugs. But I told them I was a numbers runner and they left me alone."

"A numbers runner?"

"Yeah. It's in a script I'm reading. If you're a numbers runner, you work for the Mafia and nobody bothers you." He smiled.

"So you told them absolutely nothing?"

"Look, Miss Chandler. The truth is I'm not sure what went on that night. I drove you there and I drove you home. You got into the car, changed your mind, and went back into the house. Then you came running out. You were upset. The next day you told me that he was dead. We never talked about it again."

"I know," I said. "I'm sorry."

"When they let me out of jail they started searching the car. I don't know what they were looking for but they didn't find anything so they told me to scram. I think you're basically a nice lady but I don't want to work here anymore."

"No. No, you do," I said quickly. "You have a place to live and a neat car to drive. You go out on auditions. And if you get a movie role, you get time off." I suddenly realized, as annoying as Andrew was, that I didn't want him to quit. My annual New Year's resolution to learn how to drive hovered over me like a long, accusing finger. But I never did anything about it. "If you'll only stay until all this is over," I found myself pleading, "I'll give you a raise. Yes, that's what I'll do. You need a raise."

"How much?" said Andrew cautiously.

"Let's see. You get thirty-five now. I'll pay you forty."

"Wilson Gumbo gets forty-five."

"Who's Wilson Gumbo?"

"He drives for Gene Kelly."

"Forty," I said firmly. "If you stay on, maybe I'll consider more."

"And overtime for being in jail all night." Andrew stood up.

"Wait a minute—the cookies. I wonder if I should send you back."

"I don't have the cookies. When the cops stopped me, I told them I had to deliver cookies to Mr. Hearst. One of them said, Oh yeah? I said yeah. Then he said he'd do it."

"A cop took the cookies?"

"Uh huh. He drove off in the patrol car. The other cop got in with me."

Andrew gave me that annoying little smile of his.

"He said he always wanted to ride in a Bentley."

20

Sometime around four, I was jarred awake by the ringing of the telephone. I lifted the receiver, figuring it would be Nick. It was Tee.

"Just wanted to check. Any better?"

"No," I said quickly. "I died. The family requests no flowers be sent."

"I wouldn't have," said Tee. "I promised you I wouldn't the last time you died. Other than that, how are you?"

"Achy, icky, ugly."

"And crabby," Tee supplied.

"I was hoping you could help me with the ugly part."

"You want to borrow one of my disguises? I have a new mustache-beard ensemble that's simply divine. It's jet black."

"Uh, I was thinking more along the lines of pancake makeup. Are you going to be anywhere near KTLA? Maybe you could stop in and swipe some."

"Wrong neighborhood. I'm driving Donna St. Clair to Palm Springs. I was just getting ready to leave."

161

I touched my nose gingerly, and winced. "I thought she was going home. I thought she'd already left."

"The insurance man's playing games, telling her it'll be a few more days before they're satisfied that Jim didn't kill himself. Or something. So she decided to go off with a friend. She met someone who has a place there."

"She expects you to chauffeur her?"

"I don't mind. I'll spend the night, probably, drive back tomorrow." Tee paused. "You'll be okay?"

I didn't buy her story. Maybe she was following a lead. Tee wasn't the type to put herself out. I said, "Sure. I'll be fine."

Tee seemed to hesitate. I figured she was going to say something more about my condition. But instead she said, "You ought to get a TV."

I glanced at the clock. "And watch test patterns?"

"No, to watch at night. It would give you something to do."

I wondered vaguely where I would put one. I began a mental trek through my house.

"I mean, you're on it. You should have one."

No place upstairs, maybe down. The living room? No. I rarely used the living room—possibly the kitchen.

"And despite what you think, Paris, a TV won't fry your brain."

The kitchen had a radio.

"You don't know that," I said.

I maneuvered myself out of bed and walked stiffly into the bathroom. I popped another aspirin-codeine tablet and dabbed some makeup on my face. It covered the yellow parts but not the purplish-black. The swelling under my eyes had gone down a little, but my nose still looked like I had mistakenly grabbed the wrong size. I sighed.

In the bedroom, I slowly pulled on a pair of black cotton slacks, custom-made at Jax. I tucked in a white shirt and slid a black mohair V-neck out of its plastic bag. I was debating what shoes to wear when the phone rang.

"I've been trying to call you all day," announced Nick. "Your phone is always busy. You should have been an operator. Are you okay?"

I smiled. "I am an operator. And I'm sort of okay."

"Tell me more."

"It's just the flu, really."

"No, about how you operate."

"Slyly. Will you be all right without me tonight? I'm sorry to do this to you."

"You can't imagine what you've done to me. You've created a scandal."

My heart began to race. It was out. Someone had discovered I was the mysterious blonde. Tomorrow, Wednesday, it would be in all the papers. Or maybe even the early editions tonight. I said, "I can't imagine what you're talking about."

"The worst part is, Etta is overjoyed. She hated you for what you did."

I sank down onto my bed. "Oh."

"Don't worry. I'm trying to help you save face. I'm going to lead off the show with it, attack the story head on."

"How—did you find out?" my voice said woodenly.

"First, Warner Bros. called and denied everything. Then Cooper called. He actually called in person. He was pretty nice about it, considering."

"You mean," I said hesitantly, "Cooper isn't going to Warner Bros.?"

"That's what they're saying."

I had to put my hand over my mouth to keep from laughing.

"They're saying," Nick went on, "the bungalow is for Alan Ladd."

"Oh dear."

"What I think happened was that Cooper was getting ready to bolt. But Paramount didn't believe him. Then, when they saw your Item, they sobered up fast and gave in to his demands. Anyway, that's what I'm going to say. It'll sound good on TV."

"You're terrific, Nicky. Thanks."

"Can I come by after?"

"Er, I think not. I've got a bit of a fever. I'm going to try to sleep it off."

There was a pause. "I miss you."

"Well," I said. "Um, I miss you, too."

I put down the receiver. Trying to decide if I really did.

"Park on a side street," I instructed Andrew. "Actually, park a few blocks away. No. Park one street away."

"I'm not the elevator man, Miss Chandler. You ought to make up your mind. Hopefully soon. I've been circling for some time now."

"Sorry. I just don't quite know where one parks for a break-in. I wish Walter were here. He'd know exactly."

In the end, Andrew parked on the side street just north of the alley that ran behind the St. Clair house. It was dark by now and we were able to creep along the alley and turn in through the back gate without worrying that anybody would spot us, including the nosy neighbors. The air was warm and sweet, still fresh from the latest blast of Santa Anas. Occasionally a car went by, or leaves rustled, breaking the comfortable stillness of Hancock Park. The hinges on the gate creaked as we pushed through. We waited a moment, standing just inside. Then we moved quickly across the lawn to the kitchen door.

I took my old key from my pants pocket and slid it into the lock. The door opened and we stepped inside.

The house was dark.

Andrew switched on his flashlight. I took it from him and swung it around the kitchen. A dish towel lay on the Formica counter beside the sink. I walked over to it. A cup and saucer and two glasses sat in the sink, waiting to be washed. I began opening the white wooden cabinets. One contained a cheap set of dishes that Jim had bought at Landis's Department Store over on Larchmont, but the other cabinets were bare. Crumbs crunched underfoot as I moved over to the table. I glanced at the salt and pepper shakers, the sugar bowl and a telephone book. In the pantry, I found corn flakes, five cans of soup, three cans of peas and a box of crackers.

I led Andrew through the dining room, across the marble rotunda and into the living room. It contained only the furniture that had been in the house when Jim rented it: two couches on either side of a coffee table in front of the fireplace, a card table with four chairs over near the French doors, a lounge chair with a floor lamp in the corner opposite. I stood there for what seemed a long time. Wondering. If that other person had arrived shortly after eight, and I sometime before nine, she would have still been here I had to assume. Is this where she had been sitting? Where Jim had come hurrying out from when he heard me enter the kitchen, having forgotten I would come, trying not to look surprised. Or had she, this interloper—Barbie?—been waiting in the study? I tried to remember if there had been a light coming from the living room. But my mind would only give me a trick answer. I could never know for sure.

I motioned Andrew to follow.

A pair of double doors at the far end of the living room led into the study. Yes, she had probably been in here. With Jim. He and I had never sat in the living room. Despite the fireplace, it was a cavernous, uninviting room for two. The study was small and cozy, with dark green wallpaper and two cheap landscapes of the English countryside. We would sit on the worn beige couch, drinks in hand, surrounded by piles of newspapers and magazines. Propped up against one wall you would find Jim's polo mallets; he was an accomplished rider and played in a match on Saturday mornings.

The mallets were gone. So were the newspapers and magazines. The English landscapes hung crookedly on their hooks. On the small desk, shoved up against the wall in the corner, stacks of manila folders and loose papers lay in disarray. I dropped the blind over the single window and pulled the heavy flowered draperies closed. I switched on the desk lamp. "That's better," I said.

Andrew was standing in the doorway, the flashlight still on. "Would you mind going upstairs?" I asked. "You could go through the rooms up there."

"Looking for what?" said Andrew quietly.

"A folder marked 'freeways.' Or any papers that look interesting. Or—"

I stood there very still. Why hadn't I thought of it before? His briefcase. The one I had brought in from the car. That would be where the freeway file was, assuming it hadn't been stolen out of the KTLA office, or commandeered by the police. Yes, surely. If he were meeting someone in connection with the freeways that night, he would have thrown the file into his briefcase. He might have scribbled careless notes on a pad while interviewing someone, but knowing Jim's obsessiveness, he would have wanted all his information handy, either to check previous notes or to add new ones to his file.

Andrew was watching me expectantly, as if he were awaiting some major announcement.

Suddenly, as if synchronized, we flinched in unison as the stillness of the house was broken by the sharp ring of the telephone. We stared at each other as we waited for the ringing to stop.

"His briefcase," I said. "See if you can find it. And use the flashlight, no room lights."

Andrew switched off the flashlight. He shoved his free hand in his pocket and stared at the floor. Finally he looked at me.

"I didn't hear a gunshot, Miss Chandler."

"No," I said.

"I was asleep, I think. But if there had been a gunshot . . . well, I suppose it could have been a muffled one. But a normal gunshot would have woken me up."

"I know." I walked over to the closet and peeked inside. It contained only a two-drawer file cabinet. I opened each drawer. But there was nothing in them.

"You did go back, though."

"I forgot my book."

"The Fountainhead, wasn't it?"

"Yes, *The Fountainhead."*

"And you brought it into the house with you? Maybe you only thought you did."

"No, I had the book. There was a passage I wanted to show Jim about city planners. I thought he could use it on the air."

"You didn't get it back though. I would have noticed. It's a fat book. I was thinking maybe you had forgotten something. But when you came out, you just had your purse."

"Yes." I glanced at my watch. "We'd better finish here. I'm feeling a little jittery."

"The briefcase," said Andrew.

"Thank you," I said.

I stared at the mess of papers and file folders. Probably they had been neatly stored in the empty file cabinet. But if the house had been ransacked, chances were the papers had been dumped. Mrs. St. Clair had picked them off the floor but hadn't bothered to reorganize them.

Clearly these papers represented the bulk of Jim's work during the war. There were typed stories with date-lines from London, Sicily and Tunisia, stories Jim had delivered on the air. Also there were dispatches to him from various army units and from NBC Radio in New York.

I glanced at my watch. We had been in the house thirty minutes.

A glossy brochure caught my eye. *"Why rent . . . when you can buy this beautiful, modern duplex home . . . for approximately $35 monthly!"* Below were sketches of houses and blocks of type explaining each home's selling points. At the bottom of the brochure in large letters, it said, *"Contact: The Barnathan Group."* An address in Encino was listed along with a phone number. I put the brochure aside.

Floorboards creaked above me as, I presumed, Andrew made his way from room to room.

I picked up another handful of papers and hurriedly flipped through them. Suddenly I found myself looking at a pamphlet put out by the Highway Commission giving facts and dollar amounts for its proposed new freeway system. I put the pamphlet on the floor and began thumbing through the headings on the folders. Most of them were empty, the papers they once contained having spilled out. There must have been fifty. But none was labeled freeways. Disappointed, I went back to the loose papers.

Which is when I found Lucille Wills's letters.

There were two, each written on delicate pale blue stationery and folded into a matching blue envelope. In beautiful script the letters were addressed to Mr. James St. Clair at KTLA. She did not include a return address.

I slipped the letters, the housing brochure and the highway pamphlet into a folder marked "D-Day," switched off the lamp and started back to the kitchen. I was thirsty. I would have a glass of water and then I would have a quick look in the first-floor closets. At the foot of the staircase, I glanced up and softly called, "Andrew?"

From somewhere upstairs, I heard a door close.

It was pitch black as I felt my way into the dining room. Once I reached the kitchen, I could open the refrigerator door for a bit of light. But now, groping, my outstretched hand at last found the back of a chair, and I followed the chairs around the long, oblong table. Letting go, I took small steps, reaching out for the door frame. I stepped onto the linoleum floor. A beam of moonlight came in through the kitchen windows. I could hear footsteps above me as I moved toward the refrigerator.

Suddenly there was a loud click. The sound of a key in the lock. Then—unmistakably—the front door opening.

Instinctively, I held my breath. A light went on, filtering into the kitchen from the rotunda. My god, had Mrs. St. Clair returned?

Slowly, I walked to the kitchen's back door, carefully opened it and slipped out. I hurried across the backyard to the gate and ran into the alley. From there I stared at the back of the house. Andrew was a sitting duck. If he timed it right, he might slip down the stairs and go out the front door, the kitchen door or the French doors in the living room. I didn't know what to do for him, or for myself.

After a moment, I started up the street toward the Bentley.

21

◆

"You would have been quite proud of me," I said to Walter. "Although I must admit, it occurred to me later that I forgot the gloves. I know how you feel about gloves."

"And Chanel No. 5," Walter put in.

"No perfume, no cigarettes."

I had gone on my first break-in—or B & E, as he put it —with Walter. It wasn't exactly what I would call a seminal event in my life. A fledgling actress named Anne Bardon had been murdered at the beach and Walter came up with the trite idea of searching her house in West Hollywood for "clues." I don't recall that we actually located one, but Walter had used the occasion to lecture me on the delicate art of detection.

"So Boy Wonder's upstairs about to get caught red-handed," Walter said impatiently. "Tell me he came swinging out the window on a rope like Tarzan."

"You keep forgetting," I said. "Me, Jane."

"Sorry. So you climbed up a rope. Obviously."

"Don't be silly. I rang the doorbell."

170

"Uh-huh," Walter said. "Naturally."

"I didn't care who was in the house, as long as it wasn't Tee. I didn't see her car. Maybe she had dropped Mrs. St. Clair off. Or maybe she had parked down the street somewhere. Anyway, I took a chance."

"Thinking you would serve as a decoy so Superman could fly away."

"Exactly."

"And?"

I felt a tap on my shoulder. Constance McPhee Estevez was standing above me, her face scrunched in a questioning frown. Even in Los Angeles, most people did not wear sunglasses indoors. I put my hand over the mouthpiece. "Eye infection," I said.

She made a *tut-tutt*ing sound and sashayed off.

I said to Walter, "If it was Mrs. St. Clair in the house, or even Tee, they would have answered the door. Right? But nobody answered. Nobody came to the door."

"But you distinctly heard a key in the lock? It could have been a crook with a skeleton key."

"Let me finish, Walter. I kept ringing. Then I started banging. But nothing happened. Not even the nosy neighbors turned up. But it worked. Cause just when I was about to give up—"

"Yes?"

"Andrew . . . hissed."

"Gee, that's great, kid. The guy hissed."

"From the bushes. He'd gone out the French doors in the living room. For a dope, Andrew's pretty swift sometimes."

"And he never saw the intruder?"

"He saw her from behind. Standing at the front door while I was banging on it. A blond woman."

"Who?"

"I don't know yet. We waited until she came out and got into her car. We followed her home. Or at least to an apartment house on Burton Way. We waited for half an hour but she didn't come out again. I'm betting it's that Barbie person."

"So now what you do—"

"Right. Andrew is camping out at the building this morning."

Theresa McKenzie waltzed in, gave me a look, shook her head and sat down at her desk, which was right behind Nick's museum-quality one. Nobody could remember during what age it had last been used.

"There's more," I said to Walter, "but my neighbors are arriving." I wanted to tell him about Albert Aubrey-Brown. Theresa stared at me hostilely.

"All right, Paris, let me give you this. You may find some kind of connection to Whatshisname."

"Who?"

"That guy. The one who's married to the floozy."

"Norman Wills?"

"For whatever it's worth, Wills is interested in running for district attorney. Which explains why his wife's in a panic. As in S-C-A-N-D-A-L."

"Oh yummy. Anything else?"

"Yeah," Walter said. "Give my love to Andrew," and he hung up.

I glanced at Theresa, wondering what her problem was. "So how's the party circuit?" I said, giving her a plastic smile. Chubby Theresa used her press card to bust into every party in town.

"I was about to ask you the same, dear."

Ah. She had interpreted my sunglasses as a cover-up for a major hangover. Obviously, I had been to a smashing party that she hadn't. I began to wonder if Etta's neuroses were contagious.

"Private bash." I smiled sweetly and headed for the kitchen.

The briefcase had not turned up, which troubled me. Andrew swore he went through the upstairs like a human suction cup, but he hadn't found it. The police might have taken the contents of the briefcase, but it was a big clunky case; would they have confiscated it, too?

Even more troubling was something else Andrew had said.

He had said, "Well at least you got the book."

I had said, "What book?"

"The Fountainhead. I saw it in the guest room and put it at the top of the stairs. But later, when I started down, it was gone. I thought I heard you come upstairs."

I hoped that Andrew had simply overlooked the book in his panic to get out of there. Otherwise, the St. Clair house had been busier than Union Station. Or infested with ghosts.

I finished making tea and went back to my desk. Not thrilled with either possibility.

Aside from Gene Tierney's walkout at Twentieth Century-Fox, reportedly because she felt Linda Darnell had the better role in *The Walls of Jericho,* and Mrs. Walter Slezak's new ten-carat diamond ring, it was a dormant day for gossip. I sat at my desk thinking about Lucille Wills—and getting nowhere. The two letters I had swiped were more intriguing than damning. The first, dated August 19, said simply: *"Yes! Tomorrow. Beachwood Canyon. Noon. Have what you need. Yours, L."*

The second was more provocative:

"Darling—I am desperately trying to find out what you wanted to know. But it isn't easy. He's at the office late all the time and when he comes home, he's exhausted. It would be helpful if you could tell me more. I do have one name though. Can't wait for Wednesday. Don't disappoint me. Love L."

Neither her name nor her address appeared on the letters.

I picked up the phone, gave Jo, the switchboard operator, the number for Esther Lubinow, and hung up. A moment later, Jo put me through.

"How's the packing going?" I asked.

"Mama's had a setback and I can hardly leave her bedroom," Esther reported. "I think she just can't stand the thought of leaving this house."

"I'm sorry. I know how difficult this is for you. And I apologize for being a nuisance."

"Oh, please. It's nice hearing from you, Paris. Usually when the phone rings it's the doctor or Mr. Sims from the Division of Highways wanting to know when we'll be out."

"Are they going to demolish your house?"

"They're holding an auction. But if nobody buys it, the state will either demolish it or move it."

"Could you buy it back and move it yourself?"

"Not now. We've already used the money they paid us to buy a place in Studio City. It's got a nice backyard. It will be good for Mama."

I said that sounded great. Then, "I was wondering if I could drop by and take a look at the contract you signed with Richard Walken."

"Sure, Paris, any time."

I told her I would phone first. I hung up and wondered why I hadn't heard from Andrew.

It was six o'clock before I made it over to Esther Lubinow's house. She was wearing an olive corduroy jumper over a white blouse and the same tired smile she had on the last time I dropped in. I handed her the bakery cookies and flowers I had picked up on the way over. Her sad life brought out the guilt in me.

"Oh for gosh sakes, look at this," she said smiling shyly. "Really, you shouldn't have."

"The flowers are for your mom," I said. "The cookies are for you."

"I'm afraid she's asleep now. But please come in."

Even through my sunglasses, I could see that the messy living room was, if anything, even more of a mess, with packing cartons wedged between the spills of magazines and balls of yarn on the floor. The sour smell of medicine and sickness permeated everything. Houseplants, shoved in a circle in front of the radio, drooped, as if they, too, had taken ill. Esther disappeared into the kitchen and returned holding the contract.

She looked at me quizzically. "Is there something wrong with your eyes?"

"Allergies. I always get them this time of year." I took the contract from her and squeezed onto the couch.

It was three pages of legal double-talk as far as I could tell. I quickly thumbed to the third page. At the bottom, Richard Walken's name was scrawled. Under it were the words, "Right-of-Way Agent, Los Angeles."

I said, "I'm running a bit late. Would you mind if I took this? I could have it duplicated at the office tomorrow. I'd like to have a copy."

"Sure. Then just drop it in the mail to me." She smiled wistfully. "I wish you could stay."

"We'll get together soon," I promised. "When are you moving?"

"Next Thursday, I hope."

"If you need anything . . ."

"We're fine. Let me see you out."

Feeling guiltier than ever, I slipped into the backseat of the Bentley. She stood on the front porch and waved as Andrew drove away.

Life was something I still didn't get.

"Well, Andrew, did you have a pleasant day?"

These were the first words I had spoken to him, other than, "Miss Lubinow's house, please."

"Yes, ma'am. And you?"

"Divine."

Andrew swung onto Sunset and headed west. At this hour, traffic on the boulevard was sparse.

"Some music?" Andrew asked formally. He sounded like William Powell in *My Man Godfrey*.

"The only music I care to hear," I replied, "is you singing."

"I didn't goof up, Miss Chandler."

"Are you speaking of your duties for me, or your audition?"

"I told you, I told you at the airport. I wanted to try out for the pilot role."

"How silly of me. To forget."

Blocks flew by. My bad humor was exacerbated by the pain from my cracked rib. Which reminded me of Albert Aubrey-Brown and made me wonder if he would come back.

"I think I got the part," Andrew informed me. "I saw the cockpit. They built this whole cockpit and it's *groovy*." He glanced at me in the rearview mirror. "I would have third billing."

I would need protection. I looked at my watch. Quarter to seven. "Please stop at a phone booth, Andrew. I have to make a call."

"Pretty soon," said Andrew, "you'll be able to call from the car. Someone invented a radio telephone for the car."

"So cars can talk to each other? Pull over at the corner, I see a box."

I got out and dropped a nickel in the slot. Tee answered on the third ring. I asked if she would like to meet me at Schwab's. "Telepathy. I was just going to call you," she said. "I'm on my way."

As we rolled into Hollywood, the traffic went into its usual snarl. We sat at the corner of Highland waiting for the light to change. Even at this hour students from Hollywood High school were milling about, puffing cigarettes with panache. "So," I said to Andrew. "Is there anything else you would like to report?"

"I know you think I shirked my duties, Miss Chandler. But I didn't."

"Uh huh."

"I mean I sat in front of her building till ten o'clock when I had to leave for the audition."

"Uh huh."

"She never came out."

"So I gather."

"Yeah. Anyway, I went in."

The light turned green at Fairfax. Two blocks up, Andrew found a spot across from Schwab's. I could see through the big glass windows that the drugstore was hopping. I reached for the door handle but didn't press it.

"I looked at the names on the mailboxes. I would have written them down, but I didn't have a paper or pencil."

"Equipment failure, eh?"

"But I think I know who she is."

"Really."

"One of the names sounded familiar anyway." Andrew turned round to face me. "It was Martens. Ursula Martens."

22
◆

I bought a *Hollywood Reporter* and settled into a booth in the area behind the heavily trafficked counter. I glanced over. A pair of peroxides in tight sweaters were sharing a chocolate sundae and eyeballing the crowd for somebody to discover them. They must have been new in town. Most of the men at the counter were deadbeats—out-of-work actors and producers hoping to pick up a tip. The boys with the bucks tended to eat in the booths. I scanned them, but I only came up with the actress Norma Shearer sitting with a suntanned man half her age.

I ordered a cup of coffee and plowed into "Rambling Reporter," the gossip column on page two. I was heavily into Melvyn Douglas's party to introduce Mayor Humphrey of Minneapolis to Hollywood when—a jolt—something thudded onto the table. I found myself staring at *The Fountainhead*.

"When you're done," said Tee, sliding in across from me, "I'd like to borrow it. Looks interesting."

"It is." Idly, I flipped open the cover. My name was

printed in ink on the first page. "It's about an architect whose ego is bigger than his buildings. His designs are brilliant. But after a while, his strong individualism is seen as a threat to the system and he is brought down. It's meant to be a polemic against communism." I closed the book. "You set me up, Tee."

"Cup of coffee," Tee said to the waitress. "Then I'll order." She grinned. "I like your sunglasses. Veddy glamorous."

"Where were you? In a closet? Disguised as a lamp?"

"Paris, calm down. We need to talk."

"Oh god, I just remembered. I forgot to feed the cat." I reached for my purse.

"Will you please listen for a moment? I'm your friend, remember?"

I leaned across the table. "No, *you* listen. I came to you asking for help. But you couldn't help your friend Paris. You were helping Donna St. Clair. Then, when it occurred to you that maybe *I* could help *you,* you didn't just ask. You set me up and you spied on me."

I started to get up, until Tee grabbed my arm. "I also lied for you. I told the police I was with you that night. Which is why you haven't heard from Gladstone this week."

I sank back against the upholstery. A guy in overalls waltzed up behind the two peroxides at the counter and held out a pack of chewing gum.

"You girls know what you want now?" The waitress, a plump, gray-haired woman who had probably worked at Schwab's since the gold rush, stood above us tapping her pencil on a pad. Her name tag read Ethel.

"Cheeseburger," said Tee. "French fries, cole slaw and a chocolate milkshake. Lord, I'm famished."

"Jell-O," I said.

"Whip cream?"

"No. And more coffee." I opened my purse and excavated a cigarette. "Just think, I wasted a dime on the *Hollywood Reporter* when, if I had only waited, I could have been titillated for free."

"Try listening," said Tee. "Several days after the police

searched the house, the latest batch of canceled checks arrived from the bank. One was from Brahm's, the jewelry shop on Rodeo. I stopped in and had the girl go through the sales checks. Jim had bought a gold bracelet. He left it at the store to be engraved, then delivered. The name of the party and her address were on the sales check. Ursula Martens, Burton Way. Bingo! I followed her for a few days. She works as a secretary for a landscape place called Sunset Estates."

I opened my mouth to correct her, then decided not to.

"She's blond. It seemed possible she was the woman who was with him that night. Chapter one. Chapter two—"

The waitress arrived with Tee's cole slaw and my Jell-O. I sipped my coffee.

"I went through Jim's files next. One was marked Los Feliz. In it was a letter from a woman named Lucille Wills inviting Jim to attend a neighborhood meeting of concerned citizens who had heard the freeway was coming through."

I picked up my spoon and began mashing the Jell-O.

"Several other letters followed. I suspect they were having an affair."

"Which is what you're so good at—tracking down affairs."

"Thank you. Though somehow I missed yours. Didn't I?"

I put down my spoon. "Are you asking me if I had one with him?"

"Instinct and circumstantial evidence suggest you did. But I have no actual proof."

"Well," I said, picking up the spoon again, "you have time."

"Don't be snide with me, Paris. None of this is my fault."

Ethel was back, unloading a fairly heavy tray with Tee's gluttonous order. I finally got a spoonful of Jell-O into my mouth. "Look, I'm sorry," I said.

"It's just that a cop I know who's connected in all the

right places told me they were interested in your where-
abouts the night St. Clair was murdered. That, and your
consuming interest in freeways, made me wonder. Anyway."

Tee slathered ketchup on her burger and took an
enormous bite. I let my eyes roam. Milton Berle and
Henny Youngman had just come in. I watched them
"hello-hello" their way to a booth across the room.

"It was possible one of them shot Jim," said Tee,
bringing my attention back. "So I decided to stir up the
pot. I called Ursula Martens, Tuesday, at work. I told her
we knew about the bracelet and the affair, that we had
the receipt at the house, along with several other items
that connected her to Jim. I said that in her bereaved
state, Mrs. St. Clair hoped by meeting her husband's
lover, she could handle her grief better. I—"

"Handle her grief better?"

"Whatever. And I told Ursula that Mrs. St. Clair
would be back in town on Wednesday. Could she stop by
Wednesday evening?"

Tee bent over the straw. The milkshake line plunged
like an elevator.

I said, "Figuring that if she were guilty, she would
come before Mrs. St. Clair returned to retrieve the incriminating evidence. Clever."

"I got hold of Lucille Wills—who is married by the
way—with a similar story."

"And me."

"No."

"Ah." I ate a spoonful of Jell-O and watched Berle
put a napkin on his head.

"I called to ask how you were and see if you needed
anything right away. I knew I would be unavailable last
night. I told you the Palm Springs story because that's
the story I was spreading around. The last person I expected to show up was you."

I pushed the Jell-O aside and grinned. "Well you certainly hit the jackpot."

"What I hit was Pandora's box." Tee went back to
work on her cheeseburger, but the gusto was gone. Half-

eaten, she pushed the food away and blotted her mouth. "I talked to Ursula Martens last night."

"In the house? You cornered her in the house?"

"Scared the living daylights out of her."

"So what was her song?"

Suddenly, a loud whoop broke through the din. The room fell silent. Milton Berle had thrown a piece of pie in Henny Youngman's face. Berle was laughing hysterically.

"That gives me an idea," I said gaily. "Do you prefer lemon meringue or cherry?"

"You do, I'll knock you on your can," Tee replied cheerfully.

Youngman got up and began dancing toward the men's room.

"Ursula told me she'd arrived at the house with Jim at eight-ten, as reported," Tee continued.

"Lucky her."

"About half an hour, forty-five minutes later, another woman shows up, comes in through the kitchen door."

"Not Lucille whatshername?"

"Ursula claims she never saw who it was. She and Jim were in the study. Jim said he'd be right back. But according to Ursula, he took the woman upstairs. After a while, she left. Ursula was furious."

"Who left," I said. "The woman?"

"Ursula. She didn't like being two-timed."

"Oh boy," I said.

"End of story. Next day, Ursula reads that Jim's dead."

"And the police buy this story?"

"The police don't seem to know about her. She said that's why she came to the house. To collect the evidence."

I lit another cigarette and casually blew the smoke away. "So that leaves Lucille as your mystery woman?"

"Lucille isn't blond and she doesn't drive a Rolls-Royce."

"The blonde in the Rolls could have been a coincidence. Driving by at an inopportune time." I inhaled.

"Maybe Ursula lied to you and didn't leave when she said she did. Which raises another question. If Jim drove her there, how did she get home?"

"The neighbors claim the blonde left the house at ten-thirty or so. Ursula insists she left at least an hour earlier."

"Well it sure confuses the hell out of me."

"What confuses me," said Tee neutrally, "is why the police are interested in you."

Her attention wandered then, but I knew it was a calculated act. She was trying to lighten the moment. I waited her out.

Tee's eyes were on Norma Shearer, who was running her fingers across her companion's arm, as she said, almost as an afterthought, "You really ought to try to remember where you went that night." She turned back to me and smiled nicely. "In case I'm asked again—or you are."

I watched Youngman, with a clean face, return to his table. Our waitress was at the next table, taking an order. I caught her attention.

"I'll do that," I said to Tee.

"And I'm curious about last night. What made you go over there?"

"I'm curious who's asking. Mrs. St. Clair's private dick, or my friend, Tee?"

"You didn't have to do that, Paris."

"Sorry. I'm still looking for the freeway file. I believe Jim knew of improprieties." I hesitated. "I'm trying to find a way to transfer out of gossip."

Tee gave me a sardonic look. "Right."

"You misjudge me, Tee. I'm more downtown than you know."

Ethel arrived. "Can I get you girls anything else?"

"Yes. A piece of pie, please. Cherry."

"Okeydoke. One fork or two?"

I grinned at Tee.

"None," I said.

23
◆

I removed Albert Aubrey-Brown's address book from the toolbox in the garage, where I'd stashed it, and was perusing it in bed. It was early, but due to the rib problem, my batteries were still running low.

Under "S" I found Sunset Estates, and beside it, a Beverly Hills exchange. Aubrey-Brown worked for a construction company called Consolidated Developers. Maybe. Ursula Martens worked for a landscaper. Unlikely. And Richard Walken was in real estate—one way or another. Three distinct dots, but did they connect? More to the point, how did Ursula stumble onto Jim?

Walter, I thought, *call me.*

I ran through the book page by page looking for a Barbie. Not there. At least, I thought, if Jim were mixed up with her, too, she wasn't, perhaps, mixed up with them.

At ten o'clock I switched on the radio. *"The forward echelon of America's sons who fell in World War II will return home tomorrow after an absence of nearly six long years,"* a solemn voice intoned. *"Their people will receive them with humble homage they will not witness, with the booming of guns they cannot hear, with the droning of planes they will never see. They are the advance phalanx of more than 228,000 American war dead who will be returned in the next few months. . . .*

"The weather for tomorrow . . . rain, possibly heavy at times. . . ."

Like a foreboding of weather doom, the phone suddenly crackled. I grabbed it. "Walter?"

"You're joking," said Nick. "You've still got that bum?"

"Oh." I paused. "Well not at the moment. At the moment . . . I've got you." Nick had no use for Walter. Walter wasn't Hollywood.

"Would you like me in person?"

"Perhaps. What do you look like?"

"Come with me to Romanoff's tomorrow night. You'll see."

"Romanoff's?"

"Etta said to. Michael is having a party for Princess Alexandra of the Volga. She's just arrived in town."

I said, "Oh my god."

"So while you're lapping up caviar, I'll be trying to bare her royal fakeness. Then we can go to a spot and dance."

"Another phony Russian royal? How many do you suppose there are?"

"They're leaving Russia in droves. Stalin terrifies them."

"But why do they have to come here? I mean, it's not like we have *winters*. All those furs gone to waste. You'd think somebody would tell them."

"*You* can, my little chambermaid of commerce. I'll pick you up at, say, seven?"

"Um. Could you hold for a second? I'll be right back."

I walked into the bathroom and switched on the light. I studied my face in the mirror. The swelling was definitely down. Maybe I could convince my father to get the Warner's makeup people to do something.

I got back on the line. "Princess Paris accepts."

"Needless to say," said Nick. "Prince Charming is delighted."

I couldn't fall asleep.

I hadn't been straight with Tee. Or with Gladstone. There were parts of the story that, maybe because I couldn't accept them, I couldn't reveal to anyone else. Even Andrew. The guilt I'd inherently felt about seeing Jim had been magnified by his death, then bent into a whole new shape as information about his other infidelities surfaced. I had carelessly and blithely waltzed into his life, or allowed him to waltz into mine, without a second thought. And now I was trudging out of it, shamefaced and humiliated, burdened with the knowledge that I was not an innocent victim. Just a stupid one.

It was midnight.

I went into the bathroom and drank a glass of water. Then I picked up the new issue of *Life,* glanced at the cover photo of Notre Dame quarterback Johnny Lujack, yawned and curled up on the window seat. I raised the window to let in fresh air, but the air blew chilly and damp. The royal palms outside were rustling up a racket, and in the distance came the low rumble of thunder.

I began turning pages. Suddenly, big, loud drops of rain began battering my window. As I stood and leaned over to close it, I looked out to the street. In the shadows, I could see something move. Quickly I went over and switched off the light.

Huddled now inside the gray silk draperies, I saw him immediately. The black figure. Gliding leisurely down the middle of the street. He seemed oblivious to the rain, skating fast now, head down, arms stretched behind him. Then slowing, and going into his figure eights. I was mesmerized.

When he was directly in front of the house, he paused. Highlighted by the street lamp, the rain was coming down in long, sharp needles. He threw his head back as if exulting in the downpour. Then, almost languidly, he began twirling—spinning faster and faster.

Suddenly, he lost control. He grabbed the air for balance, but his feet shot out from under him and he landed
in a heap inches from the curb. He didn't move. One leg
was flung out, the other bent back under him. No movement still. I wondered if he had hit his head. I went to
the closet, grabbed a big terry-cloth robe and trotted
down the stairs. As I opened the front door, I realized I
had forgotten to put on slippers. Walking carefully, I
went down the four steps and started along the driveway.
In a second I was soaked to the skin. A zigzag of light-
ning turned night to day, followed by an ear-splitting
clap of thunder.

I was standing on the sidewalk, pushing my hair out of
my face.

The street was deserted.

The black figure was gone.

Inside the house, I peeled off my white satin nightgown
and dumped it, along with the robe, on the kitchen table.

Upstairs, I poked at the bandages around my rib cage.
They were damp but still holding tight. I wrapped my wet
hair in a big white towel, slipped into another nightgown
and crawled into bed.

I fell asleep listening to the steady pommel of rain.

"I don't know if you remember me. We met briefly at the
Downtown Athletic Club."

"Ah yes. The girl who was interested in freeway
ramps."

I glanced up. The copy boy was clattering through with
the coffee cart. I said, "I think I found one I like." I held
up my hand, but he didn't see me.

"It was a joke. They're not for sale."

Men with no capacity for humor really sent me.
"Look, I was wondering if I could see you today. We
need some information on this freeway relocation business. Just a few minutes, later today."

"I'm afraid not. You'll have to speak to one of our community relations people. Orders from the top."

"We already have," I countered. "But the questions concerning contracts nobody seemed able to answer. I have just a few."

"I'm terribly snowed under, Miss—?"

"Chandler." I waved again and this time the kid saw me. He began wheeling the rattletrap my way. "We're doing a whole spread on the relocation business so the public understands exactly what's happening. You'd be doing us all a great service, Mr. Wills."

"Well . . . Perhaps we could do it now. What, for example, do you need to know?"

I debated the offer. "I have something to show you," I said, declining it. "You name the time. What's best for you."

"Miss Bell, bring me my calendar."

The cart creaked to a stop. I put my hand over the mouthpiece. "No cream," I said to the boy. "Just a little arsenic."

"—Ah, here we are. All right, Miss Chandler. If you can be here at eleven, I'll see what I can do."

I thanked him and hung up. If Norman Wills planned to run for public office, he was going to have to brush up on his charisma. Lucille really ought to tell him.

I killed time by reading the "9 A.M. Final," which wasn't the final at all. The paper would be updated twice more before tomorrow's edition hit the streets.

The lead story concerned the return of 3,028 war dead from the Pacific. It had taken six years for the bodies to be sent home, and it was believed that in the coming months another 225,000 would follow from all the battle-fields of World War II. The story, out of San Francisco, began with guns booming and bells tolling as the transport *Honda Knot* sailed into San Francisco Bay. A sidebar listed in alphabetical order the names of the slain heroes. I began to scan them.

My phone rang.

"Miss Chandler?"

"Yes, it is." Automatically, I reached for a sheet of copy paper and a sharpened pencil.

"You don't know me. I got your name from a friend."

That kind of opening usually spelled trouble. I put down the pencil and reached for the cardboard cup. "Yes," I said matter-of-factly, "please go on."

"Not long ago, I was forced to sell my house to the state because of the freeway coming through."

"I see."

"The man who appraised my house told me at the time that it was not in good condition and the state would have to demolish it."

"Did he pay you a good price, Mr.—?"

"Renfeld. Tim Renfeld. It was a fairly large house, two stories, about eight rooms. But it was a bit rundown. Old icebox, floors kind of sagging, if you know what I mean."

"Uh huh."

"I had no idea what it was worth. But seven thousand sounded good."

"Are you still in the house?" I asked, wondering where he was going with this.

"Oh no. I moved out about six months ago. They gave me two weeks to get out."

"Are you serious?"

"It was just me and my wife, so it didn't involve a lot of trouble. We moved in with her folks for the time being, out in Cheviot Hills. We've been looking for our own place but prices are kind of steep around here."

"Is there some kind of problem, Mr. Renfeld?"

"I'm not sure. Last Sunday Iris and I were out looking at houses. We went over the hill because they say houses in the Valley are cheaper. You wouldn't believe all the development going on."

"Yes, I've heard."

"Well this is the thing. While we were driving around, we saw my house. Sitting on the corner of Moorpark and Laurel Grove right there in Studio City."

"What do you mean you saw your house?" I put down the coffee. It was vile.

"The one we'd been living in. The one in Silver Lake that we sold to the state."

"Are you sure?"

"Yeah, it was all fixed up real nice. They stuccoed over the wood and put one of those red Mexican tile roofs on it. There was a white stucco wall, too, maybe three feet high, running around the edge of the yard. They'd planted some flowers under the living room windows. The property could use some trees though."

"You're sure this was your house?" I repeated.

"Oh yes. I know that house, right down to the two chimneys. They took away the front veranda and put in a couple of nice wide steps with a wrought-iron rail. But that's my house. We went in."

"You talked to the new owners?"

"Yep. We rang the bell and said we were admiring the house and mentioned how we were looking for one ourselves. Maybe they could put us onto one like theirs. They showed us around. Now here's what galls me. They said they paid fifteen grand for it. Can you imagine? Why, I could have moved the house and fixed it up myself for the seven the state paid me. Instead, I got seven grand won't buy me nothing."

"Did they tell you who sold them the house?"

"They said they had moved from Boston and saw a "For Sale" sign out front. They called the number and a gentleman came out and showed them the house."

"His name wasn't Richard Walken, was it?"

"Nope. Clark Smith. I got his number right here. It's WE-4101."

"Mr. Renfeld, who is this friend we have in common?"

"Edna Herbert. She's the one who told me to call you."

I took down Mr. Renfeld's number at his in-laws and said I'd see what I could find out. I hung up and realized I was smiling.

At long last I was on the road to somewhere. It didn't bother me that I still didn't know where.

24

◆

I crossed to the middle of Broadway and stood there cooling my heels, waiting for a Red Car to materialize out of the glinting mirages in the distance. I had on a long navy wool skirt, a white sailor blouse and my navy roll-brim hat. The rain had washed the foul air and an early morning sun had dried it. The air felt light as a feather.

Eventually, a street car screeched up. I hopped on, dropped a dime in the coin box and found a seat near the back. As we clanked north along Broadway, I reviewed the questions I wanted to ask Norman Wills. I would have to be careful, and I would have to save the best for last.

After six or seven blocks, I could see the big mounds of dirt and the tractors off to the left where freeway construction was underway. I tried to imagine how it would look when it was finished; wide, coursing rivers of concrete shooting through the heart of Los Angeles. Already some city planners were warning that the freeways would not be big enough to accommodate the projected

191

number of automobiles. But they were being branded as slippery-fingered crooks, on the take from the Firestone Rubber Company, which, naturally, hoped to sell substantially more tires.

I jumped off the Red Car at Second Street and crossed to the State Building.

I left the rumble of bulldozers outside.

Mr. Wills's waiting room contained two beat-up brown leather couches, yellow walls hung with framed documents spaced around a personally signed photograph of Governor Warren, a table with magazines and ashtrays, and a wooden floor. I parked my soles on the wooden floor for forty-five minutes.

"I'm so sorry," Miss Bell kept apologizing, as men in mainly brown suits shuffled in and out. She fingered the bow knotted under her high collar. "Are you sure you wouldn't like some coffee?"

She was a thin dishwater blonde with a plain face and a prim manner. A little makeup and an injection of sauciness might have made her marriage-bait. But as it was, she was earmarked for spinsterhood. I smiled and shook my head.

The ticking of the round clock on the wall was synchronized with Miss Bell's typewriter.

"I was thinking of buying a blouse like yours," she spoke up suddenly. "I saw one in the new Sears catalogue. Is that where you got yours? I think it was fourteen ninety-nine."

"Er, no." Mine had come from Magnin's in the latest shipment of clothes my mother had trucked over. The shipment, the seamstress and my mother arrived at the beginning of each season. I still had some things from last fall that I had yet to put on. "My mom got it for me, but I'm not sure where."

It was eleven forty-nine. I took off my gloves.

"Mr. Wills's office," recited Miss Bell into the phone. "Oh yes, Mr. Walken." She listened for a moment. "He knows. But I'll remind him again. Surely. Thank you."

"Excuse me. Was that . . . ?"

At once, the door to Wills's inner office flew open. "Miss Chandler? Come in. Miss Bell, I'll be leaving at noon for my lunch appointment. Make sure the car is ready. This way, Miss Chandler."

I stepped past him into a sunny square room dominated by a large desk with only a blotter and a telephone on it. Behind the desk, a framed picture of Lucille and a smaller one of the boy sat on top of a long credenza beside a row of leather-bound law books.

"Please sit down."

Wills walked over to the windows. Looking out, you could see the bulldozers chewing up downtown. Wills pulled a cord and the blinds came crashing down, obliterating the sight. He pulled a second cord to let in narrow slats of sunlight.

He turned. In the darkened room at the Downtown Athletic Club, he had appeared younger. But now I could see, through the lenses in his horn-rimmed glasses, dark circles under his eyes, and below, the deep creases around his mouth. He was, perhaps, forty. "Have you always worked for the government?" I inquired.

"No." Wills sat down in the high-backed swivel chair behind his desk. "Before the war, I was in private practice. Two of the partners were killed in action and we disbanded the firm. This came along and it interested me. It meant a new direction in my life and it seemed fitting. The whole country is off in a new direction."

I flipped open my notebook. "Perhaps you could begin by explaining how your department works." The notebook was for show. One of my talents as a reporter was being able to recall conversations verbatim. But people, I had learned, became uneasy if you didn't write every word down. I poised my pencil meaningfully.

"Of course," said Wills. "The Right-of-Way Department for District Seven has a number of divisions. Appraisal, acquisition, demolition, transference, people and contracts. Once a route is planned for a freeway, an appraiser is sent to each home or building. He checks the condition of the property and assigns a value to it. Often, a second appraiser is sent out as well. In the meantime, someone from the people department pays a personal call to the dweller and goes over any concerns the dweller may have. As you can imagine, having to move can be quite upsetting."

"Sure," I said.

"That person also assists the dweller in finding a new home, if necessary. If the building is in disrepair, we mark it for demolition. If . . ."

"Who, exactly, demolishes it?"

"Private companies. Practically all the work that's done is let through the bidding process. Sometimes the fire department will come in and do the demolition, but normally it's private companies."

"The same is true for moving a house?"

"No. After we purchase a house, if it's in movable condition, we hold an auction. Whoever purchases the house takes over the responsibility for relocating any tenants. He must help the tenants find suitable lodging within six months and pay each one fifty dollars toward the relocation. It's also the new owner's responsibility to move the house."

"Why would anyone go to all that trouble?"

"Many of these houses can be bought at auction relatively cheaply. Especially if there are no tenants. You move the house, fix it up and you can have quite a nice home. Also, it will be years before enough new housing can be built to take care of the shortage we currently have."

"And your role in this, Mr. Wills?"

Wills glanced at his watch. "I'm sorry . . . I'm running late. Well quickly, I look over all the contracts between the state and the individual. Actually, that's no longer true. I can't possibly do it myself. I run the department. We have a staff of lawyers who do most of the work. I parcel the contracts out and if I have time, I go over some of them myself."

He pushed back his chair. "I'm afraid . . ."

But I was quicker than he. I held out Esther Lubinow's

contract. "Like this? Would this be what you're talking about?"

Wills furrowed his brow as he took the contract. I watched his eyes scan it. "Yes, this is one of our contracts." He looked at me questioningly.

"We thought we might use it. For art."

Again he looked at the paper. "Perhaps we can make one up for you. This might be considered invasion of privacy."

"Oh, Miss Lubinow doesn't mind. And the only other name on it is Richard Walken's."

Wills handed the contract back to me. I said, "Is he here in the building?"

"Is who in the building?"

"Richard Walken. I thought I might speak with him."

"I have no idea, Miss Chandler. There are hundreds of right-of-way agents."

He strode quickly around the desk, stopping at the door, waiting impatiently for me to hurry it up.

I turned in my chair. "You mean you don't actually know him?"

"I may have met him, I don't recall. Like I said . . ."

"Well, who sends these men out? I mean who actually says, 'Mr. Walken, you go to Green Street today'? "

"One of the department heads, I imagine. Look, if you need anything else, you'll have to call back." He pushed his glasses up his nose and turned his head. "Miss Bell?"

"Mr. Wills, I'd like to clear up this confusion now."

His head swiveled back. "What confusion?"

"Mr. Walken's name is on this contract."

He frowned. "Yes. So?"

"Your personnel department has no record of him."

Norman Wills stared at me. "Our records can't always be trusted, Miss Chandler."

"Oh, that's nice."

His face reddened. "You're making a mountain out of a molehill and I simply won't have that. We're doing our very best to serve the public. Now that's *all.*"

I smiled. "As a public service, I just thought you might like to know."

. . .

In the anteroom, I made a production out of adjusting my hat and putting on my gloves. "How exciting it must be to work here," I gushed to Miss Bell.

"Yes, it is. Mr. Wills is a very important man."

"I suppose he deals with very important people. Like . . ." My eyes traveled to the photograph of Governor Warren.

"Oh the governor is rarely *here*. But yes, we have city officials in and out constantly. Once"—she lowered her eyelids—"John Wayne came in. Right into this room."

"Oh golly." I paused respectfully. Then, "I heard you on the phone before to Mr. Walken. Was that Richard?"

Miss Bell reacted with surprise. "Why, yes. Do you know him?"

"I met him once. He does something in real estate, I believe."

"Actually," said Miss Bell, her voice cooling a degree, "I don't really know. I believe he's a friend of Mrs. Wills. But I must get back to my typing now."

Outside, I stood on the steps of the State Building, a light breeze ruffling my skirt. It seemed unusually quiet and I realized the bulldozers must be on lunch break. A beggar holding a tin cup slouched against the building rattling his change.

Connecting Wills with Walken made me feel charitable. I dropped in a dime.

On the streetcar, I realized I had given away my last coin. The conductor gave me a scathing look—along with change for a five.

"Hi, Paris. Grab a seat."

I pulled up a chair and wondered what Fred Dickinson wanted. Fred was the city editor. All around me, typewriters sang against the clangorous symphony of wire service machines. Out of habit, I glanced over to the rewrite pen. But Walter, of course, was not there.

I watched Fred scan a piece of copy. He had nice gray

eyes and a wide, friendly smile, two attributes that masked a lunatic edge. In one of the drawers of his desk he kept a cap gun. Whenever Fred wanted someone's attention, he began shooting off the gun like a madman.

"Be right with you," he said absently. I couldn't imagine why he had summoned me.

"I see we've added a little class to this joint." Purvis Winn, who wrote about farm matters and had been at the *Examiner* since before time, collapsed in a chair at the next desk over. "You busy tonight, doll?"

"Unfortunately, Purvis, I am."

"God, my chompers are killing me." Purvis stuck his thumb and forefinger into his mouth and pulled out his teeth. He grinned at me toothlessly.

Fred Dickinson leaned back in his chair. "So how are things going, Paris?"

"Fine."

"Etta keeping you busy?"

"Sure. But I'd be happy to do something for you."

"Gets a little old going to all those hat parties, eh?"

I smiled and said nothing.

"I got a call a little while ago from Norm Wills over at the Division of Highways. He said you'd been in asking questions. He wasn't quite sure what we were doing. The problem is, neither am I."

I knew what the truth would bring me. I had been through this before when the actress who died at the beach had come to see me in Society shortly before her death and I had certain information that no one else had. The paper shooed me away and turned the story over to that guttersnipe crime writer George Healy. What I had now was far more tenuous.

"I did go to see Mr. Wills," I admitted, "but he made an understandable mistake. I met him last week when I was doing an item for Etta. So even though I told him I was only doing research for KTLA, I guess it went right by him."

"Freeway research?" Fred said dubiously.

"Yes. You know how after the newscast, KTLA has that fifteen-minute show, *Eyewitness,* where they interview people in the news, or have discussions on an issue? They're planning to devote a week to freeways and they've asked some of us to get background dope."

Fred leaned forward. "Now listen, Paris. You do that little show with Nick, no problem. It helps promote Etta's column. But anything else is a *big* problem, understand? You tell them over there, we don't allow our people to help them out. If they intend to be in the information business, let them get their own informants. Is that clear?"

"You're saying . . ."

"I'm saying you take stuff from Etta's column and babble it on the TV, I don't care. You go talking to people like Norm Wills, I do care. I'm smelling a real conflict of interest here. We're in a circulation war with the *Times.* We've got a slight edge, but it's a cutthroat business. You start helping some two-bit TV outfit, using your *Examiner* credentials, I'm gonna get real mad. Got that?"

A loud cackling made me turn. Purvis Winn was grinning maniacally at his typewriter. His teeth lay diabolically next to his beat-up hat.

I looked back at Fred Dickinson. I told him that I did.

25
•

Late in the afternoon, Andrew ferried me over to KTLA.

"I got it, Miss Chandler. I'm going to play D. V. Turner, pilot. I even counted the lines. I've got twelve!"

"Why that's terrific," I enthused as I tried to calculate how many shooting days it would take Andrew to say twelve lines. "I suppose you start pretty soon?"

"I'm waiting to hear, but I have to go in Monday for wardrobe." Andrew spun around in his seat. "Isn't this exciting, Miss Chandler?"

In spite of myself I smiled. It wasn't, after all, his fault that I'd hired him. Or pleaded with him to stay on at forty dollars a week. Nevertheless . . .

"You wouldn't know of a replacement?" I said anxiously. "I can't bear the thought of Mrs. Keyes." Mrs. Keyes, in her last life, had surely driven in Rome and thought that the same daredevil maneuvers were required in L.A.

"I'll ask around," Andrew promised, pulling up behind the black panel remote truck camped outside KTLA.

I told him I would only be a minute.

. . .

At five o'clock, KTLA looked more like a gypsy camp than ever.

The long hallway was clogged with performers nervously rehearsing their acts. Gladys Rubens, who operated a children's talent school, was running through a dance number with a group of eight- to ten-year-olds for the weekly show *Sandy Dreams*. Nearby, Dick Lane was calming a terrified tuba player who undoubtedly would appear on his musical talent show, *Hits and Bits*. In the midst of this frenzy, two edgy-looking cops in uniform leaned against the wall smoking cigarettes. Perhaps they would appear on *Eyewitness*, discussing some torrid local crime.

I squeezed past a cowboy twirling a lariat, and nudged my way along to the back of the garage. May Rivers, the makeup lady, was bending over a table set up in the hall, laying out powders and rouges, lipsticks, pancake makeup and mascara. The lineup of pale faces would soon begin.

She straightened. "Paris. What are you doing here? Although, who knows what day it is anymore." Her carrot-colored hair was clamped behind her ears by two metal barrettes. Her white apron was already spotty with makeup.

I sat down in the high chair. "I need a favor, May. Could you do my makeup? I'm, uh, a little banged up."

May stood over the chair and examined my face. Gently, she touched the area under my eyes. She stood back and frowned.

"I'm going to an affair tonight and I can't look like this."

"Not unless it's a costume party."

"What happened was—"

"Spare me. You'll just shock me. What color is your dress?"

Fifteen minutes later I popped out of the chair and held up May's big hand mirror. The false eyelashes she had glued on—"to steal attention from the rest of your face"—accentuated my green eyes and made me look seriously glamorous. "This is great, May. I can't thank you enough."

I started back past advertising and the art department and was approaching the newsroom when out strolled Harry Gladstone. Down the hall, the two cops I had seen earlier were stamping out their cigarettes. I had guessed wrong. They weren't going to be guests on *Eyewitness;* they were accompanying their boss. I stepped into the police chief's line of vision.

"Paris!" He grinned. "Ooo la la."

"Hello, Chief."

Gladstone grabbed my arm and pulled me aside. "I was just talking to Truman. He told me as soon as he could find a hole, he'd plug me in. Loves the idea of me having my own show." Gladstone beamed. "Isn't that fabulous?"

I said oh yes.

"You know, I really think this is where my future is."

I said, "Ah ha."

"I was even thinking, well, looking down the road a ways, that I could do an armchair detective show."

A clown came somersaulting down the hall. I stepped aside to avoid being kicked. "Um, you mean—?"

"Why—I know. I'll get Raymond Chandler to write the scripts."

I batted my new eyelashes appreciatively. "You're some kind of guy, Chief."

"Call me Harry. Now here's what I'm thinking—"

"I don't know if I can take any more."

"Maybe we could get together and you could teach me the ropes about being on camera."

My mind began to race. If I were a suspect, would he be associating with me? On the other hand, he could be setting me up. I smiled enigmatically and lowered my fake eyelashes demurely. "You know where to find me. *Harry.*"

I patted his tie and walked away.

·   ·   ·

Truman Stone was hanging up the phone when I swept in through the sheets. "Hi, there."

"Lo."

"I'm sorry I missed the other night." I sat down in Jim's chair.

"We all get sick," he said. "Sometime."

"I just ran into Gladstone. You're going to put him on?"

"God, I hope not." Truman leaned forward. "You don't suppose he could lock me up for obstruction of his TV career?"

"That's something to consider, certainly."

Truman gave me a level look. "Just in the neighborhood, I suppose?"

"I got fitted for eyelashes." I batted them. "Mike Romanoff is having a party for Princess La Di Da. An escaped Russian."

Truman grinned. "We should get Klaus to send the remote truck."

"Nick would love *that*."

"Yeah."

"So Gladstone came in to ask about a job? He says he's going to be the next Philip Marlowe."

Truman glanced away. "He came looking for Jim's freeway file."

I said nothing.

Truman began drumming a gnawed pencil on the desk. "Let me ask you something. Remember you came in last week, looking for it? Well I had it. It was buried under this mess on my desk."

"Really? That's great."

"I found it that afternoon. I wanted to take it home. Then you came in asking about it. I decided not to say anything until I'd gone through it."

"Did you find anything?"

"Nope. I never took it home. I left it here because I didn't want you to see me carrying it out." Truman began fiddling with the pencil again. "It was gone when I came in the next day."

"And you think . . . ?"

"Naw. You wouldn't be going through my desk. I was just wondering though . . . did you happen to see anybody else around that night?"

I hadn't. But I told Truman I thought I'd heard footsteps.

He smiled sheepishly. "Could have been me. I had a quick one at O'Blath's and came back. But you were still here, going through the file cabinet." He paused. "Maybe somebody came later."

It was possible, especially since the St. Clairs' house had been ransacked the next night. Not finding the folder here, they would have gone there. I looked at the piles of papers spilling across Truman's desk. "You're sure it's not buried somewhere?"

"Yep."

Truman's story sounded screwy. But I had no reason to doubt it. What was interesting was that he had thought the folder might be important. And now, apparently, the police thought so, too.

"Princess Alexandra, may I present Miss Paris Chandler."

The woman had the gall not even to hold out her hand. Forced into a subservient position, I did a minor curtsy, which I felt was totally uncalled for. "So pleased to meet you, Your Highness," I murmured. "I hope you will find L.A. pleasing to you."

The Introducer, a short man with a monocle, smiled broadly. Princess Alexandra smiled briefly. It was possible she knew no English. But I doubted it. More likely, she was a starlet-hopeful from the Midwest hoping her air of mystery would capture some major mogul's fancy. It had been tried before. Then again, her nose was too large. I smiled sweetly and backed away.

Nick, who had been introduced right before me, continued hovering about the princess as if he were a bee extracting nectar from a fragile blossom. If anyone could undo her, Nick would. I shot him an evil grin and turned away.

The whole back room of Romanoff's had been given over to the party. And one quick glance indicated that *everybody* had turned out. Dressed to the eyebrows. I quickly learned to detect the Russian hoi polloi from the local ones; *they* were wearing tuxes. The natives made do with dinner jackets and bow ties, while the women wore everything from floor-length taffeta gowns to shimmering cocktail dresses. I adjusted my one-strap black velvet dress, which Mrs. Keyes had poured me into, snatched a glass of vodka from a floating tray and plunged into the pond, flinging out my lines, waiting to see what I could hook.

I felt a tug almost immediately. "Paris? Is that you? It's been so long."

I turned and found the delicate face of Virginia Grey smiling up at me.

"Virginia." I gave her the required kiss on the cheek. "You look *sensational.*" A petite blonde with porcelain skin and long dark lashes, Virginia Grey was a B-movie actress who had never been able to make the Big Jump. "Is Clark around?"

Immediately I knew I had said absolutely the wrong thing. But then, keeping track of the Virginia Grey-Clark Gable romance would require round-the-clock surveillance.

The small red mouth plumped into a perfect pout. "Don't write this, Paris, but we're going through a temporary separation." Her eyes flashed. "You-know-who's in town."

You-know-who was Dolly O'Brien, Gable's East Coast paramour. Whenever Dolly arrived, Virginia was dumped. It had been going on for years.

I said, "I saw *Smooth as Silk,*" hoping to get out of hot water. "You were terrific."

"But I *hate* being killed," Virginia sulked. She hesitated. "So—you thought I was good?"

"Virginia, darling!" Erich von Stroheim wedged in between us, giving me a chance to slip away. I spotted Dore Schary, the head of production at RKO, making an entrance. Ronnie Reagan beat me to him by an out-stretched arm.

"Did you hear?" a heavyset man was saying. "Sinatra dropped thousands on the Series."

A woman brandishing a terrifyingly long cigarette holder, replied, "You mean—he bet Brooklyn?"

"So I hear."

"Poor Frankie."

Across the room, I spotted Mrs. Howard Hawks. Word was rampant that her marriage to the director was on the rocks and that she had taken up with the agent Leland Hayward. I edged around the cigarette holder. "Slim" Hawks was an industrious social butterfly who had actu-ally commanded a whole story in a recent issue of *Life*. If anybody knew what was going on in town, she did. As I elbowed closer I saw that she was chatting with Mrs. Lucien Tindle, the wife of the car wash magnet. "Ah, Paris," said Slim. "Surely you can help us out. You do know Mrs. Tindle?"

"Of course, how are you?"

"Splendid, my dear. I was just saying I had heard that Mr. Hearst is well enough to talk on the telephone. If so, I really ought to call him."

"Oh it's true, I'm afraid." I laughed and told them an edited account of my cookie story.

"You mean," said Mrs. Tindle, "the police stopped your chauffeur and *stole* Mr. Hearst's cookies?"

"All I know is they were never delivered. It was only a few days ago." I smiled charmingly. "I'm hoping I won't get fired."

Mrs. Tindle waved her hand. "Don't be silly, dear. I hear his memory is nearly gone."

"Oh look," cried Slim. "George Burns."

"Excuse me," said Mrs. Tindle. "I *must* talk to him."

"Have you spoken with the princess?" I asked Slim.

"I did." Slim tossed her dark hair. "But *she* didn't speak back." In tandem our eyes swung over to Princess Alexandra. George Burns was speaking to her while Nick hung in the background. Mrs. Tindle was a distant third.

"Do you think . . . ?" I began.

"Did you *see* her jewels? I could swear they're fake. Paste and glass," said Slim with certainty. "If you can imagine."

"Seriously? How dreadful. I'm tired of these people trooping through."

"That's it!" A devilish smile spread across Slim Hawks's face. "Listen, we'll have a dinner party at my place for her and her companion, that greasy little man with the mustache over there. I'll have Mike arrange it. Then we'll get to the bottom of this Russian business." Slim lowered her voice. "I've heard they are actually spies. Communist spies. It's the only explanation, don't you agree?"

"Mrs. Hawks?"

An absolutely ravishing blonde in a white satin dress touched Slim's arm. Ruby red lips dominated a face otherwise covered by the veil from her black pillbox hat. The two women managed to kiss each other's cheek without leaving a mark. "I'm delighted to see you here," said Slim.

The young woman laughed. "I have to admit I wasn't invited. But Victor Klopstein asked me. We're doing his property up Benedict Canyon."

My eyes wandered. Then pulled up short. Standing by the bar were—my parents. It had never occurred to me that they might be here. I took a sip of vodka and turned back to Slim and the woman in white.

"Do you two know each other?" Slim was saying. "Paris Chandler this is Ursula Martens."

I nearly choked on my vodka.

"Oh," Miss Martens exclaimed. "How fabulous! I always watch your show. I envy you so much."

I managed a smile but could think of nothing to say.

"Why look at you two," Slim said suddenly. "You could be twins."

Ursula laughed. "Except for the eyes maybe. Mine are blue. And she's taller. How tall are you, Miss Chandler?"

"Five-six, I believe."

"Well I'm five-four. But I hear that you can actually stretch yourself a whole inch."

"No!" gasped Slim, her eyes canvassing the room.

"*Yes.* You know those chinning bars? You just dangle for a half-hour each day. I read it somewhere. Gosh, this is sensational. Meeting Paris Chandler. Would you think it silly if I asked for your autograph?"

I was studying her like a foreigner reading a road map. Even I could see some resemblance. The nose, for example, and the mouth. Our builds were similar, too: small-boned and slender. Our hairstyles, shoulder-length and bouncy, could have come out of the same beauty parlor. Only her hair had waves.

"I'm afraid I don't have a pen."

"Oh, look," said Slim sighting over my shoulder. "My god, it's Hedy Lamarr. Excuse me, girls."

"Perhaps one of the men has one," Ursula Martens said.

"I really don't think I'm autograph material." Was she serious? Did she not know we had been in the same house at the same time on two separate nights? I sipped my vodka. "Did I hear you say you worked for Mr. Klopstein?"

"I work for a company that's doing his landscaping. Sunset Estates. I act as a go-between and make sure the work is done on schedule."

"How fascinating. I suppose you have a green thumb. Or something. However did you get into *that* line?"

"I needed a job," Miss Martens said without taking offense. "I answered an ad for a secretary and this is what it turned out to be. It's okay. But it's not terribly exciting."

I grinned wickedly. "Oh, but I hear Mr. Klopstein is *very* exciting. I believe he's in ladies' garments. I imagine his house is quite, er, large."

"Yes."

"So you see, Miss Martens, your job may not be exciting but it does have endless . . . possibilities."

"Oh, here he comes. Victor!"

Victor Klopstein's face lit up like a neon sign at the

sound of being summoned by Miss Martens. He pushed
through the crowd like an eager puppy hearing his master's voice. He was almost bald, except for the barest
white fringe. His head rested on his collar like a soft-
boiled egg in its cup. Victor arrived a bit dampishly. He
was at least sixty. And a recent widower. More to the
point—Victor was filthy rich.

"There you are, cupcake." Victor's fleshy lips swooped
down on Miss Martens's neck. "I couldn't imagine where
you'd gone to."

"This is Paris Chandler, Victor. From the TV show."

Victor stepped back and appraised me. "Ooh such a
dish, if you'll excuse my French. The girls nowadays
are—"

"We need a pen," Miss Martens broke in. "Miss Chandler was about to give me her autograph."

"No, really," I protested mildly.

"You need a pen? I got a pen."

Victor reached into his pocket and produced a gold
fountain pen. He handed it to me. "So maybe you'll
write down your phone number for me?"

"Oh yes," said Miss Martens. "Do. I would love to see
you sometime."

"I'm afraid I have no paper," I hedged, holding out
the pen to Victor.

Victor, clever man, snatched a paper cocktail napkin
off a passing waiter's tray. Resignedly, I signed my name
and wrote down the number at the *Examiner.* I wanted to
tell Miss Martens that my landscaping was already quite
nicely done.

But I knew I would have to see her.

I handed her the napkin and Mr. Klopstein his pen.

"So delighted," I said.

"And—good luck with your trees," I also said.

"Darling," my mother cooed, eyeing me sharply. "Your
lashes. Paul, doesn't Paris look divine?"

My father grinned and kissed me. "As always. How
are you, baby?"

My father, who hated dressing, had obviously been co-erced by my mother into the entire dinner jacket routine. His broad shoulders and growing girth gave him a rather stuffed look, but with his gray crewcut and tan, unlined face, he looked rather dashing. My mother, whose exqui-site body seemed oblivious to gravity, was wearing a low-cut beige peau de soie gown. A black velvet cord around her neck supported an enormous emerald and diamond pendant that nestled dramatically between her breasts. Her short taffy-colored hair was brushed behind her ears to show off her favorite diamond earrings. She did not, somehow, look overdone; just her usual elegant, beauti-ful, perfect self. She *always* wore false eyelashes.

"Tell me," said my mother, clutching my elbow. "Who are you here with?"

"Nick."

"Ooo—wonderful." My mother adored Nick. "I was afraid you'd come with that boring Ted person." She sur-veyed the crowd expertly. "Though really, this isn't his kind of soiree."

Ted Stein was an assistant district attorney, a boy I had gone to high school with, dated several times, then lost track of until recently. "I don't think it's mine either," I responded. Then I caught myself. My mother and I rarely agreed on anything, but I wasn't in the mood for one of our tiffs. "Really, Mother, don't you think she's a fake?" I quickly put in.

My mother's eyes drifted over to the princess. "It's possible. But it never hurts to get to know those people." She looked at me. "They're often well connected, fake or not." Her eyes went back to the princess. "Oh, there's Nick. You must bring him over, Paris. In fact, you must invite him to dinner. Doesn't he look handsome?"

He did, in his black formal wear. Nick, like my mother, was a major dresser. He was now talking to the man Slim had identified as the princess's "escort." I smiled.

"Nobody's gotten the princess to talk. Perhaps you should try."

My mother put her drink down on the bar and followed me through the crowd. When we reached the royal party, I tugged on Nick's sleeve. He turned.

"Mrs. Masterson. What a surprise." He kissed her hand. "I'd like you to meet Major Popov, Princess Alexandra's consort."

"Escort," I whispered.

"How you do," the major said heavily.

"My pleasure," said my mother coquettishly.

"Your jewels are—how you say?—*delicious*," declared the major in a thick accent. "Jewels are, you know— everyzink."

I pulled Nick aside. "Well?"

"Later. We can go soon." He took my hand. "I don't have to report in tonight."

"Really?"

"Etta said it would be better to write a separate story tomorrow. For the afternoon papers. It's more than a column note."

"What fun," I said.

Nick's eyes wandered for a moment. "There's a girl here who looks amazingly like you. White dress. Ah, over there."

I followed his gaze to Ursula Martens. She was talking with a couple I did not recognize. I said to Nick, "Well that's not very flattering. Being compared to someone else."

Nick smiled. "A hat with a veil for a formal affair. *Tsk, tsk.* You would never make such a mistake."

"But then," I said smoothly, "*my* hair isn't dyed."

Nick hadn't had a moment to eat and announced, as we entered my house, that he was starving. I searched the refrigerator and came up with a slab of leftover meatloaf. It was one of the few dishes Mrs. Keyes hadn't learned to ruin. I made him a sandwich, brought him a bottle of beer and watched him eat.

"You missed the sister," Nick informed me between bites. "That was one of the giveaways."

"Meaning?" I said eagerly.

"Well the princess only said things like, 'how var you?'
And, 'dahlink, a vodka,' and 'zeese shoes hurts my feet.'
Maybe she thought that would legitimatize her, wearing
fashionable shoes. But what had me convinced she was
real were her teeth."

"Her teeth?"

"Like a mule's. I suppose they don't have orthodon-
ture there?"

I giggled.

Nick took a swig from the bottle of beer. "But there
was this girl hanging around, who also had bad teeth. A
bit chubby and pimply. At first she wouldn't talk. Just
kept shaking her head. So I said I ran Paramount Pictures and I was terribly struck by her. Was she a Russian
royal?"

"You didn't!"

"And the girl nodded. So obviously, she understood
the language." Nick held up his sandwich. "Want some?"

I shook my head. Thinking, only Nick could have
pulled this one off.

"Anyway, I said I was casting a big picture and maybe
she would like to audition. Just the thought of it gave her
another pimple."

"You are a cad."

"I told her she certainly had the looks. But we'd have
to see about the accent. She and the princess were obviously star material. But Americans are not tolerant of
accents."

"I don't believe this."

"The whole time I kept hearing Walter Winchell."
Nick cleared his throat. "'Bulletin . . . And on the
Coast, the sisters Karamazov were feted . . .'"

"Nicky. Continue."

"So I said to the girl, who was absolutely heaving at
this point, 'Do you know if the princess would be interested? I mean, do you know the princess?' And she burst
out, 'She's my sister.'"

"In English?"

Nick grinned his spectacular Nick grin. "In English
twang. One of those middle of the country twangs."

"I knew it," I declared.

"The only princess there," Nick said, "was you."

After a while, I told Nick I was beat, still weak from the flu. I had taken the bandages off my rib cage, but even a gentle hug was more than I could bear. And I had on enough makeup for the entire cast of *The Ten Commandments*.

"My mother wants you to come to dinner," I murmured, as we huddled at the front door. "Will you?"

Nick kissed my nose. "Any time. But not this weekend."

"No?"

"I'm going to Palm Springs. To play golf. I'm leaving tomorrow night. But I'll call you when I get back on Sunday."

We kissed some more. "Will you miss me?" Nick said.

"I'll let you know," I said. "On Sunday."

As I watched him walk to his car, I rather thought I would.

26

Friday arrived with more news of the war dead returning to San Francisco.

Reports of bodies being carried off the ship dominated the front page and were followed, on succeeding pages, by accounts of families that had come from across America to take the bodies home.

The stories acted as sharp needles, pricking the bubble of optimism sweeping the country. Los Angeles, like many cities, was bursting with energy: new buildings, new roads seemed to spring up overnight. Men who had come home from the war intending to return to their jobs as clerks now found they could go to college instead. The GI bill. Families that had lived in cramped apartments could slap down some cash and own a home. The VA loan. Gas was flowing at the pumps; Detroit was churning out cars at a record rate. And housewives were discovering the joys of washing machines and dryers right in the home, along with freezers that stored prepackaged dinners—ready to heat up.

Some people had been able, after the war, to pick up

213

their lives where they had left off. Others, as the newspapers darkly illustrated, had not.

I looked up.

"There's a gentleman to see you, Miss Paris."

I put down my coffee cup and followed Mrs. Keyes along the hall to the front door. A man in a Mafia-style chalk-striped suit, and holding a weighty briefcase, stood on the welcome mat, tapping a foot.

"Yes?"

"Mrs. Chandler, I'm Edwin Oakes with the law firm of Allerton, Sands, Kresky and Oakes." He paused, waiting for a reaction. I let him wait. "As you may know, I'm representing the Chandler family in the disputed matter of your house. May I come in?"

I studied his face. He had a high forehead, emphasized by a widow's peak, with dark hair slicked down behind his ears. His cheeks were flushed; a razor cut, still fresh, underlined his lower lip. Below his thin brows, unfriendly eyes looked back. "I think not," I said.

"We have an offer to discuss with you."

"Perhaps you have made a mistake."

"You are Mrs. Russell Chandler?"

"Yes."

"And this is the house currently owned by the late Mr. Chandler's parents?"

"That, I believe, is being disputed, Mr. Oakes, as you well know." The Chandlers were claiming that because they had made a sizable down payment on the house, leaving Russell to pay off the small, remaining mortgage, the house, which was in their name *and* Russell's, belonged to them. My attorney maintained the down payment was a wedding gift to us both.

Oakes gave me a tight, condescending smile. "But that is why I'm here. We may have a solution to this, uh, dispute."

"Then surely, in your eagerness, you have made a mistake. Thomas Whitehouse is the man you must see. He is my attorney, as you also know."

"Mrs. Chandler, we would like to get this settled right away. I thought . . ."

At that moment, I noticed Mr. Oakes's car, parked in the drive. A highly waxed gray Oldsmobile. From the backseat, a man and a woman stared out the window at me.

"Who are those people?" I said angrily.

Another condescending smile. "A lovely couple. They may be interested in purchasing this house. You could do very well, Mrs. Chandler."

"I'm already doing very well, thank you." I stepped back and gently closed the door in Mr. Oakes's face.

An unwelcome intruder. The long reach of the war had grabbed hold of me, too.

"Mr. Smith, please."

A woman on the other end of the line said he would be right with me.

I fiddled with my pencil. Having run into a dead end with Richard Walken, at least temporarily, I decided to try another approach.

"Hello! This is Clark Smith. How are you today?" Instinctively, I held the phone away from my ear. He sounded like a man who was going to ask for my vote.

I cleared my throat. "Mr. Smith, this is Miss Chandler. I understand that you show properties in the Valley."

"Absolutely. It's the up-and-coming place to be. Let me tell you, Miss Chandler, the Valley's been given a bad name. In five years, it will be *the* address in town. Mark my words."

I tried to imagine Bel Air and Beverly Hills defecting to the Other Side. The image I came up with was fuzzy. "I'm sure you're right," I said haltingly. "In fact, I wanted to ask you about a house. The one you sold recently to—" I realized then I had neglected to ask Mr. Renfeld the names of the new owners. "Um, the one in Studio City at the corner of Moorpark and Laurel Grove."

"Of course! Superb house. You certainly have an eye, Miss Chandler. I think I can safely say that. And if you liked *that* house, you and I are in business, cause I have another one, similar but—are you ready for this? With a swimming pool! I must show it to you immediately."

"Actually, Mr. Smith, what intrigued me about the house was learning that it had been moved. I understand it was trucked over the hill and remodeled. Is—that possible?"

Some of the exuberance drained out of Mr. Smith's voice. "It's possible. It's being done routinely these days. But whether the Perry house was moved, I don't recall."

"Oh dear."

"Let me ask you something. You're looking to buy a house? I can show you many. Some of them brand new, built on the spot. Why don't we make an appointment? The way houses are selling, you won't want to waste a minute, Miss Chandler. And . . . *only ten percent down.*"

"No, no, you misunderstand. I don't want to buy a house. I want to sell a house."

"Well that's fine. I'd be happy . . . where is this house?"

"That's the problem, Mr. Smith. I want to do the same thing. I want to move my house into the Valley and fix it up and see what I can get for it." I stopped. A headline suddenly leaped to mind: BEVERLY HILLS WOMAN SCANDALIZES CITY; MOVES HOUSE TO THE VALLEY. I bit my lip. "But I don't have anybody to do the work. That's why I thought you could tell me who moved and renovated the Perry house."

"I see." There was a pause. I figured he was calculating how to wring some money out of me. I moved to speed up the process. "If you can provide me with the names of the people who did the work," I said cheerfully, "then I shall ask you to be my agent when I'm ready to sell."

"Can you hold, Miss Chandler? I'll have to check my files."

"For the seller's name."

"Yes. One second, please."

I selected a burnt umber crayon and began drawing a sad-looking house. I had the sagging roof on and was reaching for a green to start the landscaping when Mr. Smith came back on the line.

"Sorry. Let me see now. The seller—oh. Of course. I remember now. It was Angela Walken. Would you like her number?"

"Yes, please."

"It's Crestview 6429. Or was. This transaction took place some months ago."

"Do you know if she did the work? I mean, was she living in the house at the time she sold it?"

"No, I believe the house was empty. In fact, the painters were just finishing up."

"I see. Did she say where the house had been moved from?"

"No, why?"

"Because I was wondering how far you can move a house. I suppose that's a silly question."

"I'm afraid I can't help you there. But I'm sure Miss Walken can. Now, if I could have your number . . ."

"Perhaps she moved it from Hancock Park, do you suppose? I mean your address on Wilshire is in that area. Why else would she have come to you?"

"My firm is very well known. There's no mystery here. And we have branched out into the Valley. Like I said, Miss Chandler, the Valley is the vista of the future." He cleared his throat. "That's our motto."

"I'll remember, Mr. Smith. And thanks." I hung up before he could ask for my number again.

Then I stared at the one Clark Smith had given me for Angela Walken. It rang a bell.

I dialed it. A woman wished me good morning and announced I had reached Sunset Estates.

"Angela Walken, please."

"I'm sorry," said the woman, "she's not here."

"May I leave a message?"

"I'm saying we have no one here by that name."

"Your company does not employ her?"

"I'm afraid not."

"Is it possible she once worked there?"

"Nope. I've been here the whole time. Two years last

August. It started with just me and Mr. Aubrey. Even now, there's only the four of us."

"Mr. Aubrey," I said. "Mr. Albert Aubrey?"

"Only he's not here anymore. I think he went over to construction."

"Is there an Ursula Martens? Perhaps I have the wrong place."

"Ursula? Why didn't you say so? I'll connect you."

I disconnected first. I sat there, staring into space. Had Ursula Martens given a false name on the sales contract? That didn't make sense. Anybody could call the number she had given and find out that Angela Walken didn't exist. I would check the leather address book when I got home for Angela's name. I would also, I decided, copy all the names and numbers and mail the book back to Al Brown. Albert Aubrey-Brown.

"Miss Chandler?"

A copy boy pulled up breathing hard and handed me a slip of paper. "This came in while you were on the phone. It sounded important."

I looked at the scrawled words. "From RKO publicity. Urgent! The leopard from *Bringing Up Baby* is dead."

27

Ursula Martens continued to haunt me as I sleep-walked through my Item-collecting chores. At some point, a scheme began to hatch. By the time I had it worked out, it was after twelve, too late to put into play just now. Besides, I wanted to consider the consequences over the weekend. I phoned Esther Lubinow.

The sad-cheerful voice greeted me with a packing up-date: she had, by now, made a dent. A mover had been found, which wasn't easy. Trucks were hard to come by, given the sharp increase in the moving business. And— she added, Sunday was going to be a nightmare.

"They're holding the auction," she said.

"Already? But you're not moving until next Thursday."

"They told me they like to hold auctions on weekends so people can come," Esther said. "Next weekend somehow is booked."

"Maybe I'll stop by. I'm curious."

"That would be great, Paris. I was thinking of taking Mama out for a drive so we wouldn't have to be here.

Before the auction starts they let people walk through the house."

"That's awful," I sympathized. "Look, I'll definitely come. What time?"

"Ten o'clock they start letting people in. I think the auction is at eleven."

"I'll bring the contract with me." Returning it to her was the reason I had called. "Cheer up," I said. "The worst is almost over." My voice sounded hollow, even to me.

I stood up and walked to the waist-high wall that separates Society into its own little fiefdom. On the other side is the cracked linoleum floor that serves as both hallway and neutral zone between us and the newsroom. The dividing wall helps the newsroom pretend Society doesn't exist.

I went around the wall. Most days I strolled through the newsroom at least once to read the bulletin board humor and glance at what was coming over the wire machines. As I walked in, a copy boy, carrying a stack of freshly printed noon editions, handed me one as he hurried by. I sniffed the ink then glanced at the front page.

Under a story out of San Francisco harbor, concerning the return of the dead soldiers, was a box. L.A. WIDOW HELPS POOR BRING WAR DEAD HOME, read the headline. By Walter Ainsley. There was no dateline. It took a moment to register.

I looked up. Against the back wall stood the copy desk, a horseshoe arrangement of six desks planted directly under a pinup of Betty Grable. "The patron saint of copy," they had dubbed her. At the moment, only Arlie Johnson sat under Betty's come-hither gaze. Against the right wall, mid-room, just after the bank of wire machines, a lone figure sat at a desk, his back to me, hammering out a story. He had his shirtsleeves rolled up and his hat tipped back on his head. A cigarette burned in the ashtray.

Walter.

I stood there watching him from thirty feet away. He

never once looked up from his keyboard. After a while, I slipped away.

At my desk, I had Jo, the switchboard operator, put me through to Western Union. To Walter Ainsley, *L.A. Examiner,* I said.

"The message is . . .

" '*The time has come,*' *the Walrus said,* '*To talk of many things: Of shoes—and ships—and sealing wax—of cabbages—and kings—And why the sea is boiling hot*' . . . *And whether murderers have wings. Stop. Reply soonest. Paris.*"

28

◆

Outside the Pantry, the line stretched half a block. It didn't seem to be in a hurry.

Twilight was deepening into night, etching the brightly lit restaurant into sharp relief while the people on the sidewalk dimmed—like an audience beholden at the foot of a stage. A gentle breeze brought cooler air, along with the bus fumes from over on Figueroa. Hungry, and growing irritable at the molten progress to the Pantry's front door, the line had fallen silent. Only the clanging metal wheels of the streetcars broke through the eerie quiet—and Tee's Southern drawl.

"I can't stay long."

"You weren't asked to," I said.

"I'd like to think I had something better to do." She sounded wistful. "But it's just another Friday night stakeout."

"The radio guy?"

"His girl is two-timing him all right. Even though he suspected it, he acted real shocked. They always act shocked."

222

"Anyone interesting?"

"The sound engineer."

"You mean . . . she threw over the Silken Voice for an engineer?"

"Ex-Marine. They still think they own the world." Tee glanced at her man-sized watch. "His tattoos are something else." She shook her wrist and frowned. "Six-ten?"

"Twenty," I corrected.

Tee grunted. "So what's the story, morning glory?" She began fiddling with her watch.

"I met Ursula Martens last night. At Romanoff's. Slim Hawks said we could be twins."

Tee tapped the crystal with her fingernail.

"Nick thought so, too."

Tee looked up. "Nick? Where is Nick? I haven't talked to him in a week."

"Palm Springs. How come you didn't tell me I look like her. I hate that I look like her—do you think that I do?"

"No." Tee held the watch to her ear. "But someone who isn't your close friend might. You have guile written all over your face—she doesn't."

"I suppose she's just little Miss Muffet, all innocence and lace."

"We don't know if Miss Muffet wore lace." Tee smiled at her watch, then pulled the sleeve of her black sweater over it. "Why are you so hot under the collar?"

"It's obviously mistaken identity. People are mistaking me for her."

"Like who?" said Tee.

Her eyes were wide and questioning with just a hint of amusement shining through. Underestimating Tee was dangerous. She knew I'd been at Jim's house the night of the murder and she'd undoubtedly guessed why. Whether she believed Ursula Martens's story that she had left first was another matter. Tee also knew I had held everything back from her. But she probably had figured that one out, too.

Out of the corner of my eye I could see him from a block away. "Listen," I said quickly, "Donna St. Clair's got to be paying you a lot. Or have you given up? But you never give up, do you? I need to know what's going on."

Tee tossed her head sending out a dazzling shower of magnificent red hair. She ran her fingers through it casually. "Urse didn't do it. But I think she knows who did. I have not given up. You want to know what's going on? I get to know what's going on back. Oh—I see Walter coming. I think I'd better warn him."

"Warn him?"

Tee raised her arm in a throwing position. "They serve pies here."

"I didn't throw it at you."

"Only because you lost your nerve. Henry Fonda walked in."

"Well—"

"And saved me. Just like in the movies."

"Right. Theodora Jones, damsel in distress." I made a face. "Spare me."

"It's a lonely life, stakeouts." Tee smiled enigmatically. "Our minds can wander, too."

I watched her walk away, long-legged, graceful. She stopped and gave Walter a big hug. According to Tee, Walter used to patronize her brothel before the war.

The line inched forward, carrying me along. I watched Tee cross the street.

I couldn't imagine where her mind might wander to.

"Here, try this steak." Walter nudged his plate toward me.

I shook my head.

"No, go on. The chicken's not as good. You shouldn't have ordered the chicken."

"I'm fine, really. So you told them you wouldn't write about the returning war dead?"

"War dead, war alive. No war stories, period."

"Uh huh."

"Besides, I was trying to come home. Six months in Sacramento. They called it a trial period, I called it a sentence. The time was almost up. And my work, I think, has been good." Walter raised his eyebrows, then reached for the glass of iced tea.

"Your work has been sensational. I've heard the comments. You wrote about the Statehouse like it was the Führer's inner circle." I smiled. "You should be writing literature."

"I am," said Walter emphatically. "That's what good journalism is. As I keep trying to tell you. Liz Taylor's pet turtle escaping the pool house is not."

"And James St. Clair is?" I bit into a piece of bread. "They'll never let me."

"You haven't exactly tried. At least that I'm aware of."

I raised my napkin to my mouth. "I can't. I only got curious because of—the circumstances. I'm in no position to write stories."

"No one is. From what I hear, they've thrown a blanket over the investigation. They're either onto something or they're trying to hide their own incompetence." Walter pushed his plate aside and shook a Camel out of the pack. "Jeez, it's great to be back at the Pantry."

We had come here because it didn't serve liquor. Apparently Walter had yet to go to Musso and Frank's, his former stomping ground.

"You haven't finished your story," I prompted.

"They told me I could pick up a family at the boat and travel with them back to L.A. I said hell, no."

"It's hard for me to understand, frankly."

"Is it?" Walter blew a smoke ring and watched it drift over the crowd at the communal table. We had a table for two just behind it. In Walter's silence, I lit my own cigarette.

"It's like a little black box that's been sitting around," Walter said. "It's an eyesore and it's beginning to stink up the joint. But you can't bring yourself to open it up, clean it out. So you tiptoe around it—maybe tomorrow."

"Obviously tomorrow came."

"As it does," Walter said, "about once a day."

"You're driving me crazy. Just tell me."

"I'm trying to." Walter sounded testy. He puffed on

his cigarette, then mashed it in the ashtray. "There's a guy called Joe Barney. Real sweet fellow. He'd been a welder up in Sacramento. Came back from the Philippines with a wooden leg. And third-degree burns. His face is a road map of scar tissue. Nobody'll give him work. They say he can't do the physical stuff and they won't give him a desk job because he might scare the nice customers away. I met him at a jazz joint. Kid named Ray Charles sings, plays the piano there. Blind guy. Sometimes, when they're short-handed, they let Joey wash dishes. He put me onto iced tea with sugar. I used to help him out."

"The blind leading the blind?"

"No, not Joey. The singer. Ray Charles."

"Sorry."

"Yeah." Walter tore a strip off his paper placemat. "So what happened to the contracts guy? You shake him down yet?"

I nodded. I could see Walter was fidgety, the way he was shredding the placemat. "I wouldn't mind some fresh air," I offered.

Walter grinned. "You're looking good, kid. Did I tell you? You're really looking good."

We skirted the line, which stubbornly remained half a block long. I fell into step with Walter. "Joe Barney, poor fellow. Tell me more."

"Yeah."

We walked along in silence, crossing Figueroa and wandering past a tattoo joint that was shuttered. Walter had two. The Marine insignia on his left bicep, the word MOTHER on his right.

"I told him," Walter said suddenly.

"About not wanting to write the stories?"

"Yeah."

"The smelly black box?"

"We're at the jazz joint, 2 A.M., and Joey goes berserk. Sweetest guy in the world, suddenly he's screaming at me like a lunatic. Saying whatsa matter with me? I come home, all parts working. I can earn a living, have a family, a real nice life. And I say yeah, writing about the guys who came back with no parts working."

"That's good, Walter."

"Joey keeps ranting like he's Richard the Third. He says, 'Listen, pops. You already done the hard work. You done the war and now you've shaken the booze. And still you won't stop feeling sorry for yourself.'" Walter paused. "Do you think I've been feeling sorry for myself?"

I didn't answer.

"Then Joey says—I'll never forget this. He says, 'You think you're helping me out, getting me little jobs, having me run errands for you, buying me dinner. But what you're really doing is making me feel like a handout case.' Do you believe that, Paris?"

"Well—"

"Joey says, 'You really want to do something grand for me, Walter, write that story. Wrench it outta your gut. Write that story about this family, four kids, no father. Then you go back to the paper and give 'em hell.'"

"Joey said that, huh?"

"Yeah. Said *then* I'd be doing him some good. Making him see it's okay to dream."

I slipped my arm through Walter's. "So you're back now?"

"They said I could work on the copy desk."

"That's not fair. You should . . ."

"I figure I'll give 'em a month. Then I say, gimme my beat back. They say no, I'll go over to the *Times* maybe." Walter turned his face and grinned at me. "You like that?"

"Don't you dare. You can't go to the *Times.*"

"Problems?"

"The Chandlers are trying to sell the house from under me, if you call that a problem."

"*I* don't," sang Walter happily. "You should sell it. Collect some money, go buy yourself a place in a respectable neighborhood."

I smiled. To Walter, Beverly Hills was a town for unregenerate phonies married to materialistic reprobates. He said he felt compelled to wear a tie, just to drive in. "So where are you living these days; no—let me guess. Some turn-of-the-slum, dollar-a-night hotel. Right?"

"Next door," Walter said. "The YMCA."

"Well that won't do. Come stay with me. I have a guest room."

Walter stopped short and just looked at me.

"You could think about it."

"I could, huh?"

"You could."

"Great," said Walter. "I survive Bataan. I survive the Japs. I survive that goddammed hellhole in the desert where guys who think they're Sigmund Freud tell you you only want a drink *in your mind*. All so I can end up in —*Beverly Hills*?"

Suddenly Walter began to laugh. The laughing grew convulsive. Walter Ainsley stood under a street lamp and laughed until he cried.

29

I made a cup of tea and carried it into the study. Mrs. Keyes, typically, had gone off with her sister for the weekend, leaving me the run of the house. It was a toss-up which one of us looked forward to her departures more.

I twisted the radio dial until I caught the strains of "Rhapsody in Blue," then I settled behind the leather-topped desk with Al Aubrey-Brown's address book, and a fresh reporter's notebook. I flipped immediately to the Ws. Walken Realty was listed along with a phone number. Under it, was R. Walken, followed by a different number. After that came a Walker and a Wilson.

I checked my watch. Nearly nine. I lit a cigarette, thinking. After a while, I went out to the center hall and dialed the phone on the table by the stairs. A woman picked up on the fourth ring.

"Hello?" Her voice was cobwebby, as if she had climbed out of a hole to answer the phone.

I said, "Angela Walken, please."

"This is her."

I hesitated, not having expected this. I was certain Angela Walken didn't exist. "You don't know me," I improvised. "But I've been looking at houses and I happened to notice the Perrys' on my rounds. I learned you were the seller. And I wondered if you could refer me to the people you used for the fabulous renovation."

"No, I can't," said Angela Walken. "You'll have to speak to Richard. Richard can tell you all that. Except he's not here."

"Richard," I said. "That's your husband?"

"Oh no. My husband passed away. Richard's my son. Maybe I should find a pencil and paper and take down your name. Surely, he'll call you back."

"And he would know about moving a house and renovating it?"

"Oh my yes. Richard does it all the time. I'll have to go to the kitchen to find a pencil."

"Don't bother, Mrs. Walken. I'll call again tomorrow. I'm sorry if I disturbed you. It's just that Mr. Smith at the real estate office looked up the Perrys' contract and told me you were the seller. So I thought . . ."

"You'll have to talk to Richard. He knows his business real good. He's adding a new room onto this house for me to do my sewing in. Maybe he'll let you come over, take a peek."

"That would be great. Well, look, thanks again."

Just before I hung up, I heard an explosion of sharp, loud barks. The dog, Jessie. I put down the receiver and went back to the pilfered address book.

Several dozen people had already collected on the sidewalk outside Esther Lubinow's house when Andrew pulled up shortly before ten. Most of the men were wearing white shirts and ties, and some had on hats. The women wore suits or dresses and tried to keep track of their children. Parked at the curb was a red pickup truck containing a noisy family in jeans and straw hats. Slowly I got out of the Bentley. I sighed and nudged my way up the steps to the wooden veranda.

A large white sign had been hammered onto the house to the left of the screen door. In big black letters it proclaimed: FOR SALE. TO BE MOVED. INQUIRE RIGHT-OF-WAY DEPARTMENT, DIVISION OF HIGHWAYS, STATE OF CALIFORNIA." An address and phone number followed.

I rang the bell.

A man immediately intercepted me. "Can't go in yet, miss. Not until ten."

"I'm a friend," I said, "not a bidder."

I rang the bell again and called, "Esther?"

The door swung back. "Oh, Paris. Come in."

Esther was wearing a red plaid shirt and jeans; her hair was in braids. She stepped back and quickly shut the door. "Don't you think this is undignified? I feel like a dead horse with buzzards circling overhead."

I took her hand. "In a couple of weeks, you'll have forgotten all about it. Is there something I can do?"

"Esther! Who's out there?"

I followed Esther into the living room, which had now fallen into a new state of disarray. Cardboard boxes were stacked against one wall, furniture was heaped everywhere else. A narrow path had been carved out to allow passage to the kitchen.

"Mama? This is my friend, Paris Chandler."

A stout, buxom woman in a shapeless black dress stood frowning in the door frame. Her coarse gray hair was pulled back in a severe knot, setting off a pasty, bulldoggish face: all jowls. Her eyes saw only herself. "I can't find my handkerchief," Mrs. Lubinow snapped. "Stop dillydallying and help me find it."

"Paris has come to be with us," Esther said cheerfully. "Isn't that nice?"

"Tell her to come back another time." Mrs. Lubinow turned on her heel and marched back into the kitchen.

Esther sighed. "I'm trying to take her out for a ride. It makes Mama cranky to go somewhere."

I suspected Mrs. Lubinow was always a crank. "Is there some way I can help?"

"The only thing I can think of, could you keep an eye on the place when the people come in?" Esther glanced skeptically at the pile of furniture. "Not that anything is worth stealing."

"I'd be happy to. Go get your mom and leave right now. You'll both feel better when you get on the road."

Esther trooped into the kitchen and emerged a few minutes later with a recalcitrant Mrs. Lubinow. The doorbell rang.

"I'll get it." I walked through the living room and opened the front door.

A pale man in a black suit tipped his hat. "How do you do? I'm Mr. Otto from the Division of Highways." He looked like an undertaker, which he was. For dead houses. He smiled quickly. "Shall we begin?"

The only place I could find with enough room to stand was the kitchen. I took up my position and watched the people troop in.

They were, on the whole, a respectful lot. The men, silent and appraising, merely stood in the doorway, nodding. Their wives, pushing in past them, spoke excitedly of the kitchen's possibilities.

"Harry, we'll have to get a new oven, I can see that. And—oh goodness—is that an icebox? Excuse me, miss, is that an icebox? Can I look?"

I smiled and said sure, go ahead.

"I didn't know they even had ice deliveries anymore, Harry, we'll have to get one of those new Frigidaires they have now, the ones with the separate freezer compartment."

"Oh, look, Arthur. Look at all the cabinets!"

"Yellow wallpaper, George, don't you think?"

"Jeremy, do you suppose we could add a pantry onto the kitchen? I really would like the extra space."

Eventually, I moved some pots off the one chair at the kitchen table and sat down. I was lighting a cigarette when Richard Walken strode in.

"Excuse me. I was looking for Miss Lubinow."

We had only met for a few minutes and he obviously didn't recognize me. Also, I was wearing a gray floppy brimmed hat and had tucked my hair underneath it. Take away a good view of my eyes—and no hair—and I became, past experience had taught me, a blank page. "I'm sorry," I said. "Who?"

Richard Walken looked at me for a long moment. Then he shook his head and walked out.

I puffed on my cigarette. A pregnant woman wearing a billowing yellow cotton dress stuck her head in. "Hi," she said shyly. "I—"

Her dark hair was pulled back in a ponytail, her face drained of color.

I stood up. "Are you all right?"

"I'm a bit dizzy. I was looking for somewhere to sit down."

"Please, sit here. Let me get you a glass of water."

Gratefully, she sat on the chair, while I scrounged through the nearly empty cabinets. Finally I found a coffee cup. I filled it with water from the sink and carried it over to her.

"Thank you. All of a sudden I felt faint."

"Perhaps it's so many people, all crowded together," I commiserated. "It's a bit warm for this time of year. Better?"

"I think so." She put the cup down and studied my face. "That man you were talking to. Do you know him?"

"The man who was just in here? Why no. He was looking for somebody."

"Oh."

"Why do you ask?"

She smiled and shook her head. "Just curious. I've seen him before."

"Really?"   ·

Now that her color was coming back, I noticed a light sprinkling of pale freckles across her nose and cheeks. Her heaviness made her look older at first glance. But now I could see she was quite young.

"My husband and I have gone to several of these auctions. I think it's crazy, buying a beat-up old house and moving it. I want something new, like they're building over in the Valley. But Leon says it would be fun to fix something up."

I rerouted her train of thought. "And you've seen that man at other auctions?"

"That's the thing. He always bids. Usually, a lot of people bid in the beginning. Then they begin to drop out. He'll stay in right to the end. Just him and another party. Then he quits."

"Maybe he gets cold feet. That happens sometimes."

"Maybe," said the woman. "But did you look at him? I mean he looks kind of fancy compared to the others. You'd think he could go another five hundred or so."

"Yes you would." I hesitated. "You don't think he's somehow driving the price up? Why would he do that?"

"I was thinking maybe he wants to make sure his friend wins."

"But his friend could just keep bidding, he wouldn't need that man's help."

She smiled suddenly. "You're right. Well look. I'd better be finding Leon. Who knows? Maybe today will be our lucky day."

Her bright smile masked the sarcasm in her voice. I wished her well and watched her go out.

"All right, folks, let me tell you what's going to happen."

Mr. Otto paused, waiting for the crowd to give him its full attention. He was standing on the front porch. Gathered on the Lubinows' bit of lawn and spilling onto the sidewalk, were maybe forty people. Roughly eighteen were men. I was standing at the back of the crowd, around the side of the house.

"Bidding will start at one thousand dollars. We'll move up in increments of one hundred dollars. Whoever comes in with the highest bid must be prepared to pay ten percent on the spot. You will then have ten days to come up with the rest, or get a mortgage. You have thirty days after that to move the house out. Now. You've seen the house and it's a good one, let me tell you. And the beauty here, it comes with no tenants. So you won't have to spend the fifty bucks to relocate each party. We, at the Division of Highways, are set up to help you in any way possible. We can recommend movers. If you haven't found a place to relocate to, we have people who can advise you of available land. Please keep that in mind when you are bidding. You must be able to purchase a lot in addition to covering the moving costs. Now." Mr. Otto's practiced eyes scanned the crowd. "Any questions, folks?"

"Boy, this is weird," Andrew whispered.

"How much will it cost to move the house?"

"Usually not more than two, three hundred bucks," replied Mr. Otto. "Depending."

"I mean really weird," Andrew emphasized.

"Hush," I said. "And keep your eyes open for Al Brown."

"I'll circulate," said Andrew importantly. He drifted off.

Just as the bidding began.

I doubted the auction would take long. The price the state had paid for the Lubinow house—$2,250—was prominently posted and the state was not allowed by law to make a profit. If the bidding reached the selling price, and two or more interested parties remained, the auction entered its second phase: The parties wrote their names on pieces of paper and the winner was drawn from a hat.

"Fifteen hunnert . . . do I hear sixteen?"

"Sixteen!" shouted the man who had brought his family on the flatbed truck.

"Seventeen," uttered a curly haired man in a plaid jacket. "Ralph!" hissed his wife. "Don't."

"Seventeen. Do I hear . . . eighteen?" A momentary hush fell over the crowd. Richard Walken, who had been leaning against a car parked on the street, straightened and stepped forward.

"Eighteen," he declared.

All heads swiveled, taking in this turn of events. As my

eyes followed the crowd's, I noticed a slick-looking man in a dark suit, wiping his face with a handkerchief. Carefully, he folded the white cotton square and slipped it into his jacket pocket. Perhaps sensing he was being stared at, he turned his head and glanced at me. Quickly I looked away. I had seen him somewhere before, but— where? My eyes went back to Mr. Otto on the front porch. Below him, to the right, the pregnant woman was clasping her husband's arm. I saw her give him a worried look. He straightened his shoulders. "Nineteen!"

The man in the plaid jacket seemed to be holding back. The man with the family raised his hand tentatively. "Two thousand."

Richard Walken came forward a couple of steps. But he said nothing.

"Two thousand . . . do I hear twenty-one hunnert?"

Someone touched my elbow. "Paris Chandler?"

I hadn't noticed him before, a young man, neatly dressed, V-neck sweater and beige pleated pants. Dark hair, mustache, nice white teeth.

"Yes?"

"There's a phone call for you. I was in the kitchen getting a drink of water, and the phone rang. A woman asked for you."

"Oh."

"You can use the kitchen door around the side of the house," the man said. "You won't have to interrupt the auction."

"Thank you."

"Twenty-one," sang out the man in the plaid jacket.

I walked around the side of the house, across the small backyard and entered the kitchen. The phone was sitting on a carton beside the back door. The receiver was off the hook.

"Hello?" I said. "Esther?"

But it wasn't Esther Lubinow. It was the dial tone buzzing in my ear. I pushed the disconnect. "Hello?"

It happened faster than my brain could register. The receiver was wrenched from my hand and clattered to the floor. From behind, someone grabbed my arms and yanked them back. I started to struggle and scream at the same time, but the scream never came, dislodged in my throat by a gasp as my arms were jerked harder, sending a shot of pain through my bruised rib.

A hand clapped itself over my mouth. "Don't," a voice warned.

There had to be two.

Something rough, a piece of cloth, came down over my head, drawn tight across my eyes. They were trying to pull my hat off, but it was pinned and wouldn't budge. The rough cloth was knotted behind my head, below the hat.

"Get that dish towel," the same voice said. I heard a ripping sound. A moment later, a strip of cloth was tied around my mouth.

"Let's get outta here."

At that precise moment, as I was being muscled out the door, a loud cheer went up from the front lawn, as if the crowd had come to applaud my abduction. I liked the timing of it. If the cheering meant the auction was over, the crowd would be breaking up, and someone might see me.

Dragging my feet, not helping at all, I was shoved and yanked across grass . . . behind the house perhaps, to the side . . . I didn't know where. Pain shot through my sore rib with every step. They had me by both arms, big men, taller than me, one on either side—two goons making a Paris Chandler sandwich.

My shoes scraped pavement, just as the one on my left let go. He must have stepped forward to open a car door, for the one on my right said, "Watch your head," and pushed me in.

The same man slid onto the seat beside me. The backseat.

There was a lot of room, maybe a Cadillac or a Lincoln. The engine turned over. A metallic noise, the driver shifting into gear. We began to move.

I could not see or speak. But my hands were free. I felt for the armrest on the door and grabbed hold of it. Neither man spoke. I had no idea the streets we were driv-

ing, and couldn't even guess, since I didn't know Silver
Lake at all. Andrew would wonder what had happened
to me, but what could he possibly do? "Oh, I suppose
Miss Chandler's been abducted, oh well."

Somewhere along the way, a ghoulish thought poked
through. This had to be about freeways. And freeways
meant big construction equipment. They could do away
with me, gangster-style. Bury me under some godforsaken stretch of road, blanket my grave with concrete.
My spirits sank, along with a mental picture of my
corpse. I was scared.

Suddenly, a voice cut into my gloom. *"This is the Reverend Tilden O'Toole, my friends, your shepherd through
the Kingdom of the Lord, beseeching you, begging you,
praying that you, yes you, all of you! will lend me your ear
and allow me to guide you down the path of righteous glory.
Now you ask yourselves, who is he? Who is this man before
me, who believes he knows the Way? And you are right. I
am only the Lord's humble servant. I know wherein lies
goodness and strength of character, and I can lead you
there, yes I can! But first, I want you to hear from a young
lady, a lady with a cross too big for any soul to bear, and
she will tell you how she found the Lord, just when she had
no earthly reason to believe any more. Sister Arlene, where
are you, sister? Come . . ."*

The car stopped.

The driver got out and slammed the door. The man
beside me didn't move. But I could hear him breathing. I
could hear him breathing, I realized, because of the
deathly silence that enveloped the car. Wherever they
had taken me, not even the sound of traffic intruded. A
stretch of new freeway; my burial ground.

The door opened. Grabbed by the arm, I was pulled
out of the car. The grabber ushered me onto a hard
surface. "You have three steps now, miss." His voice,
which I hadn't heard before, was pleasant. My right shoe
bumped a stair. I lifted my foot and ascended the steps.
A few more feet and I was inside—somewhere. Wooden
floorboards creaked, then gave way to carpeting. The

man leading me stopped and backed me up. My legs brushed against a chair. I was told to sit down. I sat.

It was a deep, cushiony armchair, with a tall back. I laid my head against it gratefully and tried to slow my breathing. I could hear retreating footsteps on the wooden floorboards and a door softly closing. The sickly sweet smell of dying flowers permeated the room.

"Miss Chandler."

I flinched. I had not been aware of anyone else present. The voice was low and had a hard New York edge to it. It seemed to be coming from a spot directly in front of me.

"You won't be able to speak," the voice continued, "but when I ask you a question, you will nod or shake your head. Got it? You're going to cooperate with us. Fully."

The man fell silent then. And once again I was aware of the ghostly stillness of the place. I had no idea how long we had driven, or how far.

"We could kill you, that's one option. What we'd do is . . ."

But the man did not continue. Verbal torture, was that it? I began counting in my head. At least two minutes went by.

"We would make it look like a terrible accident. The police are easy to fool." I heard a chuckle. "Clever of you to cozy up to Gladstone, Miss Chandler. That's when I realized you would have to be handled, uh, carefully."

I hadn't cozied up to Gladstone. Nonetheless, how could he have known that the police chief and I had chatted? Who *was* this man?

I crossed my legs.

"You were at St. Clair's house the night he was iced. You're the blonde everyone's looking for. Whether you've spilled this to Gladstone, I wouldn't know. But I do know that whatever you told him, certain pieces of evidence can suddenly turn up that will finger you, beyond a doubt, as the murderer. Got that?"

I was so captivated by his words that it took me a

moment to realize this was a place in the script designed for me to nod. I nodded.

"Good."

More silence. I folded my hands in my lap.

"So you see," the voice said eventually, "whether we arrange for a tragic accident or frame you, the problem of you has been solved."

The problem of me? If I hadn't had the gag on, I would have volunteered to rewrite this scene. No actor could possibly agree to talk like that.

"So this is the deal, Miss Chandler. You will keep your nose out of affairs that don't concern you. That includes anything to do with St. Clair's death or any stories he was investigating. St. Clair made a mistake and he paid for it. You make a mistake, you will, too. Got that?"

This time I took my cue like a pro. I nodded.

The man did not respond. The silence went on so long, I began to wonder if he had left the room. I heard a click, then caught the scent of cigarette smoke. I believe he smoked the whole cigarette before he continued.

"Not only will you instantly forget you ever knew St. Clair, you will not tell anybody about today. Do you understand *that*?"

A harsh note had crept into his voice. I nodded.

"Furthermore, Miss Chandler, you will do whatever you must to get that gawky private eye pal of yours to get lost. She keeps snooping, you won't have a pal anymore. Got that?"

I sighed inwardly. And nodded.

"And finally, if you make the mistake of trying to prove what a cute little cookie you are, you may also be minus a chauffeur. We'll rub out anybody we have to, any way we have to. And we can. You see how easily we got hold of you today. You are a sitting duck, sweetheart, and there ain't nobody, believe me, can stand in our way. Not even the cops."

Not even the cops? Is that why nothing seemed to be happening in Jim's murder investigation? Had the police been somehow bought off? What on earth had Jim tumbled to?

The man said, "The boys will drop you off now. You will forget you ever were here. You will not keep looking for St. Clair's killer. You will have no more interest in the freeways than the average citizen. Got that? The murder will be forgotten, the freeways will be built. And someday when you try telling someone about this long ago chapter in your life, everybody will think you're nuts. Are we agreed now on all of this?"

I nodded until I realized I had nodded too long. Then I stood up. I understood, yes. He could now let me go. If he really intended to.

I heard the door opening behind me and footsteps on the floorboards. A hand took my arm. As I turned and was led away, the voice trailed me.

"We'll be in touch, Miss Chandler. Bye-bye!"

Again I was shoved into the backseat. The engine came to life and off we went. The radio was still carrying the incantations of the Reverend O'Toole. From time to time I caught the sound of a car passing.

Eventually, we bumped onto gravel and stopped.

"End of the line, lady," the driver's voice said. "After we pull away, you count to a hundred, slow as you can, before you take the blindfold off."

I opened the door and stepped carefully out of the car and onto the gravel. Just before the door slammed after me, the radio sobbed, *"Yes, my lambs. Everybody on your feet! Hallelujah! Glory be! Follow me!"*

The sound of the engine faded into the distance. I counted to one hundred as slowly as I could. Then I untied the blindfold and removed the gag.

I was standing beside an empty stretch of road, surrounded by orange groves as far as I could see. The silence, and the smell of the fruit, rose up around me.

Resignedly, I stepped out onto the road.

Waiting to hitch a ride.

30

◆

"Listen," Roxy barked into the telephone, "you've got to get to Cary Grant right away. This item is *top priority.*"

"You'd think Etta would snare him herself," I belligerently told Etta's overly protective, mean-spirited secretary. "If this item is *so* top priority."

"Etta's got to get ready for her radio show. You know that. Just be at the Brown Derby at six o'clock. Cary always eats dinner at the Brown Derby on Sundays at six o'clock."

A grim silence followed, as each of us hastily plotted our next tactical maneuver. "It's not like I'm supposed to do your job *for* you," Roxy volleyed first.

I balanced the phone between my chin and my shoulder and pulled out my hat pin. Then I removed my hat. It was three-thirty. It had taken two rides—one in the back of a truck with five raggedy migrant orange-pickers and a second, stuffed between three squabbling children in the sticky backseat of a De Soto, to get to the *Examiner.* Etta's column was due at five-thirty and Roxy had left three panicked messages, the first one called in at noon.

I gazed at my wrinkled cotton dress. "Well look," I said. "I'll think of something."

"Get there early," Roxy coaxed. "Tell them you need to be a waitress."

"Right."

"Etta had a legman who did that once. He spilled soup on Alfred Hitchcock. Then he took him into the men's room to clean him up and he got the scoop."

"On Alfred Hitchcock."

"It was something, kiddo."

"Fine. I'll dress up like a waiter, drag Cary Grant into the men's room and get the scoop. Shall we have a photographer hiding in one of the stalls?"

Roxy hung up.

I had spotted Walter in the newsroom when I came in, and I was anxious to speak to him. But I suddenly remembered Andrew. I dialed my house, trying to picture what he might have done about the missing me. He answered on the first ring.

"Hi," I said.

There was an audible gasp. "Miss Chandler? Wow, it's Miss Chandler! Are you all right?"

"I'm fine. I'm sorry . . ."

"She says she's fine!"

"Calm down. I'm at the office and . . ."

"No, she's at the office!"

"Andrew," I said exasperatedly, "who are you talking to?"

"The police. All the police are here. They just put out an APB. That's an all-points bulletin."

"I know what it is." I hesitated. "You called the police?"

"And they came right away. Two squad cars and Chief Gladstone. But he left. They're going to get a dog to sniff your clothes."

"Yuk. Tell them to go home. And I'll need you about five-fifteen. Okay?"

"But where were you, Miss Chandler? Were you kid-

napped? I half-thought this call would be Sydney Greenstreet demanding a ransom."

"You've been watching too many gangster movies, I'm
afraid."

There was a moment of indecision. As if—hope
against fading hope—the voice of a gangster might still
break onto the line. The hope faded.

"Just when it was getting good," Andrew sighed.

A little past six, I was led to a table near the front of the
restaurant, next to the row of circular booths so coveted
by the big shots—and deposited. A napkin was placed
across my lap. The maître d' vanished and, a moment
later, a waiter appeared. "May I bring you a drink while
you're waiting, miss?"

"A Perfect Manhattan, please. Thank you."

I was facing the back of the restaurant. To my right
was a booth. In the booth was Cary Grant, seated with
Randolph Scott. You had to hand it to Roxy. Camped
out in the Bentley, I had observed Grant arriving precisely at six o'clock.

The waiter delivered my drink. I opened my purse and
removed my cigarettes. I laid the pack on the table and
began to fish for my matches. After a while I closed my
purse and leaned slightly toward Grant. He was wearing
an elegant navy suit, crisp white shirt and a navy and red
striped tie. He turned his head.

I smiled. "Forgive me. But do you have a light?"

"Forgive you?" he said sternly. "Whatever have you
done?"

"Oh I mustn't ruin your dinner by telling you. It's . . .
shocking."

With long tapered fingers, Grant picked up a gold
lighter off the table and leaned toward me. "But if you
don't tell me," he said genially, flicking the lighter, "you
won't be able to enjoy yourself. Will she, Scotty?"

Randolph Scott looked bored. "I dare say."

"See?" said Grant. "It's unanimous." He smiled
charmingly.

I began to melt. There was something about movie stars—what, I didn't know—but somehow they always looked even better in person. This one looked criminally better. I leaned away and exhaled. "Perhaps later. It shall take me a while to compose myself."

Grant laughed. "Well whoever the fellow is who is keeping you waiting should be shot. I'd be more than happy to oblige when he comes in."

I managed to look horrified. "Oh you mustn't do that. He's all I have, really."

"Ah. Well I think he's just arrived."

I looked up. Walter, who had crossly acceded to wearing a tie—carelessly knotted and tucked inside his safari jacket—stood at the chair opposite. "Sorry, I'm late, sweetheart. Couldn't find this joint." He sat down.

"It's all right," I murmured. "I didn't wait long."

"Long enough to order yourself some booze, I see."

"Just one." I hesitated. "Are you hungry?"

"I'm fine. So. What did you do all day? Laze around, listen to the radio probably."

I smiled. "It's Sunday, darling. But actually, I helped my friend Esther move."

Walter grunted.

I put out my cigarette. I gathered, from the words floating over from the booth, that Grant was encouraging Scott to take a role in a new Western. "I have to decide what to do about Theodora," I said. "By the way, do you know where she is?"

I had phoned Tee from the *Examiner* twice. She wasn't home, and the answering service lady who picked up her calls on the office number was not one of the more helpful ones.

"No idea." Walter signaled a passing waiter.

The Brown Derby was filling up. It was one of the few restaurants that did a good Sunday night business. Most people either ate at home or in someone else's. "I'm not quite sure how to handle the situation," I continued.

The waiter arrived carrying two menus. "Sorry to keep you waiting, sir. Would you care to order a drink?"

"No," said Walter flatly. "And she won't be having

another." His voice carried. I sensed Grant glancing over.

"I'll bring the water and the rolls right away," the waiter said cheerfully.

Walter glanced at his menu. "Frankly, I don't know what you see in her. Nobody needs a friend like that." He lit a Camel.

"But she's a wonderful friend," I protested. "I wish you would get to know her better."

Walter gave me a disparaging look. "Undoubtedly, I will."

"Now, sir. Have you decided?"

"Yeah. Steak, medium rare. Baked potato. Salad, french dressing."

"And the lady?"

"She'll have the same," Walter stated.

"Actually, I was thinking of having . . ."

The waiter looked at me in confusion.

"That will be all," Walter declared. The waiter bowed his head and departed.

"I was thinking the baked chicken might be nice for a change," I said unhappily. "It's awfully good here, darling."

"Takes too long, the chicken." Walter grinned nastily. "And I, sweetheart, have other plans for the evening."

"Walter, please."

"What's wrong with that? We're going to be married, aren't we?"

"Yes, but— When? Why can't we set a date?"

"Do we have to go through that *again*? Sometimes I think you have no brains."

I gulped. "But it's been eight months."

"And I told you. A divorce takes a year. That leaves four months to go, *if* you can subtract."

"But we could at least set a date, couldn't we? Mama . . ."

"I don't want to hear about Mama. Now cut it out."

We fell silent. And I realized that Grant and Scott had also grown quiet. They were concentrating on eating and —the entertainment coming from the next table.

"I can't say I'm crazy about that hat," Walter said. "It reminds me of one my maiden aunt used to wear."

"It's brand new from Paris. A Lilly Daché."

"Ha! Someone sold you a bill of goods. Hat was probably made in Brooklyn."

I said nothing as the waiter served our salads. I picked at mine. I hate french dressing.

"I suppose you had a bad day," I said eventually.

Walter laughed harshly. "I guess you could say that."

"Really bad?"

"I was doing great till the seventh race. Then I blew it all on a favorite called Dillinger's Deal. So I borrowed a C-note from Louie the Nose and blew that, too."

I put down my fork. "You borrowed a hundred dollars, and lost it?"

"Eat your salad, doll baby. It's no big deal."

"But where are you going to get a hundred dollars? And—"

"How am I going to pay for this feast?" Walter grinned. "That's what I've got you for."

Walter plunged his fork into his salad. I just stared at him.

"Aw, stop looking at me like that and eat your salad. You know I'll pay you back."

"That's not the point."

"Oh? What's the point? Which, I'm sure, you're about to bring up."

I leaned across the table and whispered, "I've really had enough."

Walter slouched back in his chair. "I'm a little tired of taking orders from you, you know that? You don't want to pay for dinner, fine. *Waiter!*"

Walter's voice boomed across the restaurant in sonic waves, jolting dozens of eardrums. I sank lower in my chair. Hurriedly, as if spotting a flame and hoping to put it out before it could engulf the place, our waiter dashed over.

"Cancel our dinners," Walter commanded. "Then bring the lady the check. You can handle that, can't you, doll?"

With Grant and Scott openly staring, Walter stood up, threw his napkin on the table and walked out. I sat there frozen, eyes downcast, desperately hoping that nobody in the restaurant knew me.

"Uh, miss?"

Slowly I raised my chin. "I'm terribly sorry," said the waiter. He was holding the check awkwardly. "Is there anything I can do?"

I smiled meekly. "No, thank you. Just the check . . . well, actually." I hesitated. "You could bring me another Perfect Manhattan."

"Of course, miss. Right away."

A busboy whisked away Walter's plates and silver, a magician trying to make a bad scene disappear. I told him to take my salad. When my drink arrived, I sipped it slowly. Then I slid a cigarette from my pack.

"You see, Scotty, I *am* losing my timing," Cary Grant said. "I promised to shoot the blackguard on sight and here I missed my cue entirely." The lighter clicked. "May I?"

I partially turned toward Grant but did not look at him directly. "Thank you."

"I was eavesdropping of course."

"Oh."

"I sympathize with your friend," Grant said. "I bet on Dillinger's Deal myself."

That won him a direct look from the obviously distressed young lady. He grinned. "I couldn't resist the name."

"You mean—you bet on him because you liked his name?"

"Well," said Grant, "I did the usual homework. I saw that he had a beginning and an end and four legs in between."

I smiled. And inwardly admired his grace. By turning my bone of contention with Walter into a joke on himself, he had expertly defused the entire appalling scene. "I hope I haven't ruined your dinner, Mr. Grant."

"Not at all. Now, Scotty, which one of us is going to

drive this lady . . . oh. Sorry. This is Randolph Scott, Miss—?"

"Paris Chandler. And you mustn't worry about me. I'll call a cab."

"You'll do nothing of the sort. Where do you live?"

"Maple Drive."

"Then I win," said Grant agreeably. "Scotty's driving to the beach and I'm going not far from you. Shall we?"

The check had not come back. Two salads and two drinks. I left a generous five on the table and—amid a restaurant full of stares—exited. At the curb, Grant said good night to Scott and ushered me into his white Cadillac, which an attentive valet had instantly produced. Parked across the street, in the shadows, was the Bentley containing Andrew.

"I can't imagine why a beautiful girl like you would put up with that kind of behavior," Grant commented, easing into traffic. When I didn't reply, he added, "But then, I'm not one to talk. I'm not sure where I fare worse. The racetrack or the altar."

"A metaphor?" I said.

"Perhaps."

"Is there no one in your life now?"

"No one I intend to marry."

"I heard that you are no longer seeing Miss Hensel."

"That's true." Grant gave me a sharp look. "What else have you heard?"

"You—you are always the subject of so many rumors."

"Yes. Every leading lady and—well, the makeup ladies too!"

I laughed. "Exciting life you lead."

"Why if I had a dollar for every rumor, do you know how rich I would be?"

"Fort Knox?"

"Or Fort Cary Grant. Now, listen, young lady. Are you going to be all right? I mean, he won't come pestering you, will he?"

"No, no. Anyway, by now my housekeeper will be back. She terrorizes Walter."

At Sunset and Maple, he turned left and I directed

him down the street to my house. Which was dark. "Oh dear, she's not back. What time is it?"

"Nearly eight."

"That woman . . . She's supposed to be back by five o'clock. But she never is."

Grant pulled into my dark driveway. "Then you must fire her," he declared, braking at my front door.

"Fire her? Oh I couldn't do that."

"Why not? She's being paid to serve you. If she isn't carrying out her duties, you must find someone else."

"I don't think I could fire her."

"Of course you can. I fired my housekeeper just the other day. Same thing."

"You did? What had she done?"

"Among other things, stole my canceled checks and sold them to autograph hunters. And several times when I was away, she let strangers in to have a look around."

"I'm shocked."

"Well don't be. It's rare to find help you can trust anymore."

"So now I suppose you have to find someone." I grinned. "My housekeeper's name is Willa Keyes. If I fire her, you'll know not to take her on."

"Actually, I've already got someone. I made sure before I fired the one I had. Now I'll wait here until you're safely inside."

"Thank you so much, Mr. Grant. You've been very kind."

I drank in that final woman-slaying smile, hesitating a moment too long, I suppose, before I remembered to reach for the door handle.

"Best of luck, Miss Paris Chandler," he called after me.

"You, too." Gently I closed the car door and floated up the front steps, fumbling for my key.

Feeling heady and guilt-ridden. Objective accomplished.

31

◆

Walter and Mrs. Keyes were sitting at the kitchen table in the dark when I walked in. I switched on the light.

"Did he drive you home?" Walter asked eagerly.

"Of course."

"Cary Grant?" gasped Mrs. Keyes. "Oh my heart."

I smiled. "He was nice."

"So how'd I do? Pretty good, huh?"

"As usual, Walter, you were perfect."

"Yeah I should have been an actor, you think? Grant's nice looking. But Scott. He ain't got nothing on me." Walter fluttered his eyelashes.

"I'd better phone Roxy. Be right back."

I went into the center hall and dialed Etta Rice's number. "It's Paris," I said when Roxy answered.

"It's about time. Whaddya got?"

"Sorry it took so long. But we lingered in the driveway. I—"

"Who lingered?"

"Cary and I. He drove me home."

There was a heavy silence. "He *didn't*. I don't believe you."

"He did, too. Are you ready?" I cleared my throat. "Once again Cary Grant has broken off a relationship." I paused dramatically. "He's fired his housekeeper."

I found Walter in the study staring into the open liquor cabinet. "Mrs. Keyes is bringing in some sandwiches," I said. "Would you like a Coke?"

Slowly, Walter closed the cabinet. "Fine." He walked over to the couch and sat down.

"If you had been alone, would you have?"

Walter leaned forward, hunching his shoulders. "Nah." He stared at the floor. "I dunno. Maybe."

"I'm very proud of you, Walter."

He brightened. "Food, huh? Geez, I could eat a horse."

"You may. With Mrs. Keyes it's always a possibility."

As we gnawed through the suspiciously sinewy brisket sandwiches, I told him how I'd been forced into a car and driven, gagged and blindfolded—somewhere—and warned off. And then I told him how they had threatened Tee, too. I told him about Angela Walken, who was wrongfully cited as the seller of a property, and about Ursula Martens, who, as far as I could tell, was the last person to see James St. Clair alive. Barring the killer, unless it was her.

"You know that? You know she was there for certain?"

I nodded uneasily.

"You never told me this. How do you know?"

"It isn't important, Walter. Can we move on now?"

Walter watched me with those penetrating eyes of his. But after a moment, he realized I was not going to explain. "So what we've got," he continued, "is a bunch of people involved in freeway relocation who are dancing around the corpse. What we don't got, is the kingpin. The guy calling the shots."

"He could have been the man who threatened me to-day."

"And you couldn't find the place again?"

"Not the building, no."

"Maybe we'll set you up." Walter said it nonchalantly, the same way he might have said, "Maybe we'll run to the store." I started to open my mouth. But Walter had already moved on. "By the way, whatever happened to St. Clair's widow?"

"Good question."

"Could she have knocked off her old man? Find out if there was an insurance policy."

"Oh please, Walter. That's as old as the hills."

"Most motives are."

"If it was Mrs. St. Clair, then why are all these people pushing me around?"

Walter began scraping his teeth with a fingernail. The phone rang. I ignored it. Walter cocked an eyebrow. "It might be Cary Grant."

"Then we'll hear a big thud," I said, "when Mrs. Keyes faints." The phone continued to ring. "You haven't answered my question."

"Never underestimate greed," Walter said knowingly. "The dame's got a husband on the other coast, helping himself to a little on the side. She wants revenge. Money heals a lot of wounds." Walter paused and listened to the phone ring. "Five bucks it's Cary Grant."

The ringing stopped. A moment later Mrs. Keyes, looking quite cross, appeared in the doorway and announced, "It's Romeo."

"Ha," said Walter, "I told you."

I went out into the hall and picked up the receiver. I said, "Hi, Nick."

"So you survived the weekend without me."

I smiled. "Just barely. Tell me about Palm Springs."

I curled up on the stairs and listened to a rather drawn-out account of a hole-in-one missed at the seventeenth with none other than Walter Pidgeon looking on.

"An inch and a quarter? How do you know it was *exactly* an inch and a quarter? I mean . . ."

I looked up. Walter was standing at the front door. He doffed his hat and went out. "Uh, Nick? Can you hold . . ."

"You just know these things. Golf is a game of inches. For instance, on the second hole . . ."

I heard Walter's car cough and wheeze, followed by the gnashing of gears. I sighed inwardly and listened to Nick prattle on. At last, he wound down. "So anyway, will you have dinner with me tomorrow night?"

"Sure."

"How about Chasen's? I'll pick you up at seven."

"Great."

"I missed you, Paris."

"Yeah," I said, "I missed you, too."

Having worked the weekend, I was entitled to two days off. On Sunday, I had informed Roxy that I would be taking them the beginning of the week. I was exhausted. My rib was killing me. I needed the sleep. I awoke Monday morning at eleven feeling like a newer model. I rang Mrs. Keyes on the phone intercom and asked her to bring up my coffee. Then I dialed the paper.

"Morgue, please."

After a moment, the begrudging voice of Penelope Potts grumbled, "Liberry."

"Hi, Pen. It's Paris. How are you today?"

"You mean other than my bunions? Someone swiped my radio."

"Oh, I'm sorry." I hesitated, unsure how to continue.

"I think it was the new janitor, Harley."

"You do?"

"Got mad when I wouldn't take a drive with him."

"Harley, er, Harley's got a car?"

"A truck. That's what I mean. Chump thinks I'm going to take a spin in a truck? The front seat's all torn up besides. I told him a stroll through the garbage dump sounded better to me."

"Er . . ."

"But I'll fix him. See I know where he parks his truck.

So right before the end of his shift, I'm gonna go down and pour glue all over the front seat. It's the clear glue, takes a while to dry. Then when he . . ." Suddenly, there was a raucous barking. I finally realized it was Penelope laughing.

"Er, Pen? Could you do a small favor for me?"

"What?" she asked sharply, returning to her normal malevolent self.

"There's a man named Norman Wills who's a lawyer for the Division of Highways. He handles right-of-way contracts. I couldn't find anything on him in the files and I was wondering if you could check *Who's Who* or some other reference book we might have."

"You broke your leg?"

"I'm at home, Pen. And I need the information." I paused. "Please."

A new chorus of noises filtered through the line, which I interpreted as grumbling acquiescence. A loud bang followed, jolting my eardrum. I gathered she had dropped the receiver on her desk. Mrs. Keyes waltzed in and handed me a cup of coffee. I sipped it and waited.

Penelope came back on the wire all business. Wills was not listed in *Who's Who*, but a few lines about him appeared in something called *The City Directory of Public Officials*.

"Born in 1909, San Diego. San Diego State University. Law degree from UCLA. Married Lucille Brady, December 1939. One kid. Partner, Evans, Kramer, Wills and Hostetter. Chief lawyer, Right-of-Way Department, Los Angeles, January 1946–. Member of the ABA, the Elks, the Downtown Athletic Club and Conservatives for a Better America. That's a political action group that's an offshoot of the Birch Society. You want anything more, try the Division of Highways."

Penelope hung up.

I considered calling the Division of Highways, but the information in the *City Directory* must have come from there. I debated trying to locate the former law firm partner who had not been killed in the war. But I needed to know about Wills in the here and now, not the then and there.

I put down the coffee and dialed his wife.

"You're sure it was the pregnant people?"

I spoke to the back of Andrew's head as we scooted along Franklin, heading east.

"I already said so, Miss Chandler. I think you're just trying to avoid the subject." He cast me an evil eye in the rearview mirror.

I sighed. "The subject. All right, let's hear it. What have you cooked up?"

"His name is Jackson and I've told him all about you. He's very reliable. He used to drive for one of the Marx Brothers."

"Which one?" I asked suspiciously.

"I'm not sure. But he's very large."

"The Marx Brothers are not large."

"No, Jackson. I think he played football for some team."

"Football players usually do." I lit a cigarette. "Where did you find him, anyway?"

"In the parking lot. Some parking lot. Many parking lots. I'm always seeing Jackson." Andrew swerved left onto Vermont.

"And he knows how to drive a Bentley? I'll kill you if he doesn't drive it properly."

"Miss Chandler," said Andrew exasperatedly. "I took him out for a test spin, did you think I wouldn't? You continue to insult me."

"Well let me insult you once more. You're absolutely sure the pregnant lady and her husband got the house?"

The sign for Griffith Park loomed up ahead. "As sure as I am my name is Andrew Bigelow."

A hush fell over the car as we both, in silent unison, considered Andrew's words.

I'm not sure who burst out laughing first.

• • •

I wound my way down the grassy slope to the playground. The early morning fog had given way to damp afternoon gloom. I glanced up at the sky. Solid gray. No sign of rain clouds. But the lack of an afternoon sun meant, perhaps, that cooler weather was at last on the way.

She was sitting on a bench with her back to me. A blue scarf, tied in a bow on top of her head, held back her hair and matched the blue knit suit she was wearing. A whiff of perfume floated up as I came around the side of the bench. "Lucille?"

Calmly, she turned. "Hi." Her lips parted in a small smile, but it stopped before it reached her eyes. "Thank you for coming here. I know it was out of your way."

I sat beside her. She bent over and flipped open the lid of a wicker basket that lay at her feet. Inside were a Thermos and four plastic cups, red plaid napkins, a Three Musketeers and a small bag of potato chips. Also sandwiches in waxed paper. She held one up. "Ham and cheese?"

I shook my head. "You go ahead."

She put the sandwich in her lap and turned her attention to a sandbox some fifty feet away. In it three children were building something. Two women were seated on the edge of the sandbox talking. I gathered one of the kids was Lewis.

"You said you had the letters."

"I do."

"May I have them?" There was a tension about her that hadn't been there the first time we met. Her eyes, as she turned them on me, looked glassy.

"Of course." I opened my purse and took them out. I handed them to her. Quickly she opened the two envelopes and glanced at the stationery. Satisfied, she slipped them into her purse. Her shoulders seemed to relax.

"I found them at his house."

"Really?" She opened the waxed paper and looked at the sandwich. "How did you manage that?"

"It's not important."

Her eyes traveled to Lewis. "I told you I would pay you."

"Yes. But first you ought to know something, Lucille."

"What?" Her tone was sharp, her eyes wary.

I stretched out my legs and gazed around the playground. Nearby, twin boys rode the swings, their mother, standing behind them, pushing one after the other. I could feel Lucille's eyes on me.

"There was another letter."

"What letter? Did you bring it? I don't remember how many I wrote."

"It wasn't a letter from you."

"Then why should I care about it?" Lucille picked up the sandwich and bit into it.

"It seems like such a coincidence. Here you are, married to a lawyer who works on relocation contracts. And then you have an affair with a man who is attacking relocation on TV."

"That's none of your business," Lucille snapped.

"It's like you were a spy. Or at least you were in position to inform one man what the other was doing. To live like that must have made you jumpy as hell."

I turned and looked at her questioningly. But Lucille was staring straight ahead, gripping the sandwich tightly in her fingers like a horn player watching the conductor, waiting for a cue.

"It's possible that Jim was using you. You two met, he saw an opportunity to get inside information. Or—" I opened my purse and shook out a cigarette. "You saw an opportunity to use him. Forgive me, but all this fascinates me."

I lit the cigarette and dropped the matchbook into my purse. "Just for fun, let's say you were trying to help Jim because you were hopelessly smitten. How could you help him, I asked myself. Well, if your husband, or the Division of Highways, was doing something wrong, you could pass that information along. Otherwise, what would there be to tell?"

Lucille put the sandwich back in the paper.

"Then again, if Jim were uncovering a possible scandal, how nice to be able to keep your husband informed. Did you actually tell him you were romancing Jim to get that information?"

Lucille's head whipped around. "How dare you speak to me like that. This is none of your business. It was . . . just a fling. If he hadn't died . . ."

"Been murdered, Lucille."

"What are you saying, that I murdered him?"

"Of course not. Absolutely not."

I reached down into the basket and peeked under the bag of chips. "Anything besides ham and cheese?"

After a moment I straightened. "Look, I'm sorry. I know you must have adored him. I knew him pretty well, too. And he was a charmer. But he was also ruthlessly ambitious. I'm not saying he wasn't interested in you, but I suspect part of the attraction may have been your husband."

Her hand came up so quickly, I had no chance. I heard the slap before I felt it. The surprise of it and the sting on my left cheek made my eyes smart. I sucked in my breath and blinked hard at her.

Rage burned in her hazel eyes. "We were both going to get divorces. And you can go to hell." She stood up. "Lewis!"

I sat there in silence. Lewis looked up but seemed to need coaxing from one of the mothers. I stepped on my cigarette. Now was the time to play the one card I had, slight as it was.

I said, "I sincerely doubt that, Lucille. Your husband knew about the affair. And you are too clever to be so careless. He knew because you wanted him to."

"Lewis, come quickly!" She turned to me, frowning. "What?"

"There was another letter. From your husband to Jim. Alluding to the affair, threatening him."

"There wasn't. I don't believe you."

"Why? He knew. Your husband knew, didn't he?"

Lewis came romping into his mother's arms. She patted his head, murmuring to him. After a moment, she sent him back to the sandbox. Then she sat down, turning to look at me. "You mustn't tell anyone. I'll pay you anything you ask."

I didn't respond.

"We started meeting for coffee. I could tell he wanted to have a fling. We began seeing each other, I'll skip the details, but he told me he was worried about me because my husband was involved in something. He said he would do what he could to protect our name, but he needed information. Norm never discusses business with me so I had no idea what James was talking about. I couldn't imagine that my husband could be mixed up in anything. He has political aspirations."

I nodded.

"So I told Norm that I'd met James for coffee and that he'd hinted there might be a scandal in the division. Norm said it was probably the Democrats trying to set him up. He wanted me to stay in touch with James, keep on top of his investigation."

"Uh huh," I said. And thought, how clever. She had actually managed to get her husband's permission to be with James St. Clair.

"I kept putting James off, telling him I couldn't find anything out. After a while, he stopped seeing me. I told Norm that if we wanted to string James along, we would have to give him something. But he said it was okay, the problem was taken care of."

"When? When did he say that?"

"I don't remember. But it was weeks before he was murdered." She turned away. "Norm didn't do it." She said the last words in a flat voice that made me wonder if she truly didn't know whether her husband had been involved or not.

"You never told your husband the coffees had become an affair?"

"No! My god, he would have killed—" She bit her lower lip. "That's not what I meant."

"Lucille, what did Jim think was going on?"

She bent over and began packing up the basket. "I don't know. He never exactly said. Anyhow, it doesn't concern you."

"Oh yes it does. I have the letter your husband wrote threatening Jim."

She sat up fast. "Where is it? Give it to me."

I opened my purse and slid a corner of the envelope into view. Then I pushed it back and closed my purse.

"I want that letter."

"I know."

She slumped back against the bench. "James said some of the right-of-way agents were conspiring with homeowners to get more money for the houses than they were worth."

"How?"

"I think the agent would say the house was worth five thousand dollars but he could get the state to pay six if the owner would hold out for it and maybe supply some phony bills showing there had been improvements made. They would split the extra thousand."

"And Jim thought your husband knew about this practice?"

"Norm told me he would look into it, go through all the contracts himself. If it was going on, he'd find out about it."

"I see." Lewis seemed to have had his fill of sandboxes, or of his mates. He picked up a bucket of sand and dumped it on another kid's head. The other mothers jumped into the sandbox. Lucille seemed not to notice. "And is that where Richard Walken fit in?"

"What?" Lucille turned and looked at me.

"Your friend Richard Walken, the real estate agent. Who is also a right-of-way agent. Although nobody can find his name on the rolls."

Lucille was on her feet. "What's the matter, baby?" She got down on her knees and opened her arms. Lewis flew into them and burst into tears. She stroked his head. "What, baby, what?"

I stood up. "You want to talk further, call me. I've really got to run."

"Wait! I must have that letter." She looked up at me with frantic eyes.

"Sure, anytime. As soon as we finish our conversation."

She stood up slowly, holding Lewis's hand. "I only met him once or twice, I believe. He's a real estate agent, that's all I know."

"And Ursula Martens?"

I saw it in her eyes, a quick, burning flash, then a slight tightening of the mouth. "Sorry, who?"

I smiled. "Not good enough, Lucille." I pointed to her purse. "The letters, you owe me." I started to move away.

Her face crumpled. "All right, look. It was Richard's idea. To send Ursula to find out what James knew. He thought—he and Norm thought—she could get more out of him than I could."

"And what did she get out of him?"

Tears began to well up in Lucille's eyes. Lewis, sensing something was wrong, stood watching his mother quietly. "I don't *know* what she got out of him. I only know . . . she got him."

I took the sealed envelope and knelt, slipping it into the picnic basket. For a split second, I really felt rotten. The carrot I had dangled before her, the letter from her husband to Jim, was a blank sheet of my own notepaper.

I straightened. "You never saw me today, Lucille. If you tell your husband, remember, I have something to tell him back."

I smiled. "I can play as dirty as you can."

32
◆

I was feeling draggy when I got home and thought I might take a nap. But before I could start up the stairs, the phone rang.

I reached over the banister and grabbed it. "Hello?"

"Hi, it's Constance. I'm sorry to bother you, but—"

"It's okay. What's up?"

"A girl named Ursula Martens is trying to reach you. She said it was personal and could you please call her. She's at Crestview 6429."

"Right."

"Also, if you don't have plans for tonight . . ."

"I do," I broke in quickly. God knew what society event Constance was leading up to.

"I've got two tickets to Louis Armstrong at the Palladium, which I can't use. The ambassador to Luxembourg is hosting a dinner and Mr. Estevez insists we go."

"Louis Armstrong?" I said in disbelief.

"The tickets will be at the box office. Can you use them?"

"Are you kidding? Thank you so much."

"My pleasure, dear. Your Cary item was so delicious, I've been in ecstasy all day. By the way, the concert's at eight."

I thanked Constance again and could hardly hold still to dial Etta Rice's number. Marilyn, Etta's No. 2 secretary, in charge of appointments, answered and informed me that Nick was out. "I don't think he's coming back. But I know he'll be calling in."

"Will you give him a message? Ask him to pick me up at six-fifteen, not seven. Tell him I have a surprise for him."

Marilyn promised she would. I bounded up the stairs and into my room, only to remember Ursula. I picked up the phone on the bedside table and dialed Sunset Estates.

The receptionist put me through and Ursula's girlish voice came on the line. "Oh, Paris, hi! I'm so glad you called. I really want to get together with you."

I wanted to see her, too. But I hadn't yet figured out how to deal with her. On Friday, I had plotted to set up a lunch with her, then have Esther Lubinow waltz in. Esther would remember her as the woman trying to buy her house. We would put the squeeze on her. But after Sunday's threats, I abandoned that idea.

"Sure," I said, "let's." Leaving it up to her.

"I'm tied up with Mr. Klopstein's project this week and I can't get away for lunch," Ursula said. "But what do you say to a drink?"

"Fine."

"Tonight? We could meet at the Polo Lounge."

"Well—it would have to be early. I need to be somewhere by six-thirty."

"How about five? Will you be going far?"

"Only to Chasen's. That would work."

"Hey, that's swell. You wouldn't be meeting Nick Goodwin, would you? I saw you with him at Romanoff's. He's adorable."

Ah, but not as adorable as Victor Klopstein, I thought. "Yes, I am." I hesitated. "So I'll see you at five?"

"Great. And maybe we'll double-date sometime. Unless I'm being presumptuous. He *is* your beau, right?"

"We seem to spend a lot of time together." I began examining my fingernails. They were long and looked good. I said I'd see her later.

I phoned Marilyn and asked her to tell Nick to meet me at Chasen's at six-thirty instead, Then I lay back on the bed. Thinking.

Just try it, sister.

I'll scratch your eyes out.

Dressed to kill in a low-cut red taffeta sheath, high-heeled red satin shoes and a mink stole, I swept into the Beverly Hills Hotel like Cleopatra in search of Antony. Bellhops and guests fell back, gaping openly, as I marched through the lobby to the Polo Lounge, eyes straight ahead, refusing to bestow upon anyone the gift of a single glance. I was cooking.

I pulled up short at the reservations' desk. "Hello, Morrie."

The solidly built majordomo looked up. For once, his toupee was on straight. "Why, Miss Chandler. How nice to see you." His eyes grazed my bare shoulder. "Are you . . . meeting someone?"

"A young woman. A Miss Martens."

"Of course. Right this way."

I turned down the dial on my routine and swayed sedately behind Morrie to a round, leather-padded booth in the alcove to the right of the door. About half the tables were already filled. The room had a buzz and haze of smoke.

She was wearing a simple black wool dress and a hat with a veil and puffing on the end of a long pearl cigarette holder. A white-gloved hand held the cigarette holder to dark red lips. I mentally erased the cigarette holder and idly wondered if that's how I looked to the world at large. "Ursula."

"Paris!" She jumped up. "Wow. Look at you."

I allowed Morrie to seat me. Ursula fell back into the

booth with a sigh. "You look just like a movie star. Everyone in the room is staring at you."

I laughed self-consciously. Now that I had apparently achieved the desired effect, I wasn't sure what to do with it. "I believe," I said, "I must have a glass of champagne."

"Champagne," I told the waiter. I peeled off my gloves, rested my chin in my hand and gazed at Ursula as if she were the Mother Divine. "You must tell me all about you, Ursula. I'm dying to know *everything.*"

Ursula squirmed and emitted an embarrassed laugh. "Gosh, there's nothing really to tell. You're the one with the exciting life."

"Don't be silly. Why, you are creating the landscapes of Beverly Hills. I mean, years from now, *decades* from now, your ideas will still define how Beverly Hills *looks.* How smug that must make you feel." I smiled radiantly. "Now. Do tell me *everything.*"

She should have blushed. She did not. She tapped her cigarette in the ashtray. It was the first tiny crack in her armor. Miss Giggly-goo became cool as the ice cube in her Campari and soda. "Let's see. I grew up in Omaha. Daddy is with an insurance company there. We're just a typical Midwestern family. I have three little sisters and a mama who's ill. I came out here to be an artist. I could always draw pretty well. But it takes time to establish yourself and Mama's bills were more than Daddy could handle."

She removed the cigarette from the holder and stubbed it carefully into the ashtray. I broke my look of utter enthrallment to take a sip of champagne.

"That's how I ended up at Sunset Estates. I needed a paying job. A friend told me they had an opening for a secretary. It's really as simple as that."

"Oh no. You must be *terribly* talented, Ursula. Tell me how you design a garden. Really I can't imagine."

She laughed nervously and turned her head. Her eyes moved quickly around the room.

"Are you expecting Mr. Klopstein?"

"No, I just thought—I'm sorry. I thought I saw Betty

Grable over there." She grinned. "I'm such a sucker for movie stars."

"You were telling me about your work. What's your boss like?"

Ursula seemed to relax again. "He's very nice, Mr. Cochran. When I began showing him sketches of gardens, he really seemed interested. Then he let me try one. It's wonderful when someone gives you a chance like that."

"Mr. Cochran? He owns Sunset Estates?"

"No, he just runs it. It's a small company. There are two landscapers, a receptionist and me. Mr. Cochran takes care of the business side."

"But who owns it? I ask because I've lived here all my life and I'd never heard of Sunset Estates."

"I think it started after the war. I've never met the man who owns it. They call him Mr. B., or The Boss. He's a big businessman who owns lots of things."

Again, her eyes traveled the room. I continued to bide my time. My plan of attack was not to attack. She had a reason for bringing me here and I was determined to wait, like a sitting duck, for whatever tricky little scheme she had concocted to play out.

Her eyes came back to mine. She laughed self-consciously. "We must be losing our touch, Paris. You'd think someone would have tried to pick us up by now."

"I suspect dear Morrie is making sure nobody tries."

Ursula leaned forward. "Now tell me about your work. How did you ever get to be on TV?"

I sipped my champagne and told her about the column and how Nick had somehow parlayed this into us having our own show.

"So you must have known James St. Clair."

Just like that. Through the veil her wide blue eyes radiated a harmless innocence. It was a question she would naturally ask, that anyone would ask. She asked it at ten minutes to six.

"Yes," I said. "I knew him. It's been an absolute *nightmare.*"

"Poor man." She slipped a cigarette out of a metal case and worked it into the holder. "Do they have any idea who did it?"

"Not that I know of." I watched her light the cigarette and inhale. "The investigation seems to have dried up."

Her eyes lingered somewhere across the room. Then she said, "The word is there was a love triangle." I waited for her to go on. But she only looked at me questioningly.

I smiled dismissively. "This is Hollywood, Ursula. Everyone's always looking for a story."

"But you knew him. Was there—"

"Why hello!"

I hadn't seen him come up to the table. He stood there smiling in his nice camel jacket and brown slacks, holding a pair of gloves in his hand. "Ursula, I thought it was you. I saw the cigarette holder the moment I walked in."

"Richard, meet Paris Chandler. Paris, this is Mr. Walken."

"How do you do? May I join you for a moment? I seem to be early for my appointment."

He borrowed a chair from the next table and slid it up to the edge of the booth. He turned to Ursula, saying, "I hear you have the Klopstein account. How's that going?"

I listened to her mumbo-jumbo wondering how they were going to try to pass him off. The waiter came over and took Walken's order for a martini. Ursula asked for another Campari. I passed. I glanced anxiously at my watch.

"Paris, Mr. Walken is in real estate. He often recommends us to his clients."

For the first time, Walken turned to me. His brown eyes sighted down his beaklike nose at me. "How amazing. Is this your sister, Urs? But why didn't you tell me?"

"Oh we're not sisters," I said pleasantly. "We met at a party only last week." I paused. "I believe I know you."

Walken arched an eyebrow. "Really?"

Ursula said, "Will you two excuse me for a moment?"

She stood up. "I'm trying to remember where the ladies' room is."

I told her she had to go out and cross the lobby. It was just down the hall after that.

"Yes, I believe I was in your office recently, Mr. Walken. In Silver Lake? You have a dog and you were rather cross."

"Oh my, yes. I remember now. Forgive me, Miss Chandler. I was in the middle of a crisis of sorts and I— oh thanks." He watched the waiter put down his drink on a paper Polo Lounge napkin. Walken raised his glass to me. "My sincerest apologies."

"I accept. Real estate seems like a business of crises. Especially where you are. The freeway coming in must present all kinds of problems."

"Actually, the freeway presents all kinds of opportunities."

"Does it?"

"Sure. I figure the best way to help my neighborhood and my business is to try to relocate people. I've been working with the Division of Highways."

"You don't say."

"Yes. I facilitate the state in buying properties. Then, if I can, I help the people find new homes." He raised his elbow along with his glass. "It's been terribly rewarding." As he sipped, his Adam's apple bounced.

"I can imagine. So you act for the state in buying a home and then you try to sell those people new homes? You must be a very clever man."

"Industrious, Miss Chandler. The state is short of right-of-way agents. Most realtors won't get involved because there's no commission. So the Division of Highways is very happy to have a helping hand."

"But if you don't get paid by the state . . . ?"

"I collect at the other end. I have already established a relationship with these folks. They know they can trust me."

"Well of course." I sipped my champagne. "I understand that some people actually move their houses."

"We try to encourage that. The housing shortage is so bad right now, we don't want to waste any usable buildings."

"And you help in that area, too?"

"If I can. I will suggest movers and people to do renovation. I can also sell them lots."

"And the movers and the construction companies pay you a fee?"

"My my. A girl with a business head. Do you work?"

"Yes." I glanced at my watch again. It was six-twenty. "I help Etta Rice with her gossip column at the *Examiner*. I'm going to have to run in a minute. I'll just wait for Ursula to come back."

She had been gone a bit too long. And his "appointment" still hadn't arrived. But I couldn't figure out what they were up to. Unless I was supposed to come away with a new impression of Richard Walken. Hero to the Removed.

"I forget why you came in to see me," he said mildly. "Perhaps there's something I can still help you with."

"Perhaps there is. But I'm afraid I can't go into it now. May I call you?"

"Please do." He reached inside his jacket and pulled out a small leather case. As he did so I caught sight of a handle protruding from a shoulder holster. He had done that on purpose, showed me his gun. Nice, very nice.

I took his business card and saw that it was identical to the one he had given Edna Herbert. I slipped it into my purse. "Whatever has become of Ursula?"

"Oh she probably ran into somebody she knows in the lobby. Let me ask you something, Miss Chandler. Are you looking to buy?"

"It's a thought."

"Then I must encourage you. Real estate is the best investment anyone could make. Just between you and me, it's going to go through the roof."

"Is it? Well we'll have to talk more. But I must go. Will you tell Ursula I'm sorry I couldn't wait?"

From inside his ivory tower, he gave me an insincere

smile. "I can't get over how much you two look alike. Surely you're related. Cousins, perhaps?"

I slid to the edge of the booth and stood up, quickly scanning the room. Ursula wasn't in it.

I said, "Let's just say we're related by blood."

33
◆

Andrew braked in front of Chasen's at six-forty. I followed two couples inside and waited for them to be seated. Maude Chasen returned. "Yes?" No matter how many times I had been there, she never seemed to know me.

"I'm meeting Nick Goodwin."

"Nick?" She look unconvinced.

"Has he arrived?"

"As a matter of fact, he came in a little while ago." She turned and glanced over her shoulder into the restaurant. Then she stared blankly at me as if she were waiting for me to say the secret password.

"Could you please show me to his table?"

"Excuse me. I'll be right back."

I stood there wondering what the sentence for strangulation might be. Eventually, she reappeared. "Nick must be in the men's room. Why don't you have a seat?"

Perhaps he was using the phone. Still, why couldn't I have been shown to his table? I sat down in a little velvet chair. Five minutes must have passed.

272

I stood up. "Mrs. Chasen, could you please check again?"

"I just did. I didn't see him."

"May I take a look?"

She seemed to debate this. Finally she shrugged. "But make it quick. And don't bother any of the guests."

I checked all of the booths in the front of the restaurant; I made the rounds of the back. No Nick.

I detoured over to the rest rooms. A man was coming out the mens' door. I stopped him. "I'm looking for someone and wondered if he might be in there. He's about six—"

The man shook his head. "I was the only one, miss. Excuse me."

By now I was completely confused. I knew I couldn't stay in the restaurant by myself so I went outside and found Andrew parked around the corner. I climbed into the backseat. "Nick seems to have disappeared."

"Disappeared?" Andrew turned round and stared at me.

"You didn't see him come out?"

"Uh uh. But I wasn't looking."

"Let's drive around the block and look for his car. Maude says he came in. But he doesn't seem to be anywhere."

Andrew started up the Bentley and we tooled around the block. The green MG was nowhere to be found.

I went back into Chasen's. I left a note for Nick telling him to meet me at the box office. Then Andrew and I stopped at Dolores's Drive-In for a hamburger before heading over to the Palladium. Nick still did not turn up.

In the end, Andrew took his seat, tenth row center.

He said the concert was really groovy.

The mystery of the vanished Nick unraveled the moment I got home.

He was sitting in my study—sitting, actually, in my red leather wing chair—feet up on the ottoman, holding a snifter of brandy. Billie Holliday moaned softly in the background.

He grinned.

"I hope I didn't keep you waiting," I said acidly.

"I've been here about an hour and I've had a chance to calm down. Paris, you're not going to believe what happened."

I edged into the room. "Are you all right?" His shirt collar was open and so was his beige jacket. A strand of hair fell across his forehead. He looked a bit rumpled for Nick.

"I'm fine. Can I pour you some brandy? You're going to need it."

He started to get up, but I waved him back down. I went over to the liquor cabinet. The bottle of Courvoisier was out. I filled half a snifter and walked over to the couch. "You missed Louis Armstrong."

"Mrs. Keyes told me. How was he?"

"Great. I guess." I sat down. "Maude Chasen said you were there, so you did get my message. But—where did you go?"

Nick was giving me a funny look, which I ignored. The record ran out. I got up and turned the phonograph off. Then I went back to the couch, kicked off my shoes and tucked my legs under me. He was still giving me the look. I met his eyes but said nothing.

"The message said to meet you at Chasen's at six-thirty. There had been a change of plans. You had a surprise for me."

"That's right, that's what I told Marilyn."

Nick sipped his brandy. He put the glass down on the round cigarette table and said, "This story is going to upset you. Just bear with me, Paris. I got there a few minutes early. I told Maude I was meeting a young lady, Miss Chandler, had you arrived? The phone rang. As she picked it up she pointed into the dining room. I thought that was odd because she always gives me a booth."

Suddenly, I felt my fingers go numb.

"So I walked back there. At the far end, I saw you

sitting at a table. You had your black hat on with the veil and you were smoking a cigarette."

"In a holder," I said woodenly.

Nick blinked. "Do you know then—what happened?"

I shook my head.

"I started toward the table. It's a long room. Suddenly, you stood up. You motioned me to follow and you turned and walked out the back door. By the time I got outside, you were getting into a cab. The cab began to pull away. But it stopped just before it turned onto the street. I gathered I was supposed to follow. My car was parked back there, in that little lot behind the restaurant. So I hopped in and—I followed."

"It never occurred to you that this was odd?" My voice had a scratchy quality to it—like a record that had been played too many times. I wet my lips with the brandy.

"Sure I did. But maybe the Bentley broke down or Andrew was sick. Anyway, I followed you to an apartment building on Burton Way. By the time I parked, you were inside. I went in and you were at the top of the landing. I followed you up two flights of stairs. On the third floor, I walked down the hall. One of the apartment doors was open."

"And still nothing went off in that nimble little brain of yours?" I reached for the cigarette box on the coffee table and tried to beat my anger down by lighting up.

"You said you had a surprise for me, remember? And I must say, this was all very provocative."

I disappeared behind a cloud of smoke. I wasn't going to kill him just yet. "So now you're in the living room."

"The dimly lit living room."

"Of course."

"But you weren't there. A door was open. I heard a sound, a kind of rustling sound. Naturally I walked in."

"Excuse me. We're now in the bedroom?"

"Er, it was very dark. And—"

"I don't believe this, Nick. Really, it's too much."

"Stop glaring at me. I told you you weren't going to like it. But let me remind you of something. You're the one with the shady underside to your life. All the time

I've been sitting here waiting for you I've been thinking, who the hell is this girl?"

"You mean me?"

"You."

I reached for the plaid blanket at the end of the couch and burrowed into it. "Please go on."

"She said my name softly. She was in the bed, under the sheets. She had taken her hat off and I think her dress. Anyway her shoulders were bare, that's all I could see. I sat down on the other side of the bed. I must have said something like, 'Paris, what are you doing?' She touched my cheek and laughed. She said, 'I'm not Paris. I'm better. Why don't you see for yourself?' "

"Must I hear *all* the details?"

Nick flushed. "Yes, you must."

He picked up his brandy and stared at me with angry eyes over the rim of the glass. He cleared his throat. "I said, who the hell are you and I turned on the lamp. Boy, was it weird. The resemblance is so strong. She even had on Chanel No. 5. But obviously she wasn't you. Her mouth is different and her eyes. And—"

"Are we going to catalogue the whole her?"

"All right. So I asked her what the hell was going on?"

"You remembered her from Romanoff's?"

"Of course. And I'd seen you talking to her. For a moment I had this wild notion that you two were up to something."

"How I adore men's fantasies. They send me right to Mars." I tugged my arms out of the blanket and reached for another cigarette. The old one had burned out.

"She said to turn the light off. We'd discuss business later. I got up and went into the living room."

"Uh huh."

"And then she came out."

"And what, may I ask, did she want? Besides the treasure of you."

Nick's feet flew off the ottoman. He got up and marched over to the cabinet. I could hear the gurgle of brandy as it sluiced into his glass. He stood there, with his back to me, raising the snifter to his lips. Looking at him, I was suddenly reminded of a fight that Russell and I once had in this room. He'd been standing in the same spot, pouring himself a Scotch and telling me about plans to spend Christmas Day with his parents, along with a cast of thousands of Chandlers. I had protested, not wanting to.

"You never told me about James St. Clair."

Nick walked back and sat on the edge of the ottoman. I squirmed under the blanket. I had this overwhelming desire to scream at him, the way I had screamed at Russell. I said, "Should I have? Why should I have?"

"I don't know. Maybe it just would have been nice."

"Fine. I had an affair with James St. Clair. Which maybe wasn't anybody's business."

"Except you are the mystery woman seen leaving his house the night he died. You could have told me, Paris."

"If it's true, maybe I could have."

"Are you still going to play games with me?"

"What did she want, Nicky?" My nerves had reached the breaking point and I now felt so very tired. I pulled the blanket up to my chin.

"She said she was also at St. Clair's house that night. She said she got there first. Then you showed up. Apparently there was a fight. St. Clair told you his wife was arriving the next day and he wouldn't be seeing you anymore. You were furious. You reminded him how he'd sworn he was going to dump her for you. She heard two shots and a door slam. When she came out of the den, she found St. Clair dead."

"Oh boy," I said.

"I know," Nick said. "I didn't swallow it either."

"So why would she tell you all this?"

"Apparently the police found a nightgown at the scene of the crime."

"They did?"

"It was in a closet. They thought it might be Mrs. St. Clair's. But then she showed up and said it wasn't. The police confiscated it. They later found a bill for the nightgown, charged to him, sent to you."

I said nothing.

"But according to Ursula, St. Clair also bought one for her. She went with him, tried it on and took it with her. That's the nightgown the police found."

"I suppose there's a point to all this." I yawned.

"However many of these nightgowns Saks had, they're all gone. They came from Italy and it would take four months to get one specially ordered."

"So? If the police have one and they think it's mine, what does she care?"

"She cares that you can prove it's not yours."

I tried to digest this. Maybe it was the weeks of tension, or the beating my body had taken, or simply the result of a long, strenuous day. But my brain seemed all tangled up. I couldn't track what Nick was saying. "What does this have to do with you? What message are you supposed to be delivering?" With a great deal of effort, I leaned forward and got hold of the brandy glass.

"The thing is," said Nick, "if you can prove it's not your nightgown, the police are going to wonder whose it is. They'll go to Saks, find out if St. Clair bought any other nightgowns. Ursula's afraid the saleswoman could identify her. That would present problems. But if you can't produce a nightgown, the police will be satisfied that the one they have is yours and they won't go looking for another one."

I studied the brandy glass. "I'm not following you."

"She wants me to steal your nightgown."

"What?"

"That, from what I gather, was what tonight was all about. Get the nightgown. Oh, and also to let me know, in case I didn't, that my girlfriend is a murderer."

This got me sitting straight up, brandy glass rattling onto the table. "So you're supposed to just waltz in here and *steal* my nightgown?"

For the first time since I walked in, Nick smiled.

"But what could possibly make her think you would?"

"She told me," Nick said, "that ten thousand dollars would."

34
◆

"Mr. Cochran? This is Mrs. Joseph. We've never met."
My voice had an early morning huskiness that I rather
liked.

He cleared his throat. "How can I help you, Mrs. Joseph?"

The money Ursula dangled had to be coming from
somewhere. I doubted it was coming from Norman
Wills.

"It's about landscaping, but . . . I'm terribly embarrassed. You see—"

"Oh, please, don't be. Whatever problems you have,
let me tell you, you aren't alone. For instance, white fly is
something we're all having to deal with these days."

I forced a giggle, which, after all the alcohol Nick and
I had consumed, and having not quite poured down my
first cup of coffee, was a somewhat heroic event. I said,
"If I have white fly, Mr. Cochran, I'm sure you can cure
me." I wriggled my toes on the faded green carpet. "Or
so I've been told. You come *very* highly recommended."

"Why thank you. May I ask who was so kind to recommend Sunset Estates?"

I giggled again, setting off a major disturbance in my head. "Now you've hit on my problem. I was at a party recently, mainly friends of my husband, you see, and I began chatting with someone, quite a lovely man, and he told me he was in landscaping. I nearly died right there because Mr. Joseph and I just moved in and we were saying that very day, what are we to do with this tangled mess of a garden? And presto! I encounter a man who can help me. Isn't that something?"

"Extraordinary," said Mr. Cochran.

"I know. Things seem to happen that way for me. I think I have a problem and presto! Here comes the answer."

"You say the man was in landscaping?"

"Yes, that's what he said. He told me he owned a landscaping firm and that I should call right away. He said I must ask for you and that he would tell you I would be calling. I wrote your name on a cocktail napkin and stuffed it in my purse and I only just came across it this morning. But I was so silly. I totally forgot that nice man's name." I paused. "They say the air out here makes you lightheaded."

Mr. Cochran chuckled. "Now that's something I hadn't heard. But I can tell you, we'd be most happy to come take a look. Where is your house?"

"In Beverly Hills. Let me get my appointment book and we can set a time." I rested the phone on my knees and let time pass. Then, "Here we go, Mr. Cochran, let's see. This is what month?"

"October. We could come out this afternoon, how's that?"

"Ah, here we are. Tuesday. Oh dear, I have this charity thing. In fact, I was telling that nice man about it. Wait a minute—B. His name begins with a B, right?"

"Mr. Barnathan, he owns Sunset Estates."

"I *knew* it. Barnathan. He seemed very important."

"He is. He's quite a businessman. Everyone knows Mr. Barnathan."

Right, I thought. Except for his employees.

"What is your address, Mrs. Joseph?"

"It's 1415 Doheny Road, just above Sunset a bit."

"Fine. Is tomorrow convenient for you?"

I hesitated. "Why yes. Say right after lunch?"

"I'll send our very best man up to see you. Now give me your phone number in case we need to call."

I pulled one out of my imagination and gave it to him. "Mr. Cochran," I added, "whatever you do, don't tell Mr. Barnathan I forgot his name. It will be our little secret, promise?"

"I swear on my mother's petunias," Mr. Cochran vowed.

I sat on the stairs grinning to myself until myself reminded itself that it had a prodigious hangover. I dragged upstairs, stepped carefully over the red taffeta dress and one fallen high heel and started the water running in the bathtub.

We had finished the bottle of brandy.

I had asked Nick how come he didn't swipe the nightgown and take the score? Because maybe, he had replied slyly, *I* would be willing to pay him even more.

He had carried me up the stairs, somehow.

I remembered the moonlight streaming in through the windows and all of the tantalizing smells: the hair tonic, the after-shave and finally, just Nick. I asked him how much.

"Quite a bit," he had said thoughtfully. "Double."

"And what would you tell Ursula?"

"That a terrible pang of guilt prevented me from accepting her offer, such as it was."

"And I would get a kickback, naturally. After she went even higher. Tricky Nick."

Which is when, I believe, he suddenly remembered some other tricks that he knew.

I climbed into the tub. The hot water soothed my rib cage. I closed my eyes, one hand gripping the coffee cup on the edge of the tub like a lifeline.

The key question was: *How had she known?*

Okay.

I had left Jim's house, not knowing she was there, in the den. She might have gone upstairs first; no, he must have come right down. How long was I gone? Less than five minutes. Walking around back to the Bentley, then remembering I had forgotten my book, going back.

They had been downstairs, in the rotunda. Perhaps they had moved upstairs then. He would have heard something—a noise, possibly, or the doorbell—and come back down. Or maybe they had stayed downstairs a few minutes more—and he was shot.

Either way, she could have fled through the kitchen door as I had, out of sight of the nosy neighbors on the other side. Or, she could have left right after I did. She could have come back and rung the doorbell. Or she could have left before the killer arrived.

But none of this was really the point. No, the point was her nightgown. Where was it that night? In a closet, where I wouldn't have looked? Or had she brought it with her, brought it upstairs sometime after I had left? No matter. What did matter was that she had left it behind. Ursula seemed too calculating to have done that unwittingly. But—and this was the big question—how could she have known that I had one, too?

I leaned forward and turned the faucet, drawing more hot water, but not any insight. I swallowed the rest of the coffee.

Two sources could have told her.

Jim, which I doubted.

Or the police.

I kicked aside the implications of the latter and focused on the one answer I had found. The completion of the chain. Richard Walken at one end, Matthew Barnathan at the other. And little Ursula Martens flitting somewhere in between.

Wrapped in an old pink robe, I spent the next couple of hours working the phone. Tee Jones received the mes-

sage I had left with her service and called me from a pay
phone near the Arizona border—collect. "Guy welched
on a bill," she said. "I'll be back tonight." She said she'd
meet me at KTLA after the show.

I also spoke with an assortment of voices at the Division of Highways. I chatted briefly with Nick. And finally,
I put in a call to Chief Gladstone.

He wasn't in. I told the doddering Miss Percy I would
try again later. When I hung up, I found Mrs. Keyes
standing in the hallway, kerchief on her head, looking
discombobulated.

"I don't know what to do about that man," she com-
plained. "He just paces back and forth, back and forth,
behind the kitchen. I can see him through the windows."

I stood up. "What are you talking about? I have to get
dressed right away. Is it warm, cold, soggy?"

"Like some kind of animal staking out his territory.
You know who I mean. I hope he doesn't expect to come
in the kitchen because I won't let him."

"Who? Oh—the chauffeur? Um, Jackson?"

"Jackson! Is that his name? Well I won't have him
skulking around *my* house."

I followed her clumping footsteps down the hall to the
kitchen. Outside, pacing back and forth just as she had
described, was a Negro dressed in a crisp beige uniform.
He was tall and quite muscular. He had a little goatee
and he was wearing sunglasses.

I opened the back door.

"You can't go out like *that,*" said Mrs. Keyes hysterically. "I won't let you. It's indecent."

I slammed the door behind me. "Jackson?"

He had been walking toward the swimming pool. He
halted and turned slowly back. The closer I drew, the
larger he became. His neck, instead of going up and
down, mostly went sideways. A grin broke out on top of
it. An array of dazzling white teeth flashed before me,
except for an upper front one, which flashed in gold.

"Yes, ma'am. At your service, ma'am."

"I'm Miss Chandler, how do you do."

"Yes, ma'am." He stood there, still grinning.

"Have you been here long, Jackson?"

"Oh yes, ma'am."

"Well I'll be ready to go out soon. Um, is there something that you need right now?"

"No, ma'am."

"Fine. Why don't you wait for me over by the garage?"

"If it pleases you, ma'am."

"Thank you. I'll be out in a minute." I started to turn back to the house then stopped. "Excuse me. Is Jackson your first name or your last?"

He wrinkled his forehead, as if the question required concentrated thought. "Yes, ma'am. It's both, ma'am."

"Your name is Jackson Jackson?"

The reflection of a cloud passed across his sunglasses. "I was gypped," Jackson said sadly.

It was, I supposed, divine retribution from the chauffeur god that, after having one chauffeur with too many names, I should now get one with too few. I sank into the backseat and tried not to giggle.

After a few blocks, I didn't have to try. This Jackson drove like a true professional, which meant he drove like a turtle.

"Jackson?"

"Ma'am."

"I realize you don't know me. But if you did know me, you'd know that I am not a fifteen-mile-an-hour girl. I'm more like a thirty-five-mile-an-hour daredevil."

That was a *big* mistake. Jackson stepped on the pedal with a shoe that had to have been made out of concrete. We took off with such a lurch I feared we had left the ground.

"Uh, Jackson!"

But by then he had the radio on and was singing at the top of his lungs.

I gritted my teeth and thought evil thoughts about the mean-spirited, duplicitous chauffeur god.

• • •

A floorwalker in a black suit with a white carnation in his lapel slithered up to me. Floorwalkers, I have always suspected, are failed maître d's, though I'd never actually done the research. "May I help you?"

"Thank you. I'm going to the second floor."

"Yes, madam. The elevator . . ."

I knew where the elevator was. I took it up, stepped off and walked through Dresses to Lingerie. No one was there. I bent over a glass counter and studied a collection of racy red garter belts, the latest from France, a small card read. I began tapping my foot impatiently. Eventually I hollered, "Hello?"

A woman, rubbing her tongue over her teeth, came hurrying through the curtains. "Sorry, I was just grabbing a sandwich." She ran a thumb across the corner of her mouth. "Egg salad."

"Perhaps someone else can help me," I said. "I'm looking for the head saleslady."

"I guess that's me. The other girls are only part time." She was middle-aged and a bit lumpy through the middle. She cocked her head and peered at me through harlequin glasses. There was something in the look I didn't like.

"You're in charge then?"

"Yes. I'm Mrs. Benton. Is there something I can show you?"

She was still looking at me like I had runny mascara or lipstick on my teeth. I said, "What I need is some information." I stepped closer. "It's a matter that's quite private."

Mrs. Benton brightened immediately. "Ah—we're getting married, are we?"

"Not exactly. This is about a black lace negligee from Italy. A friend gave me one as a present. I understand you had only a few. Is it possible"—I looked over my shoulder—"to find out who bought the others?"

The woman was still giving me the runny mascara look.

"Look, is something wrong?"

"You're Paris Chandler, right? From TV?"

Oh *that*. "Er, yes," I said awkwardly.

Mrs. Benton shook her head. "I swear, sometimes I think I'm losing my mind."

"What do you mean?"

"Someone came in, just last week. Asking about the same negligee. I could swear it was you."

"Did she say she was me?"

"Nope. She didn't say who she was. But she wanted to buy the negligee. I told her we had only gotten four and we were all out. I said, 'Besides, I already sent you one. From Mr. St. Clair.'"

So that was how Ursula knew. She had come in hoping to replace her own nightgown and through blind luck had found out that I had one, too. I didn't like that. I didn't like people with blind luck.

"Mrs. Benton, did this woman say anything else?"

"I don't believe so. Is there some kind of problem?"

"Yes. But not with the nightgown." Two women strolled by and paused to look through the girdles displayed on a table. I lowered my voice. "I know this is a strange request, but I really need to find out who else bought the nightgowns. Would it be very much trouble?"

"Let's see." Mrs. Benton pursed her mouth. "We got the negligees, I believe, in August. So I'd have to go through two, three months of sales slips. It may take a while."

"Could I help?"

"No. The problem is I'm here by myself. But maybe I can take them home. I got nothing better to do. It's Edgar's bowling night."

"It would mean a lot to me if you would, Mrs. Benton. I'd be terribly grateful."

"You want me to call you?"

"Yes, please." I wrote down my number for her.

On my way out, I bought the red garter belt.

35
◆

A message from Police Chief Gladstone awaited me when I got home. I called back immediately. After a momentary hold, he came on the line. "So how's my favorite little star?"

"Not as bright as you." I slid a tiny pout into my voice. "You never come to see me anymore."

"I never did. Is that an invitation?"

"Well," I said, "I think so. I'm a person of my word. And I promised I would teach you TV."

Faster than Jackson could hit the accelerator, Gladstone asked, "Tonight?"

I calculated quickly. "It would have to be on the late side. I've already promised to have dinner with someone after the show. I probably won't be home till nine."

"Nine it is. And then you can explain to me what happened to you the other day. Your boy acted like it was the second kidnapping of the Lindbergh child."

I laughed. "I apologize. And appreciate your speedy response. I foolishly went off with a friend and forgot to tell Andrew." I paused. "Andrew has no concept of real life. He assumed Sydney Greenstreet had absconded with me."

"Of course," said Gladstone, unconvinced. "You're a weird bird, you know that? Anyway, at nine we'll shine. Adios."

I hung up smiling. And went looking for Mrs. Keyes.

A fierce battle was being conducted in the KTLA newsroom when I parted the sheets a few hours later. Truman Stone was leaning forward across his desk, gesturing emphatically to Klaus Landsburg. Klaus's back was to me but Truman glanced up and gave me a quick shake of his head. I backed away. A battle with the general manager had to concern money.

I retraced my steps to the front of the garage and stuck my head in Studio One. It was just before airtime and the studio was in its usual madcap frenzy. Two men each were wheeling the two clunky cameras into place in front of the news desk, while the lighting engineer trucked over two large light stands to sit on either side of them. The soundman was placing vinyl disks on his round tables; they would provide background music for newsreels of floods, troop movements or whatever the world had unleashed three days ago. I watched for a moment or two, until the overhead lights came on and the ovenlike heat drove me out the door.

I began strolling along Marathon Street. Across from the main Paramount Gate stood a row of apartment houses. Most contained a shop, four steps down from street level. I passed Mr. and Mrs. Hersh's laundry, a bakery and a gift shop. Next door, the lights were still burning in Hjalmar's barbershop. A man in a British bobby's uniform was in the chair having his hair cut. I watched Hjalmar, a Swede, snip away. Rumor had it that he was actually a leading Communist spy. Everyone went to Hjalmar, hoping to get real proof.

I returned to the station and found the news director alone.

"Listen to this," Truman greeted me. He began reading a wire service story. " 'The Department of Justice Anti-trust Division is investigating how the new long hemline style came to be decreed as the latest fashion, and whether the New Look is a dark, sinister plot in restraint of something or other.' " He paused. "Do you think it's a dark, sinister plot?"

"Yes, definitely. Christian Dior is a dangerous Communist trying to subvert capitalist ladies." I sat down. "What did Mr. Landsburg want?"

Truman reached for another story. "It's what *I* want."

"Which is?"

He glanced up sharply. "Did it ever occur to you it's none of your business?"

"Never. I'm a gossip by trade, that's why you hired me, remember? You kill me, Truman, you really do."

Truman smiled in spite of himself. "I'm pushing to do the real estate show. Klaus isn't interested."

"I can't say that I blame him. Why pay Matthew Barnathan to go on TV to sell his own houses?"

"Oh thanks. Aren't there any festering infidelities you could go run down?"

"I wanted to talk to you. About Barnathan, actually."

"Frankly, I don't care to hear your ideas on the subject."

"You won't get them. This is something else. I've been thinking about Jim's freeway folder."

"And I thought you were supposed to think about gossip."

"You told me you pulled the folder from the file cabinet and put it in your desk. But then you didn't want to take it out in front of me, so you left it, and the next day it was gone."

"So?"

"Are you sure it was the day I dropped in?"

Truman gave me a long, hard look but said nothing.

"Because I went through your desk right after you left. I'm sorry, Truman, but I did. I went through all your drawers. It wasn't there."

"Why were you snooping?" He didn't sound angry.

"I wanted the folder because of Mrs. Wills. Her husband is the chief lawyer in the right-of-way department. It struck me as odd that she would be having an affair with the man who was attacking what her husband was doing. It made me *very* curious. I couldn't find the folder in the cabinet so . . . I went through your desk."

Truman was looking at me like a man who couldn't decide whether to shoot the rabid dog or continue to watch it with fascination.

"Truman, right before I came in, you were talking to Barnathan and his yes-man. Did you run out for a moment and leave them alone in this office?"

"So they could steal a folder they didn't know existed?"

"You said Jim discussed his investigation with you."

"But he didn't discuss Matthew Barnathan with me."

"What about Norman Wills?"

"Negative." He grinned crookedly. "I said I put it *on* my desk. You haven't been hitting the laudanum, have you?"

I studied the piles of folders and papers on his desk. "No, but maybe I will." Had he really said *on*? I could have heard him wrong. I glanced at my watch and stood up. "We'll talk more in the next day or two, okay?"

"Sure. Maybe we'll have tea."

I smiled. "That's all you can say?"

Truman tapped his ruler on the desk. "The night you went through my desk, you didn't see a gold fountain pen, did you? My wife's going to kill me."

When the TV lights are on, they are as blinding as the harsh rays of the setting winter sun. You learn not to look directly into them, but even so, you are seeing bright, white halos. These lights form a solid wall between you and the studio audience sitting in the rows of folding chairs. Sometimes you can hear them. A coughing sound, a laugh—from a roomful of ghosts. But you can never see them.

I saw him a second before the explosion of lights flashed on and effectively blacked him out.

He was wearing a dark suit. A stocky man with thinning black hair fringing a high bald dome. A round face with a cigar in it. Hard, nearly black eyes. Taking off his hat, sitting down, aisle chair, back of the studio.

"Ladies and gentlemen! Live from the KTLA studios in Los Angeles, it's *Nick and Paris on the Town*! Brought to you . . . every Tuesday evening by . . . Rancho Soups—when you want a soup like Grandma makes, reach for Rancho—here are Nick Goodwin and Paris Chandler!"

"Good evening, Paris. I hear you went to a fabulous party over the weekend," is what Nick said.

"And I can't wait to tell you all about it," is what I said.

So. He had come here to meet with Truman, maybe. Or maybe not. But suddenly, as Nick began talking about *his* weekend in Palm Springs, it flashed into my head that the man at Esther's house auction who looked familiar but whom I couldn't place was Matthew Barnathan's yesman; the dope who needed change for the Coke machine.

"Walter Pidgeon and Joel McCrea were there, Paris. But don't mention it to Joel." Nick grinned. "He lost his ball in the trees. Twice."

"Knowing Joel," I said, which of course I didn't, "he probably wanted to get a better look at the ladies in the gallery." *I* grinned.

The fifteen minutes allotted to our show dragged into forever. When at last the TV lights went down, when the moment it took for my eyes to adjust to the room light finally passed, the chair he had been sitting in was vacant. Matthew Barnathan was gone.

"What did he look like? Tall, short?" Tee pushed her hair behind her ears and threw an annoyed look in the direction of the waiter. The waiter was standing calmly behind the bar, running a finger across his Errol Flynn mustache. He didn't look like Errol Flynn.

"A mobster," I said with certainty. "He was in the back row, chair nearest the door."

"I was standing by the door. But I must admit, my eyes were glued to you." Tee grinned. "You're a real kick on TV."

I glanced nervously toward the men's room door. "Lots of this stuff Nick doesn't know. We're going to focus on Ursula when he gets back. That's mainly the part he knows."

"Which part of Ursula are we speaking of?"

"Don't get me started." I lit a cigarette. "Which reminds me. Is Mrs. St. Clair still in town?"

"Still here."

"I thought she hated L.A."

"Likes it better now. She's got a fella."

"That was fast. Maybe Walter is right. He wonders if she killed him for the insurance."

Tee tried waving at the waiter. But he didn't want to notice. "If she did, she had him killed. She really was on that train. Never got off. Police checked that out."

"Insurance policy?"

"Only fifty grand. They didn't have kids. Probably she'd have done better just spending his paychecks."

"But who is this guy? Maybe they planned it together."

Tee screwed up her face. "Which movie are you speaking of? Anyway, it's Fred Golden. Of the jewelry shop. You know him?"

I shook my head.

"Well, let me put it this way. If Donna saw a mouse, he'd be the one standing on the bed hollering."

We had taken a table in the back of O'Blath's, in the bar area, which was not the place to talk. The bar was jammed at this hour with people from Paramount, who kept bumping into our chairs. I spotted Nick coming out of the men's room. He stopped to talk to an old man dressed in a hat and tails. He looked like Gabby Hayes playing Dracula.

"To bring you up to date," I said, "Ursula found out I was meeting Nick at Chasen's last night, got there first and lured him to her apartment. Prince Charming thought it was me putting on the moves." I stubbed out my cigarette. "You warned me about him once, didn't you?"

"So when did you ever listen to me?"

"Did you order me a Scotch?" Nick sat down and surveyed the drinkless table unhappily.

"You and Walter Pidgeon birdied *which* hole?" said Tee sardonically.

Nick smiled beatifically. "Look, it's TV. You can say anything you want. It's not like anybody's gonna check." Nick leaned over and squeezed my hand. "Right?"

"I don't know. I'm kind of the checking type. If I followed some guy home, I'd sort of check to make sure he was who I thought he was."

Nick made a face and said to Tee, "She's cute, isn't she cute?"

"I know how cute *Paris* is. I want to hear how cute *Ursula* is."

Nick jumped up. "Waiter! We need drinks." He sat down. "I can't take on the two of you thirsty."

I grinned. "Just remember that, Nicky. The next time you tumble into one of your steamy, sticky little fantasies."

"Oooh, what fantasies?" cried Tee, delighted.

Nick tugged at his shirt cuffs. "I understand they've hired a new chef," he said.

At precisely three minutes past nine, Police Chief Harry Gladstone, hatless and wearing a tweed suit with a white linen pocket handkerchief, rang the doorbell. I was absolutely ready for him. I had turned on the lamps in the living room, a part of the house I rarely inhabited, and set out silver bowls, which I rarely used, filled with chocolate-covered bridge mix, cashews, and a platter with cheeses and crackers. Cigars filled the humidor on the coffee table, and a tray with two brandy snifters and a fresh bottle of Courvoisier loomed nearby. I had debated changing into my black silk lounging pajamas, then decided that would be wrong, wrong, wrong. Instead I put on a red cashmere sweater and skirt, black suede open-toed shoes and black silk stockings with seams up the back. Ten minutes before he arrived, I stood nervously in the kitchen repeating my instructions to Mrs. Keyes. Jackson had long ago departed. Andrew was up in his room over the garage, intoning his lines for tomorrow.

Just another typical night at home.

Gladstone stood on the front stoop actually holding a bouquet of flowers. He held them as if they might explode at any minute.

"My, my," I said, "how sweet." Thinking, would this guy give roses to someone he thought was a murderer? "Well come in, *Harry.*"

Mrs. Keyes, outfitted in her serious black house-keeper's uniform, fidgeted uncomfortably in the foyer. I handed her the flowers and led Gladstone past the study, down the hall to the living room. I sat him down, poured him a brandy and held open the humidor. "No, thank you," he said.

I sat at the other end of the couch. "You look tired."

"I don't know why I took this job. It's a lot of thankless work and the newspapers are always gunning for me. You'd think I was a Nazi war criminal instead of a—" He raised the snifter. "Cheers."

"I guess there's a lot of pressure to solve this murder case, huh? It must be frustrating to hit a dead end."

"Who told you that?"

"I don't remember. Anyway, that's the word. Truman Stone said he'd love to have you talk about the case on TV. Maybe you could. It would be good experience for you, Harry."

Gladstone grunted. "The St. Clair case is only one of many. Important, yes. But we have other murders to solve and we've got bunko and illegal gambling operations. This city is rife with crime. And next year's an election year. The politicians are crawling all over me."

"Oh dear. You're speaking of the mayor?"

"The mayor, the city council, the district attorney, the attorney general, the freeway people. You name it."

"The freeway people? What do they want?"

"Roadblocks, traffic officers, special permissions for this and that. But you don't want to hear it." He gave me a meaningful look. "Tell me about you."

"No, really," I protested. "Police work fascinates me. It's so . . ."

"Fascinating," Gladstone supplied.

"Just between us, Harry, are you still looking for the mysterious blonde?"

"You mean the girl with the mole on her knee?"

"Oh." I raised my glass and took a sip of brandy. "So you still think it's me? Forgive me, Chief. But it's so unbelievable to me that I could be considered a suspect. I keep forgetting to take it seriously." I glanced up. "What?"

Mrs. Keyes had come into the room and was shifting from one foot to the other. "I'm sorry, Miss Paris. But I think there's someone lurking out back. I heard a noise and I saw something shadowy."

"Is it Jackson? Maybe he came back."

"Who's Jackson?" said Gladstone, getting to his feet.

"My driver of the moment."

"And I don't like him," Mrs. Keyes declared.

"Jackson? I thought the guy's name was Andrew."

"Jackson's filling in for a few days. Um, Mrs. Keyes, I'm sure there's no one out there."

"I'll take a look anyway," Gladstone announced. "Where?"

He followed my unhappy housekeeper down the hall. I sashayed along behind them. The kitchen, when we arrived, looked like a camp for vagrants. The ironing board was set up. One of my blouses lay across it, half-ironed. Mrs. Keyes had also strung up a clothesline, stretching from one side of the kitchen to the other. Hanging on the clothesline were three of my slips, a robe and—the black negligee.

"I'm sorry about this mess, Harry," I said, as he ducked under the clothesline and scooted round the

ironing board. He reached for the knob on the back
door. Suddenly, a gun appeared in his other hand. It was
a smooth, practiced move. "Get away from the window,"
he called over his shoulder. He went out.

We stood there for a moment, on the far side of the
kitchen table. "Let's go down the hall a bit." I took Mrs.
Keyes's arm. "You look so unhappy."

"What's he going to think of me? Why couldn't I iron
in the utility room? I always iron in the utility room."

"I know. Come along now. We'll just go back to the
living room and wait."

"For what?"

"For him to make sure we're safe. Policemen like to
do that, I think. Then you can fold up the ironing board
and go to bed."

I arranged myself on the couch and waited. After a
long while, the kitchen door slammed. I waited some
more. Eventually, Gladstone's footsteps sounded down
the hall. He filled the arched doorway. He was still holding the service revolver.

"Anything?"

"You're okay." He slipped the gun into a holster on
his belt and smoothed his tweed jacket over it.

"See?" I said to Mrs. Keyes. "I don't know why you're
so jittery lately."

Mrs. Keyes sniffed.

"Come sit down, Harry. That will be all, Mrs. Keyes."

Gladstone sat on the couch, quite a bit closer to me
than before. He put his arm around the back of the
couch and leaned his face into mine. "Frankly, I envi-
sioned a different scene. I have to say, I'm disappointed."

My eyelashes fluttered. "What do you mean?"

"The nightgown. See, I figured you'd put it on for
me." He gave me a wolfish grin. "My hunches aren't
usually wrong."

Instinctively, I leaned back against the cushions. "And
that's why you brought the flowers? To hurry your
hunches along?"

Gladstone laughed. "I like smart women. They really

get my juices going." He stood up and the smile faded. "Just don't get too smart, Paris. I've got to run along."

"Already? What a shame." I lifted my glass and sipped the brandy, not taking my eyes off Gladstone. "You knew I had the nightgown all along."

"Wasn't that the point of Sunday's little melodrama? To get me over here when you were gone?"

"No. Please stay, can't you?" I was suddenly feeling panicked. Why had Gladstone come here?

"I've got a guy in the car. Got to run him downtown."

"You brought a policeman?"

"This ain't no cop. This is who I found prowling out back. I cuffed him and threw him in my car." He walked to the archway. "It's a nice car."

"Are you serious? Who is it?"

"Little twerp says he's Albert Aubrey." The police chief turned. "Know him?"

I sat forward, gaping at Gladstone.

"Says he got lost. You think he got lost?"

He took a step back into the living room. The clock on the mantle ticked a soliloquy.

"He beat me up last week," I said.

Gladstone continued standing where he was. "Is that so?"

"Yes. Right here in my house."

"You don't say."

"I met him on a plane from San Francisco. We played cards. He told me his name was Al Brown. It was—a week ago Sunday. A day or two later he showed up here and tied up Mrs. Keyes. When I got home he said I had stolen his address book. I said I had not. So he beat me up."

"Maybe we'll all go downtown. You can press charges. Funny you didn't mention it before."

I stared at my lap, watching my fingers nervously playing with each other. "I'd rather not."

Gladstone started to come back over, then thought better of it. "Why would he think you swiped his address book?"

Suddenly I saw an opening, and how to play it. I smiled offhandedly. "Maybe I did."

"You stole this guy's address book?"

"But I mailed it back right away."

"Uh huh."

"I went to San Francisco for the day. To see Walter Ainsley. Walter picked me up at the airport and we had lunch at the Fairmont. Walter noticed this man get off the plane, sit at the next table while we had lunch and follow us out of the hotel. He got to the airport a minute after we did. Walter said I should sit next to him on the plane and try to find out what his game was."

"What was it?"

"I don't know. He said he was in sporting goods. He said he had a business appointment but the party didn't show. Anyway, when he went to the rest room, I opened his briefcase and all I could find was the address book. I took it hoping it would tell me something. It didn't."

"I'm afraid you're going to have to come downtown, Paris."

"Uh, I have a friend upstairs, Harry."

Reflexively, his eyes rolled up to the ceiling. "Who?"

"I'd rather not say." I stood up. "Look, he can't prove I took his address book. He didn't see me. He came into my house and searched it. Didn't find it. I mailed it back, he has it. But I can prove he tied up Mrs. Keyes and beat up me. I have a bruised rib. I went to the hospital."

"What are you saying? That you won't press charges if he won't?"

"That's what I'm saying."

Gladstone pressed his lips together, then shrugged. Once again his eyes combed the ceiling. "You really have someone up there, huh?"

I smiled sheepishly.

Gladstone shook his head. "My hunches usually aren't wrong," he said.

36

Tee and I sat on my bed drinking Cokes and brandy. Not together, but alternately. And munching on potato chips. "So now Gladstone can roast Albert Aubrey-Brown," I said cheerfully. "He can find out about Richard Walken, if he hasn't already." I chewed on a chip. "I don't know what he knows, except I think he knows more than I know he knows."

Tee was frowning. "What about the nightgown?" She seemed a little crabby. Maybe because she had driven all the way from Arizona. She still had on her driving clothes: a man's plaid flannel shirt over a T-shirt and black cotton trousers. Her long, wild hair snaked down her back in a thick braid. Her creamy skin looked a bit green in the lamplight of my bedroom.

"He saw it. Maybe I didn't have to run it up like a flag for him. But for sure he knows I have it."

"So?"

"Right." I stared at the two glasses on my bedside table and went for the Coke. "I guess all it means is that the nightgown at Jim's house wasn't mine. Which doesn't mean anything. I could have killed Jim anyway. Only I didn't."

"So now Nick delivers the nightgown to Ursula?"

I grinned. "And collects ten grand." I put the Coke down and threw myself back against the pillows. "I get half."

"Sure," said Tee.

"You don't think she'll pay?"

"She's a very crafty girl."

Tee was sitting cross-legged at the foot of my bed. I got up and went over to the gray-and-white striped silk chaise near the windows and curled up on it. I needed the distance. The time for games was over. "Let's talk, Tee. Okay?"

She swiveled round to face me. "Ursula?"

"Ursula. Tell me what you know, how you found her."

"And in return?"

"I'll tell you what I know. How I found her." Tee gave me a look that said *nice try*. "You'll want to know this," I promised.

She pulled the braid forward, over her shoulder, and began fiddling with the ends. Tee needed to play with her hair in order to think.

"Okay. A neighbor saw a blonde get out of the car with Jim a little past eight, like I told you. Someone else saw a blonde leave the house about ten-thirty. So I'm wondering, if this blonde came with Jim, how did she get home? Maybe, if I wasn't going to be lucky, she got someone to pick her up. But if I was going to be lucky, maybe she took a cab. I thought about the cab after I realized you could walk from Jim's house over to Larchmont, and there's usually a cab in front of the drugstore. If I was going to be lucky."

"Of course," I chimed in. I, too, had been wondering how Ursula had made her escape.

"Turns out a blonde got in the cab of a Bobby Roper about the right time. And lucky me, Bobby didn't turn the meter on. He was getting ready to quit for the day and he figured he'd make the run and not report it. So I got Bobby to think real hard and remember the address. It was the same one on the bill from Brahm's."

"What else did Ursula tell you?"

"She said that Jim, being the man he was, working the hours he did, was always busy. That night was the only time he could meet with her about his *lawn.*"

"Ah." I lit a cigarette. "The lawn. So she wasn't there as a, um, friend?"

"Of course not. The blonde showed up, she and Jim went upstairs. Ursula left."

"So when did the cabdriver take her home? That should prove if she's telling the truth."

Tee's smile faded. "That's where my luck ran out. The guy had been dozing, couldn't be sure. His car clock doesn't work. All he knows is that he got to the cab stand a little before nine and kept the engine running until Phil Silvers was over. He made one short run, came back, dozed and woke up to Miss Drop-Dead jumping in the backseat. After he let her off, he went home. To Boyle Heights. He got there just as the news was ending and Steve Allen was coming on. That would have been sometime before eleven-fifteen."

"How long would it take to drive from Ursula's to Boyle Heights?"

"Depends where. Thirty minutes."

"So she didn't leave at nine-thirty. See? She had to have left much later."

"It probably doesn't matter, Paris. She didn't kill Jim."

"But how do you know?"

"The gun and the shirts were found in a trash can two blocks west of Muirfield. Larchmont is three blocks east. I doubt she would have made that detour. If she had killed him, she would have wanted to get out of the neighborhood as fast as possible." Tee hesitated. "Course I could be wrong."

She stretched out, laying her head on the pillow closest to me, and sipped her brandy. She had discreetly moved out of my line of vision so I wouldn't have to look at her while I told her.

"I didn't know about her," I said quietly. "Or any of

them. Lucille Wills and Ursula and somebody, I think, named Barbie." I hesitated. "Have you come across a Barbie?"

Tee shook her head.

"Jim may have met her after work that night." Again I stopped. "This is really hard to talk about."

"Take your time."

"Okay." But I didn't go on. I lay back on the chaise, taking one of the throw pillows and hugging it to my chest. From downstairs I could hear Mrs. Keyes moving around, probably shutting off lights.

"When I got to Jim's house, I had no idea anyone else was there. They must have been in the den. I used my key and opened the kitchen door. He heard me and came out and took me upstairs. Everything was like it always was. I knew his wife was coming, he had told me. That's one reason I wanted to see him that night. Or he wanted to see me. He said things were bad between them and he didn't know if she was going to stay in L.A. or go back, that this was something they would have to resolve."

"Yep. Ursula told me that, too."

"Then, when I was getting up to leave, the phone rang."

"Wait. You got up to leave from where, the bed?"

"Come on, Tee."

"But, Paris, how did you feel? Knowing it might be over?"

I didn't answer. I tossed the pillow on the floor and stood up. I went over to the window seat and pushed up one of the windows. Then I sat down on the edge of the chaise, facing Tee directly. "I'm not sure. I mean I wasn't in love with him, I don't think. There was something we were both holding back. Besides, sometimes you don't realize what someone means to you until they're gone."

Tee nodded.

"I never spent the night. I always went home. So after a while I got up and got dressed. He wanted me to bring his briefcase in from the car, which I did. I locked the front door behind me and went back around to the alley where Andrew was. I don't remember if I actually got in the car, or just opened the door. But I realized I had left my book. So I went back."

"You entered through the kitchen? Or the front door?"

"The kitchen. It was dark, but I could see my way to the kitchen table where I'd left it."

"Go on." It was a whisper.

"I heard voices talking softly. For just a moment. Then it was quiet. I edged into the dining room. The light was on in the rotunda. I knew I had turned it off. I edged a little bit closer. His back was to me. And—" My voice trailed off as the picture flicked on in my mind.

"Tell me."

"A pair of arms were around his neck."

"They never saw you?"

I shook my head.

"You're sure?"

In my silence, I could hear a car drive slowly up the street. But the image in my mind was of them, so wrapped up in each other. He hadn't even rushed me, or suggested in any way that I leave, as if he knew she would wait, however long it took. Or maybe, the coldness in him precluded him from caring—one way or another.

I cleared my throat.

"They wouldn't have noticed King Kong."

After a while, we went downstairs and took up new positions in the living room. Tee was unusually silent. I began telling her about Sunday, and the warning intended for her.

"They know about *me*? Hell, who are these people? Did you tell Gladstone?"

"No."

I then described my phone call to Sunset Estates, and finished with the news that Matthew Barnathan was trying to get on TV. "He was the one in the audience tonight. Do you know anything about him?"

Tee bent forward, grabbed a handful of bridge mix and popped it in her mouth. "I'll ask around."

In Tee's life as a madam, she had been hostess to some of the city's most powerful men. She had taken good care of them up in the mansion over Sunset, keeping her mouth shut, telling the lies that needed to be told to protect them. In return, she had a townful of friends whom she could call on if she needed to.

The phone rang. I jumped up and went off to answer it.

"Paris? It's Mrs. Benton from Saks. Am I calling too late? My daughter dropped in and . . ."

"No, this is fine. You went through the sales slips?"

"Yep. The first negligee was bought by Mr. St. Clair and sent to you, August nineteenth. Then a lady in Beverly Hills sent one to her daughter in Seattle, Washington, on the twenty-first. A Mrs. Dornak. On September first, Nancy Nightingale bought one. She sings on the radio. Both those ladies used charge accounts. The last negligee was sold on September sixth. It must have been paid for in cash, because we don't have a name on the sales slip. I may have written it up, I just don't remember."

"Would you have remembered if Mr. St. Clair had bought it?"

"Oh yes, definitely. But the one he bought he sent to you. I sold that one myself."

"So if he had come back, you would have remembered, right?"

"Sure. If you want, I'll check the time cards and see who else was working that day. Oh wait."

There was a pause. Then, "I just remembered something. I personally sold the first three. Ah, now it's coming back. Then someone came in looking for a real nice gown and I went to show her this one thinking there was still one left. But there wasn't. So it must have been sold by someone else."

"If you could find out, I'd really appreciate it," I said. She promised she would call me the next day. I thanked her and hung up. I went back to the living room and reported to Tee.

"She'll only tell you he bought it. What difference does it make?"

"None, I guess. Actually, I'll be happy to get rid of mine. I don't think I want that particular reminder anymore."

Tee sat up. "Listen, Paris. Don't give it to Ursula. She's setting you up."

"How? Gladstone knows . . ."

Tee was shaking her head. "The police don't know about her."

"But you do. And I do."

"Hush. She will go to the police herself. She will tell them she was there that night, that you were there. You had all these opportunities to tell Gladstone the truth. They will think less of your story because you didn't."

"But what's *her* story?"

"Whatever she wants it to be."

"And they'll believe her? That's ridiculous."

"She'll say it's your nightgown they found. She can say what she told me. She was there about his lawn. If Jim bought the other nightgown without her, nobody will know he gave it to her."

"In that case, why would she want mine?"

"Mainly to get it away from you. That way you wouldn't be able to prove the one the police found wasn't yours."

"So I outsmarted her. The police know mine's here."

"Not necessarily."

"For God's sake, Tee . . ."

"If she did go to Saks with Jim, then she has to worry that the salesgirl can identify her."

"Uh huh."

"Luring Nick to her apartment was really clever. Believe me, you'll never see the ten grand."

"I don't understand what you're saying."

"Ursula will say that Nick followed her home, charmed his way in and wound up in her bed."

"*On* her bed," I said testily.

"And then"—Tee began batting her eyelashes—"can you believe this, Chief? I come out of my bathroom and . . . the guy's *gone*."

I stared at Tee, finally getting it. "You're kidding," I said.

"And, Chief Gladstone—guess what?"

I felt my throat tighten. "She wouldn't," I whispered.

Tee picked up the bowl of bridge mix and stared at it bleakly. "Let me ask you something." She put the bowl down. "Is there anything else to eat?"

37

◆

I was sitting at my desk, skimming a self-congratulatory editorial in the *Times*. A unified smog control district had been approved by the state legislature the day before, thanks to a *Times* crusade, of course, and now conquest of the dirty air could proceed in an organized fashion. Constance McPhee Estevez leaned over my shoulder to see what I was reading. "L.A. was so great before the war," I said wistfully. I glanced back at her. "Remember?"

"Remember? I get nauseous driving to work. All this construction. The traffic is insane. The count wants to buy a horse ranch in Santa Barbara."

I put down the paper. "Sounds nice."

Constance was a blaze of orange. Orange suit and an orange cloche and sunset orange lips. Some of the lipstick had rubbed off on her teeth. She sighed. "Anyway, dear, Etta wants you to get hold of Clark Gable. The rumor is he's agreed to do a series of magazine articles called, 'The Women I've Loved.' Hollywood is hysterical."

"Oh what *fun*. Where is he?"

"On the set of *Homecoming*. But call publicity first."

I called MGM and left word with Kate Levine in publicity, then I went to work on my own list of numbers. I had started the day before, trying to get the names of subcontractors the state used in its relocation program. The Division of Highways was its usual unhelpful self, so, with the yellow pages at my elbow, I began blindly phoning contractors, companies that did demolition work and those that moved houses. I asked the same question of all: Did they know who was doing work for the state? Interestingly, the name Barnathan was not listed anywhere in the yellow pages.

But it did come up in conversation. Repeatedly.

"Some of the demolition's done by the fire department," one man told me. "But I think Matt Barnathan does some of it, too."

"I'd guess there's thirty, forty companies moving houses," another man told me. "These firms are springing up like mushrooms."

"What about Barnathan?"

"Oh yeah. He's got a whole vacant lot filled with houses, like used cars."

"He does?"

"See, he buys houses cheap at auction and hauls them out to his lot. People come in and pick out a house. Barnathan moves the house and renovates it. Or he does the work first then puts the house on the market."

"He can do that, huh?"

"Why not? All the state wants to do is get rid of the houses. And because he's a big contractor, he can use his own men to fix them up cheaper."

I heard the same report from five different people.

But only one knew where the lot was located. I took down the address and hung up, stunned.

.   .   .

"Bingo!" I said to Walter.

"Naw, it's not my kind of game."

He was sitting at the copy desk, working the *Examiner* crossword puzzle, waiting for stories to start flowing in. He looked up and raised an eyebrow. "Mah-Jongg?"

"You're awfully chipper today." He had a bit of a tan. His white shirtsleeves were rolled up to show off his muscular forearms. Walter was quite proud of his arms. "I'm not sure good humor really suits you."

"Did you see the paper this morning?"

"Sure, why?"

"Front page story, 'Fiend Attacks Handcuffed Woman in Park'? I worked on that. I *love* stories about fiends."

"In that case, there's a fiend I must tell you about."

"Goodwin?"

"Very funny. Barnathan."

Walter's grin faded. "Christ, I forgot. I've got something for you, too." He looked at his watch. "Let's run out, get a cup of coffee. I'm waiting for a car theft ring to come in."

"Mm." I smiled languidly. "I'm waiting for Clark Gable."

Walter tossed his pencil down. "Obviously, I win."

The counter at Gallagher's was filled, the early lunch crowd having already claimed it. So we took a table near the back.

Mort, the string-bean waiter who boasted he was heading for a major career as a drummer, brought us coffee and toast.

"How old do you suppose that bread is?" said Walter, as I spread a little strawberry jam across one piece.

"Three or four weeks?"

"You look so elegant in that Dior or Pucci or whatever. And you sit here lapping up junk like a common soul."

"My soul isn't elegant, Walter. And it needs food more than my outfit. Which is really just off the rack." I had on an Elsa Schiaparelli brown-and-gold plaid suit. It had been an expensive rack. I laid my knife across the plate. "You were going to tell me something."

Walter stirred sugar into his coffee. "The grand jury's meeting. Guess what they're looking into?"

"Matthew Barnathan?" I said, biting into my toast.

"Right-of-way agents making illegal profits on sales of houses to the state."

I put down my toast. "Oh boy."

"The word is indictments are going to come down by the end of the week."

"Barnathan?"

"My information isn't that good. How's the toast?"

"Delicious. Listen to this. Barnathan is doing big business buying houses at auction, warehousing them, finding buyers, then renovating them. He uses his own companies to demolish, move and renovate."

"Doesn't mean he's doing anything illegal," Walter said.

"Unless he's somehow connected with Walken or Norman Wills. I've been thinking. Suppose Wills tells Walken where the freeway is going before it becomes general knowledge. Walken sends Ursula to buy property. The seller pays a commission to Walken, who acts as broker. Then Walken, acting for the state, buys the property from Ursula. At an inflated price. Ursula makes a killing, which she shares with Walken."

"Wills, too?"

"Maybe. He has to be getting something out of this. But I don't see how Barnathan fits in. Yet somehow these houses end up with him. And I think that's what Jim found out."

Walter sipped his coffee but said nothing.

"What I'm thinking is for us to try to link up all of Barnathan's dealings and see where they lead."

Walter shook his head. "Wait for the indictments. You may be way off base."

"The point is not to wait for the indictments. The point is for you to break the story first."

"It's not my beat, kiddo."

"Is this the new Walter Ainsley speaking?"

"There isn't a new Walter, sorry."

"Oh yes there is. Or will be. Look, I can't do it. You know how they regard me. I'm just this silly society reporter who can't even . . ."

"Drive," Walter said.

"If you can break this story," I continued, ignoring him, "you'll be back in the game, doing what you love, instead of rotting away on the copy desk."

"Oh yeah? And what's in it for you?"

"To find Jim's killer and get me off the hook. I don't trust Gladstone. The police are corrupt."

"Not necessarily. He's been cleaning the department up."

"How do you know?"

"You've got it all figured out, eh?" Walter gave me one of his annoying indulgent grins.

"I've got one thing figured out." I licked some jam off my thumb. "Everyone's been looking for a woman named Barbie, the name Jim scrawled on a scrap of paper. Remember?"

"Yeah."

"Guess what? Barnathan's got a lot in East L.A., where he's stockpiling houses he buys at auction."

"Uh huh," said Walter, watching me smear jam on the second piece of toast.

"The lot happens to be located on Barbee Street. Two ee's."

Walter just looked at me. Then he smiled, little by little. "Did I ever tell you what an elegant soul you are?"

Mort arrived and began drumming his fingers on the table. "Can I get you folks anything else—be bop a hee hop, dum, dum, dum."

"More coffee, please."

"Me, too," said Walter. "And bring me some toast."

Kate Levine returned my call shortly after I got back to Society. "You want to speak to Clark?"

"Can you arrange it?"

Kate Levine could generally arrange anything she

wanted to. She was one of the sharper publicists on the MGM lot and she had figured out right away that doing favors for me got favors in Etta's column in return. I had done more than my share of dumb starlet Items so that once in a while I could land a Clark Gable.

"Just between us," Kate confided, "he's really grouchy today. Can it wait?"

"No."

"What's it about?"

"Just tell him I'm checking out a report."

"I *know* what to tell him, Paris. But you've got to be straight with me."

I told Kate about the rumored magazine articles. She began to laugh. "I'm sure he was joking. But let me catch him during lunch break. Will you be there if he wants to call you?"

"Not even an earthquake could move me," I said.

Sometime during the afternoon, between the phone call from Mrs. Benton and the one from Clark Gable, I decided to get tricky. I would call Barnathan's office. I had memorized the number from the brochure I had picked up at Jim's house. It was a Valley number.

I got Jo to ring it. After a woman sang the name of the company, I asked for Mr. Barnathan.

"He's not in. Who is this?"

"Could I speak to his secretary, please?"

"Nancy isn't here either. Can I help you?"

"I'll call back," I said and disconnected.

I hoped Nancy wasn't an old girl. I dialed Norman Wills's office. The spinster, Miss Bell, answered.

"Hi, it's Nancy," I said, squeezing my nose. "Do we have a meeting with you this afternoon? I have something written down here."

"Nancy?"

"Mr. Barnathan asked me to check."

"Oh, *Nancy.* Gee, you sound awful. It must be that flu that's going around."

"Tell me," I moaned.

"Well, honey, I think you got confused. They're at the DAC having lunch right now."

"Oh. So that's what this scribbling means." I laughed. "Hookay. Thanks, dear." I hung up. Grinning a devilish grin.

And dialed Lucille Wills.

"Hi, it's Paris Chandler. I have some news for you."

I hadn't. But I didn't want her to hang up on me, which she probably was all set to do.

An icy silence followed.

"Lucille, I'm sorry about the other day."

"What do you want?"

"Some help."

"You expect me to help you? Lewis, quiet down, honey."

I could hear the kid bawling in the background. "I tricked you and you have every right to be angry. But I did get those letters for you, remember?"

"And what about the other letter, Norman threatening Jim? Was that a trick, too?"

I stared at my crayon pot and finally selected a bright red. "No," I lied. "It wasn't a trick, too."

"Then where is it? I want that letter."

"I want something first."

"What?"

What I wanted were answers to two questions. There was no reason for her to answer them, except as payment for a letter that didn't exist. She was probably a nice lady. But both of us had been pushed into corners and I was going to have to keep muscling her if I hoped to get out of mine.

I said, "I understand you are trying to protect your husband. He wants to run for district attorney and neither of you wants to be connected to James St. Clair. Correct?"

"Are you threatening me?"

"No. Listen, Lucille. Did you know that Ursula Martens was at Jim's house the night he was murdered?"

In her silence, I could hear Lewis babbling idiotically. "I didn't know. Are you sure?"

"The *Examiner* has a team looking into this."

"Do the police know?"

"I can't say. Personally, I don't know if the police care who killed Jim. Someone may be sitting on them. Which brings up an interesting thought. If the papers start screaming about the lack of police initiative, and the D.A. hasn't been heard from either, a few people could lose their jobs."

"Wait—are you saying it's to Norman's advantage if they don't catch James's killer?"

"I said it's an interesting thought."

"Well your interesting thought has nothing to do with Norman or me. Unless—"

"That's right, Lucille. Unless I tell the reporters what I know."

"You're trying to blackmail me."

"But not for money. Do you know Matthew Barnathan?"

"He's a real estate developer in the Valley. I've *heard* of him."

"Never met him?"

"Not that I remember. Norm's mentioned him."

"In what connection?"

"Lewis!" There was a loud crash. Then, "Just a moment. Lewis knocked a plate on the floor. Can I call you back?"

"I'll wait."

I used the red crayon to draw a devil. I put a skirt on the devil. The devil, at the moment, was me. Lucille eventually came back on the line sounding like she was going to cry. "He was a colicky baby but he was supposed to grow out of it." Her voice carried a whine I didn't begrudge her.

"Have you thought of getting a nanny to help out?"

"Yes. But Norman doesn't understand what goes on here all day. He says we can't afford one."

"Running for office is expensive."

"That's it," said Lucille suddenly. "I think that's how Norman knows Mr. Barnathan. They're both members of the Better Los Angeles Committee."

"What's that?"

"I think it's a group of lawyers and doctors and businessmen who work toward improving the city, something like that."

"Why would your husband have mentioned Barnathan?"

"Norman was talking to me about raising campaign funds. I think that's when his name came up. But what does this have to do with you, or with James?"

I looked up. Constance was dancing in front of my desk, mouthing the name Clark Gable.

"Lucille, you're not going to believe this, but I have to take a call from Clark Gable. We'll talk again."

"But—"

"Listen, you'll be okay. I promise."

Another lie. I felt like a real heel. I should have been badgering her husband, not her.

I hung up and waited for Jo to transfer the call.

"Miss Chandler?"

"Mr. *Gable.*"

"And how is the lovely first lady of gossip, Etta Rice?"

"Fine, I believe." I lowered my voice conspiratorially. "She put me up to this."

"In that case, the next time I see her, I'll beat her silly."

Officious, bullying and irritating, Etta nevertheless managed to win the affection of those off whom she earned her considerable living. It always amazed me. I said, "We'll all want tickets to that. Now, about this other thing. How much are you getting paid? I hear it's quite a sum."

Gable laughed. "We could make one up. How much do you think I *should* be paid to spill the beans?"

"Oh lots. Thousands."

"Maybe I should do it then, do you think?"

"Oh yes. Do it."

"Seriously, I was just kidding Lana. We were on the set waiting to do a scene and I told her I'd been offered a large hunk of dough to write these articles. 'The Women I've Loved,' I think I called it."

"Lana Turner? How did she take it?"

"I said, I can spill a lot of beans if I write about you. And about the others I've loved in celluloid, such as Greta Garbo, Joan Crawford, Myrna Loy, Hedy Lamarr, Greer Garson, Norma Shearer, Vivien Leigh, Deborah Kerr—"

"How about not in celluloid?"

"Fat chance, my dear."

"So are you going to do the articles, Mr. Gable?"

"No. I refused the offer. After all, I have to live in this town."

I said good-bye. I had wanted to ask him if he would say it just once, "Frankly, my dear, I don't give a damn." But I couldn't bring myself to actually ask.

I stared at my scribbled notes and wondered: How could I be such a sap for a movie star—and such a conniving, lying bully to a poor defenseless woman?

It spoke of a dark side to my personality that I wasn't sure I cared to explore.

38
.

When Mrs. Benton had phoned earlier that afternoon, she confirmed Ursula's story. The part-time salesgirl had indeed sold the last black negligee to Mr. St. Clair, whom, she said, was in the company of an attractive blond companion. The news depressed me.

I finished typing the Clark Gable Item and phoned Etta's house. Roxy said Etta was at that moment squabbling with her hairdresser and why didn't I just send the Item through and the copy desk could stitch it in. I rolled up the piece of paper, walked over to Constance's desk, slid the Item into a metal cylinder and shoved it into the pneumatic tube. The Item would be whisked by air pressure straight downstairs to the printers. Did he have to buy her the exact same nightgown?

I returned to my desk and tried Tee at her office in Hollywood. She answered on the second ring. "He really did. He bought her the exact same nightgown," I said.

"Not necessarily. The police found the negligee hanging in the closet. He could have bought it for his wife."

"He would have had it gift-wrapped."

"Men don't always think of those things."

"Oh really," I said crabbily.

"Tell Nick to offer Ursula your negligee and see what she does. How much do you want to bet she reneges?"

"Nothing. My instincts are on the blink. In the meantime, Walter and I are going for a little spin. I've found the mysterious Barbee."

I gave Tee the details and told her I'd call her later.

I phoned Nick at Etta Rice's house and we made plans to meet up at Ciro's at nine. By then, presumably, he would have talked to Ursula.

It was only five. I lit a cigarette and suddenly wondered why I hadn't heard from Chief Gladstone about Albert Aubrey-Brown. But my thoughts soon strayed.

If he'd bought it for his wife, I wouldn't have felt so blue.

A sliver of moon hung in the sky as we drove through downtown, then swung over to Main Street and headed east.

We kept driving east, over the sad Los Angeles River and into a neighborhood called Lincoln Heights. It was just north of Boyle Heights, but it didn't mean anything to me. My life's border stopped at downtown.

"Are you sure we haven't left the country?" I said to Walter.

"You'll know when you see the cannibals."

Actually, Lincoln Heights looked pretty much like Los Angeles, that is, street after street of little box houses all squished together, some wood, many stucco. Occasionally, I spotted a tree.

"Check the map," Walter said. "I should be turning somewhere around here."

I held up Walter's city map and tried to catch the intermittent street lamps. "Jackson would have known," I said grieviously.

Jackson had been the source of a major argument in the parking lot across from the *Examiner.* Walter had a fit when I started to get into the Bentley. "You don't go to knock over a place in a limo," he had bellowed.

"It's not a limo," I had replied coolly. "It's my car."

"If it's got a driver, it's a limo."

The Bentley stayed put. As did Jackson.

"You want to turn left on Griffin Avenue. No. Take Eastlake. That's just beyond." I put down the map. "I think."

"I suppose," said Walter, "some people find your helplessness endearing."

"Me? You're the one who had to be dragged into this story if I remember correctly. You still think you can't do it."

"Because it isn't my story."

"There. I made my point. Here's Eastlake."

Walter turned left. Two blocks later he turned right. "Barbee Street," he announced with a flourish.

It was a disappointing destination. All this time, Barbee had taken on a mysterious allure. But in real life it was a street only two blocks long. On the first block a warehouse commanded the south side and four ramshackle houses the north. The second block had three sagging houses on the north and the Barnathan Collection on the south. The Packard coughed and expired at the curb.

"Will you look at this?"

We peered out the windshield. The lot contained row upon row of houses on wooden blocks, one crammed up against the other. Piles of rubble littered the front of the lot. Except for the moon slice, the only available light glowed dimly from two street lamps.

"This could be your lead, Walter. Have you ever seen such a sight?"

Walter grabbed a flashlight from the glove compartment and didn't respond. We got out of the car and walked along the broken sidewalk of Barbee Street. The houses, like little soldiers all in a row, faced the street. At the center of the lot, a wide gap had been left between houses, forming a path to the back. Walter switched on the flashlight and played it on the ground as we walked single file along the path, making crunching noises on the gravel stone. It was a deep lot. Six rows of houses had been shoehorned in. At the back stood a chain-link fence.

Walter frowned. "No trailer. I'm surprised they don't have a trailer. You'd think they'd have some kind of office."

"Maybe they're using a house."

A light breeze kicked up, carrying with it dampness from the ocean. I pulled the belt of my trench coat tighter around me.

"If they're using a house," Walter said with certainty, "it would be along this path or in the front."

He clumped up the steps to a little box house with an arched doorway. He tried the knob and came back down. He went over to a window and peered in. From somewhere in the neighborhood, a dog howled.

"Maybe we should go," I said dubiously.

"I'll try a couple more."

"What do you expect to find?"

"That, my dear Watson, is the point."

I didn't know what that was supposed to mean and I doubted Walter did either. I watched him try another doorknob and began to wonder who had lived in these houses and if they, like Esther Lubinow, had felt the pain of being shoved out. The strange lot with its sad remnants began to feel like a graveyard for a dead way of life.

Walter came back to me. "I have another lead for your story," I said. "The strange lot with its . . ."

Walter held up a finger.

From somewhere behind me came the faint sound of a door creaking, or maybe it was the rustling of leaves in the breeze. "I think someone's in the last house with a flashlight," Walter whispered. We crept further along, past the final row of houses, then along the chain-link fence to the last house on the lot. It was a strange-looking building, two narrow rooms protruding, each under a triangular roof, with the front door set back in between. Walter walked up the front steps and rapped softly on the door.

Carefully, he turned the knob. The door opened. He stepped inside. "Anybody home?"

The blackness swallowed him.

Nearby, a car engine turned over. I stood there uncertainly. Then I walked up the steps. As I stood just inside the doorway, a light suddenly came on to the left. I followed it into a musty room. Walter was standing beside a desk with an old oil lantern on it. A small flame flickered. "I thought I saw a flashlight through the window. But it could have been this."

I took a step into the room. It was rectangular, the length running from the front of the house to the back. It had probably been the living room, now stripped bare. The wooden floorboards looked worn and scratched. The paint on the walls, a drab yellow, appeared fresher. In the middle of the ceiling, two wires dangled, the remains of some kind of lighting fixture. In the corners of the room, large cobwebs added to the eerie decor.

"Which means somebody is here, or was here," Walter said.

"I heard a car engine a moment ago. Perhaps he left."

"I shouldn't have left the car out front. They'll see it."

"Who will?"

But Walter didn't answer. He was staring across the room. My eyes followed his. I hadn't even seen it, a small, two-drawer wooden file cabinet. Walter picked up the lantern and carried it over, set it on the floor. "See what's inside, Paris. I'm going to look around."

He switched on the flashlight and turned away. But I was already cross-legged on the floor, pulling open the top drawer. It was filled with folders, neatly aligned. Each folder had a four-digit number printed on the front cover and appeared to contain information about a house. I pulled three at random and set them on the floor.

The bottom drawer contained more folders, but these had been carelessly thrown in. The first two I opened contained architectural drawings and building plans. I put them on the floor.

"Paris, you about ready?"

I opened a big manila envelope and pulled out a handful of papers. "Oh boy." I turned and glanced up. "I think these are freeway plans. They're stamped Division of Highways."

"Take it, we'll look later."

I pulled another folder out. In it were two receipts for plumbing supplies. That left two fat folders on the bottom of the drawer. I opened one. A thick sheaf of papers, stapled, with the words "Geological Survey."

"Let's go." Walter's hand was on my shoulder. I grabbed the last folder.

"Give me another minute."

"I'm going to move the car. I'll be right back."

I heard the front door close softly. But my attention quickly drifted. Unlike the other folders in the drawer, this one was labeled. I stared at the neat printing on the tab. *Freeways-One.* I opened it. "Oh god," I whispered.

It was James St. Clair's freeway file.

I began thumbing through it. It was filled with sheets of copy paper, scraps of paper, printed material from the Division of Highways. Also letters. I became so engrossed that I must not have heard the door open. But something—a sound, a movement—made me turn my head.

Standing in the doorway, smiling genially, was a large blond man in a cheap leather jacket, blue jeans and scuffed brown workman's boots. He wore a cap. "Hi." He took a heavy step toward me. "Whaddya doing here?"

"Hi. Er—"

"Get up."

I smiled. "Okay." Slowly, I put Jim's folder on the floor and got to my feet. Just then the front door opened and slammed. I held my breath, waiting for Walter to appear. But it wasn't Walter.

"Well well, look who's here," said Albert Aubrey-Brown.

I stood perfectly still, staring at his pointed gun.

"My knuckles long for your ribs, did you miss me?" I screamed.

Which was a mistake. They were on me in a flash. One hand flattened itself on my mouth, another yanked at my hat. The long hat pin that secured it tore at my hair. Another hand, the big blond guy's, began dragging me, pulling me out the door, down the steps. The chain-link fence curved around the side of the lot for only a short distance. They pushed me along to the opening and out to the side street. A battered truck was parked at the curb. The big guy shoved me onto the front seat and squeezed in beside me while Brown hopped in on the driver's side. He switched on the ignition and we were gone. I doubted the whole incident had taken more than three-and-a-half minutes.

"I know a nice empty lot," the blond guy said, "not far from here."

"First we check with the boss."

"What for?"

"Shut up."

"Jeez, Al, why mess around?"

"Shut up," Aubrey-Brown repeated.

"And take your hand off my knee." I tried to elbow the lout, but there was no room to maneuver. He kept his hand where it was.

I sat there rigid as a corpse—hoping I wouldn't become one.

Thirty minutes and one pay-phone call later, we pulled into the parking lot of the Players' Club on Sunset. Brown steered the truck along the lot to the west, double-parking in front of a row of shiny, well-kept sedans. My spirits rose. Instead of ending up in the godforsaken Valley, I was back on home turf. Ciro's, where I was to meet Nick, was just down the street.

Brown switched off the ignition and pocketed the keys. "No monkey business." He got out and slammed the door. Behind me, I could hear cars pull up and doors slam. I stared through the windows into the restaurant. Questionable-looking men in shiny suits and women in tight dresses swam in circles around the bar. Years ago, it was the place to be seen, but now it had fallen into disrepute, a hangout for tourists and mobsters and con men on the lam. I felt the blond guy's hand creep up my leg.

"Watch it, buster."

I crept closer to the steering wheel, wondering what my chances were of barreling out the door. The hand came off my leg and grabbed my shoulder, jerking me into him. I tried to push away, without a whole lot of force. I didn't want to get into a boxing match with this creep. He tightened his hold on me and forced his scummy face into mine. He reeked of body odor. I began to struggle as he tried to jam his tongue into my mouth. But he had my arms pinned against me and my legs were in a tangle pointing toward the driver's door. I kept my teeth clenched and finally he gave up.

"You stink," I said.

"You love it," he said.

I slapped his face, and reached behind me for the door handle. But he grabbed me first. And then I saw Brown trotting toward us. He opened the door and climbed in.

"He'll meet us across the street."

Brown pulled out onto Sunset and made a U-turn. We drove east past Crescent Heights and turned right into the Garden of Allah. He parked in front of a row of hedges, bordering three of the hotel's bungalows. I was yanked out and shoved down a path. We pulled up short in front of Bungalow 10. Brown rapped on the door.

It swung back. A peroxide case in a purple negligee leaned against the door frame. "Oh it's you." She turned on her high-heeled slippers and swung her ample hips into the room.

"Get dressed, Ginger, and then get lost," said Brown.

She picked up a pack of cigarettes off the desk and lit one. "Where is he?"

"He's got business to conduct. Come back in an hour."

She eyed me suspiciously. "Who's this?"

"The business. Now scram."

Ginger slunk into the bedroom and banged the door shut. "You," said Brown, "sit over there."

I walked over to the drab gold couch and sat down. "How about giving me a cigarette," I said.

Brown tossed me Ginger's pack. I shook out a cigarette and picked up a book of matches from the coffee table. The lug went over to the desk and switched on the radio. He got Jack Benny and Phil Harris. The lug began to laugh.

I didn't. "Who's coming? Barnathan?"

Aubrey-Brown grinned. "It's a surprise party."

"Look, Jack, I'm figuring on buying a small ranch," Phil Harris was saying, *"and I got most of the dough but I need a little more to swing the deal and I was kind of wondering if you'd lend me ten thousand dollars."*

"Mary, tell him I'm not home, will you please?"

The lug chuckled.

"Wellll," said Benny, *"are you willing to put up security?"*

"Yeah," said Harris. *"But not like the last time. We* missed *the kids."*

That cracked the lout up. He gaffawed loudly. The bedroom door opened and Ginger, wrapped in a snug gold cocktail dress, slunk out. "Say, fellas, I have no car, no moolah. Someone wanna buy a girl a drink?"

"Yeah," said Brown. "Come on, we'll go to the bar. Mikey, I'll be right back."

"Bring me a beer."

"Sure."

After they left I put out my cigarette. The heavy glass ashtray was one weapon, but it would be a job grabbing it at the right moment and coldcocking the creep. He was watching me now, from across the room, his attention divided between me and Jack Benny. In a moment, he would be on the couch.

Casually I lifted my arms and pulled my hat pin out, cupping my right hand around it. Then I took off my fedora, set it down and shook my hair. I smiled at him.

The pin had a large piece of purple glass, shaped like

an acorn, at one end and five inches of pin shooting out of it. I rested my hands on the couch on either side of me and slowly, seductively crossed my legs.

He stood up.

"Leave me alone," I said.

He walked toward me.

"I mean it, go away." I edged away from him, to my right, hoping he would sit down to my left.

He stood above me, grinning dopily under the bill of his cap. I held up my left hand protectively. "Get lost."

He grabbed my hand and hauled me to my feet. "Time for beddy-bye," he grunted. And began dragging me toward the bedroom.

In the doorway, I resisted. There was a large unmade bed pushed up against the far wall. Beside it, a lamp was on. He shoved me into the room and knocked me onto the bed. "Strip."

"Do you mind turning out the light?"

His eyes widened at my sudden acquiescence—what a jerk. He turned his back and went over to the nightstand. I stood up, preparing to attack. But I got cold feet and, instead, bolted for the door. I was out into the living room before he realized what had happened.

"Hey!"

Fifteen feet. I switched the pin to my left hand and dodged around the desk chair, grabbing it with my right hand and knocking it down behind me. He stumbled and swore. I reached for the doorknob and ran out, but I forgot there was a step. I lost my balance—couldn't catch myself—and fell to my knees. He was on me instantly. I tried to kick him, squirming, flailing helplessly. But I couldn't fight him for long. "Okay," I breathed, going limp. "Stop. Please."

He crouched, sitting back on his heels. Slowly, I struggled into a sitting position. Then I brought my right hand up and jammed the pin into his neck.

It hit just below his Adam's apple. I shoved my hand against the acorn, making raggedy little sobbing noises, and drove the pin in further. I jumped to my feet. He made an "aaahh" sound as he grabbed for the hat pin. Fascinated and horrified, I stood over him a moment longer. Then I took off on the run.

Canned laughter from the radio followed me into the night.

39
◆

"You're late and you're cross."

"Not cross." I gave Nick my best smile as I sat down across the white tablecloth from him. Then I turned. "Why, hello, Ursula."

Actually, I didn't have to turn at all. She was draped all over Nick, her and her cream silk dress.

"Hi, Paris. What fun running into you here." She smiled brightly, her lips glistening red. The same red as the lipstick mark on Nick's cheek.

I said to Nick, "You look divine."

"Yes, I think you're right." He smiled impishly. "The woman in the plunging dress, two tables over, has been drooling at me all night."

"All night?"

"Well, once or twice. During the last fifteen minutes. Is that a smudge on your cheek?"

"Possibly. Why don't you order me a drink and I'll be right back."

"Oh have some champagne," said Ursula breezily. "We must have *some* left, don't we, hon?"

"If not, a martini will be fine." I stood. Nick gave me a quizzical look. I had never had a martini in my life.

Inside the ladies' room, I stared miserably into the mirror. The maître d' had impounded my trench coat and now I saw what a mess was underneath. My pale green wool dress was wrinkled and had pouched out in all the wrong places, making me look like a frump. Sighing, I went out to the pay phone, located on the wall between the two rest rooms. I realized then I had no purse. I went back in and begged two nickels from the bathroom lady. Mrs. Keyes answered on the fourth ring.

"Were you asleep?"

"I'm trying to listen to 'The 39 Steps' on *Mercury Theatre,* but every other minute, this thing rings."

"Who called?"

"Do I have to tell you now? Try me back in fifteen minutes."

"Mrs. Keyes, tell me this minute."

"Walter. Walter called."

"When?"

"A few minutes ago. He said he'd call back. And that girl, Theodora, called. You're supposed to call her back. Okay?"

"Yes. Now listen. Tell Walter or Tee that I'm at Ciro's. But don't tell anybody else. Make sure all the doors are locked. Do not open up for anyone, unless it's Tee. I'm going to try to reach her now. Also, is Jackson there, or Andrew?"

"Jackson is *not* here. He brought the car back and left. If Andrew is in his room, I don't know about it. All right?"

She was so put out at my interruption that it didn't occur to her to ask what was going on. Which was probably for the best. I told her I would be home soon, reminded her again to check the doors and not to let anybody in. "Okay?"

She hung up. I dropped another nickel in and dialed Tee at home. No answer. I left a message with her answering service.

Back in the ladies' room, I tried to make do with the

powders and lipsticks displayed on the counter, but my hands began to shake, followed by my knees. I sat down on a small pink chair and started to breathe deeply. The bathroom lady was glued to the radio. She, too, was listening to Orson Welles. I tried to get interested, but my mind wouldn't focus. Suddenly, the door swung open and in flounced the notorious Princess Alexandra.

She was embalmed in a cloud of heavy perfume and was wearing—how shall I put it?—this *dress.* Layers of multicolored taffeta, red, yellow and green, descended from her waist like tulip petals to just below her knees. Over the black taffeta top of the dress, she wore a large, crinkly taffeta stole, bright purple, secured above her bosom by an enormous jeweled brooch. I stood up and slid down the makeup table, eyeing the brooch, trying to decide if the jewels were real.

She caught me staring as she began foufing her hairdo.

I smiled. "Your brooch is lovely."

She smiled in return. And kept foufing.

I picked up a lipstick brush and, with still quivering fingers, began applying Red Rose, saying, "Princess Alexandra? I believe we met at Romanoff's."

"Ah," said the Princess. "Nice men, Mr. Romanoff's."

"Are you happy in Los Angeles, Your Highness?"

"Hoppy? What mean hoppy?"

She opened her little beaded bag and pulled out a lipstick. I glanced quickly at her shoes. Chunky black leather pumps, which, considering the dress, were hideously wrong.

"Princess," I said, turning toward the door. "Forgive me. But you have a run in your stocking. The left one"— I pointed—"right there."

She regarded me with chilly black eyes. "A run?" She hiked up her dress, bent over and examined her leg.

"Goddammit to hell," the princess said.

"Nicky, I must phone it in. Clearly, she's an imposter."

"On lesser evidence have men been hanged. But the *Examiner* won't print 'goddammit.' "

"They can say 'a swear word.' "

"Perhaps. But tell me about the smudge. *You* are never *smudged.*"

"Later. I really must phone. And I want to eat. And then I want to dance. Her perfume, by the way, nearly asphyxiated me. I must mention that, too."

"Sir?" A waiter leaned over Nick and presented him the sight of a new bottle of champagne.

"We finished the other one," said Ursula carelessly. "I love champagne."

"A toast," said Nick.

"To Princess Alexandra," sang Ursula.

I raised my glass. "Whoever she is."

"And there she is," announced Nick, catching sight of her as she flounced out of the ladies' room. "I must ask her to dance."

"Ask me first," I said. "The floor isn't too crowded."

Ursula put down her glass. "But Nicky, you promised me." She ran her finger down his tie. "Remember?"

Nick gave me a gee-what's-a-fella-to-do? look and stood up. Ursula shimmied to her feet. "I hope you don't mind," she said sweetly.

I watched them sail off, darkly thinking.

I had used my hat pin on the wrong neck.

They were into their third dance when the maître d' came up to the table and placed his hands on the back of Ursula's chair. "Miss Martens?"

Thinking he meant, Was that her chair? I said, "That's right."

"Come with me, please. You have a phone call."

I started to correct the mistake, but he was already walking away. I followed him to the front of the restaurant. When I reached the reservations' desk, he handed me the phone.

"Hello?" I said cautiously.

"It's me, sweetheart, what's cooking?"

Despite the din, the voice had the same New York in it

that I had heard, blindfolded, in the Valley. I injected some of Ursula's giggle into mine. "I can't hear you."

"Did he take the bait?"

I hesitated as my eyes traveled across the room to the dance floor. Nick had his arms around Ursula's waist and was tipping her backward. "Yes."

"Good. Is the chick there by any chance? We're looking for the chick. She might run to her boyfriend."

"Here? Uh uh."

"Call me if she does. I've sent a couple friends over to her house. See if Goodwin knows where she is. Check?"

"Er, yes."

"Urse, you okay? You sound funny."

"I really can't talk. I have to go."

"Call me." The man hung up.

I returned to the table just as Nick and Ursula arrived. "Did you call in the Item?" asked Nick.

"Yes, I was calling it in." I extended my hand to Nick. "It's my turn now."

But at that moment the band broke for intermission. This meant at least fifteen minutes. I sat down, trying to think what to do. Ursula had already thought what to do. She tucked an arm through Nick's and rested her blond head on his shoulder.

I needed to separate them. And I needed to get home. The waiter came over, lifted the champagne bottle out of the ice bucket and began to refill our glasses. I lit a cigarette and attempted a smoke ring, while Ursula nuzzled into Nick's neck. The smoke ring collapsed.

The waiter left. I leaned across the table to grab the ashtray and clumsily knocked over Ursula's glass. A sudden shower of champagne splashed all over her dress. "Oh heavens," I said.

Ursula jumped and sat bolt upright, looking positively stricken. "Oh! Oh no! Look what you've done."

I passed her my napkin. "I'm so sorry. Nick, get some napkins. I'll buy you a new dress, Ursula; I promise."

"My dress," she moaned. "It's all over my dress."

I waved frantically to the waiter, while secretly eyeing

my handiwork. The champagne had flooded her lap, too.
There were times, I had to admit, when I adored myself.

"Waiter," I cried, "we need some napkins and a big
bowl of salt. Right away."

Ursula glared at me. "What?"

"If you rub salt into the stains, it will make them go
away. Trust me," I said.

Ursula stood up. "Nick, take me home. I can't stay
here like this."

"I'll get my trench coat," I volunteered, ever helpful in
a crisis. "You can wear it."

We trooped to the door. I retrieved my coat from the
cloakroom girl and offered it to Ursula. "Poor thing," I
cooed.

Nick ushered us out saying, "Paris, I'll call you later.
Your car is here, right?"

"No. I sent Jackson home." I grinned. "We're just going to have to squeeze into your car."

It was all rather brilliant, I decided. We'd drop Ursula
off and go back to my house. I started to get into the
passenger seat.

A car honked.

I turned.

Walter jumped out of the Packard and waved excitedly
at me.

I sighed and removed my foot from the MG. The trouble with being so clever is that sometimes you outsmart
yourself.

As we turned off Sunset onto Maple Drive, Walter
switched his headlights off. We rolled slowly down the
street. No one was out, nothing moved. The Packard slid
to the curb three houses north of my house and across
the street. He switched off the engine.

The front door and driveway lights were on, and a
light shone from my bedroom window on the second
floor. I picked up my purse from the floor of the car,
where I'd left it earlier.

"Give me the key, I'll see what's going on," Walter said. "You stay here and lock the doors."

"Uh-uh. I'm coming with you."

I trailed Walter down the street. We circled the house, peering in the windows. At the front door, he took my key and slid it into the lock. Slowly, he pushed the door open. I stepped in right behind him. And practically into the barrel of a .38-caliber gun.

"It's about time," Tee Jones said.

Tee volunteered to take up watch outside the house. Walter went back to the car to bring in the folders he had swiped from Barnathan's lot after returning to the house and finding me gone. Having prowled around for half an hour, he had finally accepted the fact that I wasn't coming back. He had grabbed the loose folders and raced to the paper, where he phoned, first Mrs. Keyes, then Tee. Tee, out having a cocktail somewhere, had finally received both of our messages. Walter called Mrs. Keyes again and got mine.

"A hat pin?" said Walter from the couch in the study. "Where the hell did you learn that?"

"A Victorian novel I once read. Those girls were big on hat pins. I always thought it would be a gas to use one."

"Uh huh," said Walter. "Was it?"

"No. It was icky. This little trickle of blood started oozing out. And his face got all horrible."

"You didn't ice him? Jesus, Paris, do you think he's alive?"

"Only a little blood came out."

I hunched down in the wing chair and toyed moodily with my cigarette. Now that I was safe, a feeling of sadness swept over me.

"Don't worry, kid. It'll be okay."

"Russell gave me that hat pin," I said.

.   .   .

It was after eleven when I started on Jim's folder and I kept on going long into the night. From time to time, Walter went out to take hot coffee to Tee. If Barnathan had sent his goons to find me, they hadn't shown up yet. By 4 A.M., I had begun to nod off. I sent Walter home, but Tee stuck with her watch.

I had, in the end, finally found what I was looking for. But it didn't help me to fall asleep.

Four o'clock in the morning. And still no word from Nick.

40
◆

I slept fitfully. And dreamed badly. But in those dawn hours, as the demons cavorted, two slender threads of thought connected. By nine-thirty, when I dragged out of bed, I had already turned my mind back in time.

All along I had overlooked the significance of the phone call Jim received as I was preparing to leave his house that night. His tone had been affable, his voice calm and reassuring to whoever was on the line. He had not acted like the call was important and I had taken his cue. But standing under the shower, soap forgotten in my hand, I now recalled the words he spoke.

"Just getting ready to go to bed . . . Can we talk in the morning? Sorry I haven't gotten back to you . . ."

It was this subtle dismissal that had made me indifferent. The party had not been important enough for Jim to return an earlier call.

He listened for a moment and I remembered how he had looked over at me and smiled, as if he were politely indulging the caller. He had said, "Well I wouldn't worry about it." And he had yawned. I sat down on the end of the bed to put on my stockings. Jim said, "Where is he now?" And he had listened some more. I finished dressing, thinking he would be off in a moment. But then Jim grew more animated. "They're going to call me? He told you that?" He wiggled a finger at me and I came over to him. He was saying, "I'm a newsman, they can't touch me. Hang on." He had lifted a hand toward me and I had bent down. We kissed. He whispered, "I'll call you tomorrow."

Now, with water streaming down my face, and prompted by a nagging instinct nudged loose in the night, I was certain the caller had been Lucille Wills.

The address, listed in the phone book, was on St. George Street. Jackson slid the Bentley into the curb and cut the engine. Set back on a wide front lawn stood a two-story white clapboard house that looked as if it had been there quite a long time. Los Feliz was an old family neighborhood inhabited by old family money. In broad daylight, the old families were nowhere to be seen. I skirted a little red wagon, stepped up to the front door and rang the Wills's bell.

I picked lint off my black suede gloves as I waited. I rang the doorbell again and pressed my ear to the door. The lack of Lewis noises made me wonder if anyone was home.

At last footsteps. "Who is it?"

"Paris Chandler."

"Oh." The door crept open reluctantly. Lucille Wills stared at me with a mixture of surprise and annoyance. Like the day in the park, her long brown curls were tied back with a scarf. She was wearing a cotton print housedress, white anklets and loafers. Her wide hazel eyes softened. "I was afraid you were the sitter."

"Afraid?"

"She took Lewis to the park for a couple of hours. So when I heard the doorbell I was afraid something had happened and she was bringing him back." I watched her eyes travel beyond me to where, undoubtedly, they alighted on the Bentley.

"I thought we might talk for a moment."

"I suppose I'd better invite you in." She stepped back hesitantly. "But I must get dressed and get out. Come this way."

There was a center hall with a light blue hand-woven rug over a wooden floor. We passed through it into the living room. It looked as if a mad interior decorator had been imprisoned in there too long. A large beige Oriental rug with a vaguely Chinese motif anchored two dark green brocade couches with a gold leaf print. A black lacquer coffee table sat between them loaded with gee-gaws. Behind the far couch, a long table supported an elaborate brass lamp. Two side chairs with orange, green and white stripes bordered the third side of the coffee table. A blue-and-white enamel-topped table sat between those. The windows were covered with long print draperies, whose only relationship to the rest of the room was a splash of green. A fireplace held the wall between two of the long windows. It was framed by white pleated curtains that went up and across the wall above it—something I had never before seen—and, hanging in the middle of the white curtains . . . the *pièce de résistance*, a large canvas of an imposing man who was, perhaps, somebody's ancestor. Other paintings, sconces and small shelves covered every square inch of the walls. It was the kind of room that might have been photographed for some high-class magazine, but the busyness of it, the constant movement of the eyes to grasp each detail, would have had me in a straitjacket by dinnertime. Lucille pointed to one of the couches. I sat down. She chose one of the chairs.

"You seemed like a nice girl. I had no idea you would turn into such a troublemaker."

I removed my gloves. "We're both innocent victims, Lucille. We're at odds with each other because we're both trying to get out of a mess. I have to ask you some questions, not because I'm trying to hurt you, but because a man was killed and his murder is directly affect-

ing me. I told you Ursula was there that night. What I
didn't tell you—I was, too."

Surprisingly, Lucille didn't react to the news. She
merely shrugged. "It has nothing to do with me."

"I was there when you phoned Jim, about ten-fifteen."

She curled her hands in her lap. "I did not."

"You told me you weren't in touch with him anymore,
but you called him. Why? To make sure he was home?
Because not long after he hung up, someone shot him to
death."

"I don't know who shot him, if that's what you're asking."

"Who told you to phone him?"

"Nobody." Her eyes traveled to the coffee table. On it
were several art books, a Chinese enameled bowl, an
arrangement of dried flowers and a black candle growing
out of a cinnamon-colored candlestick. None of the
props came to her rescue. "I wanted to warn him."

"That he was to be murdered?"

"Of course not." Her hazel eyes flashed angrily. "It
was—I wanted to tell him he was going to be called before the grand jury."

"Your husband told you that?"

"Yes. He was worried."

My mind, which was racing ahead, came to a dead
halt. For the first time, Lucille Wills had indicated she
knew her husband was culpable. I opened my purse. "Do
you mind if I smoke?"

She shook her head.

From somewhere in the house came faint voices. Radio voices, I presumed. I lit the cigarette. "Has your husband been called?"

"He must appear tomorrow."

"Matthew Barnathan?"

"I don't know."

I would have to find out when the grand jury had begun meeting. Someone like Wills, or Barnathan, would
be well-enough connected to get inside information. If
Jim's name had gone on the list as early as mid-Septem-
ber, it was conceivable he was murdered to prevent him

from testifying. *"I'm a newsman. They can't touch me,"* he had said. They might have guessed he would plead protection of sources and reveal nothing. But would he have done that? Would he have saved his information, assuming he had it, for his own broadcast?

"Your husband asked you to phone him?"

"No. I told you. I wasn't supposed to be in touch with him. Ursula was the one pumping him, to find out what he knew."

"So why did you phone him, Lucille?"

"I told you."

"At ten-fifteen at night? I don't believe you. I still think you were checking to make sure he was home."

"I wasn't. Do you think I could? Have a nice conversation with him knowing he was about to die?"

"Where was your husband?"

"At the office."

"Really? You told me you were supposed to have dinner with Jim, except you canceled because your husband was coming home."

"We had made the date several days before. I wanted to tell James then. But that morning Norman told me he was coming home for dinner. So I called the station and left a message canceling." She leaned back in the chair, gazing at me steadily. In her lap, her hands were still. "After dinner, Norman went back to the office. To clean off his desk, he said."

I bought the first part. Jim had said, "Sorry I didn't get back to you." It fit. "When did Norman get home?"

"Right after I called Jim. Actually, I was on the phone when I heard Norman come in. I had to hang up right away."

If she were telling the truth, I could eliminate her husband as the murderer. But then, Norman Wills hadn't seemed the type. He was the kind who would have hired someone to do it. "Did anyone call your husband that night to tell him Jim had been murdered?"

"No. He came right up to bed and we went to sleep."

She stood and walked over to the fireplace. A small clock had stopped at four-thirty and Lucille began to wind it. "We were having breakfast when Norman got a call. I can't even remember who it was."

"How did he react?"

Lucille turned to face me. "Norman? He was shocked. If I recall, he didn't even go to work that day."

"Does he know who did it? Has he said anything to you?"

"Oh yes, he knows who killed James." Lucille straightened her shoulders and looked at me without expression. "My husband said it was you."

When I arrived at the *Examiner*, I found a message from Nick. I ignored it. I picked up the phone, asked Jo for an outside line and called Chief Gladstone. While I waited for him I picked out a dark purple crayon and began doodling. So far, I hadn't been aware that anyone was following me, but I knew they would come sooner or later. If Barnathan was powerful enough to control the police department's investigation, all I could fight back with was the newspaper. But time had run out.

My doodles, which had begun as flowers, turned into scowling monsters.

"Yes, Paris. I'm in a meeting right now."

"When will you be free? I need to see you. It's important."

"Come by around three o'clock." Chief Gladstone hung up.

I went back to the kitchen in the Home Cooking Department and made a cup of tea. It was a slow day in gossip. The only Item I had to check out was Hal Wallis's attempt to borrow Jennifer Jones from David Selznick for *Sorry, Wrong Number*. I realized then, as I dropped a cube of sugar in my cup, I had forgotten all about Princess Alexandra. I went back to my desk and called Slim Hawks.

"Any new dope on her highness?" I asked.

"Yeah. Put this in your bonnet. The phone number one of her functionaries gave me was not a working number."

"No."

"Yes. So I called Mike Romanoff and told him I was dying to give a dinner party for her. And do you know what he said?"

"I'm holding my breath."

"She's in hiding."

I giggled. "What?"

"Mike says she's staying at the home of someone very, very top-drawer. But that the Russians are after her. So mum's the word."

"Do you mind if I use this, Slim? I absolutely *must* use it."

"Please, I wish you would."

"Because I ran into her last night."

"No."

"She was disguised as herself and was keeping under-cover at Ciro's."

"Well how do you like that?"

"It gets better." I took a sip of tea and went through the rest room routine.

Slim snorted. "Why that little creep, Prince Romanoff. I'm going to call him right now and give him a piece of my mind."

"Before you do, how well do you know Ursula Martens?"

"Well enough to keep my man away from her. She's going after all the prominent men in town. If you have one, chain him up."

"Actually, I was thinking of advertising him in the classifieds. In the for sale section."

"How marvelous. Instead of personals. We could start a new fad—jokers for sale."

"Ursula could have her pick."

"It's extraordinary how you resemble her."

I glanced down at my purple scribblings. They looked like the work of a demented mind.

"I plan to do something about that," I said.

.   .   .

I sandwiched a sheet of carbon paper between two pieces of copy paper and rolled them into my typewriter. With two fingers, I quickly beat out the fake princess Item. I got Roxy on the line and dictated it to her.

"Goddammit," exclaimed Roxy, peeved. "You know we can't use goddammit."

"I wanted to be accurate," I replied sweetly.

"Accuracy is no excuse for vulgarity."

"Oh."

"Hang on. Nick wants to talk to you."

Carefully I replaced the receiver. I collected my purse and gloves and went to the newsroom to find Walter.

"No wonder the police are corrupt in this town."

Walter stared belligerently at the roast beef sandwich in his hand. "Studies show that poor eating habits is one of the factors responsible for crime."

"Is that so?" I took a small bite of my sandwich. It tasted fine to me. "How do you explain that?"

"I noticed it myself over the years. Criminals never eat well. I think it has to do with sour stomachs souring the mind."

"Have you thought of applying for a Nobel Prize?"

"Look at 'em." Walter stared at the sandwich shop across the street as two uniformed officers, each carrying a brown bag, came strolling out the door. We had decided to have lunch—bought from the villified sandwich shop—on the steps of City Hall, on the theory that the safest place for me in Los Angeles was within shouting distance of the LAPD.

"Anyway, as I was saying, Walter, Jim's notes were cryptic, illegible, nonsensical, or all three. It wasn't till I found the notation 'd. billing,' that I began to get it."

Walter wadded up his half-eaten sandwich into the waxed paper and shoved it into the brown paper bag.

"So I looked at the folders for three of the houses on the lot. Guess what?"

"I need a Coke."

"Each of the printed forms was filled out. Address,

description, square footage, age, condition, etc. Also the date of purchase by the state and the price paid."

"Uh huh," Walter said, glancing at his watch.

"At the bottom it said, 'Means of disposal.' Then there were the words, 'Resale,' 'Demolition,' 'Rental,' 'Removal,' and 'Other.' I have no idea what 'Other' means. Do you?"

"The possibilities overwhelm the mind."

"Next to each word was a space to check. Then below was the word 'Explanation.'"

Walter's eyes drifted back to the sandwich shop. I touched his arm. "In each case, the word 'demolition' was checked. What I'm thinking is that Barnathan billed the state for demolition, only he didn't demolish the houses. He moved them to the lot. It's possible he also bills the state for removal. That's why Jim wrote 'd. billing.' Double billing. Either way, Barnathan gets the house for free, spends a little to fix it up and sells it. Nice profit."

"How much profit do you think there is?"

"I talked to one man, Tim Renfeld. He got seven thousand for his house, which was supposed to be demolished. Only he saw it in the Valley. Remodeled. He said the house had sold for fifteen."

"You're sure it was to be demolished?"

"That's what the right-of-way agent told him. I suppose there could have been a mistake."

Walter was drumming his fingers on his knees. "Are the descriptions on those papers good enough to identify the houses?"

"You're thinking of going back?"

"Thinking."

"I'm not sure the descriptions are that clear."

"How do you know the houses in the folders are the same houses that are on the lot?"

"Because Barnathan keeps meticulous paperwork. Stamped on the inside cover of each folder are the words, 'Sent to Barbee,' followed by a date."

"So the guy is not only collecting for demolition, which he doesn't perform, he is gypping the state out of money he should be paying to buy the houses at auction."

"Right. Though he does buy some. A woman at Esther Lubinow's auction told me she and her husband had attended several auctions and that Richard Walken would bid the houses up, then suddenly drop out. Walken and Barnathan's flunky were both at her auction. I think they work together to make sure the flunky gets the house, driving the price up till everyone else drops out."

"But why buy when they can steal?"

"Maybe to cover some of their dirty tracks. In case anyone starts asking questions, they can point to the houses honestly come by. Or—who knows—maybe something else is going on."

"And this is what you're going to tell Gladstone? I don't think it's good enough. He won't listen."

"It isn't good enough. There's a lot more checking to be done. But I've run out of time. So I need to buy more. If I can convince Gladstone of just some of this stuff, maybe he'll start putting the heat on them. And take it off me."

"And if he's covering for Barnathan?"

"You can tell he loves being police chief, Walter. And he drools at the possibility of being on TV. If he's covering, he's being squeezed. By somebody bigger than him."

"He'll protect himself before he'll protect you."

"He may have an out. The grand jury. In which case, I have an in."

"Ted Stein?"

I didn't reply. Across the street, a bum was asking a cop for something, gesturing with his hands. The cop reached into his pocket. He handed the bum some change. I looked at my watch and stood up. "Are you going to wait for me?"

"Naw. I think I might wander over to Barbee Street. Have one of the cops drive you back to the paper."

Walter went over to a garbage container and tossed in his crumpled paper bag. He walked back, scowling.

"I see what you mean about sour minds," I said.

41

♦

I sat in the outer office listening to Miss Percy click her tongue for nearly fifteen minutes. Occasionally she typed a sentence. Mainly she just stared into space, or answered the phone.

"Paris, come in."

Police Chief Harry Gladstone filled the doorway, his right arm beckoning impatiently to me. I stood, straightened my skirt and followed him into his office. He closed the door and asked me to have a seat. His face was deeply tanned as usual, but even so, the face looked tired, the lines around his eyes and mouth more pronounced. He was wearing a navy sport coat with wide lapels and dark gray pants. His white shirt was crisp; the club tie slightly askew. He sat down behind his desk with a long sigh, as if—suddenly punctured—the air was seeping out of him. "What can I do for you, Paris?"

The intercom buzzed. Gladstone leaned forward and pushed the button. "Yes?"

The tinny voice of Miss Percy escaped. "Mayor Bowron is calling."

346

"Scuse me," said Gladstone, lifting the phone. "Sir?"

I studied the contents of his desk. Behind the shiny nameplate was a blotter, an appointment book, a container of Alka-Seltzer and a large boxy tape recorder, which hadn't been there when I visited before.

"Yes, sir, things are moving along. Let me phone you later. Thank you, sir."

Gladstone hung up with a new round of sighs. "Your friends at the L.A. *Times* have an editorial in tomorrow's paper ripping into the police department for the St. Clair investigation." He smiled woodenly. "You can see I am a desperate man."

"It must be the time of year. Desperate is my middle name."

Gladstone raised an eyebrow.

"I never found out what became of the man you picked up behind my house. I was expecting to hear from you."

"Nothing became of him. Jurisdictional problems."

"Pardon me?"

"I took him into Beverly Hills. I can't arrest a guy in Beverly Hills and haul him into Los Angeles."

"I see," I said uncertainly. "That's it?"

"No. I asked him if he got his address book back. He said he had. I said, fine. I told him to stay away from you and I told the desk officer to book him for trespassing."

"So he paid a fine and they let him go."

"You think we should have hung him?"

My eyes wandered to the tape recorder, just to the left of Gladstone's blotter. For a moment I wondered if he intended to tape our conversation. But the reels were not turning. "I've come here to talk straight with you, Harry. Can we do this unofficially?"

Gladstone sat up. "You're going to talk straight to me? Well, hell, if it isn't my lucky day."

"I'm serious. Al Brown, or Albert Aubrey, works for Matthew Barnathan, the developer in the Valley. Barnathan has contracts with the Division of Highways for demolition and removal of houses. James St. Clair was poking around into this when he was murdered. I've come to tell you what I know."

Gladstone leaned forward and ran his thumb down his desk calendar. "You've come here to tell me what you know about a murder . . . thirty days later?" He gave me a stern look. "What's your angle this time?"

"I'm frightened."

"Yeah? Why is that?"

"Barnathan's men have been harassing me."

"Maybe you should mind your own business."

"I can't. Because you're not doing yours."

"Maybe I'm doing it better than you think."

"You've got some leads?"

"Oh yeah. Wanna hear one?"

I nodded. Gladstone reached over and switched on the tape recorder. He sat back and watched me with bright, interested eyes.

"How's your drink?" said a woman's voice.

"Fine," said a man's.

Giggling . . . *"Did you bring me a present?"*

A brief silence. Then . . . *"You'll have it. Soon. As soon as I get mine."*

"Darling, you don't trust me? Come sit by me. I can't stand having you so far away."

"Okay, here it comes," whispered Gladstone. "Listen."

I nodded obediently. I was trying to keep my face expressionless, but it was hard.

He: *"Do you have the money yet?"*

"What a businessman you are. I should think maybe you could do me a teeny weeny favor. Especially considering that she ruined my dress."

"It was an accident."

"I can't believe you let her lead you around by the nose. Of course—you do have to work with her."

"Mm hm."

"But me . . . you only have to play with me. After you bring me the nightgown, I'll show you all my games."

"I'd love to play your games, Urse. But business first. Ten grand. That's the deal."

"I can't believe you could be so greedy. About money." A laugh. *"I was hoping your greed would run to other things."* A pause. *"Do you like . . . ?"*

Indistinguishable sounds. Then . . . *"I think we should clear this up first. It would be better."*

"I don't like being robbed. You're as mean as she is. Ten thousand is a lot of money. And I don't even know if you have the nightgown. The two of you could be trying to put one over on me."

"You sound like you've changed your mind."

"Rub my back, Nicky, okay? Just for a while. It will help me to sleep. Please?"

The voices grew distant. Fading away. After a moment, the only sound was the static of the tape.

Gladstone switched off the machine. "Cup of java?"

"Thank you."

He got up and left. I couldn't think straight. Where, how? Her apartment? Yes, of course. She had planted the tape recorder and scripted a conversation that made it sound like I was holding her up. I had no illusions what the rest of the story would be.

I stood and walked over to the window. Down on Temple Street, traffic had come to a standstill. Making a wide turn from Main onto Temple was a house. It was on wheels and was being towed by a yellow tractor-trailer truck. A few pedestrians had stopped to watch, but most went on their way. The sight of a moving house was becoming commonplace in L.A.

I sat down again, stiffly holding my gloves in my lap until Gladstone came back.

He returned, trailed by Miss Tut-Tut, lurching forward with the same wobbly tray. As it clattered onto the desk, coffee from the two cups lapped over the edges, spilling into the saucers. She stood there, wringing her hands, mumbling. "That's fine, Abigail. Thank you, dear."

I lifted one of the cups carefully and nearly scalded my

tongue on the boiling-hot coffee. I put down the cup and laughed. "I think it's not my day."

"No," Gladstone agreed. "Not today."

"Whose idea was the tape recorder. Yours?"

"She said she could prove you stole her nightie. I said great."

"Don't you mean Nick?"

"Right. He stole the nightgown. You put it on display. I was truly impressed."

"But why did I do it? That's what I can't figure out." I opened my purse and found my cigarettes. "I mean, you couldn't arrest me on that basis."

Gladstone smiled agreeably. "That's why I never came looking for it."

"But you said you did look. The day Andrew thought I had been kidnapped."

Gladstone smiled wider and nudged a big glass ashtray across the desk. "Yeah, I looked. So Goodwin had already stolen it."

"Ah."

"All it does is help corroborate her story."

"Did I kill him? In her story."

"No way to tell. She had left."

I leaned forward. "Chief . . ."

"Aw, no more Harry?"

"Harry. Ursula Martens was in the house the entire time I was. And I *can* corroborate that. If I need to."

"Is that a question?"

"Yes, I think it is. Actually, the question is, am I really a suspect?"

"Exactly how would you corroborate when Miss Martens left?"

"A neighbor across the street saw her arrive sometime after eight with Jim. She saw Ursula get out of Jim's car. So when she left, sometime after ten-thirty, how did she get home? She walked over to Larchmont and took a cab."

"Somehow I'm missing a few hundred pieces," Gladstone said dubiously.

"Wouldn't it interest you if I could prove she took a cab at that hour?"

"You never know. Anything's possible."

"How about if I tell you what Jim was working on and how some people didn't like it?"

"Hey, it's a free country. So they say."

"Harry, please." I could hear the frustration seeping out of my voice. "Tell me at least what you're thinking."

He turned a knob on the recording machine and the tape whirred noisily backward. He seemed fascinated by the mechanical workings of it all. When it jolted to a stop, he looked up with satisfaction.

"I'm thinking," he replied, "that it's still not your day."

Someone named Sergeant Ranger dropped me off at the *Examiner*. When I got upstairs to Society, I found Nick sitting at his desk. He looked up from *Variety* and watched me unhappily. I tossed my gloves and purse onto my desk and began thumbing through the messages that had collected in my absence.

"Most of them are from me," said Nick, standing up, coming over.

"I can see that."

"You should at least let me explain."

"I will." I reached for the phone. Nick put a hand on my arm to stop me. I turned to face him. Faint shadows underlined his nice blue eyes. "Did you know," I said quietly, "that she had a tape recorder running at her apartment last night? Gladstone played me the tape. The way it sounds, *I'm* holding *her* up."

"Then you only got part of the conversation. She agreed to pay. Tonight."

I raised an eyebrow and pulled my arm away, again reaching for the phone. "I have to call Tee. Then we'll talk."

While I was running through the Gladstone exchange with Tee, Nick's phone rang. He stood talking for a moment, then leaned over and began scribbling.

"Can you find that driver, Bobby Roper?" I asked Tee.

"Probably. But I'm more inclined to trail that slime Ursula. Let me wrap up something here then I'll hit the street."

I hung up just as Nick did. "Etta," he said grievously. "I have to run by a cocktail party for a few minutes."

I walked over to his desk. "When are you meeting Ursula?"

"I don't know. Later. She said she'd call me at home."

He seemed distracted. Or maybe he was just tired. Nick's favorite role in life was the bon vivant. Just now the role had slipped away from him and he seemed unsure how to get it back.

"Maybe I'd better come by . . . about seven?"

"Make it seven-thirty."

"But don't do anything till we talk, Nick. She's setting you up, too."

"Somehow," said Nick resignedly, "I got that impression."

I wandered into the newsroom. A knot of reporters had tied itself around the radio near the wire machines. I moved over to the edge of the crowd. "It's Congressman Lyndon Johnson," whispered a reporter, "warning us about the Communist threat." He yawned.

I grinned and stepped closer.

"We live in a world," LBJ drawled, "where a plane'll fly itself from the capital of the United States to the capital of Europe. We live in a world where I had lunch in London one day and lunch with my wife and two babies in Washington the next. We live in a world where there is manufactured, this moment, instruments of atomic warfare which, if strategically placed on this nation, two of them would . . ."

I felt a thump on my shoulder.

I followed Walter out of the newsroom and into the hallway. "You were right, kid. The folders are for the houses on the lot. I conned a confession out of one of the salesmen."

Walter pulled a pencil from behind his ear and used it to flip pages in his notebook. I said, "How?"

"I posed as a buyer."

Walter had driven over to Barbee Street, not sure how he would proceed. But as he pulled up to the curb, a couple was getting out of a car parked in front of his. They were standing on the sidewalk, looking somewhat confused, when a salesman spotted them. Walter heard the woman say they had come to look for a house, that Ray had sent them. The salesman, now seeing Walter approach, said he would send someone out to help him right away.

"So the guy comes out and I say I'm maybe interested in buying something. Ray sent me."

Walter had dutifully gone through three or four houses and then—wow!—he found just the one he had to have. The salesman, a Bill Hurley, went into the "office" to get the paperwork. He came back with one of the folders. After reviewing some of the information, Walter asked to see the papers. Sure enough, at the bottom of the page, the word "demolition" was checked. Walter inquired what that meant.

"This Bill's a nice kid. Just out of USC, his first real job." Walter thumped the notebook with his pencil. "He said the house had been purchased by the state and had been marked for demolition. But then Barnathan offered to take the house off the state's hands. Bill said all the houses on the lot were like that. That's how come they were selling them so cheaply."

"How cheaply?"

"It depends. If I wanted the house as is, haul it away myself, I could have it for ten grand. If I wanted some remodeling, I would work out the details with another member of the staff. They would also sell me a lot, if I didn't have one. He said the work generally took three months to complete, but maybe he could speed things up for me." Walter grinned. "He wasn't a bad salesman."

"Do we have a story yet?"

"We'll meet with Dickinson. I'm not sure we're quite there."

"But almost, Walter. All we have to do is prove two things. That Barnathan is billing the state for demolition work he's not doing. And that Norman Wills leaks him the freeway routes ahead of time."

Walter stuck the pencil behind his ear. "You just forgot the forest, kid." He pointed a finger at me, like a gun. "Somebody pulled the trigger, remember? That makes three."

It was after five when I placed the call. It was possible that he had already left and, as the phone began to ring in his office, I silently hoped he had.

"Stein speaking."

I took a deep breath. "Ted, it's Paris. I—" I what? *I just thought I would give you a call?* "How are you?" I said lamely.

"Up to my eyeballs. As usual. And you?"

"Needing something. As usual."

"Some women never change."

"And some men?"

"I think I'll table that one. But I am happy to hear from you. Why do you suppose that is?"

I didn't answer for a long moment. I had no answer that I could think of. "The truth is, I can't explain anything. I couldn't before. And I still can't."

"Sorry. My secretary's left and the other phone's ringing. Can you hold a minute?"

"Of course."

Ted Stein was the nicest, smartest man I'd ever met. I'd known him since high school when I stood him up for the senior prom and ended up marrying one of his closest friends. I hadn't seen him since graduation, or, I had to admit, once even thought about him. Then last January, when rumors flew that a high-stakes poker game in Beverly Hills was fixed, and the D.A.'s office might be investigating, I remembered Ted worked as an assistant D.A., and called him out of the blue. Reluctantly, he had slipped me some information he shouldn't have. We had gone out several times. And then, for reasons that still eluded me, I had disappeared on him again.

"Hi. Sorry. Are you at work?"

"Yes. Do you have time for a drink?"

"Not really. Tomorrow's bad, too. What about lunch on Saturday?"

"I need to talk to you tonight. I may actually have something that will help you."

"Wanna give me a hint?"

"Norman Wills."

A long silence followed. "Paris, can you come here? Now?"

"I'd rather not. Someone may be following me who might not be happy to see me walk into the Hall of Justice. And it just occurred to me, if you could come to the *Examiner,* someone else may have something to tell you, too."

"Give me fifteen, twenty minutes."

"I'll be waiting downstairs," I promised.

It was nearly six when Ted came through the heavy glass doors into the ornate lobby of the *Examiner.* He was wearing a gray double-breasted suit, red tie squarely knotted at the collar of his white shirt. With his tortoiseshell glasses and the dark hair, slicked back and parted high, Ted Stein reminded me of Clark Kent. He was carrying a battered leather briefcase and wearing a tired smile.

"Sorry." He stooped to kiss me on the cheek. "It's not enough that local crime is booming, the FBI's in town working on some stuff."

"Stuff?" I said, smiling.

"Stuff." His eyes wandered up to the vaulted frescoed ceiling. "How magnificent. I had no idea reporters worked in such elegant quarters."

"They don't. It's a front for the pigpen where we slop news and toss garbage on the floor." I grinned. "Wanna see?"

I decided to save Ted the thirty-seven stairs up to the

second floor, but probably didn't do him any favors by crunching him into the tiny elevator that shook and rattled alarmingly all the way up. We escaped onto cracked linoleum littered with cigarette butts. "Feel better?"

I brought Ted into Society and the newsroom, then led him back down the hall to the library. It was the only place I could think of to talk. "It's called the morgue," I explained, pushing through the glass door. "It contains a lot of dead newspapers."

Penelope Potts, hat askew, lethal scissors in hand, glanced up sourly and warned, "I'm locking up in five minutes."

I took Ted's arm and led him over to her desk. "Pen, this is Assistant District Attorney Ted Stein. Ted, our indispensible librarian, Miss Potts."

"My pleasure," said Ted.

Penelope grunted.

"Pen, we need a place to talk. I'll lock up if you leave me the key."

"How will I get in tomorrow?"

"I'll leave the key at the switchboard."

"You'll probably forget."

Ted smiled. "I'll remind her."

Penelope glared at me. "Just don't make a mess."

We walked over to a far table. "How could we make more of a mess?" whispered Ted, as I pushed newspapers and magazines aside and swept cigarette ashes onto the floor.

"Don't be snotty. *This* is where I work." I sat down and smiled. "It's good seeing you, Ted. I mean that."

Ted took a chair across the table from me, but he didn't reply.

"Walter Ainsley will be in with more information but I'm going to start. James St. Clair was a close friend and I knew some things that I began looking into. Let me tell you what I've got."

"Why?"

"I need help in return."

"Then just ask for it."

"I'm an outsider, Ted. I don't know what Chief Gladstone is doing and I don't know what's going on in the grand jury room. But I have information that suggests Matthew Barnathan has been double billing the state for removal and demolition work, possibly with the help of Norman Wills. James St. Clair was looking into this when he died."

"What do you need back?"

"I need Gladstone to cross me off his list of suspects for St. Clair's murder. And I need Barnathan's men to stop beating me up."

"They beat you up?"

"Once. Cracked a rib. Twice they abducted me, once blindfolded to warn me off, and again last night to . . . I don't know what. I ran away. But I'm frightened."

Ted shook his head and snapped open his briefcase. He withdrew a large pad of paper and two sharpened pencils. He seemed angry.

I couldn't tell if it was personal or professional.

It took nearly an hour to go through the information with Ted. He made notes, asked questions, but revealed nothing about the grand jury proceedings. When Walter came through the door, Ted glanced at his watch and asked to use the phone. I told him he could use Penelope's.

Walter turned a chair around and sat on it backward. "Has he told you anything?"

I shook my head.

"Did you know Norman Wills testifies tomorrow?"

"Yes. His wife told me."

"Richard Walken went today. Swore he'd never heard of Barnathan, but admitted doing work for the right-of-way department. He said he would go there and get a list of houses that had to be removed. Another agent would have already made the rounds. Supposedly, the first guy appraises the house and the second guy, that's Walken, makes the offer. He said he knew Wills, but not well. He . . ."

"How do you know this, Walter?"

"I've got a friend, too." He grinned. "A better friend than yours, apparently."

Behind me, I could hear Ted speaking softly into the phone. Telling someone he was sorry . . . "I'll have to meet you there. Take a cab."

"Anyway, they got Walken to admit he sold at least two houses to the state after they had been recently purchased by someone else."

"Ursula?"

"I don't know. They're now questioning him on the prices he negotiated. I think they're going to try to prove he kicked back money to the seller."

Walter glanced up. Then he stood up.

"Hi. Ted Stein."

"Walter Ainsley."

Ted shook Walter's hand. "I used to read your stories before the war. The way you tracked down criminals, I keep thinking you should be working for us."

"Then you'd have to pay me. Sit down, Ted. I'll give you what I got for free."

When Walter finished, Ted asked if he could have the folders we took from Barbee Street. "This is what will happen," he said. "We'll go through them. If there's information pertinent to our case, we will have to serve each of you with a summons. In the course of testifying you will have to say how you got these folders."

"It's called theft," Walter said.

"There are ways to elicit answers from witnesses," Ted went on, "that may not make it necessary to involve you."

"And me?"

"We're looking into possible fraud. Gladstone's looking into homicide. So far, we're not working together. But if you ask him, Paris, maybe he'll get Beverly Hills to post a couple of cops at your house."

"I wouldn't bet on it," Walter said.

42
◆

Nick's apartment was on the ground floor of one of those two-story complexes built around a garden in that rather awful Spanish-cum-Barracks style that was the rage among local architects before the war. The building was on Wilshire, near the university, and filled mainly with university people. Nick's was one of the few front doors that didn't have a pennant on it.

That door swung back and Nick motioned me inside. He went over to the couch and picked up the receiver from the end table. "Outside of them, it was mainly a bunch of Republican fat cats. Big bucks, small names. Hearst never showed up." He looked at me and grinned.

The decor, such as it was, could best be described as eclectic Brown Hodge-Podge: stained wooden floor, a worn brown couch, two old leather armchairs of undetermined dark color, really horrible gold-and-brown flowered drapes and, in the corner to the left of the fireplace, a card table with a government-issue typewriter that Nick had bought for ten dollars after the war. To the right of the front door stood a nice credenza, which contained Nick's extensive record collection and upon which sat his prized phonograph. Filling the wall above were bookshelves; they housed a decent library, shelved in no particular order that I could fathom. Between the living room and the kitchen was an alcove with a dining table and three chairs; the fourth, he said, was broken. On the other side of the room from the kitchen, a short hallway led to a bath and then his bedroom. The entire apartment was accessorized with a careless blizzard of magazines, newspapers and foolscap covered with scribblings. Nick's fastidiousness extended to fashion but not, apparently, to furnishings. He hung up.

"The copy desk. Etta left instructions that she wanted six names. Why six? I only had four."

"Christmas," I volunteered. "Maybe she's hoping for a bigger haul than last year."

"Bigger? Did you see her living room? It was wall-to-wall, ceiling-to-floor. There was enough liquor to stock Ireland on St. Paddy's Day."

"Which reminds me," I said.

"Right. You'd probably like a Perfect Manhattan about now."

"Can you fix me one?"

Nick grinned. "I'm out of vermouth. Second choice."

"Oh you know," I said, "whatever Ursula drinks."

"She drinks Scotch. Which you don't like."

"Guess what else I don't like?"

"You could sit down. Or are you going to have a tantrum standing up?"

I was suddenly angry. I hadn't arrived angry, but I was now. I walked over to the coffee table and glanced at some of the magazines strewn across it, trying to let the anger go. "There isn't room to have one." I looked at Nick. "Anywhere."

"Are you going to hold that against me, too?" He gave me his best boyish smile.

"Yes. You're cramping my style."

Nick took a step closer. "You could shrink it."

"My style?"

"Yes. Minimal style is the newest rage."

"I'm an old rager. I'm not sure I can adjust. Bourbon and water?"

"Sure."

"In an old-fashioned, very maximal glass."

I lifted Nick's jacket off the couch and hung it on the back of a dining chair, then I sat down and waited. He came back carrying two glasses with a box of pretzels tucked under his arm. He handed me the bourbon, put down the pretzels and clinked my glass. "Cheers."

"Has she called?" I asked.

"Not yet. What shall I tell her?"

"Fill me in about last night."

"Right." Nick took a swallow of Scotch. He leaned back against the cushions but didn't go on.

I said, "It was an unseasonably warm night in October. The sweet scent of night-blooming jasmine filtered in the living room window as Nick and Ursula sat, tête-à-tête, on the couch. Um—it was the couch, right?"

"Don't be cute, Paris."

"Then tell me what happened."

"I'm trying to figure out where the tape recorder was."

"It ended with Ursula asking you to rub her back. Naughty of you to move away from the microphone just then."

"I wanted the money."

"Yes, of course. That's why you were there. All night."

Nick leaned forward. "I wanted her to think I was on *her* side. So I told her I'd explained her situation to you, thinking you would understand."

"You told her I *knew*?"

"Yes. I told her you weren't as nice about it as I thought you would be. That while you agreed to give her the nightgown, you insisted on the money."

"Painting me the bad guy."

"Good cop, bad cop."

I nodded thoughtfully. "What did she say?"

"It forced her to change tactics. She couldn't just sweet-talk me. You were the obstacle. Once she understood that, she said she would have the money. Tonight."

"Well I don't believe it. Why would she think the nightgown is so important?"

"Obviously, she's trying to frame you."

"It's a flimsy frame. Did she say anything else? Did she mention Barnathan or Richard Walken?"

"Barnathan. She said she was afraid he'd fire her if he knew she was having a dalliance with a client."

"Phooey. I don't believe that, either." I swallowed some bourbon. "So how did you leave it?"

"I said if she brought the money tonight, I'd have the nightgown."

"*When* did you leave it?"

"Late." Nick reached for the box of pretzels. "Say, would you like to hear the new Basie, 'Drowning in Your Deep Blue Eyes'?"

I didn't answer. Nick went over to his phonograph. He slipped the record out of its sleeve.

"You slept with her, is that what you mean?"

The record clattered to the floor and broke into pieces. Nick didn't move; he stood there, holding the sleeve, staring at the black vinyl chards. My glass was frozen in my hand. Somewhere out on Wilshire came the bleating of a police siren.

The phone rang.

We both flinched, as if the ringing had set off a current that caused us to move again. Nick turned toward the phone.

"If it's Ursula, tell her you'll call her right back. Tell her, Nick."

He came around the coffee table and picked up the phone. "Hello?"

He listened for a moment. Then, "Let me call you right back, Urse. The messenger from the paper is here. I've got to give him some copy." A pause. "Sure. Five minutes. Bye."

Slowly he replaced the receiver. "She said she'd call back. Now what?"

I was thinking fast. "Tell her you can't see her tonight. Tell her you've been working on me and maybe I'll re-

lent. You're hoping I won't want the money after all.
Um . . ."

"Then what?"

"Tell her to meet you tomorrow night. Yes, that's it. At
KTLA. Let's see, Truman always leaves after the news.
Just to be safe, tell her eight o'clock. In the newsroom."

"KTLA—why?"

"Something just occurred to me. But I need to think it
through."

Nick sat down on the far end of the couch and finished
his drink. He didn't look at me. I lit a cigarette.

There didn't seem a whole lot to say.

. . . Where *were* they?

Twenty-four hours had passed since I poked a hole in
the lug's neck and did a no-show on The Boss. And there
had been no sign of them still. I kept my eye glued to the
rear window. I could feel myself coming unraveled. But
in a strange way, running on nerves, even jangled ones,
was all that was keeping me sane. If I was sane.

If any of this made sense.

"So. Andrew tells me you play football."

Jackson and I were sitting across the kitchen table
from each other, a plate of Mrs. Keyes's sandwiches
looming menacingly between us. Jackson was most con-
scious of his manners, and blotted his mouth with a napkin after every bite.

"Yes, ma'am. Varsity at UCLA."

"You're a student?"

"Yes, ma'am, third year. I'm thinking about medical
school."

"No." I was fascinated.

Jackson smiled disparagingly. "I'm surprised, too. But
all those injuries around me got me thinking. My biology
professor's been sort of encouraging me, so we'll see."

"What about football?"

"Yes, ma'am. We'll also see."

I had no idea if Negroes were allowed to play professional football, but I suspected Jackson's evasion meant he didn't want to talk about it. Instead, he said, "Right now, I'm out for the rest of the season."

"Are you hurt?"

He shook his head. "My mom got laid up with tuberculosis and can't work. So I dropped off the team to help her out." He blotted his mouth. "Ma'am, this sandwich is terrible."

I stole a look in the direction of Mrs. Keyes's room. The door was shut tight. I winked at him.

"I know where the cookies are stashed."

Sitting cross-legged on my bed, and working through a pile of Fig Newtons, I fielded Tee's unhelpful report.

"I guess I spooked him. But he's bound to come home some time."

"The cab company can't help?"

"He quit. Maybe he was afraid I would tell the police what I knew and the company would fire him."

Three cookies left. I took a small bite out of one of them. "Maybe he found a job with another cab company. I mean, what else can a cabdriver do?"

"Go visit his long-lost relative in Hoboken," said Tee. "But I'm checking other companies. Want me to come over tonight?"

"No. Jackson's in the guest room and I think I heard Andrew drive in a while ago. I really need to find that cabbie, Tee."

"We will. Why don't you call Nick and have him spend the night?"

I considered which of the last two Fig Newtons to eat first. It seemed important to choose the right one. They were exactly the same size.

"That isn't one of your better ideas," I said.

·   ·   ·

Later, as I sat huddled on the window seat, I sketched out a scam for Ursula Martens. I would play her game, only I would play it better.

Occasionally a car passed, giving me a scare. I opened the window a crack and was surprised at how chilly the air had become. The Santa Anas had finally gone, and soon, according to the *Farmer's Almanac*, the winter rains would come. I liked the rain.

. . . Ursula Martens. I smiled suddenly, thinking how easy it would be. But a moment later, my stomach tightening, I saw that it wouldn't work at all.

A high-stakes gamble. It would be a piece of cake—or a total disaster. Heads or tails. One or the other.

The rules of life were as old as the hills. And just as immutable.

43
♦

The second hand jerked spasmodically from number to number, getting nowhere on a schedule. I sat at James St. Clair's desk, sipping a cup of coffee, eyeing it. It was an old West Bend alarm clock that had suddenly appeared one day on top of the file cabinet. Its big round face was captured inside cream-colored enamel that gently curved into an arch above the center of the clock face, and broke into two intricate spires on either side. Rather an eyesore. Accompanying the incessant tick-tocking was the clitter-clattering of the wire service machines. People noises from down the hall grew faint as the wobbly minute hand, like Old Man Time, lumbered heavily toward the twelve.

I had arrived a little after six.

I found Ed Drake, the genial engineer, and told him what I needed. After Truman Stone left at seven-fifteen, Ed followed me into the newsroom and gave me careful instructions. It was now three minutes to eight. I had arrived too early; my nerves were warmed to a fever pitch.

366

Tee Jones still had not located the cabdriver. Walter Ainsley, his ear seemingly pressed to the grand jury room door, had learned that Norman Wills phoned in sick and his testimony was postponed until Monday. Harry Gladstone had called a press conference to announce the LAPD had uncovered the identity of the mysterious blonde and an arrest was imminent. But he hadn't arrested me. And Nick had talked to Ursula as late as five o'clock. Still, Gladstone's dramatic announcement would be the lead story in tomorrow's paper. I lit a cigarette and glanced again at the clock. Then I stood up and walked over to the UPI machine.

> *Los Angeles—The most expensive hunk of plywood in the world—Howard Hughes's $25,000,000 flying boat—was eased gently into the waters of Los Angeles-Long Beach Harbor an inch at a time today while a crew of 60 experts, engineers and workmen battled to protect the fragile giant against high winds. Hundreds of people lined . . .*

"Hello, Paris Chandler."

A gloved hand was holding the right sheet aside. She stood there, elegant and poised, as if she were a fashion model striking a pose. She was wearing a gray-and-white houndstooth dress, wide at the shoulders, nipped at the waist. White cotton cuffs melted into spotless white cotton gloves. A rose-colored scarf was tossed carelessly around her neck. The same rose was picked up again in her suede hat, which was trimmed with a gray grosgrain band. She stepped inside, dropping the sheet, and carefully removed her gloves.

"How lovely you look, Ursula. Won't you sit down?"

A cool glance. "I was expecting Nick."

I moved over to Jim's chair and pointed to Truman's. "He'll be along. He just phoned. I want to apologize again for last night. Please do sit down."

Ursula slipped into Truman's chair and tossed her gloves on the desk. I started to pick up my coffee cup. "This is the last of the coffee, I'm afraid. But I can get you a Coke if you like."

"Sure."

I took a couple of nickels out of my purse and walked down the hall. From the other end, the studio, I could hear the last of the crew leaving. *The Garry and Larry Show* was the final studio program of the night. Presumably, it being Friday, an old British picture was being run. I dropped a nickel into the machine and noticed that the fire escape hatch was slightly ajar. Once, after it had been built into the wall, they had held a demonstration drill. Two recruits from the fire department had pulled open the wide, narrow rectangular door and, one by one, rolled down the chute into the street. I pushed the chute door closed. Then I bought another Coke and walked back into the newsroom.

Ursula was smoking a cigarette and reading yesterday's *Times*. I put a Coke down in front of her and went around the four grouped desks to sit in Jim's chair. She kept reading the *Times*. I reached under the desk. As I straightened, I mentally noted the time. I had forty-five minutes. "I didn't bring the nightgown, Ursula."

She looked up from the paper, frowning. "Why not? Where is it? Nick said you would."

"I know."

Her blue eyes narrowed. "What is it that you want? I won't pay a cent more."

"I never asked for money. *You* offered to pay it. I don't mind selling you the nightgown, but I don't understand what for."

"It's none of your business." She reached for her gloves.

"Oh don't leave. We should talk. I must admit I was pretty upset when I found out Jim was also seeing you. How did you meet him?"

"At a party, I think. It's hard to remember." She smiled slyly. "I meet so many men."

"I can imagine. And they take good care of you, don't they?"

"Yes." Ursula looked at me defiantly. "What business is it of yours?"

"It's not. Except for the nightgown. Why would one

single trinket mean so much to you? I mean, Jim gave it
to me."

"He was special."

"Even though he was seeing me, as well as—"

"Who?"

"Never mind. I suppose it was Matthew Barnathan's
idea to get the nightgown. Obviously, he's the one who's
going to pay."

"You're crazy. Mr. B. doesn't even know."

"Sure he does. Don't tell me it was just coincidence
you were at Jim's house the night he was killed."

"Well it was. We wanted to be together before his
stupid wife showed up. Mr. B. didn't know a thing. Then
you had to barge in. I got sore and left. When I found
out he had been killed, I remembered my nightgown was
there and I got scared. I was afraid the police would
figure out it was mine, so I tried to buy another one. I
would tell them it was at my apartment all along."

"And where was your nightgown all along?"

"At Jim's house, I told you."

"You kept it there? Where?"

"In the closet."

"Really." I lifted the Coke bottle and took a sip. "The
police found it on the bed." They hadn't. But I suspected
she wouldn't know that, since my information had come
from Tee.

"They did not. It wasn't on the bed. I never even went
upstairs that night."

"Sure you did, Urse. I know exactly what happened.
After I left, Jim came downstairs. Then you went up to
the bedroom. A few minutes later, the doorbell rang. Jim
thought it was me, probably, and opened the door. You
heard shots. After the killer left, you ran out. Forgetting
your nightgown. I don't know if the killer was supposed
to wait for you in his car and didn't, or whether you
panicked and ran over to Larchmont."

Ursula was studying me as if I were a specimen in a jar
of formaldehyde. "That's ridiculous," she snapped.

"Barnathan wanted you there to baby-sit Jim. You
must have had a heart attack when I showed up. Then,

lucky for you, I left. Even more lucky for you, someone saw me leave. That gave Barnathan another scapegoat, if he wanted one."

"Another?"

"Though I wouldn't be surprised if he had you hand-picked to take the fall all along. One of us is going to be arrested. And I really think it's you."

Ursula relaxed. "You dope. You don't know a thing. I'm too valuable to Mr. B. More valuable than you know."

"Your value was murdered. Your job was to bleed Jim of information. Or possibly, even, to blackmail him. His wife shows up, you would threaten to go public with your affair if he didn't back off the freeway scandal. But now you have no value. You're a liability, Ursula. You know too much."

Her eyes flickered toward the sheets. "He's not coming, is he?"

"Nick? No, he'll be here. Look, believe it or not, we want to help you." I hesitated. "Well at least Nick does. He's gone sweet on you."

"You're such a liar, Paris. You're just trying to trick me."

"You've been tricked. You were tricked the moment Barnathan took Lucille Wills off the case and planted you."

"Honestly." She reached for a cigarette.

"Norman Wills was using his own wife to get to Jim. But then she fell for him. Norman was offended. So they pulled her off and sent you. The thing is, Jim was too smart for either of you. He knew what was going on. He told me."

Ursula grabbed her silver cigarette case and stood up. "I don't have to listen to this."

"Don't you know the danger you're in?" I glanced at the clock, checking the time. I said, "You know who the killer is. And they're not going to let you live."

She wet her lips. "Where's Nick?"

"Right here." The sheets parted and, like John Barrymore heeding a cue, in strode Nick. He looked dapper as usual. Tonight he had planted a red plaid pocket hand-kerchief in his navy blazer. His tie matched the plaid. "Hi, kids." He stopped. "Urse, what's wrong?"

"Oh hello, darling." She reached for his hand.

"I was just saying, Nicky, that we want to help her out of this terrible jam she's in. Seriously, Ursula, why stick your neck out for them? Forget what they're paying you. You can get a job here."

Ursula dropped back into the chair. "I can?"

"I was hoping Truman would stick around. I've told him all about you."

"Who's Truman?"

"Truman Stone. The news director. They're starting a quiz show based on current events and they're looking for a hostess." I smiled quickly. "You'd be great."

She began twisting her gloves in her hands.

"Ursula, think about it," coaxed Nick. "You'd be a star overnight."

Ursula ignored him and turned chilly blue eyes on me. "I don't know who the killer is, Paris. You're wrong."

"Let us help you," said Nick, putting his hand on her shoulder.

"Norman Wills goes before the grand jury on Monday," I pressed. "He'll sing."

Ursula snickered. "That's a laugh."

"And they're going to call you, too. Nick's right. You need us."

Ursula finally got her cigarette going. She blew out the match then curved her lips into a knowing smile. "Norman will never talk. He's been paid too much. You have no idea."

"Lucille does."

She blinked. "You talked to Lucille?"

"I talked to Jim. Poor Lucille was in love with him. She kept feeding him information. And Jim told me."

Ursula put the cigarette in an ashtray and stared at her hand, as if to make sure her nicely manicured nails hadn't been damaged. Then she looked over at me. "All right, Paris. I thought you were bluffing at first. But I delivered the checks to Lucille. You're right. She would know."

Surprised, I glanced at Nick. He was standing behind Ursula's chair, rubbing her shoulders. I said, "Every week?"

"No. There was no set schedule. I would go to the house and Lucille would give me an envelope. It would have the names of streets that had to be bulldozed. I would hand her a check. It would be made out to a dummy company. Like Acme Electrical Supply."

"Or Consolidated Developers?" That was the name of the company Al Brown had given to the bank.

Ursula nodded.

"How many thousands of dollars did Barnathan pay?"

"If you don't know, I won't tell you. But Mr. B. was giving him other money, too, that I had nothing to do with."

"Money for phonying up contracts?" I guessed.

"Something like that. Richard would buy a house from somebody and give them a copy of the contract. But the contract he gave to Norman Wills would be for more."

"And he would pocket the difference?"

She nodded. "And then when they put the house up for auction, the state could set a higher price. So they'd actually get the money back."

"Clever," Nick said.

"Not really," I said. "It's only simple greed. And Ursula was everybody's girl Friday."

She had caught my change of tone and didn't like it. "Speak for yourself, Paris. It's my word against yours, you know. Norm won't tell them anything and neither will I. And it was you they saw leaving Jim's house. Just about the time he was killed."

"You're right." I smiled. "But what you don't know is that I came back."

There was a quick intake of breath. "Came back? What do you mean?"

"Leave her alone," scolded Nick. "Can't you see she's upset?" He began stroking her hair.

"Who cares? I thought we could help her but she's way too dumb, Nick. I mean I was there. I saw."

"Saw what?" demanded Ursula.

"Everything."

The room suddenly fell silent. Even the noisy wire machines had paused, as if they, too, were eager to hear. The clock kept ticking.

"When I got to Jim's, I came in through the kitchen door," I said. "I brought a book, which I dropped on the table. But when I left, I went out the front door. It wasn't till I got to my car that I remembered the book. So I went back. I went in through the kitchen and"—I met her eyes—"I saw you and Jim. In the rotunda."

The color drained from Ursula's face. She raised her left hand to her shoulder and put it on top of Nick's. "I don't know what she's talking about, Nicky. She's making it up."

"Paris, you never told me this," Nick said sharply. "All I know is you're supposed to have the nightgown. Where is it? Why don't we just finish what we came here to do?"

Unwittingly, Nick had given a typical male response: avoid conflict and get the matter at hand over with. I swallowed a smile. "Dummy, she doesn't have the money. If Barnathan did give it to her, she'd keep it for herself and try to bamboozle you into giving her the nightgown for free."

"That's not true," said Ursula vehemently. "Mr. B. doesn't know about the nightgown. I—don't have the money."

I stood up. "In that case, this meeting is adjourned."

Ursula began working on her tear ducts. A couple of drops spilled onto her cheeks. She tilted her head back. "Nicky, can't you make her see . . ."

"Why can't you let her have the nightgown, Paris? If she thinks it will help her, why not do it?"

"Mm." I sat down and stole a glance at the clock. Twelve minutes to go. "Maybe," I said thoughtfully, "we can help each other."

"How?" said Ursula eagerly.

Now I would have to play my ace. Play it, and hope

that Tee was right. I took my time, sipping some Coke. I put the bottle down. "I can't lie to the police, Ursula. I know you were there when Jim was killed. But you can't know for sure that I was. You never saw me."

"What are you saying?"

"We'll go to the police together and tell them who the murderer is. If you'll do that, you can have the nightgown. If you still want it."

"What kind of deal is that?" She looked at me uncertainly. "Anyway, I don't know who the murderer is. I didn't see who did it."

Was she boldly daring me to accuse *her*? Well I wouldn't. I glanced at the clock. "Pity."

"Wait. Okay, you were right. I did go upstairs."

"To change."

"Yes, that's right."

"You took the nightgown out of the closet and . . ."

"I got the nightgown and started to unzip my dress. Jim was still downstairs when the doorbell rang. I came out of the bedroom and tiptoed down the hall. I heard Jim say, 'Just a minute.' Then he said, 'What's this?' Then I heard the shots. But I didn't see anybody. I swear."

"You heard the shots. You ran out. But first you went to get your purse. And maybe your wrap, if you'd worn one. You left them in the den, I suppose. Or did you bring the purse up to the bedroom?"

"I . . . I don't remember. I didn't have a jacket. I—" She hesitated. "No, wait. I ran back to the bedroom. My shoes. I had taken them off. I grabbed my shoes with one hand and my purse with the other, then I came down the stairs."

"You came down the stairs *slowly*, remember? You were afraid the murderer might still be there."

"Yes. I came down the stairs *real* slowly. I saw the front door was open."

"You went out the front door?"

"I—" She saw the trap. If I had been there, hovering in the dining room, I would have known which door she went out. She looked at me angrily. "What difference does it make?"

"Big difference. Still no deal."

"Don't be so stubborn," Nick broke in crossly. "Maybe she'll go to the police with you and tell them what she just said."

"Yes," agreed Ursula. "That's what I'll do. I'll go with you to the police."

"Uh huh. Fat chance."

"Paris—" tried Nick.

I glanced again at the clock. "You forget, both of you. I did see what happened. And with or without her, I'm going to Chief Gladstone."

Ursula jumped up. "Go ahead. You can't prove anything."

I started to say something but Nick had taken her arm and was protectively escorting her out.

Ursula turned. Her eyes were blazing. "Whatever you say, I'll deny it. You can't push me around like this."

I watched them vanish through the sheets and listened to their footsteps reverberate down the hall. I sighed. I hadn't found out the name of Jim's killer. But I had found out enough.

I pushed back my chair and reached under the desk.

The reels were still turning. I shut the tape recorder off.

44

♦

I sat there, with the clattering machines, and smoked a cigarette.

Ursula Martens had changed her story in mid-plot. In the first go-round she denied she had been upstairs that night. But when I told her I had come back, had seen her in the house at that hour, she'd warbled a new tune.

I forced myself to picture her waiting in the den while Jim and I were upstairs. Had she turned off the lamp? She might have. She would have sat there in the dark not knowing how long I would stay, or whether I would leave at all. If her purpose in being there was to baby-sit Jim until the killer arrived, why wouldn't she have left, now that I could provide the same function?

I started again.

Maybe, when they heard me come in, Jim had told her to wait, knowing I wouldn't stay the night. So, dutifully, Ursula had waited. In the dark. Smoking . . .

I straightened. The police had found a used ashtray in the den. Ashes, but no cigarette butts . . .

Ah, this was better. So she hadn't gone upstairs. No,

376

when the doorbell rang, they were both downstairs. Jim, thinking that it was me, sent her back to the den. Whether she actually went that far, or stopped in the living room, I couldn't know. But from her vantage point, Ursula had seen James St. Clair murdered.

Then—she had run into the den to get her purse. She had seen the ashtray. She picked out the butts, put them, perhaps, in her purse. And fled. Not through the front door and not through the kitchen, but out the nearest door: the French doors in the living room.

Yes, that is how it must have been. For had she been upstairs, heard the shots but not seen the killer, she never would have run back to the bedroom for her purse, *then* run through a darkened living room, not knowing if the killer was still in the house, to pick butts out of an ashtray. She would never have thought of the butts. And earlier, when she heard me leave and came out of her hiding place in the den, why would she have taken the butts with her then?

I began again.

Okay. Assume she was telling the truth when she said she went to Jim's house on her own. She had gone for a dalliance and ended up a witness to murder. Worse, she had recognized the killer. In the days that followed she would have waited for Barnathan to boast that he had ordered the hit. But either he never did or he flatly denied any involvement. Which would have been when Ursula desperately began to cover her tracks.

Given this version, her quest for the nightgown now made sense. As crime evidence, the nightgown had little standing. But if it could be traced to her, the police might keep probing; putting her inside the house, close to, or during, the time of the murder.

I switched on the tape recorder and began rewinding the spool.

From down the hall I could hear the faint rumblings of the floor sweeper. I glanced nervously at the clock. Nick was supposed to drive her home and come back. Or, if she seemed willing to talk, he would use her phone, tell

her he had to check in with the copy desk and call me
here. The spools stopped; I shut the recorder off.

Suddenly, three bells rang as one of the wire machines
began a furious clatter. Three bells meant a significant
story. I went over to see what it was.

*Los Angeles, Oct. 17—Norman G. Wills, a lawyer for the
California Division of Highways, was found murdered at his
Los Feliz home late this afternoon. Since January 1946, Wills
has headed up the Los Angeles office for the state's Right-of-
Way program, approving contracts for the removal of buildings
located along the route of the new freeway system. He was 42.*

*According to a police spokesman, Wills was apparently shot
at point-blank range as he answered the door shortly after 5
P.M. One bullet entered his neck and two more his chest. His
wife, Lucille, and their son were away when the shooting occurred, but she later told police her husband had been ill and
had not gone to work.*

*Wills had been expected to testify before a grand jury investi-
gating alleged misuse of state money in right-of-way procure-
ment for the Hollywood Freeway project. Due to his illness, his
appearance was rescheduled for Monday.*

Shaken, I ripped off the story and took it back to the
desk. Had Ursula known? Is that why she admitted making payments to Wills?

The floor sweeper cut off and footsteps sounded down
the hall, heavy footsteps coming closer. They could have
seen the Bentley out front, known I was inside. Only one
set of footsteps boldly drawing closer. I grabbed the reel
off the recorder and shoved it into a desk drawer. The
footsteps stopped. I held my breath as the sheets fluttered.

"Evenin', Miss Chandler."

Franklin, the janitor, smiled broadly. "I was wonderin'
who was down here. Is it all right, I come in and clean
now?"

I laughed foolishly. "Sure. I was just getting ready to
leave. Is the front door open?"

"Yes, ma'am. I'll run along now and get me my mop
and pail."

They could be out there, sitting in Brown's truck, waiting. I went over to the file cabinet and took a manila envelope from the supply drawer. I tried to remember if the door at the back of the garage, the one that opened directly into O'Blath's bar, was left unlocked. I slipped the reel of tape into the envelope, grabbed my purse and stole over to the sheets. I peeked out. I could hear the clanging of metal down at the studio end—Franklin folding up the chairs. I stepped into the hall and walked quickly toward the back of the garage. I turned right at the Coke machine and trotted along to the back door. From the other side, I could hear loud voices and the clatter of dishes in O'Blath's kitchen. The door was locked.

The only other way out was through the front. I turned back and stared at the Coke machine from a distance. If I stuck the envelope behind it, I could be seen the length of the long hall. My eye fell on the escape hatch. I pulled it open and carefully placed the envelope down in the left corner of the chute. Was that a noise? I turned quickly. But no one was there. Gently, I closed the hatch door and, trying to calm myself, started down the hall to the front of the cavernous building.

Nearing the newsroom, I hesitated. Walter would still be at the paper. They would be putting together the story on Wills and I wanted to pass along what Ursula had said. I ducked inside and dialed the *Examiner*.

After a momentary hold, I got through to Walter. "I just found out about Wills. Are you working on it?"

"Yeah and I can't talk, kid. I'm rewriting and stitching in some of the stuff we got. You should come in here."

"I've got more. Let me give it to you now."

"Shoot."

I repeated Ursula's remarks against the clacking of Walter's typing. The typing stopped. "Jesus Christ. When did she tell you that?"

"About eight-thirty, nine o'clock. I don't know if she knew he was dead. Do you want to hear what she said about Jim?"

"Not now. How soon can you get here?"

I said I was on my way and hung up.

It was then that I heard the *click*. Even before my head completed its ninety-degree turn to the right, I knew instinctively what I would see. Two men stood just inside the long white sheets. One was short and solid with a stomach, a band of black fringe running around the crown of his high bald dome. His plaid double-breasted jacket was unbuttoned revealing brown suspenders clamped to the waist of his plaid trousers. He had brown stains on his teeth and a cigar between his lips. His black eyes flashed menacingly. Next to him, Al Brown was pointing a dull steel pistol at me and scowling.

"Mr. Barnathan?" I said.

He took the cigar out of his mouth and came a step closer. "We came to take you for a ride, Miss Chandler."

"You missed the curtain. And the whole first act. I've already talked to the D.A.'s office."

They would have entered through the front. Jackson, hopefully, was right behind them.

"D.A.'s office isn't worth a hill of beans. Be a good girl and don't make a fuss."

"Your house of cards is falling fast. Norman Wills talked to the D.A. He turned state's evidence this morning."

"He turned to stone this afternoon." Barnathan puffed contentedly on his cigar. "The janitor's in the closet, by the way, and no one else is here. What are *you* doing here?"

"Waiting for Christmas."

"It won't come. Your chauffeur's all knotted up, having a little siesta in your tank out there. Soon you'll have a siesta, too."

"Yeah," said Brown. "For all-time."

"I hate siestas," I said. "Anyway, what's the point? What I know, what Jim knew, the D.A. knows. They want you bad."

"Not as bad as they want you." Barnathan showed me his brown teeth. "Ursula went to the police this afternoon."

"Did she?"

"She heard the fight, she heard everything."

"You mean," I said coyly, "Ursula was *there* that night?"

"In a manner of speaking. She was about to ring the bell when she heard the argument. Then she hears two shots. She runs and hides in the bushes and—guess who came out?"

"Meyer Lansky?"

"You talk a good game, sweetheart."

"A better game than you play. Your pal keeps waving that gun in my face, why doesn't he just use it? I should think you'd want to get on with it. And I happen to be sitting at James St. Clair's desk. Which adds a nice symmetry, don't you think?"

"You'll be in the cemetery soon enough. I want the folders you snatched. You got 'em here?"

"Got what here?"

Brown came over to the desk and stood behind me. I could feel the cold metal of the gun on my neck. I thought vaguely of Nick, wondering what had become of him. Walter would be no help. He would be working furiously to meet the deadline and would not even think of me until it was too late.

Barnathan said, "I'll ask you one more time. Where are the folders?"

If I told him that Ted Stein had them, they would have no further use for me. Brown started pulling my hair, which hurt.

"I don't have them. I—"

The phone rang. For a moment, we all stared at it. "I guess I'd better answer it," I said.

"Maybe you'd better not." Barnathan reached over the desk and placed his cigar hand protectively over the receiver. It had to be Nick, I thought. Which meant he wasn't coming. After ten rings, the phone fell silent.

"I don't have the folders," I repeated. "I really don't."

Brown yanked with more enthusiasm on my hair. Barnathan leaned his face close to mine. "Then where are they?" His cold black eyes bored into me. Beads of perspiration had formed on his dome.

I was about to tell him the folders were at the *Examiner* being gone through by half a dozen reporters and editors, but then another idea came to me, a far riskier gamble. "Please," I said, "may I have a cigarette? There's one in my purse."

Barnathan straightened. Tentatively, I reached for my purse. He didn't stop me. I found my pack of Chesterfields and with a shaky hand, lit one. Slowly I exhaled. "If your friend would step away from me, I'd tell you what you want to know."

I needed to buy a moment of time. The worst that could happen, I decided, was that my story wouldn't jibe and then they would only push harder. But they needed my information, which, for a while, gave me the edge that might keep me alive.

I said, "I gave the folders to Ursula."

"You did what?" said Barnathan.

"You're a liar," scoffed Brown.

I forced myself to sit very still.

"What are you talking about?" Barnathan growled. "Ursula don't have no folders."

"I gave them to her last night. I don't know what she may have done with them."

"Jesus, Mr. B., you gonna listen to this?"

Barnathan leaned over and put his smelly cigar in the ashtray. "I'm listening, sweetheart."

"Ursula told me where I could find the folders. I mean, how else would I have known? I was supposed to get them and meet her at Ciro's. So I went to that place on Barbee Street. I brought someone with me who stayed in the car. When I didn't come out, my friend went in, saw the folders and took them."

"Yeah, who was the friend?"

"Never mind. After I got away from your thugs, I contacted my friend, who brought me the folders. I gave them to Ursula at Ciro's."

Brown grabbed my hair with a sudden, hard yank. I yelped.

"Stop it," Barnathan said angrily. "I want to hear this. Why the hell would you give the folders to Ursula?"

"Perhaps you should ask her."

"Yeah but I'm asking you first."

"She, um, said she needed them to give to Norman Wills."

"Wills is dead," said Brown needlessly. "She's a goner."

Barnathan nodded. "Let's get her outta here."

"Were the files so important?" I asked innocently.

"Someone breaks into your place, steals something, you get mad," Barnathan said.

"Look, I'm sorry. Maybe she never gave them to Wills. Maybe I can get them back."

"Ursula don't have no files. You're making it sound like she was double-crossing me. Ursula's a real loyal girl."

"Oh I know," I said quickly. "That's why she wanted the files."

"Yeah? Explain that, sweetheart. Real good."

"We were both at Jim's house the night he was killed."

"Outside the house," Barnathan interjected. "She was outside."

"No. *Inside.* I saw her. She was terribly afraid I would tell the cops and then they would find their way to you. She didn't want anybody to know she had been there. Do you think I could go to the rest room now?"

"No." Barnathan came over to me. "I'm still listening, sweetheart. For about five more seconds."

"Ursula knew about Jim's freeway file and she was afraid of what it would reveal. About you. And her. That's the one I was after."

"You're not making sense, Chandler. Why would she steal the file from me?"

"Let's get outta here, boss. Someone might show up."

Barnathan's muddy eyes flicked over me speculatively. "Ursula never went in, she would have told me."

"I think she was trying to protect you. But the police know. Someone on the street saw her go in with Jim, and the police found a cabdriver who took her home."

"When?"

"Late. Around eleven."

Barnathan raised an eyebrow at Brown.

"I never seen Ursula over there. I only seen her." He thumped my head.

"The police confiscated her nightgown," I said. "Can you believe it? That cad worked us both in that night. What a guttersnipe."

"Who's a guttersnipe?"

Like a queen from hell, Ursula Martens swept into the room. She smiled unpleasantly. "Tell me. I love guttersnipe, or is it guttersnipes?"

"Hi, baby," said Barnathan. "Where you been?"

"With Goodwin, of course. Did I miss anything?"

"Naw. She won't tell us where the folders are," Brown muttered.

I lit another cigarette and gave up trying to think at all.

Ursula flounced over to the desk and sat down.

"Can't you make her? Make her tell, darling. I'll watch."

Barnathan stuck his cigar in his mouth and tried to light it. "I was thinking," he said through his teeth. "All the time you spent with her, maybe she dropped a hint?"

Oooo, cagey. Perhaps all was not lost. I continued puffing on my cigarette.

"What are you talking about, Matthew? She hates me."

"Gee, she made it sound like you girls was friends."

"Friends?" Ursula gave me a pained look. "Do you know what she did to me last night? She spilled a glass of champagne all over my lovely cream silk dress."

"It was an accident, Ursula. You know that." I smiled benignly.

"Ha. She didn't like it that her boyfriend was paying more attention to me. He's crazy for me."

Oh swell, I thought. Now Barnathan would assume my story was only a dreary tale of revenge. In a way, it was.

Barnathan narrowed his eyes at me. "You got one more chance, sweetheart. Then you're cement. What I hate even more than losing those folders is being lied to." He turned to Brown. "We'll take her out to the Riverside project, got it?"

I believed Barnathan meant it and I began to berate myself for making the phone call to Walter. Why hadn't I just left? I might have made it to my car before they did.

"I'm waiting," the builder warned.

"I'd like to show you something first. Here, under the desk. See?" I inched my chair back and pointed with my foot.

"Jesus," said Brown. "You been recording this?"

Barnathan came around and took a quick look. "It's not on. So what?"

"It was on. Before. When Ursula was here."

"She's lying, Matt. There was no tape recorder on."

"Get up," Barnathan said. "Go stand over there."

I got up and moved around the desks to the other side. Barnathan stooped down and pulled the machine out. "There's no tape in it." He straightened.

"I hid the tape." I grinned.

"*Listen* to her," said Ursula. "She's just wasting time."

"Where?"

"Down the hall. In a fireproof drawer they keep film in."

"I say we scram," said Brown. "This Paramount next door probably has guards around."

"Let's go." Barnathan pointed his cigar at me, then at the sheets.

"Okay, but it's in an envelope addressed to Chief Gladstone," I said. "It makes me happy to think you're all goners, too."

Barnathan stopped on his way to the sheets and came all the way back to me. He stood inches from my face. I could see the big perspiration drops on his bald head. Our eyes locked in silent combat. "Al, go with her. She tries something, shoot her."

Brown grabbed my arm. "I won't be manhandled," I said firmly. "Let go."

"Walk two steps behind her," Barnathan intervened. "Presumably, you won't miss."

We exited. I felt like I was exiting from a bad play. Terrible lines spoken by dreadful actors; a rotten piece of theater. I would just as soon have retired to the dressing room, removed my makeup and gone home. Instead, I had walked into, not out of, the final act, and the march down the hall seemed to be happening in slow motion. With Brown behind me, I wondered if I could suddenly kick backward, trip him or hit him with a lucky blow of my big, clunky heel and actually make a run for it. But as we approached the Coke machine, I saw that I didn't have the nerve.

We turned right and I stopped at the escape hatch. I said, "This is the drawer. It's in there. Go ahead, look."

"Right, birdbrain. You look, me and Mr. Smith and Wesson will watch."

"Okay, but stand back a bit. It pulls way out." I leaned over and slowly worked the hatch open. I stared into the dark chute. With my right hand I began patting just below the hinges. "Oh dear. It must have come untaped."

I looked back at Brown. "I can't quite reach the bottom."

"Well that's too bad." A click. He had taken the safety off.

I sighed. I bent over, grabbed the inside handle with my left hand, raised my right leg, and reached down as far as I could with my right hand.

"Hurry it up, huh?"

And then my body was moving, seemingly without my brain's consent, somersaulting forward, whipping the door closed and rolling, rolling, rolling down the gently sloped chute and out through the rubber sheet onto the asphalt. A small wimpering sound came with me—a combination of ragged gasps and cries of fear. I scrambled to my feet in the fetid darkness of the alley. The front door to O'Blath's was around the corner and down the street. I took off, made the turn and nearly knocked over a tipsy couple on the sidewalk. I flew into O'Blath's and trotted through the dining area to the bar in back. To the left were two doors: Men and Ladies.

I pushed into the men's room, breathing hard.

45
◆

Two patrolmen heeded the phone call, grudgingly dialed by the stud I embarrassed zipping up his fly.

The cops drove me downtown to headquarters at City Hall. Lieutenant Art Bolsky, the homicide detective in charge of Jim's murder investigation, was sitting in an interrogation room, waiting. Bolsky was a lanky, balding fifteen-year veteran with long, mouth-bracketing dimples that counterbalanced the skepticism in his dark, hooded eyes. He made sure I was brought coffee and a new pack of cigarettes, and then he phoned Harry Gladstone. The chief arrived half an hour later, all spruced up and reeking of cologne, in case, I supposed, he still had time to call a press conference.

They let me use the phone. Walter had left the paper, and only the cleanup rewrite men were still around. He did not answer at his apartment. Nor did Nick answer at his. I left a message on Tee's service inviting her to join the party. Jackson had a lump on his head and was taken to Central Receiving Hospital to be looked over. I told them first thing about the tape in the chute, carefully explaining how to retrieve it, and a couple of cops took off. When the stenographer was ready to go, I began my story.

At 1 A.M., Tee arrived with Nick in tow. While they were being brought coffee, I walked out of the room and picked up a phone on a vacant desk. Walter still was not home. I called my house and Andrew answered. He said that Jackson and the Bentley had arrived an hour ago and he had put Jackson to bed in the guest room. And no, Walter had not phoned.

When I went back into the interrogation room, now thick with smoke, Tee was telling of locating the cab-driver who had driven Ursula Martens home the night of the murder, and of her own unsuccessful attempt to find him again.

Nick, his tie loosened and even darker shadows under his eyes, cleared his throat and began relating his escapades with Ursula.

"After we left Paris tonight, I told her I would follow her home. But she said she would like to stop some-where for a drink. She suggested the Formosa Café on Melrose. So that's where we went."

"She tell you anything of importance?" Bolsky asked.

"At first, she was furious that Paris hadn't brought the nightgown and she blamed me. She wanted me to go to Paris's house and steal it. Tonight. She said I had let her down and she didn't think she trusted me anymore."

"Uh huh," said Bolsky. "What else?"

"When we first got to the restaurant, I tried to call Paris. But the line was busy."

"I must have been talking to Walter," I said.

"Ursula had a couple of fast drinks. She nuzzled up to me and said she had something important to tell me but it would be a big shock. She said I'd better have another drink. That's when I went to the phone and tried again. No answer. I figured Paris had left, or maybe she was in the rest room. Anyway, when I got back to the table, Ursula said she was terribly frightened. She had no idea that Paris had seen her at the house, and what must have happened, after Paris came in through the kitchen, she must have snuck back out, come around to the front and rung the doorbell."

"Oh please," I said.

Nick smiled. "Ursula said Paris was right—she had seen the killer. It was Paris. And now she feared for her life."

Nobody spoke. Bolsky began tapping his pencil on the table. I could hear Gladstone breathing.

Nick said, "Anyway, then she went to the rest room. Only she never came back."

"You mean," said Bolsky, "she skipped out on you?"

"Yeah. It took me about twenty minutes to figure it out. I tried Paris at home, but nobody answered. I also called the paper. But Walter was down with the printers and the guy I spoke to hadn't seen Paris. I left and drove to her house. Nobody was there. I waited in the driveway about fifteen minutes, then I stuck a note under the door and went home. Maybe forty-five minutes later, Miss Jones called."

Bolsky rubbed his mouth. "Ursula said nothing about Norman Wills?"

"No."

"Miss Chandler, where were you at about five-thirty this afternoon?"

"I was leaving the *Examiner.*" I didn't like the question. "Jackson drove me to KTLA."

"And you got there when?"

I glanced up at Gladstone, who was leaning against the closed door. He stared at me without expression. "A little after six."

"Besides Jackson, can anyone verify this?"

"As soon as I got to the station I spoke to Ed Drake. He's an engineer. He was in the studio, setting up for the newscast."

"And what about leaving the paper? Anyone see you?"

No, I wanted to say. *I became a ghost.* "Tony in the parking lot across the street. And Constance McPhee Estevez. She's the society editor. We chatted as I was going out."

Bolsky looked at Gladstone. "Let's round up this Aubrey-Brown joker and get Barnathan in here. I'm going to have the boys check the files and see if we have anything on either one. Miss Chandler, what else you can think of?"

"This," I said. "If Ursula did see me shoot Jim, then why didn't she tell Barnathan? She would have had nothing to fear from him. Instead, according to him, she said she had been outside the house much earlier and heard us arguing and that she had gone home. When I told Barnathan I had seen Ursula *inside* the house, he asked Al Aubrey if he had seen her there."

"Suggesting," said Gladstone dryly, "that he pulled the trigger."

"Exactly."

"All right, folks," said Bolsky. "Let's call it a night. Miss Chandler, you aren't going anywhere we can't find you. You will be available for further questioning if we need you. And Chief, let's track down this cabdriver." He grinned crookedly. "Not that I doubt Miss Jones of course."

"Miss Jones," said Tee matter-of-factly, "suggests you offer protection to Paris."

"From what she's told me, those guys need protection from her."

Bolsky smiled at his wisecrack. I didn't.

He nodded. "All right. We'll stick a car in front of your house tonight. But if we find Barnathan and Aubrey, is there any need to keep a man on?"

Gladstone opened the door and left. Tee and Nick stood up and started moving out.

I stayed put. "You're not going to look for Ursula?"

"We'll pick her up right now. She's on what—Burton Way?"

Nick paused in the doorway. "She's at my apartment," he said.

46

◆

Tee parked in my driveway. "You'll be okay?"

"I'm fine." I stared at the front door and wondered if I had the energy to make it that far. I sat with my hand resting on the door handle. "Thanks."

"Donna St. Clair went home today. I forgot to tell you."

"She did? Back to New York?"

"She decided she didn't fancy the jewelry chump after all."

"Did she pay you?"

"She paid me a retainer of two hundred dollars. I get twenty-five a day. After eight days, she paid me another hundred. She said if I found the killer she'd send me whatever she owed and some kind of bonus. But I didn't find the killer. You did."

"Did I?" I watched the next door neighbor's cat creep up my front steps and prowl the veranda. "How's anybody going to prove it? They found the murder weapon in the trash bin, but no prints on it. How can they prove who pulled the trigger?"

392

"They'll make Ursula talk."

"And say she saw Brown pull the trigger? I doubt it. Why would she?"

"If the police book her for murder, she would."

"They could book me, too, don't forget." I smiled wearily at Tee. "Can you imagine Andrew on the witness stand? He'd testify in iambic pentameter."

Tee patted my arm. "Get some sleep. And stop thinking about murder."

"How can I?" With a bit of effort, I finally got the door open. "I'm going to strangle him."

I spent the rest of the night chasing two trains of thought, while curled up on the window seat in my bedroom. I stared at the patrol car out front. It didn't move, and neither did my trains. The mysterious black figure on skates never showed up. At daybreak, the squad car drove away. I didn't know if the cop thought the sun would protect me, or if the suspects had been rounded up, or if the guy just wanted a doughnut.

At seven, the paperboy tossed the *Examiner* onto the lawn. The Norman Wills murder was plastered across the top of the front page. I sipped a cup of coffee in the kitchen and read every word of it. Several paragraphs from the top it said:

> Just hours after the shooting, Ursula Martens, an employee of Sunset Estates, a landscape outfit owned by developer Matthew Barnathan, told the Examiner's Paris Chandler that she had routinely delivered cash payments to Wills from her boss.
>
> "There was no set schedule," Miss Martens said. "I would go to the house and Lucille [Mrs. Wills] would give me an envelope. It would have the names of the streets that had to be bulldozed. I would hand her a check. It would be made out to a dummy company. Like Acme Electrical Supply."
>
> Miss Martens said she believed Barnathan made other payments to Wills for phonying up contracts. According to her scenario . . .

The phone rang. I went down the hall to answer it.

"It's Walter," said Walter.

"At this hour? I doubt it."

"Newsmen have no hours."

"Oh, are we a newsman now?"

"Did you see the story? We killed the *Times.*"

"It's great, Walter. You really are the best. I love the line about *A Tale of Two Cities,* the sparkling, hopeful city in the sun on the threshold of greatness and the sticky-fingered city fathers out to corrupt it. Jim would have loved that."

"Speaking of Jim, get dressed and get down here. We have work to do."

"Wait till I tell you about last night."

"I know about last night. I just talked to Bolsky. The sex bomb sang."

"Ursula?"

"No, Al Brown. *Christ.* You coming?"

"I suppose that's the headline you'll write?"

"Unless you got a better one."

"I do." I twisted the cord around my finger. "But I'm told the *Examiner* won't print those words."

When I got to the office an hour later, the front of the newsroom was dark. It was Saturday, and few people bothered to come in. Most of the Sunday paper, except for breaking stories, was put to bed on Friday night. It wouldn't be until late afternoon that editors and rewrite men would show up. Walter had turned the lights on in the copy desk area against the back wall. He sat there alone, under Betty Grable's seductive gaze, banging away on his typewriter.

"I wanted to get the lead nailed down," he said, as I pulled up a chair beside him. Walter yanked the paper out of the carriage and handed it to me. His shirt was wrinkled, and dark with perspiration stains; his face had a stubble.

"You worked all night?"

He avoided my eyes and pointed to the page he had

typed. I read the two paragraphs and smiled. "It's good, Walter. Tell me more about Ursula."

The police had collected her at Nick's apartment, he said, and brought her downtown. They interrogated her most of the night. She stuck to the story she had told me; i.e., she hadn't seen a thing. About five-thirty Bolsky left her alone for half an hour. When he came back, he said Al Brown in the next room had admitted that Barnathan ordered the hit. He claimed that while I was upstairs with Jim, Ursula had slipped out of the house and gone to Brown's truck. She asked for the gun and took it back to the house with her. The cops were going to book her for murder.

"Wow," I said.

"Wait," Walter said.

The cops didn't believe Brown. They picked him up in his truck, where they found a gun stashed under the front seat. "They established it was the same gun that killed Wills," Walter said. "They're convinced he killed St. Clair, too."

"What about Ursula?"

"They gave her immunity from prosecution."

"No."

"She told them she had seen Brown shoot St. Clair. She claimed Barnathan had no knowledge of the hit. She's free as a bird."

"And Barnathan?"

"The grand jury will indict him six ways from Sunday. But nothing he said to you, or did to you, can really prove he masterminded St. Clair's death."

"Unless Brown sings."

"He's got a record. Armed robbery, assault and battery. He's served time but he's never sung."

"So now what?"

"So now you roll up your sleeves and we write."

"Okay."

"Unless Pucci sleeves don't roll up," Walter said.

·   ·   ·   ·

By one o'clock, we had most of the story written. We also took time out for a major fight. I told Walter I didn't want anything in the story that even alluded to my particular relationship with Jim. It had nothing to do with his death or the freeway scandal that led to it. "I don't see why we can't just write what Ursula told me," I argued, "about being in the house and hearing the gun go off."

"Because the other reporters will find out. Ursula will tell them. Then your credibility flies right out the window."

I chewed on my thumb.

"We'll mention in passing you were a colleague of his," Walter said. "And you happened to drop in earlier that night."

"And didn't notice Ursula because I was upstairs in his bed? That's good. Oh. And by the way, dear reader, I was also the mystery blonde seen leaving the scene-to-be-of-the-crime. That should wrap it up, Walter."

"That and a page one photo of you in the black negligee." He grinned.

I got up and walked out.

I went back to the Home Cooking Department to finish stewing and to make a cup of tea. When I returned, Walter showed me what he had written.

Contributing substantially to this story is Paris Chandler, an Examiner *Society reporter who also appears on KTLA's* Nick and Paris on the Town. *Through her friendship with James St. Clair at the TV station, Chandler was aware of his investigation into the building of the L.A. freeways. After his death, she began chasing down leads on her own and turned over substantial data to both the LAPD and the D.A.'s office.*

"I'll try to get it run as a box next to the main story," Walter said. "People can draw their own conclusions. By the time Ursula squeals, if she squeals, who's going to believe her?"

I smiled gratefully and leaned over to kiss Walter's cheek. I pulled back and, for one brief second, I caught the shame in his eyes.

"I thought so. I thought I smelled it. That's where you were last night, wasn't it? How could you do this to yourself?"

He smiled indulgently. "It was just a couple of beers. No problem with that. Beers hardly have any alcohol at all. Relax."

I pointed to today's paper. "This might be the best story you ever wrote. Why—"

Walter stood up.

"Where are you going?"

"Across the street for a sandwich."

"To the Cabrillo? Let's walk over to the Pantry."

"I don't want to wait in line. The Cabrillo's fast and they make great sandwiches for half a buck."

And there's a great bar where they serve them, I thought.

"I'd like to see you polish off the story," Walter said. "You know where we're going with it and you can probably write the last five, six graphs. I'll bring you back a sandwich. Okay?"

I said okay. And watched him walk out. As soon as he was gone, I opened the bottom drawer of his desk. That's where he used to hide the brown paper bags. There wasn't one.

I wondered how long it would be until there was.

"I want to point out to you that it's now after six," said Andrew, as we roared down Sunset at a moving-violation clip.

"Thank you," I said, "Big Ben."

"I just figured with everything on your mind you might not have noticed. I mean that it's Saturday and it's six o'clock."

We passed Maple Drive and kept going. It was nearly dark and the great houses along Sunset were all lit up. It was a pretty night. "Oh, now I see. You're making a point."

"I'll just put in for overtime, Miss Chandler." Normally, Andrew had Saturday nights off, starting at five. "Jackson went home."

"He's all right?" I asked anxiously, switching on the lamp behind me and opening my compact.

"Oh he's fine. His headache's gone and everything. But they don't need me on the set for two weeks, so—"

"You're back." I started freshening my lipstick. "That's great, I'm glad."

Andrew made a left onto Beverly Glen. "Wait, this isn't right. Where are you going?"

"Um, Nick said to bring you by after work."

"He what? No, we're not going there. Turn around." Andrew drifted into the left lane and made a spectacular U-turn. "When?" I demanded.

"He drove into the parking lot this afternoon. He told me, 'Please bring Miss Chandler by.'"

Nick had called the paper about fifty-six times—well, at least, three—but Walter always answered and said, "Sorry, she's on deadline."

"If you're going to take orders from Nick," I warned, snapping my compact shut, "make him pay you well."

"He gave me five bucks." Andrew made a slow, reluctant turn onto Sunset. "So I was wondering. Do you think I have to give it back?"

I rang the doorbell with a nervous finger. I had never been up to his house before. It was a long, low wooden house way up Tigertail in Brentwood, painted gray.

"Coming!"

I licked my lips. The door swung back. "Paris."

"Surprise," I said.

Ted was wearing a knit shirt and a pair of khaki pants, socks, and loafers. I was immediately struck by the to-matoey smells that wafted out the door. He smiled. "Is anything wrong?"

"For once, no. I just thought I'd stop by. I was working on the story all day and thinking about you." Ted nodded but said nothing. "Perhaps I should have called first."

"No, no." He hesitated. "Come in. At least have a drink."

I stepped inside a small vestibule and followed Ted into the living room. A warm beige area rug sat on light wooden floorboards. A couple of beige couches flanked a fireplace that crackled with burning logs. Potted plants were scattered about. In one corner, a table was set for two. "How pretty," I said. "Have you lived here long?"

"About five months. I haven't begun to fix up the rest of the house and the garden is a disaster. What can I get you?"

Just then, a woman came out of the kitchen. She was a slight, dark-haired girl with large brown eyes, wearing a light blue shirtwaist and flat navy shoes. An apron, tied at her waist, had an orangy smudge on it. "Hello," she said shyly.

I smiled.

"Paris, this is Sarah Singer. Sarah, I've mentioned Paris Chandler to you."

"Of course." She stepped forward and extended a small hand. I shook it.

"I'm sorry to have barged in like this. I really should have called."

"No, sit down," Ted said. "We've just opened a bottle of Chianti. Okay?"

He and Sarah went into the kitchen and I sat down near the fire. Above the mantle was an oil painting in pastels that I couldn't decide if I liked or not. Ted came back alone with two glasses of wine and sat down on the couch across from me with a sigh. "I don't know about you, but I'm beat. My father always wanted me to join his law firm." Ted grinned. "Why didn't I?"

"Because you wanted to act out your childhood fantasies of doing meaningful work on behalf of poor, helpless victims. Money was never to be the goal." I sipped the wine. "It isn't too late to revise those fantasies."

"And what about yours?"

"That's the problem. I never had any fantasies. You always seemed so certain about where you were going.

Me, I just tear along, going wherever my impulsiveness takes me."

"Like here," Ted said with a faint smile.

"For no particular reason. I think. Except maybe to grab on to something steady for a moment."

"You've been through a lot. I wish you'd come to me sooner about Barnathan. You should never have put yourself in danger like that, Paris. Sometimes I think you're as reckless as Russell was."

"No. I just like to follow reckless men."

"Like St. Clair?"

"Maybe." I gazed into the fireplace. "That's why I didn't come to you, or anybody. I didn't want to have to admit what he was or—I was."

"Don't be so hard on yourself."

"So what will happen to all of them?"

"Barnathan's finished. When the grand jury gets through with him, he'll be facing all kinds of counts for fraud. And when the police get done, he'll probably be charged as an accessory to Wills's murder and St. Clair's. You could throw in a kidnapping charge if you wanted to."

"And Albert Aubrey will go to trial?"

"Definitely."

"And Ursula. Will anything happen to her?"

"She was given immunity. Besides, we're not aware that she committed a crime."

"What about buying those houses, and selling them to Richard Walken?"

"He'll stand trial, too. She might have been charged as an accessory, but legally, she bought a house, then she sold it."

"I hate that she's getting off scot-free."

"If it weren't for her," Ted pointed out, "they all might be. You got her to blow the whistle on Wills, and your friend Nick pressured her to name Brown."

"Nick did?"

Sarah came into the room carrying a steaming bowl of spaghetti. "Paris, you'll stay?"

"Oh, I couldn't. But thank you. Really I must run."

Eventually, I overcame their objections and dropped wearily into the backseat of the Bentley. Andrew expertly guided the car down the dark, winding road. "Home, Miss Chandler?"

"Do you still have Nick's five dollars?"

"Yes."

"Good."

"Do you want to go to Nick's now?"

"No. To Schwab's." I rolled down the window and let the cool moist air brush against my face. "Nick's buying us dinner," I said.

47

◆

Old Purvis Winn was sitting at his desk, clucking his tongue against his gums as he read the comic strips. I guess that meant he was laughing. My eyes fell upon his teeth bubbling in a glass of Alka-Seltzer. Fred Dickinson looked up.

"You wanted to see me?" I said.

"Pull up a chair, Paris, let me get some of this junk off my desk."

I grabbed a chair from another desk and sat down. It was Monday afternoon and the hot story of the hour concerned the handsome, twenty-six-year-old scion of a wealthy East Coast family who had fallen down dead in a corridor of the Hermosa Beach Biltmore. Foul play was suspected. Crime never rests.

The city editor leaned back in his chair. "You and Walter did a bang-up job on the St. Clair story, I just wanted to congratulate you."

"Thank you."

"You'll be getting a five-dollar bonus the end of the week."

402

I smiled.

Dickinson bent over and opened his bottom drawer. The infamous toy cap pistol that he shot off when he wanted to get someone's attention lay there ominously. He picked it up and I instinctively tensed. Was he going to shoot me as some kind of initiation rite? "I don't know if you can write, Paris, but I gather you're a dogged reporter." He began fingering the pistol. Maybe he just needed something to play with.

"Thank you," I said again.

He had the gun in his left hand. With his right, he thumped the afternoon paper on his desk. "You have any interest in this?" He was thumping the dead scion story.

"I don't know, sir. I was thinking I might keep an eye on what the grand jury does with Barnathan."

"We'll let the courthouse boys worry about that. What I'd like to do is see if I could borrow you from Etta for a while. With all the crime in this city, you can't have enough good reporters on the beat." He paused and spun the gun around his finger like they do in the Westerns. "Mr. Hearst is always demanding more crime coverage."

I glanced quickly over to the copy desk. Walter wasn't there. I hadn't seen him since I left the paper late Saturday. I supposed he was taking some time off. I said, "You've already got the best crime reporter in the city. I should think you'd want Walter on this story."

An explosion of cackling caused both of us to whip around. Purvis was rocking back and forth in his chair laughing maniacally to himself. Fred raised the toy pistol over his head and began shooting away. "Shut up, old man," screamed Fred. The city room fell silent. It suddenly struck me that everyone in it looked a fraction off-center, as if they had been photographed slightly out of focus. I began to yearn for the Princess Alexandras of the world.

Fred said, "Walter isn't here just now," and put the cap gun on his desk.

"Is—something wrong?"

"No. He called me yesterday, said he wanted to go back to Sacramento. He said with the elections next year, he felt that was the place to be."

"Walter went back?" I was stunned. "Already?"

"He left this morning, I think. He said to tell you he'd be in touch."

"Did he seem okay?"

"He seemed fine. I told him he was welcome to take his old job back, but he said he had some unfinished business up there."

I wondered vaguely if Walter went back because he felt safer in Sacramento, or because he wanted to drink in Sacramento. "Did he say what business?"

"Ask him. Anyway, he recommended you highly. Said you had mastered the puce Pucci beat, I think he called it, and it was time to move on. I'm willing to try you."

I forced a smile. "Well that's great, I appreciate it. But I'd like to think about it. I'm not sure how deeply puce runs in my veins."

Dickinson picked up the gun. I held my breath, waiting for the worst. "You think about it, Chandler, let me know. And some night, you're gonna buy me a drink and tell me the hat pin story." He pointed the gun straight at me. "Whatever that means. Walter said to ask you." He dropped the gun in the drawer.

I told him someday maybe I would.

The phone was ringing on my desk when I returned to Society. I picked it up. "Miss Chandler? The chief of police wants to talk to you. Hold on."

I recognized the wrinkled voice of Miss Percy and sat down. The early edition of Tuesday's paper sat on my desk, the ink still pungent from the presses. On the front page were two photos. One showed Matthew Barnathan walking into the court building. Next to it was one of Ursula Martens entering, with Nick Goodwin at her side. I pushed the paper away.

"Paris? How are you, my girl?" Harry Gladstone boomed.

"Fine, Chief."

"Say, listen. About the TV thing, where do you think I stand?"

I swallowed a smile. "Um, maybe we should meet with Truman. I would think he'd be happy to fill another fifteen-minute slot. You could talk about the crime of the week. Or something."

"Oh not that," said Gladstone dismissively. "People don't want to hear about bad things." He paused. "I was thinking of a half-hour show. *Hasty Harry*. I play a police detective. Every week I solve a crime. I'm not sure about the title though."

"Um—"

"You could play my girl Friday. It would be a gem."

"I don't think I can act, Harry, but look—"

"The hell you can't," Gladstone broke in.

"Did you ever *really* think I pulled the trigger?"

"I thought it was a distinct possibility."

"You did?"

"We had you tailed for a while. We were interested."

"And when did you know I didn't?"

"When Ursula Martens told us she had seen Albert Aubrey shoot him and took a lie detector test."

I glanced inadvertently at the newspaper. "Yesterday? You thought I was lying until yesterday?"

"My first show is going to be about a murderess. The subject fascinates me. I was keeping you on a long leash, studying your m.o."

"Harry," I said. "Hollywood stories are supposed to imitate real life. Not the other way around."

"Yeah, don't be so sure," Gladstone said. And hung up.

Tee came over around eight o'clock, safely after dinner was served. Tee would eat almost anything, except Mrs. Keyes's food. I didn't blame her. The pot roast had been marginal. "A beer?" I said as we walked into the study.

"Just the bottle will be fine."

I came back with the beer and a Coke for me. "I have to tell you about my talk with the city editor," I said.

"Have you heard from Nick?"

"He offered me a chance to write crime." I lit a cigarette and snuggled into the red leather wing chair. "What do you think of that?" I flicked an ash off my cashmere sweater.

"Frankly? Frankly, I don't think you have the wardrobe for it."

"Make jokes. My hat pin may have saved my life. And, besides, Gladstone thought I did it."

Tee put down her bottle on the coffee table and grinned. "He was pulling your leg. When I told him I'd been with you that night, he said, 'Yeah, I didn't figure it was her.'"

"So what do you think?"

"I think it's great."

I gave a Tee a long look. "No, you don't. Not really."

"For one thing, Paris, you would have to give up your TV show, probably. And then, oh Lord, it would be only Nick. Can you imagine unleashing him on the city like that? The stories he would make up."

I smiled. "Ted Stein has a girl. She seems nice."

"That's another thing," said Tee. "You won't meet many eligible guys hanging around the slammer. They talk a pretty game, but they never come through."

"That's all right." I glanced at my watch. "Do you want to listen to *You Bet Your Life*? It's a new show with Groucho Marx."

"Sure."

I got up and went over to the liquor cabinet. The radio was on top of it, next to the phonograph. I switched it on and began playing with the dial. The phone rang. I finally found the program and went back to my chair. The phone stopped ringing.

"This is George Fenneman, welcoming you to the premiere of a brand-new show, You Bet Your Life. *Brought to you by Elgin watches. When . . ."*

Mrs. Keyes appeared in the doorway. "It's Nick. Again."

"Tell him I'm not home. Again."

"Well I did, Miss Paris."

"So?"

"He said you're being a jerk."

". . . *Any contestant who says the secret word receives a bonus. And we conclude with a grand prize of fifteen thousand dollars . . .*"

"Wow," exclaimed Tee. "How do we get on *this* show?"

Tomorrow, I realized, was Tuesday. And our show. I would have to see him then, for sure.

"Tell me the questions," I said to Tee.

I went down the hall and picked up the phone.

ABOUT THE AUTHOR

DIANE K. SHAH, a contributing editor at *Esquire*, has written for *The New York Times Magazine*. Ms. Shah has been the West Coast editor for *GQ* and a sports columnist for the *Los Angeles Herald Examiner*, and has covered sports for *Newsweek*. *Dying Cheek to Cheek* is the second novel in the Paris Chandler mystery series, which began with *As Crime Goes By*. She is the co-author with Daryl F. Gates of *Chief: My Life in the LAPD*.